A CHILD CALLED FAYE

THE PENDALIN CHRONICLES

BOOK ONE

JESS SENFF

First published by Jessica Senff, 2021

This edition published by Wattle Tree Press, 2025
ABN 55 778 838 320
www.wattletreepress.com

A catalogue record for this book is available from the National Library of Australia

A Child Called Faye

Cover: Wattle Tree Press
Internal Artwork: Jess Senff
Typesetting: Brooke DeBono
Editor: Tara Jean
ISBN (paperback): 978-1-7640388-0-5
ISBN (ebook): 978-1-7640388-1-2

for Mrs Alice Johnson and Mr Steven Green
Oak Flats High School 1997 – 2002

A CHILD CALLED FAYE

The Orathwyn Mountains:

These mountains tower over 10 kilometers in height and act as a natural barrier between Pendalin and the wastelands beyond. No Seeker has ever returned from beyond the Mountains. Does that really mean that the world ends there??

Werritan Canyons:

These canyons span the length of the continent from the Orathwyn Mountains down to Dammond Falls. Once a vast river system that ensured every inch of Pendalin was fertile, it is now a dry ruin, home to bandits and reptiles.

The Artesian Basin:

Once a lush plain and a valuable agricultural hub, with the drying of the central river, the basin is now undergone desertification and is a dry and arid dust-bowl.

The Arythmun Divide:

These low mountains spread from east to west across Pendalin and can be difficult to navigate. The mountains are home to the Grydin Triad and some natural wonders (such as the Grotto)

The Southern Isles:

A series of islands to the south of Pendalin. They are often barren and cold, being covered in snow for half of the year. The ancient homeland of Gwyndor is said to be beyond, yet no explorer has ever returned to confirm if the original home of Humans still exists. The histories say an apocalyptic disaster caused our people to flee a thousand or more years ago, before we arrived in Pendalin.

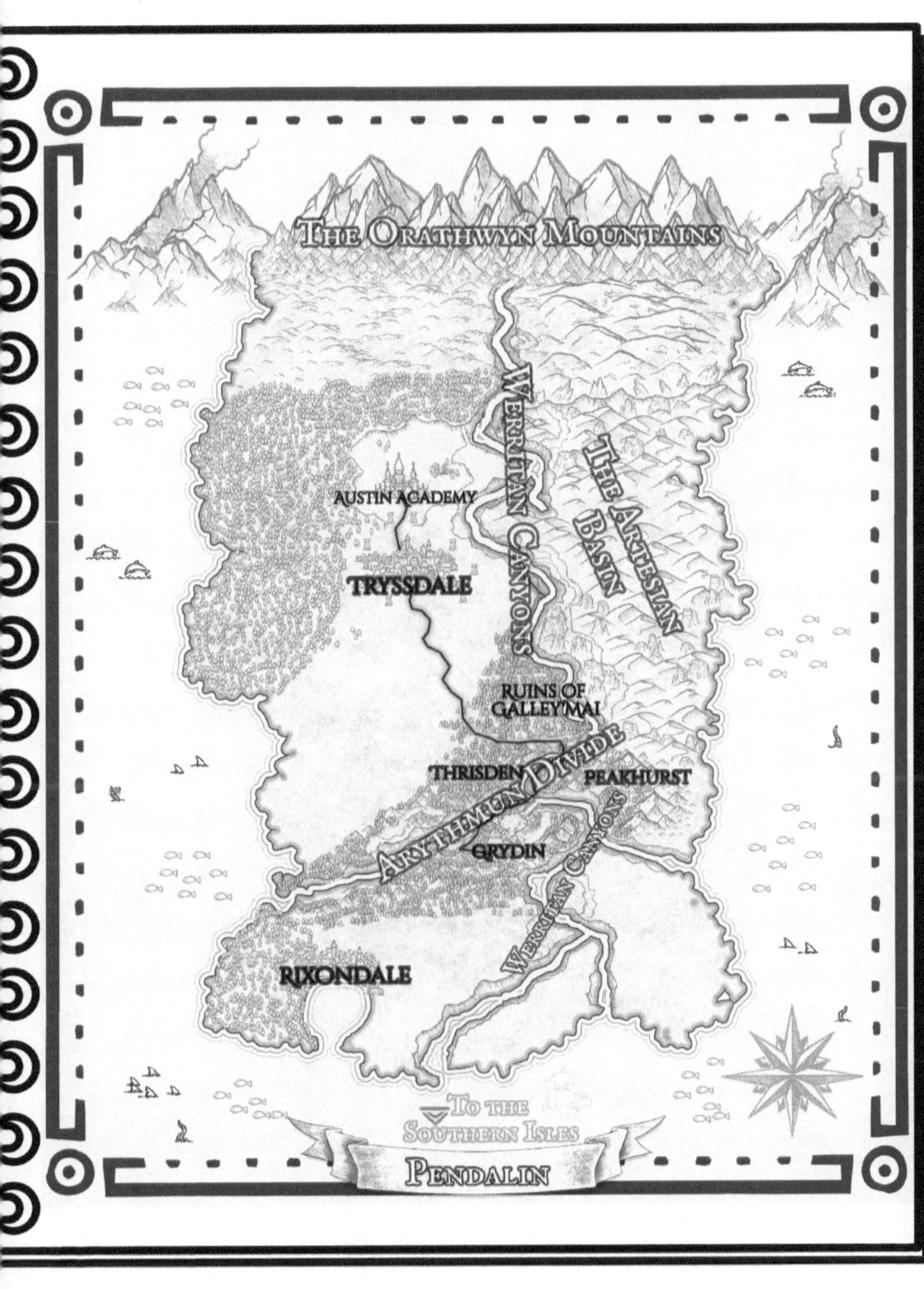
The Orathwyn Mountains
Werrian Canyons
The Artesian Basin
Austin Academy
Tryssdale
Ruins of Galley'mai
Thrisden
Peakhurst
Aurythemian Divide
Grydin
Werrian Canyons
Rixondale
To the Southern Isles
Pendalin

A CHILD CALLED FAYE

The small village of Grydin lay quiet beneath a blanket of snow. Shuddering with cold, Rhaine peered cautiously down at the simple cottages lining the single street. Yellow lights burned merrily in most windows, throwing a warm glow over the buildings and their signs.

She could see the Taylor's stout shop, the Butchers, Bakers, and Grocers. However, the one sign she sought was not there.

The wind picked up and began to moan through the branches, freeing clumps of snow. The clouds scudded across the sky, and suddenly, the entire vale was illuminated by the reappearance of the full moon. Beyond the town, Rhaine could now see the Forrester's low cottage set deep into a small wood, complete with drying racks hanging from the branches, loaded with skins.

The woman looked further on before finally locating what she had vainly searched for.

The Healer's Cottage.

Taking another shuddering breath, Rhaine stumbled down the hill, keeping to the shadows. A warm trickle snaked its way down her inner thigh, causing her to gasp painfully as the fluid turned instantly to bitter cold.

No, not yet! she thought desperately, holding her swollen belly.

The first contraction struck soon after, sending the woman staggering into a tree, grasping its rough bark for support. Exhaustion and cold began to fog her mind, but she struggled on as soon as the contraction passed and continued to slog through the snow. She had almost reached the small village when the next contraction took hold. Gritting her teeth, Rhaine managed to catch herself against a fence post until the wave of pain eased.

Gasping, Rhaine continued.

She avoided the main street of town, not wanting to be seen. Instead, she followed an icy track along its edge, behind the buildings. The contractions came closer and closer together, and she stumbled again and again, growing weaker each time.

After what seemed an age, she made it to the quaint cottage and fell on the stoop, too tired to move.

She had finally arrived.

A faint, pained groan travelled through the night air, disturbing the lonesome figure sitting close to the hearth fire. Thayrille Hogansvort, barely sixteen years of age, jumped a little.

She had just finished battling a hairbrush through her thick, brown, frizzy curls before bundling it atop her head. The girl was ready for bed, clad in a navy nightgown that made her pale skin appear almost sickly, a smattering of caramel freckles standing out starkly against her cheeks. Not that she cared for her appearance.

Thayrille had moved in only six months prior and had no one she cared to impress in her life. Nor did she want anyone! She was far better off figuring out this life alone. Other people, particularly men, were an unnecessary complication she didn't want.

A vague thump sounded near the door, causing the girl to jump again. She hadn't become accustomed to this old house's strange noises. Indeed, it was just the ancient timber frame settling? Or perhaps the wind was blowing a branch against the outer stone walls?

The youthful Healer was highly gifted, intelligent, and very young. She had graduated at the top of her class at fifteen and had been offered this placement when the previous Healer of the Grydin Triad retired. The Triad, which included Grydin and the outlying villages of Thrisden and Peakhurst, was a very isolated and small community.

Thayrille, who had spent her entire life reared in cities and crowded universities felt uneasy with the vast space and the general creepiness of being alone. It didn't help that the local villagers were backward, unsociable gits.

They believed Thayrille as too young for her post, so they didn't trust her abilities or appreciate her efforts in the slightest. They refused to talk with her or to visit for anything other than emergency treatment. The worst part was that, for many illnesses, they often sought the dubious medications of the local hedge witch — a hermit woman living in Thrisden who had only the basest of Healing knowledge. This usually led to all sorts of mischief before finally — when the illness or injury had reached almost deathly seriousness — they came to her. She fixed them right up in a matter of days.

Did they appreciate this? No.

Instead, they tried to short-pay her for her efforts and claimed she was not worth the coin because of her age and inexperience.

It fair made the girl's blood boil. She had come to hate this place with a passion.

Unfortunately, the stubborn lass was also very proud, too proud, and so could not bring herself to leave and accept a job at a Medic Ward in some city or other. As such, not only was Thayrille isolated and lonely here in Grydin Village, but she was also poor and unable to escape the self-imposed trap.

Well, almost completely lonely.

There was always Perry, Thayrille thought with a guilty start, glancing over her shoulder to the stairway that led up, up, up to the attic rooms above. She truly hoped that the odd noises hadn't woke him! She wasn't in the mood for more anxious babble or the silent, nervous shuffling from foot to foot as the child waited for her to give him a task.

Perry was a young boy from the village who had offered to assist her this winter in return for food and shelter. His previous living arrangements had been far from ideal, with a drunken, abusive father, and a harsh mother with six younger siblings living in squalor in a run-down shack at the edge of town... His mum had sent him out into the world at the tender age of ten to 'become a man'.

Thayrille had found Perry half frozen on her stoop some weeks ago, attempting to sell her some kindling he had collected from the forest. Never mind that the nearby oak trees dropped plenty of sticks she could collect herself, and Old Forrester Broc kept her cottage well supplied with timber for the merrily burning fireplace. Thayrille had felt the vice of compassion grip her heart, and she took the child in for a hot meal.

After spending a day assisting her, the Healer had soon realised that the jumpy little shadow was loathe to leave her warm kitchen and that *she* didn't have the heart to send him away. It was little wonder Perry had gratefully accepted her offer to become her assistant and stuck to her like a ghostly wraith while she completed her day-to-day chores.

Thayrille didn't hear the familiar sound of little booted feet clumping on the stairs and breathed a sigh of relief. With any luck, Perry would stay asleep.

The low moan came again, louder this time. Thayrille cocked her head slightly. It had definitely come from the front door!

Jerking to her feet, fire poker in hand, she slowly approached the small box window adjacent to the entryway. From this vantage point, she could peer out without being noticed. These past months, it had served her well in identifying potential visitors. If she didn't like who she saw, she just pretended to not be home.

It wouldn't have been the first time that some drunken man had come stumbling to her door late at night, expecting to have some extra *comforts* for a silver penny. The men of the village assumed that because she was an unattached woman living alone, despite her youth, she expected this type of attention. She, in turn, hoped that they enjoyed having their nads forcefully bruised by her trusty fire poker.

On this eerie full moon night, the girl saw not a swaying man carousing for her attention, but a dark figure slumped on her porch steps. Squinting a little harder through the fogged glass, she saw the figure move, curling around as it moaned again.

It was a woman, Thayrille realised, and she was heavily pregnant!

Hurriedly, the Healer dropped the fire poker and flung open the front door. Freezing night air gusted into the room, sending the hearth fire spitting and sputtering. The woman, a creature with the most alien of faces, looked up at her with pain glazed eyes.

"*Help me!*" she gasped, her voice harsh and raw.

Thayrille swooped down and lifted the woman to her feet, wiry curls already springing free from her tight bun as she supported the alien being through to the primary healing room. It was an ample space filled with every tool, medication, and material that a Healer could need.

Quickly, Thayrille had the woman stripped of her wet, icy clothes and wrapped in a fire-warmed blanket. She urged her unexpected patient to lie on a wide, firm mattress on the floor rather than the bench at the centre of the room. It would be easier for her, Thayrille knew, for the woman was amid a difficult labour.

Through clever architecture, the healing room shared a two-way fireplace with the sitting room. It allowed the resident Healer to prepare and warm both rooms at all hours. As custom, a large pot of water simmered on the hearth bricks. Thayrille dumped a series of small cloths into the water then fished one out. With practised motions, she used two metal instruments to wring the cloth before placing the steaming material across the woman's chest, allowing only that small amount of heat to touch her. Thayrille didn't dare to place her too close to the fire, for hypothermia had set in, and the heat would cause more harm than good.

With careful hands, the girl examined her patient.

The woman was delirious, weakened by exhaustion and cold, and the Healer noticed with wide eyes that the patient had started bleeding. Rushing to and fro between the fire, her workbench, and the woman, she did her best to stem the flow. Nothing Thayrille did seemed to work. The woman would need sorcerous healing, a treatment Thayrille was unable to provide as she only had the barest smidgeon of power beneath her control.

Within minutes, the babe's head had crowned, while the woman sobbed weakly, her body convulsing as contractions overwhelmed her sparse frame. Her gasps became shallower and fewer. As the infant slipped into the world and began letting out a raucous cry, the patient's face relaxed and her body stilled.

Thayrille held up the squirming infant, smeared with blood, offal and waxy residue.

"It's a girl," she whispered to the new mother, feeling helpless.

Blood still gushed from the alien woman, draining her of life. The small spark of yellow power Thayrille managed to conjure did nothing more than ease her patient's pain. The alien-looking woman opened her mouth but struggled to form words. Thayrille leant closer, placing her ear right next to the thin lips.

"She...Fey..." the dying woman whispered, then breathed no more.

Thayrille sat back in delayed shock, clasping the squalling child to her chest, oblivious to the gunk and mess.

The woman was dead. The child was orphaned.

A heavy footfall broke the Healer's stupor, and she turned her head to find Perry as he stood uncertainly in the doorway. The girl blinked at him for a few moments, momentarily befuddled, before being spurred into action by another of the babe's loud cries.

"Quickly, boy, down to the Forrester. Fetch him back here," she commanded.

Perry jumped like a rabbit and then raced from the cottage, his curly red hair bouncing behind him. She noted that at least the boy had the sense to put on his shoes as he hopped down the stairs one foot at a time.

Back to business. Thayrille cleaned the child, wrapped her in a warm blanket and did her best to soothe her. Once the babe had quieted, she placed her in the cloth filled basket that lay near the hearth. Uncertainly, the Healer began peering through her bottles of medicine and herbs, desperately trying to decide what she should do... She noted the empty, sterile bottles waiting to be filled with serum. She glanced down at the alien woman, her body still and shadowed in the firelight.

Feeling a squirm of distaste, Thayrille acted quickly. She used the bottles, and another spark of yellow energy, to collect the nutrient rich pre-milk from the woman's breasts. It was still warm, due to the steaming cloth she had placed there earlier, and the brush of ephemeral power appeared to boost whatever supply the strange creature had naturally produced.

Once the small bottle was full, she placed it near the hearth to keep warm. Thayrille knew the babe would feel its first hunger pangs in a few hours. The pre-milk was essential to provide the babe with nutrients and antibodies.

Thayrille sat near the basket, studying the babe, her brain awhirl with memories of the dusty pages of her textbooks. What else would the babe need in the coming days? Did she have everything to help this fragile being? Or would the tiny child sicken and die?

The babe was wide awake but silent now, comfortable with her new environment. The infant was wrinkled and ugly, as most babes were soon after birth, but she fortunately appeared more Human than her poor mother.

The baby had large, unfocused blue eyes which stared at the nearby flickering flames. Her face looked very much like her mother's; it was quite pointed and delicate. Almost alien. However, her mother's face was certainly not Human. It was the face of a creature Thayrille had never encountered before – which was unusual in a place like Pendalin. The alien woman's eyes were a glassy grey, so pale that they were almost white. Her face with its pointedness appeared almost insect-like. Her hair was a tangle of coarse pale strands, frail and white against the soft mattress, almost like cow hair.

Thayrille had been too caught up in the moment, desperately trying to save this dying woman and her child, that the Healer hadn't truly registered the bizarre appearance of her patient. Now that she had a moment to catch her breath, Thayrille's gaze was drawn to the dead woman's alien eyes, her thin lips, her cutaneous skin, her narrow insect-like face, her wiry coarse hair that shimmered purest white...

That was when the Healer noticed the object that lay tangled in the woman's short locks. It was tied with a beaded thong around her neck. Carefully retrieving the object, Thayrille found it was some sort of pipe, unlike any she had seen. It glimmered in the firelight, shining with blues, greens, and yellows. The slim instrument had some ancient indecipherable carvings over it that sent shivers down her spine.

This was beyond her experience, this strange spindly woman and her Human-like child. Where had she come from? *How* had she come to Grydin, of all places, in such a condition? The township was isolated, perched high within the Arythmun Mountains and almost impossible to navigate to during the deep winter.

Staring at those vacant eyes, Thayrille felt a shudder run through her body. The young Healer had experienced death before. It was hard not to, in such a busy Ward as the place of her apprenticeship, Tryssdale Medic Centre, but... At least there Thayrille had never been alone.

The wind whistled eerily around the house, making Thayrille feel instantly nervous. The cottage's front door flew open with a thud, causing her to squeak in fear, shivering as the open portal allowed a chill breeze to gust through the house. Perry ran into the room with the Forrester close behind.

The man was tall, broad, and covered by a swirling grey-green cloak. Most of his exposed face was wreathed with a snow-frosted brown beard, and the skin beneath was weathered and tan. Although he was dressed as any Forrester should be, he was also a stranger. Thayrille had never seen this man before.

"Wh-Who are you?" Thayrille stuttered.

It was unlike her to be anything more than calm and collected, which annoyed her. She didn't normally allow such paltry emotions to physically control her!

Where was Broc? she wondered.

The old, skinny Forrester had been rough but fair. She didn't care to have an unknown entity come into her life at this moment.

"Jack," the man replied softly, a pleasant burr accenting his voice, as he scanned the room and took in the scenario. "I'm newly appointed. Broc passed on at the beginning of winter."

Thayrille felt as though somebody had just slapped her. The village Healer she may be, but a Villager she quite obviously was not. That was becoming more and more apparent. No one had thought to tell her that the old Forrester had died. No one had thought to tell her that a new Forrester had been appointed.

No one ever thought to tell her anything!

Jack knelt silently beside the dead woman-creature and placed his hand lightly to her throat. The fact he didn't hesitate or flinch away from her alien appearance spoke volumes for his nature. Many would have recoiled from such a creature, but it appeared Forrester Jack was not easily scared. Thayrille suspected that he hardly registered this dead woman's strange appearance. He was seeing just the desperately sad situation of a new mother who had lost her life.

His shuttered expression told her that he didn't really expect much. He then gently closed the woman's staring grey eyes, shaking his head sadly.

"The child?" he asked.

"A girl," Thayrille said, gesturing to the basket, where the babe snuggled quietly.

The man briefly stared at the oddly silent infant, examining its small breath and alert responses.

"Her name?" he asked finally, satisfied that the child was alive and well.

From their proximity, Thayrille could now see that this new Forrester, Jack, was a rather handsome man. He was also quite young, not yet twenty-five was her guess. His hazel eyes gleamed with every colour of the forest and were, thankfully, resigned but not condemning. Thayrille hesitated before answering, unsure of what she had heard.

"Faye," she whispered finally.

Chapter I

House Rules

One fine summer day, some seven years later, Faye sat impatiently at her small school desk in the Healer's study. The only sound in the room was the soft ticking of an old grandfather clock; the only movement was the bright dust motes that sparkled in the morning light. Books lined every wall, tightly rolled scrolls filled drawers, and a large wooden desk stood catty-corner to her own. This room was Thayrille's study, a place where the stern Healer could read, research, and write about some medicine or healing practice as she devised it.

Faye was meant to be in here to complete a history exercise but couldn't keep her mind on track. It kept wandering out of the cottage and down the lane towards the village of Grydin. She idly twirled one bright blonde curl through her fingers as she stared out the dusty window with her large grey-blue eyes.

Not for the first time, she wished she could attend school with the other village children, but every time she asked, '*why not?*' Thayrille would answer, '*Because you're too smart for that school, they'd have nothing to teach you.*'

Faye, however, would always note the extra grimness that would line the stern Healer's mouth and the flash of anger that flushed her usually pale face. There was some other reason, she was sure, but Thayrille didn't want to say.

In the far distance, a bell tolled. It was the school bell that marked the beginning of lunch for the village children. Faye sighed, shifting uncomfortably in her wooden chair. When the second bell sounded, her foster mother would be in shortly after to check on her progress. It was the Healer's habit to ensure that Faye was securely indoors when the village children were out.

Faye looked down at the history book she was meant to be reading. She hadn't even started. With a resigned sigh, she forced herself to concentrate on the words.

The first Humans came to Almanaic – the southern lands of Pendalin – from across the Southern Ocean over one thousand years ago. When they first arrived, the magical creatures of the land were intensely curious but shy. They first saw no harm in the Humans and simply watched them. Soon after the Human arrival, the magical creatures began to retreat from Almanaic as the Humans spread, cutting down their trees and destroying their homes. Many of the species soon learned to hate the Humans. After many generations of cruel death and displacement, magical creatures finally approached the ancient, wise Elves, seeking help.

The Elves themselves travelled south to Almanaic and observed these new arrivals. They saw the great towns and cities that the Humans had built, and they wept for the needless destruction that these Humans had reaped. The Elves argued amongst themselves, torn between the Sacred

Law that forbade the slaughter of living creatures and the wish to stamp out this plague.

The King of Pendalin, a wise and powerful Elf named Fey'Ran, decided to approach the Humans. He wanted to determine if the Human's destruction transpired from malice or ignorance. He came down the mountain with his entourage of Warriors, Healers, and Scholars, and approached the great city of Rixondale. Once there, Fey'Ran demanded an audience with their King.

To his surprise, the man that greeted them was a sordid, narrow-minded Warrior. The Elves were troubled that Humans chose their leaders based on their military exploits, not by their intelligence, wisdom, or kindness. They confronted this so-called King and were unsatisfied by his responses to their questions.

'We take what we want,' the Human King told them, 'Because we are superior to other creatures. Non-Human creatures have no rights under Human Law.'

Outraged, the Elves slew this demonic Human and the other Human Warriors that challenged them.

Finally, after one week and one day of battle and murder, a Human child approached them.

The child's innocence stayed their hand as he knelt before Fey'Ran and beseeched him.

'Great Fairy King', the child said, 'please spare my people. The ones who are evil are now dead. The others just don't know any better. But we can learn, Great King, if you let us.'

Moved by the sweet boy's innocent words, the Elven King spared the lives of the other Humans. Then, in a surprise move, Fey'Ran crowned the small boy King.

He made for him a beautiful sceptre from his magics, one that could only be held by wisdom and innocence. The Sceptre of Almanaic.

He then informed the people that this child would guide their way, and if they followed his example and were good and just, then the Humans could have the lands of Almanaic as their home. The remaining people bowed, gladly accepting this peasant boy named Austin as their true King.

Austin, in turn, ruled long and wisely. The magical creatures slowly returned to Almanaic and lived amongst the Humans. The forests were re-established, and the Humans lived in peace with their surroundings...

Faye's head jerked up as the creak of the door opening disturbed her.

Surely the second bell hasn't tolled already? Faye thought, panicked.

The old wooden clock ticking on the wall indicated that only five minutes had passed. Thayrille entered the room, her usually expressionless face clouded with a small frown. Wisps of hair were starting to come loose from the twist she normally wore as she ran her hand over her head in agitation.

"Mistress Brianey is here. She's managed to cut open her leg and has delayed coming to see me by almost a week. The wound has become septic," the Healer announced, absently glancing at the page Faye was reading. "I won't have time to check your lessons. Mark the page and take the book with you to read. For now, I'd prefer you leave the cottage. I'll check your knowledge of the text this evening – the whole text, mind!"

Faye sat stunned for a moment, unable to believe her good luck! Almost an entire day to herself! With only *one* text to read! When

Thayrille's frown deepened at her ward's delayed reaction, Faye hurriedly marked her page, shut the book and leapt to her feet. With a nod of thanks, she raced from the cottage and through the back door, tucking the book into the waistband of her breeches. As she passed the primary healing room, she could hear the low, pained moans of Mistress Brianey.

Serves her right, the child thought belligerently.

Faye knew that many villagers opted only to come to Thayrille as a last resort. It displeased and secretly hurt the stern Healer to no end.

The child had no sympathy for such idiots. Especially Mistress Brianey, the Baker's wife, who had once thrown a skillet at her when Faye had peeped over the back fence out of curiosity. The girl had only wanted to see how the bread was baked!

Once out the back door, Faye looked about the large kitchen garden. Several raised garden beds lined the cobbled path, blooming with flowers and vegetables. She breathed in the numerous smells of herbs used in cooking and medicine. Faye could even name a few, as Thayrille had taken to allowing the child to sit with her as she prepared salves, serums, and other medications.

After a brief pause, Faye continued down the garden path to the back fence. There was no gate, but she scaled the stone wall and jumped down the other side with deft, practised motions. Her rugged leather breeches and linen shirt made climbing and running easy. Far better, she often thought, to look like a boy than to wear a silly, confining dress.

On the other side of the tall fence was Shepherds Lane, a path that led the back way down to the village. Thayrille had forbidden Faye from going anywhere near the other buildings, and it hadn't taken many secret wanderings for the child to understand why.

The village people were cruel.

So far, in the past year since Faye had been allowed to roam on her own, she had sticks and stones thrown at her, a broom on one occasion, and had been verbally abused in a variety of colourful ways. There was also that skillet incident, but she had always stubbornly supposed that she shouldn't have frightened Mistress Brianey by sticking her head over the bakery fence unannounced. She just didn't believe that in her heart.

At first, this callous treatment made Faye upset and angry. Her misery only increased when she had cried to Thayrille once, only to be sharply smacked and told she shouldn't have disobeyed the house rules.

Bottom stinging and her pride in tatters, Faye soon learnt to avoid the village like the plague. That occasion had been the only time Thayrille had ever struck her in recent memory.

As far as Faye could remember, she and the Healer had always had a cordial – if distant – relationship. The girl had witnessed other families and how they kissed, hugged, and laughed together... Thayrille didn't take up with that sort of claptrap and it often caused Faye to feel a pang in her heart.

Recalling her earlier wish that she could attend the village school, Faye suddenly wondered if it was the villager's cruelty rather than her intelligence that prevented her foster mother from sending her. It was food for thought.

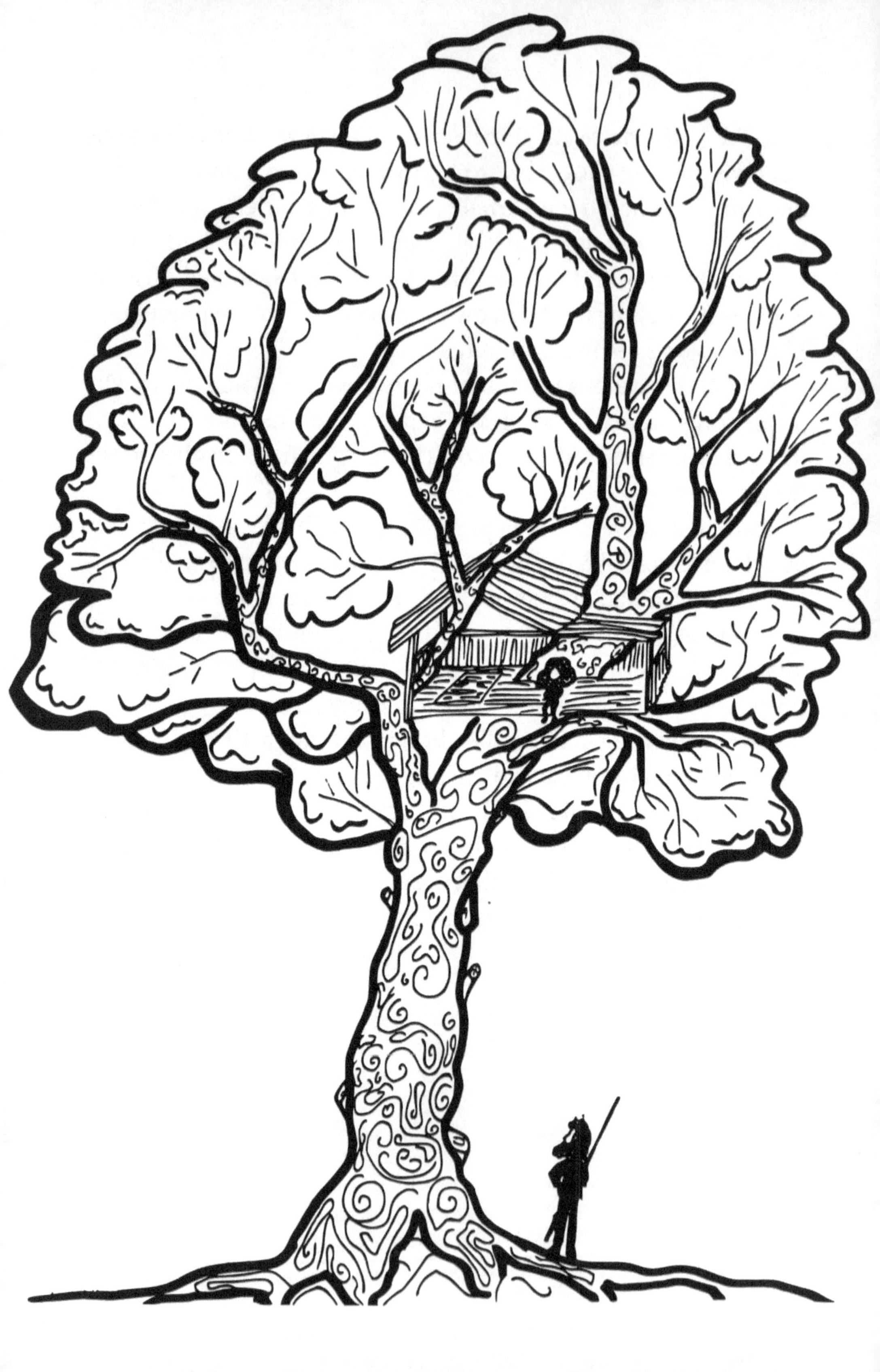

Faye glanced up and down the narrow lane before crossing quickly to enter the woods opposite. Despite the many warnings of wolves, bears, and venomous snakes and spiders, she  had always been comfortable in the forest depths. Nothing ever bothered her in here, and she felt completely safe.

A massive oak tree stood some twenty meters into the woods, along a very faint track that she carved over a year ago. The ancient tree radiated peace and welcome, filling her chest with a buzz of warmth.

Faye had constructed a large platform high in its branches, using twine and vines. She deftly climbed the tree now, reaching the platform in moments. There were many treasures stored up here. Drawings stuck on with tree sap decorated the branches, her first clumsy attempt at knitting lined the floor, and a collection of shiny colourful stones were displayed across a low shelf she had made.

Her best treasure of all sat protected beneath the bench. It was a wooden practice sword.

During one of her infrequent forays into the village, Faye had found the sword broken, having been tossed away near a woodsman's cottage. She had fixed it with sap and rock powder, which formed a rock-hard glue.

The last time she had come up here, she had used her small pocketknife to carve patterns over its surface. The designs were pretty, yet alien.

Faye couldn't remember where she had seen them, only that they were important to her. Now, the sword was ready to use.

Faye knelt next to the shelf and was about to grip the sword's hilt when her conscience pricked at her. She should finish the text first, she knew, otherwise she would forget. Thayrille wouldn't be happy about that.

With a heavy sigh, Faye flopped onto the platform as she reluctantly retrieved the book from her waistband and continued reading.

The lands of Almanaic were ruled peacefully by Austin and his descendants for many years, with the Sceptre of Almanaic being passed from parent to child.

The Sceptre would choose the successor, often alternating between first-born, middle-born, and last-born heirs. It would always glow mysteriously when held by the true heir.

Only once was the Royal lineage interrupted. The son of King Bereford jealously hoarded the Sceptre, claiming it as his right as the first-born and only son. This foresworn man, named Dex, had slain his two sisters to ensure his inheritance. When the Sceptre would not glow for him, Dex was enraged. He slew his Royal Advisors, who had plotted with him and guaranteed his success. Within days of these sad events, the Elves appeared and confiscated the Sceptre.

Driven to insanity, Dex challenged them and died swiftly. The Sceptre was passed amongst King Bereford's cousins until it finally shone again.

The Royal lineage continued.

Generations passed, and Humans began to spread further. The Elves welcomed them into the Northern Lands, known as Weirren Vale. Their blood mingled with many magical creatures, and soon, Human Sorcerers were also born. Everyone lived in peace.

After hundreds of years, the Elves slowly began to fade from the lands of Pendalin until few remained. The King of that time, Fey'Yulan, passed the ancient Crown of Weirren Vale to the Human Queen, Orchra, in a great ceremony. He and the other Elves believed that Humans had proven themselves worthy of the Guardianship of Pendalin and its creatures. Fey'Yulan conjured a great throne for Queen Orchra in the Palace of Rixondale– the Throne of Pendalin. With those three magical items, the Sceptre, Crown and Throne, the King or Queen of Pendalin would rule with great power, equivalent to the Elves. King Fey'Yulan then vanished into the mists of the northern forests.

Humans once more ruled well until two hundred years ago. King Brandon had only one son, Gerrard, who was born a natural Sorcerer. The King had also adopted his nephew, Brixton, who had lost both his parents to disease at a young age. Brixton was a quiet, sweet-natured boy and looked up to his older cousin.

Gerrard was sure that he would inherit the kingdom from his father. As such, Gerard's confidence became his doom. Gerard was so impressed with his talent that the prince began dabbling in the Black Arts, conjuring evil throughout the lands. When the old King finally passed on, Gerrard claimed the Sceptre immediately – but it did not glow for him.

Brixton claimed the Crown and placed it on his own head. The Crown glittered with silver magic, demonstrating that he was the true King of Pendalin.

Gerrard was enraged and tried to murder his cousin, but the Guards, forever loyal to the Crown and fabled Elves, stopped him. Gerrard vanished in a display of dark power and smoke, taking the Sceptre.

Brixton did his best to rule his people without the Sceptre. He divided his time equally between the southern Palace of Rixondale and the northern Palace of Tryssdale. However, the Sceptre of Almanaic was closely intertwined with the fate of Humans, and the lands of Pendalin began to slowly decline. Plague and famine increased imperceptibly, year by year.

Finally, after almost five years, Gerrard reappeared. He materialised inside the Castle of Tryssdale, aiming to take King Brixton by surprise while he was away from the magic of the Throne at Rixondale. Gerrard was far more gaunt and powerful than before. He also had his own following of Barons, Scholars, and Sorcerers.

Gerrard challenged Brixton for the throne. Brixton, however, had been forewarned of this treason and was ready. He fought Gerrard using the magic of the Crown in an epic battle. Brixton was mortally wounded during the struggle but managed to flee, taking the Crown with him. He and the Crown of Pendalin then vanished without a trace.

Thwarted once more, Gerrard was forced to return from whence he came, for the people of Pendalin revolted against him. A fortnight passed before Gerrard reappeared. He was caught searching the Palace of Tryssdale, looking for any clues as to where Brixton had vanished. An angry boy, the second cousin of the kind King, was overcome by anger at the sight of the evil Sorcerer and killed him. It is unknown how the child managed it; all records show that he had momentarily glowed with a silver light - almost as though the Elves had given him the strength of their magics.

Now, both the Sceptre and Crown are lost. The Throne, connected to both these magical Emblems, was hidden by the Brixton's loyal followers to protect it from interference.

The Throne's location was not recorded, nor revealed to anyone outside the small elite group. Now, the Throne Room remains an empty crypt.

After many sad years, the favoured cousin of Brixton turned Tryssdale Palace into Austin Academy, named for the first King. Princess Veila and her loyal government sought the most talented Healers, Scholars, and Sorcerers of the land to become Professors at the Academy, training generation after generation of Seekers.

Seekers were those who swore a blood oath, upon graduation, to search the lands of Pendalin for the lost Sceptre of Almanaic and the Crown of Weirren Vale, and the hidden location of the Throne of Pendalin. Only the most outstanding students, adept at all aspects of their training, were granted Seekership. These Seekers were indoctrinated in the ways of Honour, living by the ancient words: 'Integrity shall be my code, my life, my breath.'

Not all Seekers search for the lost Crown and Sceptre in modern times. Some comb the lands for potential students of the Academy, to increase the number of possible graduates who can take up the quest.

The Academy also offers various courses for the young and old. Students are often recruited at the age of fourteen. Admission is free, fully funded by the Royal Trust set aside by the heirs of Brixton.

Faye finished the book's last sentence and slowly closed it, her eyes glazed with imagination.

Just picture it, being a Seeker! she thought dreamily as she gazed up at the shifting leaves above her head. *Questing across all the lands of Pendalin, searching for the lost Crown and Sceptre!*

Faye sighed then glanced at her wooden sword. It seemed to beckon her, and she had a brilliant idea. What if she *imagined* a fun adventure? She could *pretend* to go off Seeking the Crown and Sceptre! A Seeker must be adept at swordplay, after all...

And there was no harm in practicing!

With that, Faye scooped up her sword and slid down the tree. Once her feet hit the ground, she began seeing the scenario in her mind's eye. She had just graduated from Austin Academy, and they had granted her Seekership. She had heard rumours – whispers! – about some great evil Guardian that was protecting an amazing treasure. She was almost certain this was the Crown, and retrieving it was up to her!

Making up the story as she went along, Faye stealthily paced through the wood, seeing ghouls and monsters that she had to slay with her wooden sword.

"Hark! I will find the Crown and restore peace and prosperity to the lands of Pendalin!" she called out into the shadowed forest, startling several birds from their roosts and a possum from its feast of ground berries.

She leapt and tumbled, raced, then hid, pranced out of cover before sliding down an embankment and launching herself onto a nearby boulder. The gloom of the forest faded, the midday sun dazzled her eyes as she performed one last leap that landed her back on Shepherds Lane, at a point some five hundred meters from the stone-and-mortar school building.

The girl didn't realise that she had drifted from under the cover of the trees and had come closer to the village. Nor had she realised that three boys, all older than her, were lolling about on an old wooden fence, watching her antics through narrowed eyes.

CHAPTER 2

I'm Not a Boy!

As Faye left the woods, unbeknownst to the distracted girl, those three boys caught sight of her small spritely figure, gracefully swinging a well-made wooden sword and calling softly to an imaginary foe. Naturally, as overgrown bullies tend to do when faced with something different or unusual, they decided to insert themselves into the stranger's path.

"Lo! The Crown is mine! Give it to me, demon, so I might return it to the true heir! No?! You refuse me!?? Then hark! I will gut thee like a pig! For Honour! For Pendalin!" Faye cried, her cheeks flushed with excitement.

"You there! Boy!" called the leader of the trio, a swarthy looking child of ten or so, with conniving brown eyes and short brown hair, snapping Faye out of her daydream. "You're that creature the Healer's taken in, ain't you? Funny looking thing you are! What is that nonsense you're babbling? Off to find the lost Crown of Pendalin? Ha! You're nothing but an orphan! No orphan would EVER be allowed to seek the Crown!"

Faye stopped dead as she heard these words. She wondered how she had managed to get so far away from the protective woods. She glanced behind herself to see if she could make it back before the trio could reach her.

Faye's stomach dropped like a stone in a still pond when she realised she would have no such luck. The three large boys blocked the path and clenched their fists threateningly. For the moment Faye said nothing, eyeing them over warily. She had the strong urge to correct their numerous mistakes – starting with the assumption that she was a boy!

"Well, ye *fungus*? Jimmy here asked ye a question. You're not allowed to go pretending to find the lost Crown," said the sandy-haired boy to Jimmy's right, a mean expression in his dull eyes.

Faye glared at the three, her jaw jutting out in a pugnacious scowl as they sauntered closer.

"Why ever not?" she challenged. "As you said, it's just pretend."

The three boys seemed taken aback that she would argue with them. They recovered quickly, and the one named Jimmy stepped closer.

"That's you being rude to me!" he shouted. "No orphan brat is ever gonna be rude to ME! Jeremy, Archie, c'mon. On him, boys." With that, the three boys leapt at Faye, but the girl was swift and agile.

She dodged Jimmy swiftly, then tripped the largest lad, Jeremy, with a flick of her leg. Using the butt of her sword, Faye conked him on the head. The blow disoriented the large lad so much that he kept moving right past her – falling straight into the nearby paddock fence before slumping to the ground, winded and dazed.

The other two boys leapt at Faye once more. She managed to evade Jimmy's headlock but caught a glancing punch to the face from Archie. She returned in kind, using her wooden sword to slash, jab, and smack.

It was a free-for-all. Legs lashed out, fists met flesh, and the three tumbled to the ground. The sword went flying from Faye's hand. Jeremy finally revived enough to stumble over to the fight. He bodily picked Faye up from amidst the fray – intending to hold her still while the others pummelled her good and proper.

Suddenly, through their skirmish, a great roar reverberated through the air. All three boys stopped what they were doing – even Faye had the grace to surreptitiously release her captor's wrist from between her teeth.

"WHAT DO YE THINK YE LOT ARE DOING!?" bellowed the shadow that had suddenly come upon them.

He was a large man, dressed in shades of grey-green and brown, his heavily bearded face almost lost within the deep cowl pulled over his head. Only his hazel eyes were visible, and they were ablaze with fury.

The Forrester!

The Forrester, the lead Woodsman of Grydin Village, was the most awed and feared person the children knew. He was deadly competent with a knife, a bow, and a sword! He was also the law enforcer since the Pendalin Constabulary didn't have a presence in Grydin.

"How dare ye! Three against one is hardly fair at all!" snarled the Forrester, his voice grating like gravel beneath a pickaxe. "Wait 'til I tell ye father, Jimmy O'Locklynn! How dare ye, picking on such a little fella, all by his lonesome!"

Faye, much sore, bruised, and tired of this affair, figured it was time to set matters straight.

"I'm not a boy, as you well know, Master Jack!" she snapped, exasperated. Although she dared say she must look a sight, with her blonde curls tangled and dusty, her face bruised and scratched...

The Forrester frowned as he peered down at her, before doing a double take as he recognised the girl.

"*Faye,*" he whispered, almost in awe, his face paling.

Then he looked at the big boy holding her up roughly by the arms. His pale face bubbled red; his speckled eyes grew murderous. Jeremy, seeming to recover some of his senses, hastily released her, causing Faye to stumble and catch her balance on Jimmy. The three boys stared at her.

A girl! their mortified expressions seemed to say.

"JIMMY!" roared the Forrester, grabbing roughly at the boy's neck as the child tried to bound away like a spooked rabbit. He swiped another hand, catching himself a second boy. Archie quailed beneath that thunderous look, too terrified to defend himself. "Just you wait, boy! Just you wait until your father hears about THIS! You too, Jeremy."

With that, he dragged the two smaller boys along, with the biggest lad following meekly behind, trembling wildly, his doleful brown eyes filled with terrified tears.

"S'rry," Jeremy mumbled quietly as he passed Faye, resolutely staring at the dirt path beneath his dusty feet.

The Forrester paused, forcing down his spiralling anger.

"You alright, lass?" he asked roughly but not unkindly. Faye managed a short nod, feeling the muscles in her neck and back twinge in response.

"Good. Get ye back to the Healer's. She'll know what to do," his gruff voice ordered.

With that, the Forrester strode on, dragging the whimpering and reluctant boys along with him.

"But we didn't know *it* was a *girl...*!" began Jimmy, only to have himself shaken like a recalcitrant puppy.

Their cries and scuffling steps faded away. Faye, not wanting to wait to see if anyone else would turn up, hobbled back to the Healer's cottage as quickly as her bruised body would allow. Shepherds Lane was thankfully deserted, and the child managed to limp around to the side gate and let herself into the back garden rather than trying to drag her sore, abused flesh back over the boundary fence.

Thayrille met her at the kitchen door, outraged by the number of bruises, scratches and cuts that covered Faye's body. She didn't yell. That simply wasn't her way.

"Tell me." Thayrille said in her firm, stern voice.

The Healer's eyes darkened as she examined every injury, her frizzy hair barely contained in the tight twist that held it away from her face. Every freckle stood out against her pale skin, testimony to her concealed rage.

Faye ducked her head, her breathing shallow as she glowered at the floor, bright spots of emotion colouring her pale cheeks. Tears glinted in the child's miserable eyes, but they did not break through her steely control. One did not *cry* because one had received a few bruises and scrapes.

With valiant effort, Faye blinked away the incriminating moisture in her eyes, her expression unyielding as she recounted, each word precise and devoid of emotion. The Healer listened, her nostrils flaring occasionally, her brows pulled down sternly as she administered ointment.

Faye was relieved that Thayrille decided she had been injured enough and didn't tan her backside for disobeying the house rules and wandering too close to the village main. Once the telling was done, Faye stood silent in her pain as every injury was bandaged – she didn't even whimper as a particularly stringent salve was placed on an ugly gash along her cheek.

Thayrille merely pursed her lip and said nothing throughout her ministrations. When she had finally finished, the Healer gave Faye a healing brew that would ease the pain and help her sleep, then ushered her towards the stairs.

"Get to bed, Faye. This day's task can wait 'til tomorrow," Thayrille instructed her in a low voice.

No matter how kind she tried to make it, her voice was often stern and unforgiving. It was just her way. Faye understood the kindness behind Thayrille's actions – allowing her to go to bed to nurse her aches and wounds instead of forcing her to stay up and finish the day's lesson... and was grateful for it.

Faye trudged up the two flights of stairs, bypassing the first landing that housed the secondary healing rooms and Thayrille's bedroom, before staggering up to the second-floor balcony that accessed the three attic rooms. The girl hesitated at the first attic door – her bedroom door – before opening and closing it again with a short *thud,* which would cause the Healer below to assume she had followed the direction to go to bed.

Instead of curling up on her own feathered mattress, Faye slid silently down the wall next to her door, out of sight from any looky-loos down below. It was time to find out just how cross Thayrille was.

The child closed her eyes, exhausted, and rested her head against the door's architrave, listening to the colourful muttering and cussing echoing up the stairs from the kitchen. One corner of her mouth kicked up in amusement.

Wow, Thayrille *was* angry! And *not* at her!

The realisation was comforting.

A knock sounded at the cottage's front door; startling Faye awake. She had dozed off in her awkward position on the balcony, slumped against the door jamb. Her muscles were now cramping painfully due to being held in an unnaturally uncomfortable position for who-knew-how-long!

With a quiet groan, Faye gained her knees and shuffled forwards to the balcony's edge so she could peer down the stairs and through the kitchen doorway. She caught a glimpse of a broad back perched on one of the breakfast bar stools, covered in a swirl of green, grey and brown.

Forrester Jack had come over.

Faye grimaced as she recalled his temper and roaring bellow. Perhaps *he* was angry with her, and she would be punished after all...

"How's the lass?" the man rumbled, an angry growl still present in his voice.

"Fine – just cuts and bruises, mainly. A sprained ankle, as well. She'll heal in good order, and she'll be right as rain in a week," Thayrille responded, her tone distinctly unhappy.

It hurt Faye's heart that she had been the cause of that unhappiness. Thayrille was the only mother she knew, and she never wanted to upset her. Faye often dreamed that Thayrille would finally hug her, smile at her, and tell her that she loved her like her own daughter.

That would *never* happen if Faye kept making mistakes like this all the time!

The Healer plonked a cup of herbal tea on the bench before the Forrester as they continued their conversation in low voices. Faye's straining ears could make out the murmured conversation.

"She's sleeping?" the Forrester asked before sighing. "Damn, was hoping to get the real story from her."

Thayrille vanished from Faye's line of sight before returning with a small brown bottle that the girl readily identified as headache medicine. The Healer sprinkled three drops into the Forrester's tea with nary a comment. He continued sipping without complaint, and within a few minutes, he let out a relieved sigh.

"Thank ye," he said softly.

The Healer made a dismissive gesture, before placing her hands deep in her apron pockets, an uncharacteristically nervous gesture.

Why was Thayrille nervous? Faye wondered curiously, her brow puckering in thought. Master Jack popped by often, and the adults always seemed to be easy with each other. Was it because of *her*? Were they angry at each other *and* her for the scrape this afternoon? Should she go down there and tell Jack the entire story like he wanted? But then Thayrille will know she had disobeyed instead of going straight to bed as directed.

The child bit her lip, tortured by indecision.

"Faye told me the story as soon as she was home," Thayrille said abruptly, saving Faye from having to make any rash decisions.

"Alright. The boys told me this, correct me where they've gone wrong." Jack began the story and paused often to watch Thayrille nod or shake her head.

His hulking form leaned closer to Thayrille across the counter as he spoke, Jack's voice softening. Faye would have expected the Healer to angrily push away as he leant into her personal space. Instead, the woman was leaning closer in return. They were so close. In fact, they were almost touching!

Faye's frown deepened. Thayrille *did not* appreciate anyone in her personal space! And yet Jack seemed to be an exception...

"The boys were sitting around Shepherds Lane, enjoying their afternoon, when another child, which they thought to be a boy, appeared along the lane," he paused, and Thayrille nodded for him to continue. "Faye, it would seem, was muttering and swinging a wooden play sword. They asked her 'what he was about', and were sassed in reply, Faye threatened them with the sword..." the Forrester trailed off as Thayrille shook her head, the loose strands bouncing around her ears.

"Faye was playing 'pretend' and acting out a fantasy of a swordfight when she was waylaid by the boys. They stopped her and began to bully her, saying that as an orphan, she would never be allowed to go on quests and the like, so she had better stop her pretending. Faye said she didn't see why, since it was just pretend. They took that as her being rude and attacked," the woman summarised her lips pursing again and her nostrils flaring.

Thayrille stepped back from the Forrester, wrapping her arms around herself as though she were afraid to ask for a comforting hug from anyone else.

Faye felt her heart sink. *She* would hug Thayrille any time the woman wanted. But whenever she tried, the Healer would impatiently set her aside and say she was *too busy* for social niceties.

Jack gave a terse nod, his large hands gripping the ceramic mug as he slumped back on his stool, clearly disappointed by the Healer's withdrawal.

"I see. Unprovoked as well, it seems. The boys must have known I wouldn't dismiss the matter," he muttered, angry colour causing his ears to light up.

Faye blinked in surprise. She didn't know a body could *do* that! Did everyone's ears glow red when they were angry? Thayrille's didn't, that was for sure. She cupped her own ears thoughtfully as she continued to raptly listen in on the adult's conversation.

"No," Thayrille gave a despondent sigh. "I bet they were counting on their parents' lack of support of you."

Jack started and a pained, guilty look came over his stern face as he glanced over his shoulder towards the stairwell. Faye froze and then shifted so the banister rail concealed her presence on the balcony. With any luck, those observant peepers hadn't spotted her.

"Aye. They did at that. I went straight to the Elders with those three, and the parents came quick-smart. Nothing was done. The whole weaselly lot of them shrugged it off as though it didn't matter." Jack's knuckles turned white around his mug, threatening to crush the clay cup.

"It is how it is," Thayrille offered with a sad slump to her shoulders, as she gently removed the now empty mug from between Jack's hands.

Unexpectedly, the Forrester clasped his hand over hers.

Faye's eyes widened, impatient for the slap that would surely follow this brazen act. Only... Thayrille turned her hand in his and thread her fingers through Jack's, her face troubled, her bottom lip gripped between her even white teeth.

"After it was dismissed, I spoke to those boys, and I let them know that the next time they picked on *anyone*, they'd be answering to me. I told them I'd be waiting, and the next time, I wouldn't worry about goin' to see their parents. I'd take care of it meself, there and then. They won't touch ye girl anymore, I promise. Neither will anyone else from the village. I've made that clear," Jack said, his voice sincere as he leaned forward again, his free hand rising to brush a strand of frizzy hair back from the woman's pale face.

"Th-th-thank you," Thayrille managed to stutter.

Faye held her breath, torn between delight and horror.

Oh. My. Goodness. Were they going to *kiss*?!

Jack's hands were moving over Thayrille's, and his thumb was rubbing her palm... But Thayrille did nothing. Just stood there staring at him, her face pensive, like a deer keeping track of a hungry wolf.

Jack released the Healer's hand and sat back again, the reluctance in that one motion palpable.

"Best be off – wouldn't do to give those namby-pambering fools another thing to talk about," he growled, then gathered his coat and hat.

Within moments, the man was out the door and vanished into the night.

Faye and Thayrille each let out a harsh sigh, confused and disappointed by Jack's abrupt departure.

The Healer's eyes snapped up and glared at the small figure crouched behind the banister.

"I *said*, get ye to bed, Faye. And I mean *now*!" the Healer snarled, anger replacing nerves. Faye bolted for her bedroom door as quickly as her abused flesh could manage, snapping it closed behind her before she scrambled beneath the covers of her narrow bed.

What on earth had that *been about?!* Faye wondered as she stared at the ceiling, her heart pounding.

Chapter 3

To Become a Seeker

Faye healed quickly and returned to normal within the week. She stayed close to the cottage after that fight, only venturing as far as her treehouse, and never following the lane any further than the cottage boundaries.

She had learnt her lesson, true and proper.

Faye worked much harder at her study tasks and soon caught up that fateful afternoon's work. She even asked for extra lessons on the trials of a Seeker. In her heart, Faye knew she had finally found her life's purpose and wanted to begin preparing now. Thayrille reluctantly lent her books on the subject, wondering if it were the best thing to encourage the girl in her fantasy.

Paradoxically, Thayrille seemed more inclined to give Faye a little free time nearly every day over that summer, as though trying to make up for the injustice of how Faye had been treated by the villagers. In the meantime, Faye used this boon to explore the forest in more depth. And always, it seemed, in the near distance was Jack, watching her. After the fifth time Faye sighted him, she finally decided to tell Thayrille and ask what the Healer thought.

"Jack's keeping an eye on you. He feels badly that those miscreants weren't punished for what they did. So, he's making sure nothing else happens," Thayrille informed her in a casual tone, as she measured herbs for a salve, then placed a pinch beneath Faye's nose. "Name this herb."

Startled, Faye sniffed, then looked carefully.

"Citrus – dried," she replied.

Thayrille nodded once and returned to her work.

No praise, no affection, no hug, pat or wink. It was just her way.

As Faye dismissed the slight pang in her heart, she further considered her problem with the Forrester and was struck by a wonderful idea. Forresters, she knew, were adept with all sorts of weapons – bows, knives, *and swords*! If Jack felt that bad about those boys beating her, she could convince him to teach her how to defend herself, just as Thayrille did each morning before breakfast. Faye appreciated the nasty tricks Thayrille had shown her this past week, with the idea that Faye could ward off further attacks if, or when necessary. Only, with Jack, there was the chance to learn a *real* weapon, which was an irresistible lure.

Faye smiled inwardly, not wanting Thayrille to notice and comment.

"Close your eyes and name this herb," Thayrille instructed once more, holding out a pinch of green. Faye complied and sniffed.

"Juniper!" she identified instantly, wrinkling her nose in disgust at the pungent odour.

The next time she was given a free afternoon, Faye dashed over the garden fence and straight into the forest. The path she followed was no longer a faint track, but a proper game trail because of how many times she had travelled back and forth to her favourite oak tree.

The limbs of the forest giant created a shielding umbrella, providing shade and privacy for Faye's makeshift cubby high up its stout frame. The girl paused at the tree's base, preparing to scramble up the trunk and retrieve her practice sword. Faye hesitated and listened carefully. Birds were singing praise to the sun, insects were buzzing with their love of summer flowers, and a nearby brook was bubbling with vigour.

All was as it should be. Except...

There! A glint of light sparkled just beyond the corner of her eye. Faye whipped her head around and caught sight of another glimmer. A shaft of golden sunlight reflected off the blade of a short hunting knife in the distance.

Faye felt her heart stop in her throat until she recognised the burly figure in its camouflage cloak. Forrester Jack was sitting nearby, just beyond the brook, sliding his knife along a thin, straight stick.

The girl barely managed to contain her squeal of delight.

Just the person she wanted to speak to!

"Yes, lass?" Jack asked when she bounded over to him, his large hands carefully whittling a brand-new arrow. There was already a pile by his left foot, testimony to the long hours he had spent in this very spot. Faye wondered briefly why he had chosen this place to sit and whittle arrows.

Jack's calico cloak melded with the surrounding forest, his tight cap disguised his curly brown hair, and his bushy beard softened the tan skin of his face. If it hadn't been for the fact that he was moving and the sunlight had been glinting off his knife, Faye would never have seen him in the first place. It almost felt... *deliberate*.

But why would a Forrester put himself in such a place, to invite her, in that silent way he had, to come to talk with him? What did he want? But then, did it really matter? It certainly suited *her* purposes to have him here so she could ask him about the very thing she wanted most.

The Forrester remained silent as he whittled, as though he hadn't a care in the world. Faye had rehearsed this moment for so many weeks! How was she meant to ask the most important of questions?

"Could you teach me?" Faye burst out after taking a moment to gather her courage.

Jack seemed to consider her request, which was an odd one by all accounts and particularly scarce of information.

"Teach ye the sword so ye can go adventuring and find the lost Crown of Weirren Vale?" he clarified, without a smile on his face, though Faye felt there should have been one the way his eyes crinkled at the corners. "Or teach ye how to whittle an arrow?"

Faye wasn't surprised he knew her deepest wishes. She was mainly focused on his acceptance. Naught else mattered right now.

"The sword, as you very well know, Master Jack!" she replied with a grin, lifting herself up on her toes and then dropping back down on her heels, barely able to contain her excitement. "I could defend myself. In the long run, it would free you up. You wouldn't have to constantly watch after me."

Jack sighed and rubbed a hand over his beard. He seemed deep in thought, as though he were weighing all sides of his decision.

"And what of honour?" he murmured, his dark eyes searching hers intently.

Her own eyes shining with excitement, Faye replied with the age-old phrase she had learnt from her history texts.

"Integrity shall be my code, my soul, my breath," she quoted, throat tight with emotion.

"So, you know the words – but do you understand the meaning?" the Forrester questioned, his deep voice stern.

For a moment, he reminded her strongly of Thayrille. Faye's mind flashed back to when the Forrester held her foster mother's hand, and they had *almost* kissed. She wondered if the two secretly *liked* each other. And if they did, what would that mean for *her*?

Faye blinked several times and tossed the ungrateful thought aside. It didn't matter. All that mattered was that Jack started training her to become a Seeker! Then she could take care of herself and not need anyone!

"It means... It means that I live by the ways of honour, to judge when to use force and when to use reason. It means I can't take revenge on Jimmy, Jeremy, and Archie and only respond to them if they challenge me again. And it also means that I'll practice being the best I can be with fighting and weapons so that if the challenge does come, I actually have the chance to win," she replied in a rush, her tone thick with desperate sincerity.

Jack nodded in agreement, the corners of his mouth kicking up beneath his thick beard.

"Alright, lass. Then let's begin," he replied before reaching behind him and retrieving two long sticks.

Faye blinked in surprise. Why would the Forrester happen to have *broomstick* handles with him out in the woods? They didn't even have a place where you could attach a brush!

When Jack set the sticks point down into the ground, Faye noted that the larger stick came to his shoulder while the other reached her chin, almost as though it had been deliberately cut for a child of just her size. Curious, the girl examined them more closely.

Made of polished wood, they were thickness of a broom handle with a soft, pliable leather grip midway along their lengths. Although they had a similar shape, the child was beginning to realise that these were *not* the average handle of a long tool, but something else.

The man gripped the larger stick and used one hand to twirl it easily, whipping it through the air with considerable force. It was a weapon!

Faye grinned, realising that Jack had fully intended to teach her, perhaps even before she had thought to ask him! She quelled the impulse to question him further, not wanting to appear ungrateful and have the burly man change his mind.

"This is known as a sparring stick." Jack said. "The first thing any swordsman learns is how to move. Only when you can effectively duck, weave, and leap to avoid your opponent, then you may begin practising with a sword." He passed her the smaller stick, quickly demonstrating how to hold it correctly. "Now, Faye. Hit me."

Faye blinked owlishly up at the man, noticing for perhaps the first time just how big he was. She was only seven! And he... He was a giant, towering over twice, or even thrice, her height!

Thayrille's voice rang in the back of her mind. *'Remember, child, if you ever face someone bigger than you, aim for a place within easy reach. But don't look at it! The flicker of your eye will give you away and you will lose the element of surprise.'*

It was the lesson on self-defence the Healer had been teaching her young ward each morning this past week.

Instinctively, Faye held Jack's gaze and swung the butt of her stick up from the ground to give a short, hard whack. It should have bruised a rather sensitive area but missed on account of the man's fast reflexes. His eyes bugged as he realised her intention. Jack managed to knock his knees together and twist his hips just in time to take the hit in his upper thigh.

He grunted in pain and grasped the end of her stick, holding it in a vice-like grip when Faye attempted to draw back and hit him a second time.

"Right," he growled in irritation. "I should have expected that."

Faye stilled and watched him with wide, panicked eyes as her heart thrummed nervously.

Uh-oh, Faye thought. *Have I ruined my one chance already?* Should she not have done that? He *had* said for her to hit him!

Jack ran his free hand over his face, and she could have sworn he muttered something about man-hating Healers, but she couldn't be sure.

"Alright, lass. When we whack someone, we don't aim for the family jewels. Well, not with our master-trainer, that is. Save that sort of nasty trick for someone who's actually trying to hurt ye," Jack said sternly. "Now I'm going to release the stick, and I want ye to whack me as though it were a sword. Right?"

Faye nodded so hard that her brain jangled in her skull.

Jack released his grip on the weapon, so Faye swung around this time, aiming for the man's ribs. Her stick clacked loudly when it was met with brute force. The Forrester easily deflected the wooden pole with his own. She noted how he held the weapon across his body, ready to meet an assault from any direction, so she mimicked him as she stood back and waited for the next instruction.

"That's it, lass. Again," Jack commanded, his tone encouraging.

Thrilled, Faye launched another attack and another, delighting in the repeated *clack, clack, clack* of their sticks. Her arms began to grow heavy, sweat beaded down her face and into her eyes, and she didn't quite manage to score another flesh-hit on Jack for the remainder of that session.

Nor in any of the other sessions that followed. However, her whacks grew in strength and frequency, her precision increased, and Faye was able to effectively evade and defend against Jack's return attacks.

By summer's end, Faye had learnt enough about evasions, attack, and defence that she was able to switch to her practice sword. And that's when the *real* work began... Especially as they had to keep her training a secret – particularly from Thayrille's disapproval.

Winter that year came in its usual flurry of sleet, hail and snow, freezing the ground solid and covering every exposed surface with copious amounts of white powder. The Woodsmen kept the cobbled main street of the village clear, with their iconic sacks of salt slung over one shoulder and a shovel in the opposite hand. Shepherds Lane, however, didn't warrant such treatment, and Faye found she had to slog through banks of snow to access her favourite cubby whenever she gained freedom from the Healer's stone cottage. The oak tree had lost its leaves and slept amongst the frozen mounds of white, yet somehow still retained that *zing* of life that appealed to the young girl.

Faye clambered up the chill branches, her breath steaming in the crystalline air, eager to collect her staff for practice. Jack had indicated the other day that, despite the heavy snow, the two of them would continue their training.

"Och, lass, ye not need it today. Leave it and come along," Jack's deep voice thundered from beneath the tree.

Faye froze halfway into her cubby and whipped her head around to peer down, down, down at the miniature figure of the Forrester at the base of the tree. He leaned casually against the trunk, grinning at her with a mischievous gleam. Over his shoulder hung a sack, not too different from the salt sacks used by the Woodsmen, and in one hand was a flat cork board.

The girl frowned suspiciously.

"I thought you said we were training," she called back, reluctant to leave her safe little nest and its stash of wooden weapons.

"Aye, that we are, lass. But not with the stick, nor with the sword. Now get ye down here, and let's get going before it grows late," Jack insisted, beckoning her back to the ground.

Faye shrugged philosophically. *Training was training*, she supposed, and if this was some sort of new skill the burly man was planning on teaching her, then she supposed she should just shut up and learn it.

Mind made up, the girl shimmied down the trunk to the ground far below. The Forrester nodded approval of her quick, economic movements and instinctive agility before turning to lead the way in a direction different to the one they usually took.

"Where are we going, Master Jack?" Faye asked curiously as she jogged every other step to keep up with the grown man's longer stride.

"Ye'll see when we get there, lass."

Faye frowned again. The grin, and that glint in his eyes, seemed rather foreboding. The girl's curiosity intensified. Where on earth were they off to?

The pair wound their way through the forest, skating over snow and ice, dodging icicles and rotten branches. The land began to dip and before too long, they had entered a broad gully she had never been through before.

"Not too far now, lass," the Forrester reassured her cheerily, whistling a merry tune that bounced off the stone walls and frozen tree trunks.

As the gully angled downwards, Faye noticed that the snow lessened, and the surrounding temperature warmed. Within ten minutes, the girl had to strip off her heavy winter jacket and the knit jumper she wore underneath, so she was left wearing only a thin cotton shirt over her leather breeches.

"What is this place, Master Jack?" Faye asked as she peered around, sweat beading along her brow.

The pair trailed around one more bend in the gully and found themselves on a pebbled riverbank. Water rushed through the canyon, its source appearing to be the multitude of waterfalls from the rim above. Rivulets trickled over the steep stone walls to collect in the rockpools below. Every pool was so full of water that it overflowed down a set of rocks into another pool beneath it and yet another beneath that one to form a stepped watercourse that vanished around the canyon's bend some distance away. The rocky edges of this secret place were lined with ferns and succulent flora that served as a home for buzzing insects and cheerily warbling birds.

It was *beautiful*.

"This, lass, is called Grydin Grotto," the Forrester murmured, his voice hushed in the dim, humid air. "During the summer, it's a series of barren, hot, muddy sinkholes, and the source of the mineral clay that some of the locals use for pottery and the like. In the winter, however, once the snowbank above grows high enough, the ice at the canyon's edge melts and runs down here, creating these hot springs. Go on, lass, take off ye' boots and dip a toe in."

His easy, encouraging smile still made the girl wary, but Faye gamely sat on a nearby boulder and unlaced her shoes. With only the smallest of hesitations, she dunked her toe, then a whole foot, into the tepid water. It wasn't hot, as she first suspected, but akin to something like a cool bath.

"This is actually quite nice," Faye commented, her wariness easing as she gazed around herself, enjoying the sensation of cool water around her ankles as she took several steps into the shallows.

The Forrester nodded in agreement, already working on his own bootlaces so he could also dip his feet in. Faye wriggled her toes in appreciation, then froze as she noted that the depth changed abruptly just a foot further along, the crystalline waters becoming murky as the pebbled ground rapidly sloped away.

"The temperature is ideal for swimming," Jack continued, his grin widening. "And that's the very reason we've come down here. It's one of Grydin's best kept secrets."

Faye stared at the tinkling water with eyes that grew wider and wider. She had both feet in, and the water lapped gently around her ankles, but she certainly had no plans on going any further!

"*Swimming?*" she demanded, affronted to her very core, the beauty of the place no longer dazzling her young eyes. "You expect me to *get in? All the way in?*"

Faye observed the small rapids in the deeper water, the murky, muddy bottom and the wafts of pungent steam rising from its surface. She whirled right around, intending to march herself up the gully, back the way they had come.

There was *no way* she was splashing around in *that* muddy water! It had to be deeper than she was high. She would drown!

The Forrester, however, had other ideas.

Faye felt a vice clamp on her upper arms moments before she was lifted bodily off the ground and swung up and out. The girl gritted her teeth against the wailing screech that built in her throat, managing to tamp down on the undignified sound as she landed with a splash in the deeper water. She plunged down into the depths before her feet found the pebbled bottom. With a bit more force than necessary, Faye kicked against the stony ground and launched herself up and out, floundering as she tried to orient herself within the murky liquid.

Jack, curse him, *laughed* as he plunged in after her, scooping her up in a tight one-armed hold and thrusting the corkboard into her hands.

"Here, lass, hold this. It'll keep ye afloat," the man soothed as Faye continued to splash and struggle against his confining grip.

Left with little choice, Faye grasped the buoyant panel and clutched it to her chest, coughing and spluttering as the warm meltwater trickled into her mouth. Her toes could *almost* touch the stones that lined the base of the rock pool, but not enough to tip toe her way out of the water and back onto dry land.

Faye glowered at her mentor, displeased by this unexpected dunking. She really wished she had ignored his orders and brought her stick! A good whack in the family jewels would indeed teach him a lesson!

The thought must have been pretty obvious, because the man laughed heartily and kept his body positioned in such a way that she couldn't effectively reach him to inflict an injury .

"Och, dinna look like such a grumpy cat! Ye'll get ye fur all dry soon enough, lass. The sack there is full of cotton towels so we can dry off when we're done. Now, todays lesson. How to float." The Forrester chuckled as he helped Faye position her body against the board so she was lying flat in the water, her chin dipping dangerously into the suffocating liquid.

"Master Jack, I don't see..." Faye began to protest, gripping the corkboard for dear life.

"Swimming can be an excellent form of recreational exercise and fitness," the man explained in a reasonable tone. "*And* it's a handy skill to have. What if ye fall into a river or a lake? What if a boat yer on capsizes? All Forresters and Woodsmen know how to swim."

Faye clenched her teeth again, her face set into a grumpy frown, but she didn't argue further. Instead, she followed all of Jack's instructions with an obstinate scowl, and by the end of an hour, she was able to float with only the smallest amount of support from the cork board and the Forrester's steadying hands.

"I think I'm getting the hang of this!" Faye finally smiled, delighted that she could now hold her head above the water, using her arms to create small counter motions that kept her afloat.

"Excellent. Now kick yer legs to move forwards," Jack instructed, an expectant look on his bearded face.

The moment the girl attempted to do just that, she lost the controlled motion of her arms and plunged down beneath the water's surface again, popping up to grasp desperately at her corkboard.

The Forrester laughed as he helped her regain balance, so she could practice the leg motion he deemed necessary for moving effectively through water. Faye continued to doggedly follow his directions, her face now permanently wearing the sour scowl that the man seemed to find so funny.

CHAPTER 4

Friend or Foe

The winter passed rapidly. Faye completed additional intensive study under Thayrille's strict guidance, her time at a desk broken only by her daily swim and weaponry lessons from Jack. Soon enough, Faye's coordination and stamina in the water improved, and she could paddle laps around the largest of the rock pools. The Forrester began to teach her several specialty strokes, one designed to increase her speed and another to allow her to creep in stealth. He even set her *study tasks*, to observe various creatures and how they moved through the water.

One memorable lesson had Faye scouring the shallow pools for tadpoles. Once captured, Jack helped her rig a tank in his Forrester's cottage so they could observe the critters morph and swim through their aquatic environment.

Faye's eighth birthday came and went with nary a blip. Thayrille lit a brand-new candle at dawn, signifying the birth of a new life, then lit another at dusk in commemoration of a life ended. The quaint custom was common amongst the local villagers and was usually accompanied by gifts and food. But, as was the Healer's way, Faye received only a pair of freshly darned socks, one new linen shirt and a new length of ribbon to bind her hair. While the girl appreciated the practical aspect of these items, they weren't exactly what she thought of as *gifts*. From what she had seen around the village, Faye knew that most children received far more exciting things. Such as a new sled, wooden toys, or other nick-nack items that could be played with. More luxury items than everyday ones.

Nevertheless, Faye thanked her foster mother and went about her day as per usual.

It wasn't until the following day, when the girl was allowed out of the house for a couple of hours of exercise, that Faye received her first-ever *proper* birthday present. She and Jack were back down at the Grotto, preparing for another round of swimming lessons. Faye had been working on freestyle, to increase her coordination and speed to navigate the rockpools as quickly as possible. As she sat on her usual boulder and removed her sturdy boots, Jack presented her with an oiled leather satchel pegged closed by a small button.

"Happy birthday, lass. Sorry it's a day late, but I dinna think Thayrille would understand if she saw I gave ye this," the big man said quickly, handing her the brown package with a friendly wink. "Don't want to raise too many of the wrong questions."

Faye's eyes widened in pleasure, turning the small package over in wonder. A gift that *wasn't* clothes!

Curious, she unbuttoned the clasp and opened the satchel to discover four odd items inside. The first three were quite similar. They were thin, hollow reeds of differing lengths that had been dried and lacquered. Strangely, the end of one of the reeds crooked into a *u* shape before fanning out into a flattened funnel.

"The funnel goes in yer mouth, lass, and the reeds connect together to form a long tube that sticks up into the air. It's so ye can breathe when ye face is under water. The contraption is called a snorkel, and it's been used by the coastal people of Pendalin for millennia."

"Well, I suppose that's handy, but why would I need that when I can swim just fine now?" Faye asked, now turning to examine the fourth and final item in the satchel.

It looked like a pair of spectacles, but the glass lenses were rimmed with cork that had been laminated with some sort of flexible resin and were connected by straps of supple leather.

"Because, when paired with ye goggles, ye can swim about and not have to keep coming up for air. It can be used for stealth and also for exploring underwater worlds," the man grinned happily. "Some of our Natural Scientists use this getup to document aquatic flora and fauna."

Faye's face lit up as she finally understood the purpose of the items. It wasn't for necessity or function, but for fun! She could swim around and explore under the surface of the rock pools!

"Thank you so much, Jack!" Faye squealed with delight, impulsively throwing her arms around his broad shoulders to give him a squeezing hug.

The man hugged her back, engulfing her in his burly arms.

"Ye're welcome, lass. Come now, it's time I showed ye how they work," he said gruffly before releasing her, a suspicious wet sparkle in his eyes.

The rest of the day was spent practising breathing through the snorkel and positioning the grippy goggles to protect her eyes when submerged. Faye became adept at using the equipment and could examine the myriads of creatures both below and above the water. She was particularly delighted by discovering the occasional precious gem nestled amongst the stones at the pool's bottom. The glints of purple, blue and green often indicated the presence of amethyst, lapis lazuli and turquoise, all of which Faye dove down to collect before resurfacing to gasp for air.

It was, perhaps, the most enjoyable pastime of the girl's life.

Before long, spring returned to the Arythmun Mountains, and the Grotto began to dry up. Faye was sorely disappointed as swimming had fast become her favourite thing to do. However, the change in season also meant a reduction in her indoor hours. As there had been no further interactions between Faye and the village children since the previous summer, the Healer would allow her ward to take books and paper out to her treehouse to complete her lessons rather than remain sequestered in the stuffy study.

Unfortunately, this time of year also meant that the Woodsmen, and by default, Jack the Forrester, were called away and spent longer hours performing their duties in the surrounding forests. This put a rather big kink in the amount of time Faye could spend with her master-trainer.

Faye and the Forrester were packing up after their most recent sparring session, stacking equipment and targets in the shelter of a nearby tree, when Jack imparted the terrible news. He was about to embark on the seasonal tour he was required to perform around the Grydin Triad and its surrounding woods. Bandits were lurking and required a show of force to move them on, bears were coming out of hibernation and needed to be documented, packs of wolves were to be culled, and venison hunted to feed the villages under his care.

"What am I meant to do for the four weeks you're gone?" Faye aimed to keep her voice reasonable instead of wheedling.

Wheedling, she knew from experience, only received a sharp tap upside the head and the terse instruction to *knock it off*. And that was just from Thayrille. The girl had no idea how her idol, the Forrester, would react.

"Well, lass, ye know enough now to carry on yer own for a time. Ye can practice ye fitness moves, ye can use that quintain we made to fence and spar, and ye can even take the frogs down to the Grotto and release them back into the shallows. They'll need to start burrowing into the mud before the rock pools completely dry out, or they won't be able to hibernate effectively come summer," Jack said with a significant lack of compassion.

"There'll be plenty to keep ye busy, and ye can start to help Thayrille a bit more around the cottage. Yer old enough to start thinking about healing and the like."

Faye frowned, unhappy with the situation...

"Yes, but *you* won't be here. It's not the same!" Faye protested. "It'll be lonely, all by myself. Thayrille doesn't like to play."

Jack ceased the task of stacking the targets and turned to face the girl, his bearded face softening in sympathy as he knelt down so their eyes were level.

"Don't be so harsh on ye foster mother. The lass is doing her best. Maybe ye should stop obsessing over the *what* and start wondering as to the *why*. Thayrille is a right prickly little woman, but she has her reasons. Her life ain't been a bed of roses," the Forrester said in a gentle tone. "Now, one last hug, and I must be off. Ye stay out of trouble while I'm gone, hear me?"

The man engulfed the little girl in his big arms, and Faye held on tightly, never wanting to let him go. She wished heartily that *he* was her father, that they had a little mother back in the Forrester's cottage to love them, and that life could be different. Only she had a feeling that Jack never felt that way. Life was whatever life was, and you had to make the most of it.

The Forrester ended the hug, ruffled her hair, and hoisted himself back to his feet.

"Yes, Sir." Faye sighed as Jack gathered his pack and strode off into the woods with one last jaunty wave.

The following week dragged by until Faye recalled rather belatedly that she hadn't fed the frogs in the Forrester's cottage, nor had she released them as she had been instructed to do.

Annoyed with herself, she took Thayrille's largest leather water skin down to the neighbouring house and let herself in the single front door. Jack's place was sparse, but his few items were of good quality. Faye particularly liked the colourful woven rug that lined the floor before the hearth. It reminded her of the first leaf changes of autumn and served as a bright focal point of the combined living, kitchen, and dining area.

Faye hurriedly filled the skin with water from the glass tank near the unlit hearth and ensured all the frogs had made their way into its dark depths before securing the neck with a large cork. She slung the bulging bag carefully over her shoulder by its attached strap, ensuring that it was snug in the middle of her back where it wouldn't slosh around too much as she walked.

She hurried back up the hill past the Healer's cottage, over Shepherds Lane, skirted her favourite oak tree, followed the faint trail that led to the gully, and down into Grydin Grotto. This was the first time she had made the trek alone, and Faye found she quite enjoyed it. The forest seemed to come alive when she was on her own, as though the inhabitants realised, she meant them no harm. Without the cumbersome form of the Forrester, the animals grew bold and would stop to examine the spritely child rather than dashing away.

Faye took her time and admired the changes the warmer weather had caused in the surrounding forests. The ground was rather muddy from the melted snow, but the trees were budding with bright green leaves, birds were flocking here and there, and small game bounded in the near distance.

Once down the gully and into the Grotto, however, Faye was less pleased to note the sulphurous stench and stagnant pools. The snow no longer supplied the series of rockpools with meltwater, and the heat of the hot springs was causing the remaining liquid to rapidly evaporate.

The place was no longer fit for swimming, although she supposed some of the outer streams would be okay to paddle in.

Faye made her way to one of these streams, noting that it was still emptying fresh water into one of the rockpools. This would be the ideal place to release the frogs!

As she crouched by the bubbling brook, the peace of the area was disturbed by a most unpleasant sound.

"*What* is *that*?" the obnoxious voice demanded, high and shrill in the still air. "Is *that* the *demon* child thing that lives with the *Healer*? Yes! See, it looks like a *boy* but has the face of a *girl*. How completely *unnatural!*"

Faye's head jerked up to find four blonde girls across the stream, all quite similar in appearance, glaring at her as though she had committed some great offence. The eldest had spoken, causing the younger three to giggle rudely into their hands. Faye decided right then that she would forever more *hate* giggling.

"My name," Faye bit out, face rigid, "is *Faye*. I am *not* a demon, nor a *thing*. I *am* a girl. Did your parents not teach you any manners?"

The four girls stopped their giggling to glare at her.

"Well, at least we *have* parents." the oldest girl spat waspishly; her bright blue eyes narrowed in intense dislike.

Faye frowned at them, wondering why they were even here. Not once had she and Jack encountered the villagers in the Grotto during winter. The locals preferred not to brave the forest's thick snow or frigid air above, despite the reward that awaited below. And, if these girls hated her so much, why did they stop to speak with her? Why not keep walking, as all the other village children did? Faye much preferred to be ignored than spoken to in such a manner.

"Come on, Hannah, let's go," the youngest girl urged, grasping futilely at her big sister's arm. "Mamma won't like us talking to this creature. We were meant to be home by now, anyway. We aren't meant to be at the hot springs without an adult."

Hannah reefed her arm away, taking a step closer to Faye.

"We'll go in a minute. But first, I think I'll have that water skin. I'm thirsty, and it's *hot* down here." the girl said, an evil glint entering her eyes.

Before Faye could protest or utter a warning, Hannah had snatched the leather bag straight out of her hands, unplugged the cork, and tipped the contents into her mouth so forcefully that the cool water overflowed down her front, wetting her dress, and coating it with strings of algae that had lined Jack's fish tank, right along with the frogs that the skin contained.

Hannah choked and squealed, dropping the waterbag into the stream, clutching her throat as though she'd been poisoned. With a mighty belch, the girl spat out the frog that had attempted to burrow down into her throat.

Hannah gave a roar of outrage and stamped on the poor, beleaguered frog, crushing it to death beneath her heavy walking boot.

"*Freak*!" she bellowed at Faye while she retched and coughed, tendrils of green algae caught between her teeth. "You've tried to kill me!"

Hannah sunk her hands into the burbling creek and reefed up a sizeable boulder, launching the heavy stone straight at Faye's head. Thanks to her relentless training with Master Jack, Faye was able to dodge the thing just in the nick of time. The stone collided with a sapling nearby and snapped the thin trunk clean in two.

If Faye had been unable to move, that rock would have cleaved her skull!

She would be *dead*, just like that poor frog!

"Just wait until I get my hands on you!" Hannah barked, already searching for another rock.

Faye, realising that the older girl had murder in her heart, abandoned the rapidly emptying water skin and dashed back through the forest, leaving the unfortunate frogs to their fate. They would either find their way into the water and the drying rock pools or perish. On the other hand, Faye chose to live another day and took herself away from the enraged, shrieking banshee just as quickly as she could. Thayrille would wonder where her largest skin had vanished too, but with luck, the girl could return another time to retrieve it.

Faye thought, half-hysterically, *So much for staying out of trouble!*

CHAPTER 5

An Unexpected Companion

The shrieking blonde banshee was Hannah Rikton, the oldest daughter of the Boarding House Mistress, Faye learned, and that day at the Grotto marked the beginning of a deep animosity between the two girls.

Whenever Faye was out and about that summer, Hannah and her younger sisters would heckle her. If the opportunity presented itself, they would throw stones, sticks and other debris as she passed. The worst occasion was when the sisters stole a dozen rotten eggs, attempting to smash the brittle shells so that the sulphuric contents would splash over Faye's clean clothes. The three were careful not to let any adults see, and Faye was at a loss how to deal with the situation.

Did she use her new-found skills to beat the girls senseless? No. That wasn't the way to handle it, she was sure. Jack would be furious because it would be a thoroughly unfair fight.

Hannah might be capable of murdering someone with a rock and had not hesitated when pulverising that unfortunate frog, but she wasn't a trained fighter. Faye felt the best course of action was to avoid the girls as much as possible… which wasn't all together difficult as Faye knew all the secret paths through the forests and could always hide in the towering limbs of her oak tree.

Nobody ever seemed to bother her there.

The remaining weeks passed at a snail's pace, but Master Jack *finally* returned home. Faye wasted no time taking herself down to the Forrester's cottage the moment she saw the telltale smoke curling from its chimney.

"Master Jack!" the girl pipped as she barrelled through his front door, launching herself into his awaiting arms.

"Och, there's the lass!" he laughed, hugging her close. "How are ye? Tell me, how are things with ye?"

Faye told him. She started with her lessons with Thayrille, excitedly prattling on about the more in-depth lessons she was made to study, and how she had learned to bottle serums when she offered to help the Healer in her kitchen.

"She said that every apprentice starts with the basics and works their way up to more difficult tasks." Faye said cheerily, helping to sort the Forrester's pack out into piles of dirty clothes and knick-knacks.

"That's about true of everything, lass. Now, I notice the tanks are empty and cleaned. Did ye get those frogs down to the Grotto alright, then?" Jack asked, pleased that the girl had taken time to scrub the algae and pond scum out of the glass container.

"Um, sure," Faye said hesitantly.

When the Forrester looked at her sharply, her shoulders slumped, and she sat down on the low coffee table with an abject sigh.

"I *tried* to stay out of trouble, Master Jack, just as you told me. I really did! But…" Faye shrugged dejectedly, scuffing the rug underfoot with her boot.

"But...?" the large man prompted, sitting across from her in his favourite armchair, before scooping her chin in his large hand, and tilting her head back so she would look him in the eye.

Faye told him the story of meeting Hannah and her sisters, the way the girl had taken the skin, choked on a frog, and all the trouble it had caused since.

The girl expected the Forrester to lecture her, or cuff her around the head, or inform her he could no longer teach her the sword, as she had failed him as a student.

Instead, his shoulders shook, and he closed his eyes, pinching the bridge of his nose between his thumb and finger of his free hand.

"Ye surely don't do things by halves, do ye lass?" he muttered, amusement rich in his voice.

"You're not angry?" Faye asked, puzzled.

The Forrester gave up on the effort to keep a straight face and burst out laughing.

"Och! I wish I'd been there to see that uppity little bully receive her comeuppance! Ye be not the only child around Grydin that Hannah Rikton has taken a dislike to. That girl is a menace," he said, his laughter simmering down as he wiped away the mirthful tears. "Now, ye did the right thing, lass. Just stay well away from that girl, and I'll do my best to keep the lads and lassies out of the forest. I'll tell the parents that a wild boar is out and about. That should do the trick!"

Faye's lips curled into a reluctant grin.

She had been hoping for a more concrete resolution to this debacle with Hannah, but she supposed the man was right. Sometimes the only thing somebody could do in such circumstances was to avoid the cause of the problem.

The seasons changed, and the years slumped by in a predictable routine. Summer melded into autumn, autumn into winter again, and Faye celebrated her ninth birthday. The day arrived and passed without any significant events, only recognised by Thayrille through the presentation of a new tome on local herb-law, and by Jack with the gift of a longer and heavier practice sword.

Nine soon became ten, and ten became eleven.

Faye read voraciously and no longer had lessons expressly set by Thayrille, instead using her indoor time to conduct her own private study by inhaling the Healer's eclectic library. As Faye grew, she became less of a child needing constant supervision and more like a small housemate to Thayrille, assisting her foster mother with various medical procedures and household tasks. Cooking lessons, particularly, were a source of fascination and fun for the girl, along with brewing herbal remedies in the Healer's stone kitchen.

Jack, as ever, circled around the precipice of Thayrille's life, assisting to mend walls, plug leaks, chop firewood, and other general maintenance while meeting the Healer's sharp tongue and short temper with a calm, unrufflable demeanour. Thayrille continued to hold herself aloof, watching the Forrester warily from within the safe boundary of her cottage.

Faye, however, continued to secretly meet with her master-trainer in the depths of the forest, often sparring in various locations to reduce the likelihood of being spotted by the other woodsmen over the summer, and continued her swim training over winter, in the lovely warm water of the rockpools.

One day, some four years after their first sparring session, Faye was waiting for Jack in their predetermined meeting place. This practice session was to take place beyond the woods, where the trees petered out and a dry canyon cut deeply into the land. Large open areas down along its bottom were shielded from prying eyes, and the sandy floor offered a perfect arena for sparring.

About a year ago, Jack had begun to formally teach Faye how to use her sparring stick as a weapon – not just for evasion and defence. She had long outgrown her original stick. The weapon she now owned was a straight, smooth limb from her favourite oak tree covered in her signature carvings. She hadn't really believed Jack when he told her the stick could become a fatal weapon... until he revealed how his own concealed sharp blades. He pressed a hidden set of buttons along the shaft of his stick, causing one end, then the other, to release a glinting blade with a deadly *snick*.

Faye had been morbidly fascinated and was now keener than ever to learn this weapon – and today was meant to be another stick sparring session! Faye sat upon a warm rock, waiting patiently. Soon enough, the sun continued to sink beyond the canyon wall causing Faye to realise that the burly man wasn't coming.

This wasn't the first time, and after three years the girl had come to accept that some days Jack would be unable to make it. She always waited patiently until almost an hour had passed. If the Forrester still had not appeared by then, she was free to return to the Healer's Cottage.

Sighing heavily, Faye realised this was one of those times.

She was about to get up from her rock when a colourful lizard slunk up onto it, slowly crawling along its warm surface. It was a large reptile, almost the width and length of her forearm, and was covered in beautifully coloured patterns. Red, green, blue, and yellow, to name a few, swirled along its scales. It glistened strangely in the sun, and as she peered at it, she realised that it had left a trail of fragments behind it. At the base of the very rock she was sitting on lay a broken egg. The egg itself seemed odd. It was almost... metallic, with a powdered coating, like oxidised magnesium. It seemed that the fragments stuck to the lizard were bits of the eggshell.

The creature must have just hatched!

Faye dismissed the remnants of the shell to examine the reptile more closely.

It must be hungry, she thought.

She had found from experience that newly hatched things often were. She wondered momentarily how big this lizard would grow, as it was rather large for a new hatchling.

Careful to keep her movements slow and steady, Faye reached into her knapsack and brought out a grape. Just as carefully, she broke the grape in half and placed it near the lizard's head.

Its bright blue tongue flicked out a time or two, testing the offering before it snapped up the pieces with relish. Faye continued to feed the thing until it ate no more. Feeling as though this should be enough to make friends, Faye reached for the animal and placed her hand around its middle, intending to pick it up.

"Don't you realise some reptiles are very poisonous to touch?" a tart voice demanded.

Shocked, Faye squeaked softly and fell off the rock.

She had let go of the lizard in fright, so it sat there complacently on the warm rock. Faye looked around frantically for the source of the voice.

The canyon was empty.

"Who said that?" Faye squeaked, fear tightening her throat.

"Come now, child, enough melodrama. It was just a casual comment. Some reptiles, especially colourful ones, really are poisonous to the touch, as well as bite," said the voice in the most reasonable of tones.

Faye looked around wildly but could see no one. "This isn't funny!" she exclaimed.

"I'd say not," agreed the voice from quite nearby.

"Show yourself," Faye returned, tilting her head this way and that, trying to target the location of this intruder.

In the meantime, the beautiful lizard had crept forward to the edge of the rock and eyed her with one beady, black eye.

"I'm right here." the lizard then said, its mouth moving in time with the words.

Faye's jaw dropped open; her breath stuck in her throat.

"But... but... but... you're a... a..." she trailed off, unable to breathe, her heart hammering in shock against her ribs.

"Yes, dear, I'm a reptile – a *lizard*, I suppose," it replied with a yawn, then eyed her curiously once more. "I don't suppose you're getting up off the ground any time soon? You're getting rather sandy."

Faye felt her head spinning, then her vision became cloudy. What was happening to her?

Just as everything faded to black, she thought to herself that someone that had forgotten to breathe for this long was bound to pass out.

Faye came to a few minutes later. The strange reptile had vanished, and the sun was noticeably lower.

It was time to go home. Shakily, she got to her feet and looked around for any sign of the lizard. Maybe she had imagined it, she thought, except that the broken shell was still at the base of the rock and there were leftover grapes still on the top.

Feeling a little unnerved, Faye grabbed her knapsack and ran for the steep trail that would lead her home. She dashed along the meandering track through the forest, briefly stopped by her favourite oak to return her sparring stick to its secret hiding place, then traipsed her way to Shepherds Lane.

Once back at the Healer's cottage, Faye faked a heat exhaustion headache and had Thayrille give her one of her famous healing brews. She really did feel unwell, just not for the reasons she told the Healer.

Thayrille pressed her to eat an early dinner before Faye went up to her room, knowing that the brew would send her charge off to sleep for the night, once she had settled into bed.

After Faye had reluctantly choked down a piece of fruit and a roast chicken sandwich, the girl dragged herself upstairs to change into her nightgown. Her legs were starting to feel heavy, and the brew had made her lightheaded.

Once she was back to her usual surroundings, safe in bed with a full stomach and the healing brew gliding through her veins and relaxing her tense muscles, it was easy to convince herself that perhaps she *had* suffered a little from the sun that day. She *had* dreamt the whole thing.

A talking lizard, really! she scolded herself.

Faye was just nodding off to sleep when a rustling brought her back to full alert. Her knapsack, which she had dumped on the floor upon her return home, was moving. Adrenaline coursed through her veins, battling with the soporific effect of Thayrille's medicine.

Eyes wide, Faye watched the sack. A few moments later, it tipped over and spilled a few odds and ends – a piece of wood, a few odd pebbles she had collected, and the empty stem of her bunch of grapes.

But the stem had been at least half filled with fruit! she thought.

Then the last item shuffled out. It was the lizard.

"How'd you get in there?" Faye demanded in a whisper, half frightened and half relieved that she wasn't really losing her mind.

"Oh, I crawled in after you fainted. Figured you'd dash off the moment you woke. Didn't want to get left behind in the confusion," the lizard said benignly, waddling across the floor towards the bed.

It had grown a little since she had last seen it. The tail was longer, too, making the lizard span the length of her forearm from fingertip to elbow.

Faye scampered back from the edge of the bed. She didn't want to find out if lizards jumped.

"Left behind? But... Why would you want to come with me?" she asked suspiciously, still whispering in case Thayrille would hear. It never occurred to Faye that perhaps summoning the Healer may well be the best thing.

The lizard didn't reply straight away – it was using its sharp claws and teeth to climb the bed covers. Once it reached the top, it settled near Faye's pillow with a satisfied sigh.

"Lovely," the little creature said, gazing around. "So, this is where we nest at night, I take it?"

"Yes... I mean, no! This is *my* bed! You still haven't said why you're here," Faye hissed angrily.

She had no friends other than Jack, and she wasn't sure she wanted the first to be some talking lizard!

The reptile appeared to smile – its lips didn't move, but its obsidian eyes twinkled a little brighter.

"I'm here because you're here. You were the one who claimed me after I hatched. That means we belong together," the creature gently explained.

"I didn't claim you," denied the girl, shaking her head in confusion.

"Yes, you did," countered the lizard. "You fed me grapes as an offering, then picked me up around the middle to carry me home. That's claiming me."

"I barely put my hand around your middle – then I got scared half to death when you spoke! I let you go pretty quickly after that!".

"Well, I wanted the message to be remembered," the lizard replied reasonably, making itself comfortable on the bed near Faye's hip.

"That 'some lizards are poisonous to touch'?" Faye recalled, frowning.

"Yes, precisely," replied the lizard, now pressed firmly against her, absorbing her body's warmth. It had curled up and appeared to be going to sleep.

"How does my feeding you and trying to pick you up make us belong together?" Faye finally asked, determined to get *some* sort of genuine answer from the creature.

"Well, as you may have guessed, I'm rather magical. No ordinary reptile can talk," the lizard murmured drowsily, kneading its claws into the blanket, like a cat might.

"Okay..." Faye answered slowly, prompting the lizard to continue.

"So, I chose to belong to you by hatching in your vicinity, then making my way to you. I offered myself by sitting a discreet distance away, and making you aware that I was available as a friend. You then fed me. I ate your offering to confirm our bond, and you, in turn, confirmed our agreement by picking me up."

The glistening reptile explained expansively, its little blue tongue flicking in and out.

Faye counted to ten beneath her breath, eyes squeezed shut and teeth clamped down so hard her jaw ached.

Patience was a skill one had to work towards, just like cooking, just like healing, just like the sword, Faye reminded herself.

She slowly released a pent-up breath, aiming to reel in her temper before she did something undignified, like shouting, screaming or some such irrational thing. That would undoubtedly bring Thayrille up the stairs quicker than a jack rabbit! And then she would have a whole lot of explaining to do!

"I didn't know about this supposed agreement – you said nothing! I didn't know you were magical. I just thought you were an ordinary lizard!"

This was just a miscommunication, Faye told herself sternly. The lizard would understand, and would return to the canyon from whence it came, then her life could return to its normal predictable state.

"Well, I thought it was rather a good surprise," the lizard said smugly.

Faye shook her head and felt it spin slightly. She was tired and becoming overwhelmed. Besides, the medicine was well and truly working now, drawing her down into the realm of unconscious bliss.

"Fine then, lizard, we'll settle this in the morning," Faye said tersely, snuggling down beneath the blanket.

She was *far* too tired to keep arguing with this... this... this *reptile*!

"Oh, my name isn't Lizard. It's Zen."

CHAPTER 6

BLENDING IN

The next morning, Faye realised that she was now stuck with this *so-called* 'surprise' of Zen, the ever-talking lizard. It refused to leave on its own, also declined Faye's offer to return it to its canyon home. But perhaps the most aggravating thing was how the lizard just *did not stop talking*!

Like now, as it explored her bedroom in the light of early morning.

"Ooooooh, my dear, have you seen this panel! It's reflective, and I can see myself! What a handy invention! I must say, what a handsome lizard you've acquired." Zen said, gushing to its reflection in the small mirror atop the dresser in Faye's attic room.

The girl sighed with frustration.

"Is there any other part of this supposed bargain I'm unaware of?" she snapped as she pulled on her usual trousers and shirt.

"You must tell no one about me," the lizard said promptly. "Or my powers will dwindle, and you'll condemn me to the dull life of an ordinary reptile."

A strange look appeared upon the lizard's face, almost of reproach, as Faye sat heavily on the edge of her bed and tied her bootlaces, resigned to her lot in life.

"You wouldn't do that to me, would you?" the lizard asked softly, seeking reassurance by placing its foreclaws onto Faye's thigh. She sighed and felt her anger drain away.

The lizard looked at her, obsidian eyes pleading and so damn irresistible.

Sure, it had duped her by not telling her of these so-called 'magical agreements', and she was over ninety-nine percent sure that this was a bogus agreement, anyway. After all, she had left the thing behind in the canyon, and Zen had *stowed away* in her knapsack to remain with her.

But, if she had known about the lizard being able to talk, rather than believing it had been nothing more than a hallucination brought on by sunstroke, would she have really left it behind? Especially if it had asked to go with her?

No way! a part of her mind said. *It was just too amazing!*

So, if she were honest with herself, she would have accepted the agreement anyway. Perhaps.

She looked down at the lizard's glistening eyes and its pleading face, torn. If there was one thing to be said about Zen, it was definitely that the little reptile was cute ... and *not at all* boring!

"No, Zen, I could never do that," she sighed, defeated.

Elated, the lizard rapidly crawled up her arm and draped itself around her neck. Faye was surprised but fought the urge to try and throw the creature off. She relaxed and experimentally stroked its smooth hide, once she realised that the lizard wouldn't claw her. A strange hot shiver suddenly flooded her skin, flowing from the point of contact with the lizard's pricking claws, filling her with a strange euphoria.

"I knew you were a good choice for my Human," the lizard crooned, snuggling into the warmth of Faye's neck.

Letting out a reluctant giggle, the girl continued to lace her boots. The odd sensation faded, and Faye dismissed it as a bodily reaction to having the reptile in such close proximity.

"I suppose I'll try," she replied, excitement replacing the annoyance she had felt until now.

She had a talking lizard! Too bad she couldn't tell anyone!

Over the following weeks and months, Faye's life began to change, all thanks to the odd company of Zen – the talkative lizard. Faye still referred to the lizard as an 'it' because she could not determine its gender. When she finally asked, Zen looked puzzled. Faye explained the fundamental difference between boys and girls: boys fertilized the egg, and girls laid the egg.

Zen shrugged and answered, "Both."

That stumped the young girl, so she retained the 'it' persona.

Faye grew bolder and more confident over these months, due to Zen's influence. Zen constantly bolstered her up, telling her she was capable of *anything*. She had never had that before. The two people in her life, Thayrille and Jack, were full of rules, regulations, cautions and consequences. Zen, on the other hand, was determined that the two of them lived life to its fullest.

The lizard accomplished this by devising so-called 'adventures'. They rescued a nest of birds from hurricane winds, fished a calf out from a raging stream, located and secretly returned a missing toddler that had wandered too far into the woods, and more besides. Grydin Grotto became their favourite haunt after Faye's favourite oak tree, of course.

There was always an element of danger in these adventures. Still, the threat would be diverted each time Zen would do something – a whistle, a buzz, or a hiss. This rare talent was all a part of its magic, the lizard had claimed.

When questioned about this chronic desire for adventure, Zen always replied, "Why, practice, of course! Suppose we make it to Austin Academy, become a world-famous Seeker, and discover the location of the lost Crown of Weirren Vale. In that case, we must get used to the adventuring part!"

Faye wondered if she would ever regret telling Zen all her dreams and secrets. However, as this was Faye's fondest of dreams, she had difficulty listening to her common-sense side. This stolid, practical voice, which she was sure she had learnt from Thayrille, told her the adventures were extremely foolhardy.

Before Faye knew it, her twelfth birthday had arrived. There wasn't much more study Faye could do to occupy her time, as Thayrille's library was finite. She had already finished the stack of books she had received as a Candlemas present from the Healer. With the cooler weather, Jack was more apt to lecture her about the topography of the Arythmun Ranges, which was the mountainous region where Grydin Village was located, rather than completing stick or sword practice in deep snow. However, Faye couldn't work up any enthusiasm for the topic.

Their swim lessons weren't as frequent now, primarily due to the fact that she could swim like a fish these days. The hot springs down at Grydin Grotto were now used for impromptu games of 'Tag Me, Find Me' that had the Forrester and his student stalking each other through the surrounding woods to build skills of stealth and camouflage.

Thayrille encouraged Faye to spend extra time bottling serums and other cure-alls for the spate of mid-winter cold and flus that would plague them before long. Even that repetitive task was wearing thin.

Meanwhile, Zen would hide away, fearful of discovery. The silly reptile *hated* the cold with a passion and didn't want to venture outside either, which meant the two could only spend time together in the privacy of Faye's room. The problem with this was Faye couldn't stand being holed up in one tiny three by four-meter space for hours on end!

Finally, as the coldest weather hit, and Zen pleaded with her for 'just one more' game of tic-tac-toe, Faye lost her temper. Her nose numb, and fingers clumsy, due to the freezing attic rooms, Faye clambered to her feet and put her hands on her hips.

"No!" she exclaimed clearly and sternly. "I'm not staying up here for one more minute, let alone another hour! I'm going down to the kitchen to help Thayrille, and you can either stay here by yourself or come along. It's up to you."

"But... but... but!" The lizard protested as it scuttled across the icy floor, its scales tinged a silvery blue on account of the room's low temperature. "What if she finds out?"

Faye rolled her eyes, no longer impressed by that argument.

"You've told me time and again, that the 'magical bargain' is only breached if someone finds out about your magical powers. Why don't you just shut your trap and pretend to be a normal lizard? I can tell Thayrille, Jack, and whoever else we run into, that you're a pet. Surely *that's* allowed?" the girl countered, tapping her foot impatiently.

"But... but... but what if you're talking to me and it gives the game away?" Zen protested weakly. "You're in the habit now!"

"So? People talk to their pets all the time. Didn't you see how Mistress Haggart was speaking to those little fluffy dogs she owns? No one bats an eye at that sort of thing," Faye assured the lizard.

"Oh... well... I suppose... As long as *I* don't actually talk..." Zen hedged before reluctantly following her down the stairs. "I suppose that won't be *too* difficult..."

The lizard's obsidian eyes darted back and forth, warily examining the other rooms as it lowered its voice to barely a whisper.

"Relax," Faye murmured, taking pity on the little creature. "Thayrille's down in the kitchen, and there aren't any patients rooming in at the moment."

"Okay, okay. Just none of that 'babytalk', dear one. If you start saying 'fwuffy wittle diddums', I might just bite you!" Zen cautioned, its blue tongue flickering in agitation.

Faye squelched a grin, knowing that the threat was an empty one. While the lizard often threatened such things, it was yet to carry out the action.

The girl bounded into the kitchen, ready to defrost her benumbed hands and feet before the fire and eager to find some sort of task to keep her occupied for the remainder of the day.

"Oh, Faye! Excellent, I was just going to call you down..." Thayrille started before all but screeching, "*What is that?*"

The ever-stoic Healer had just leapt onto a nearby dining chair, her eyes bulging in fear as she noted the brightly coloured lizard traipsing into the kitchen right behind Faye.

"Oh, Thayrille... Um. This is my... lizard. I found it over the summer and it's rather tame, so I... sort of kept it. Is that okay?" Faye asked innocently, staring in fascination as the woman she had known all her life, the most stable, sternest of all non-sensical adults, carefully and slowly put down the rolled-up newspaper and swallowed heavily.

"A pet? You brought home a pet?" the Healer asked softly, colour slowly returning to her pale, freckled cheeks. "Jack did warn me such a thing might... But then, I figured... I mean, you're always so... I never thought..."

Faye shrugged, struggling to follow the woman's mutterings.

"And it's... tame?" Thayrille pressed, seeming to gather her wits as she stepped off the chair.

"Of course! See?" Faye stooped to pick Zen up around the middle and cradled him like a baby. "See these ickle feety-kins? Aren't they adorable?" Faye crooned with a wicked smile kicking up the corners of her mouth as she tickled Zen's clawed toes.

The lizard glared at her balefully before emitting a reluctant vibrating growl, similar to a cat purring.

"Uh. Huh..." Thayrille slowly smoothed out the newspaper she had so hastily snatched up, returning it to its place on the table. "I didn't realise that lizards purred."

"Oh, yeah, this one does. Only when its happy. And it's more of a thoracic vibration, rather than a proper purr, I suppose," Faye babbled, nervously setting Zen back down by the kitchen hearth, realising that they had never quite discussed which behaviours were acceptable for the lizard to adopt. "Anyway, Zen won't be a bother. It will probably just chase mice and catch bugs or something."

"Right. Not like a cat at all," Thayrille muttered, running a hand tiredly over her face.

"Maybe it's a lizard-cat? Or a cat-lizard?" Faye suggested cheerily, aiming for a guileless expression.

Zen hissed at her in displeasure before dragging itself up the hearthstones, wishing to bask as close to the fire as it could physically manage without burning.

Faye grinned in delight. She was certain that the lizard had a hundred sassy things it wanted to say in retaliation to her teasing comments, but as per the so-called magical agreement, it was unable to - on pain of Thayrille finding out about its powers. *Now this*, Faye realised delightedly, *would be a fun game*!

"Well, as long as you're sure it won't bite, then I suppose you can keep it. It might be good having a pet. It can get rather lonely around here, especially over winter," the Healer sighed as she cautiously stepped past the basking lizard and returned to the stove. "Now, can you help bottle this latest cold remedy, or do you have more pressing things to do, child?"

Faye hopped onto a nearby barstool and dragged the prepared equipment closer. She adored the fact that there was no sarcasm in the Healer's tone. Thayrille really meant what she said. If Faye declared she had other tasks to get on with, then she wouldn't be required to help in the kitchen.

"Not at all, I'm happy to help," Faye replied candidly, eager to turn the Healer's thoughts away from the presence of their new 'pet'.

With any luck, Thayrille would become so accustomed to Zen's presence that the familiarity would mean the reptile would be easily dismissed in future.

After all, as Jack said, people don't often look for something out of place if that very thing has always been right under their nose...

Zen spent most of its time that winter basking in front of the kitchen fire, its brilliant sheen of rainbow scales a familiar sight. The lizard also fulfilled its role with gusto and made a bit of a show when catching nuisance flies, stray bugs, and sneaky mice. It would often become bug-eyed, like a thrilled kitten, and bounce around the Healer's cottage in pursuit of the stray vermin. In fact, the more obvious and noisier the lizard was in its exploits, the more relaxed Thayrille became in its presence.

"You know, Zen. I think it's working! Thayrille is very used to you now, and even Jack never commented when you came with me to his place this morning," Faye whispered gleefully to the lizard as they readied themselves for bed one evening.

"Yeah... I just... Maybe I need a break from catching pests, though," the little lizard replied, appearing a shade or two greener than normal. "Perhaps... Vegetarian... Is better..."

Faye frowned down at the thing as its scaled hide quivered and rippled.

"Uh, Zen, are you..." she began before stopping, a disgusted look on her face.

The lizard spasmed and spewed a matted half-digested mass of fur, bones and mucus onto her bedroom floor. A large rat carcass!

"That, Zen," Faye said with a nauseous grimace, "is *feral*."

CHAPTER 7

DREAMS NEVER DIE

During the quiet evenings, Faye began to spend some of her study time questing for information about 'magical agreements' with various creatures, particularly lizards – but there was nothing in any of Thayrille's books. It was the first time they had ever let her down.

Faye was determined to find out *something* because Zen was curiously lacking in specific information.

After searching another dusty volume, Faye closed it a bit harder than she intended to, frustrated. Thayrille came into the room and noted her ward's sour expression.

"Whatever is wrong with you?" Thayrille asked.

"Forgive me, Thayrille," Faye apologised sheepishly.

Faye glanced through the doorway towards Zen, basking by the fire as it did every evening. The lizard snoozed deeply on the warm hearth, soaking up the heat.

"Thayrille, could you tell me something?" Faye asked hesitantly as the Healer turned to leave when she saw that Faye was busy with her studies, wondering how to word it without breaking the agreement with Zen.

"If I can," the Healer agreed, sitting opposite her foster child with a curious lift of her eyebrows.

It wasn't often that Faye would ask for help these days, content to complete any academic activities in her own time with the aid of the plethora of books the Healer owned. Long gone were the days where Thayrille would have to spend many minutes, sometimes hours, instructing the child in various lessons. It would seem her at-home education was complete.

"While I was reading, I can't remember what now, I came across a reference to do with magical creatures... Apparently, some creatures form bonds with chosen Humans, and they enter a magical agreement of some kind. I'm trying to find more information on this phenomenon and understand how and why it happens – but there's nothing!" the girl explained, feeling her anger and frustration return.

Faye glared at the book that refused to divulge anything useful. Thayrille was frowning over the question, her face shadowed.

"I suppose you've gotten the idea in your head to try and claim a magical creature?" the Healer asked sternly.

"No!" exclaimed Faye in shock, realising how it must sound. "I was just curious. I've been trying to find out for months but haven't come across anything useful. It's been bugging me."

Thayrille nodded, then sighed as though she had come to a hard decision. Her lips were thinned, her jaw was tense. It was the very expression that made the woman look so forbidding!

Faye squirmed a little, feeling as though she had done something wrong. That look always made her feel guilty, even if she had nothing to feel guilty about.

"The roads that you will travel will bring this information to you, anyway. I suppose what I tell you now will help explain the complexity of a Fey-Human bond. And to warn you against it," Thayrille said.

Faye glanced worriedly towards Zen, but the lizard still slept deeply.

Why would Thayrille want to warn me against *Zen?* Faye wondered.

"Magical creatures existed long before our people came to Almanaic, the southern lands if you recall. The whole of Pendalin was ruled by Elves, and other magical creatures like Nyrads, Sprites, Molverns, and Gorgons. The magical Fey became curious about us. To try and better understand us, they offered themselves as life companions to a chosen few. It seemed miraculous, and soon it became the fashion to have a magical 'familiar' hanging about. They were the greatest friends a Human could ever have. However, not every Human was blessed with such a companion. Jealousy soon sprang up among the Humans, as is our nature. Humans that were not chosen began trying to steal the companions of others. When this happened, especially to the gentle creatures like Molverns, Fairies and Sprites, the Fey and their Human, would both die. Such a massacre occurred that the Elves themselves stepped in. They forbade the friendships, on pain of punishment for both the Fey creature and the Human. Soon, the magical creatures stopped offering to be Human companions, and they vanished from our history. This story is told to all that attend Austin Academy to warn against such a bond. If any Human is approached by a pureblood Fey and offered such a friendship, the Human is told to decline. To walk away. To not accept it. It opens the creature and the Human to too much pain and danger. It also risks angering the Elves... which are feared to be extinct." Thayrille paused, "Though our Scholars believe that the few who *do* remain do so in hiding, trying to preserve their way of life as best they can. We of the Academy, educated folk that revere and respect the ancient Elves, do not want to upset them by disobeying their wishes."

Faye squirmed uncomfortably and saw Thayrille's sharp gaze.

"You understand, Faye, why it is crucial? Magical creatures are gentle and simple in their ways – they do not understand. They sense the possible bond that they can form with a favourable Human. They only see the good, and do not understand the bad. It is unfortunate, and you must not seek out such a creature. Promise me, Faye," her foster-mother demanded.

Faye felt another flush of guilt then reasoned that she could make the promise. After all, she was not promising against something that was already done. It was a close thing, and Faye's sense of honour pained her greatly.

"I promise not to seek out magical creatures to form a bond," Faye said, looking earnestly into Thayrille's eyes.

One is definitely more than enough, she continued silently.

The Healer nodded, satisfied.

"What else would you like to know?" Thayrille asked, appearing reluctant to end the conversation.

"Just how are the agreements between Human and Fey made? Is there a formality to it? Like a ceremony?" Faye asked, feeling she was pushing it, but unable to help herself.

"Just a very simple ceremony," Thayrille replied. "The Fey creature will approach the Human, normally soon after its birth, and announce its presence. From our records, the creature will say something like, 'I see you, Human, do you see me?' and the Human replies, 'Yes, brother, I see you clearly.' They then exchange a magical touch, and the bond is made if both accept one another. Depending on its size, the creature will climb up upon the Human's arm or shoulder, and the Human will allow it to remain there. The physical contact seals the bond, along with a sharing of magical energy which has been described as a flood of heat over one's skin."

Faye glanced at Zen through narrowed eyes. So, the bond had been sealed when she had allowed Zen to climb onto her shoulders and she had felt that wash of heat! That hadn't happened until *after* their conversation about the agreement.

What a trickster!

At that moment, Zen opened one eye and gave her a sly wink. The lying little critter knew she was seeking answers, too!

Faye sighed and ruefully shook her head, a favourite saying of Jack the Forrester coming to mind. *What was done was done, there was no use in recriminations.*

"Thank you, Thayrille," she said, feeling that this conversation was coming perilously close to revealing the truth – if it hadn't already. "Just one last question... What species do these magical creatures include? I haven't found a compendium yet. It seems odd, if we are meant to *avoid* them, but how do we do this, if we don't know what to look out for?" Faye asked this tentatively, while studiously avoiding looking at Zen.

"Oh! Well, the usual, really," Thayrille shrugged. "Not the humanoid Fey, of course, such as Sprites, Nyrads, Faeries, or Gorgons. There aren't any purebloods left in Pendalin, and they have enough Human blood to make up their own minds about people. The rest are usually certain species of birds. I think there may be a type of cat, several native dog species, and any type of monkey or ape. And that's all I can think of. So, if you want a companion, just stick with Zen. He has quite a personality, for a lizard."

Faye nodded thoughtfully.

So, *lizard* didn't even make the short list of so-called *magical creatures*. Then why was Zen so freaked out by anyone *guessing* it had powers? Surely, if a lizard was not known to be a magical creature, then there was no risk of it being discovered, except if Zen *decided* to reveal itself as a sentient being?

Rubbing tired eyes, Faye thanked Thayrille again before bidding her goodnight. The Healer looked as though she wanted to say more and almost seemed... disappointed... that Faye had chosen to turn in early.

"Alright, Faye. I'll see you in the morning. And if you think of anything else, you can... just ask," the woman said quietly, her face less stern and impatient than usual.

Faye gave her a small smile before retiring to her room. Upon passing the kitchen fire, Zen lazily climbed to its feet and skittered behind her. If the Healer thought this was odd behaviour for a lizard, she said nothing.

Her eyes followed them both with a strange sadness in them, yet not a single flicker of suspicion.

"You lied to me, Zen. Deliberately deceived me!" Faye exclaimed in a whisper as soon as they reached the safety of her room.

The girl shut the door firmly and leant against it, glaring at her devious companion.

"I had to, Faye!" exclaimed the lizard. "I couldn't chance you rejecting me! We're meant to be together. You'll see, there will come a day when you'll be grateful for my companionship."

The girl sighed, plodded over to her bed, flipped the covers, and climbed in. She paused as she felt the heat of the bed warmer beneath the covers at the foot of the bed, realising that Thayrille must have placed it there earlier, while Faye was in the study.

Faye smiled, feeling a slight glow in her chest that her foster mother still thought to do small things like this for her.

As she snuggled down, Zen settled beneath the blankets, close to her heart.

"I already am grateful you're with me, Zen" she whispered. "I just wish you'd trust me and be honest with me."

"I do trust you. I will tell you things when the time is right, or when there is real need. Just have faith that we are meant to be together, and I love you dearly," Zen said softly.

Faye nodded, already falling asleep.

The following summer, after Faye's twelfth birthday, a most wondrous thing occurred. At the conclusion of one particularly tiresome sword practice session, Faye heard the news from Jack himself.

The two were once again hidden from prying eyes within the recesses of the sandy bottomed canyon. The makeshift arena was clear of stones and bordered by sheer rock walls in a roughly circular shape. Zen was snoozing, as it usually did, off to one side upon a sunny ledge.

Over the past months, as predicted, the lizard had become such a familiar sight to friends and strangers alike that it was rarely commented on. However, some of the more superstitious villagers felt that a lizard that followed her around was unnatural and just proved that she was a hell-spawned demon out to steal the souls of unborn children.

Wiping sweat from her brow, Faye had to ask the Forrester to repeat himself, sure she had misheard him.

"I beg your pardon?" she asked, jaw hanging open as she set her wooden practice sword pointy-end down into the sand.

Jack grinned knowingly; his hazel eyes crinkled in amusement.

"The great Seeker Rythin Batonbury is due in the town by the end of the week. Apparently, the Elders have summoned him to get one particular child admitted to the Academy, and perhaps a few other village children whilst they're at it," Jack repeated, towelling himself dry, his curly hair coming loose from its tie and springing around his face.

"Do you think that I...?" Faye trailed off as she saw the hesitant look on the Forrester's face.

"I don't mean to be negative, lass, but ye are young. They don't take anyone younger'n fourteen usually, except in special circumstances. And I just don't know if ye be ready," he said slowly, a thoughtful frown on his stubbled face. "Not that yer not clever enough in ye lessons, Thayrille has trained ye up alright, but more because of yer age. And ye not had any experience in a big city. It might be a bit overwhelming at the mo'."

Faye nodded gloomily; she had thought as much yet still hoped. When would such a chance come again, though? A Seeker might not pass through for many years...

Faye sighed, raking her sword despondently through the sand by her feet.

"Who do they want the Seeker to take?" she asked, steering the conversation away from that painful thought.

"Jeremy Bloomsbry for certain, maybe Hannah Rikton, and possibly Jimmy O'Locklynn." Jack's face turned particularly stern on the last name, his eyes narrowing in displeasure.

Faye stifled a derisive snort.

"Forgive me, Master Jack, but those last two know nothing of the code of honour. I doubt they could fool the Seeker to believe otherwise," she said when he glanced at her with a raised eyebrow.

"Point made, Mistress Faye. Be best to keep ye opinion to yourself though, especially in mixed company," he said, a warning hidden beneath his casual tone. *Mixed company* meaning herself and anyone from the village.

"Aye, I'll keep that in mind if I ever find myself invited to tea in the village, and the villagers are actually listening to anything I say," Faye replied with a slightly sarcastic tone. "Us soul-sucking demons are a stickler for convention, after all."

"Ahh, ye heard that one, hey Lass?" Jack grinned again, his hazel eyes twinkling merrily. "Ye really should'na place so much weight in all them things the Rikton girls say."

"It's hard to dismiss them when they holler out to you whenever you happen by, or when you're minding your business down at the Grotto and they won't shut up," Faye grumped, stomping over to a nearby rock so she could sit down and grab a gulp of water from the skin atop her knapsack.

"Have they tried anything physical?" Jack lost his grin as a concerned frown clouded his face.

"Nah, not the girls. And the last time Jimmy tried throwing rocks at me, I used my sparring stick to belt it right back at him. The rock smashed to powder right next to his head, and he ran off in a hurry. He hasn't tried that trick again, though," Faye smiled faintly.

Jack huffed a laugh and nodded. They stood together in silence, sipping water and watching a flock of birds soar across the clear blue sky above.

"You'd be surprised what twists and turns life sends you," the Forrester commented idly, raising his wooden sword and angling it across his chest, indicating that rest time was over. "Again."

Faye returned to her place in the practice circle, dismissing all thoughts of the village children and their vicious words. She would just try harder to avoid them, that's all.

The clatter of wooden swords clashing echoed along the rock walls, creating a rapid tempo as the two circled one another.

That night after training, Faye sat wide awake in the window of her attic room, looking out at the moonlit garden. The frame had a deep wooden seat decorated with thick pillows so she could recline comfortably to read or think.

If Faye had much to do with others her own age, she would have been somewhat alarmed that the thoughts she harboured were far beyond anything they were capable of considering for themselves. Other twelve-year-olds were thinking about dollies, cubby houses, or what so-and-so thought about their new dress. Faye, on the other hand, was sitting up late at night considering ways she might meet the famous Seeker and gain acceptance to the Academy. She had heard stories about the man her entire life, from Thayrille and from Jack, both having attended Austin Academy in their youth.

Faye loved the Healer's cottage, her little attic room, and Thayrille... but she felt as though she was ready for something more. The Emblems of Pendalin were uppermost in her mind, of course. The Lost Sceptre of Almanaic that chose the true heir, the Crown that amplified their power, and the Throne at Rixondale that secured that power to the lands of Pendalin itself. The sooner she became a Seeker, the sooner she could get to work and discover their locations. Then Pendalin would be restored, and the kingdom would be at peace once more. And, just maybe, there might be a place in that peaceful new world for someone like herself.

Even orphans could carve out their own niches, given a chance.

"Well, I for one think you should present yourself to the Seeker – let him make the judgment if you're ready or not," Zen said, trying to bolster her spirits.

"This isn't another game, Zen! It is *not* one of our random adventures. If I were to be accepted by the Seeker, that would mean that I'd have to leave here and go to the Academy. *Forever*," Faye replied, staring moodily at the night.

Did she really want to leave now? Thayrille was beginning to teach her more interesting Healing lore, now that she was old enough to handle it. It's not like she was all that bored in Grydin, what with all the lessons the Healer organised, and the swordplay and stick-fencing Faye did with Jack. And now she had Zen for company...

"Pfft, it wouldn't be forever," Zen said. "And besides, what's wrong with actually going? I thought that's what you always dreamt of?"

"Yes – but it's a dream that should come to be when I'm older, about fourteen I always thought. I'm only twelve," Faye sighed, moving away from the window and climbing into bed.

Zen crawled in after her, snuggling its cool body near her warm neck, vibrating softly.

"Sometimes it doesn't matter what we think or feel, Fate has a way of making things happen whether we're ready or not," Zen offered optimistically.

Faye chuckled weakly. "You're telling me."

"Promise me one thing?" Zen asked.

"What's that?"

"Let's at least go and see the selection process. It would be nice to know what we're in store for, when the time does come," the lizard murmured, already half dozing off.

"Very well, Zen. We'll watch. But that's it!" Faye replied, promptly closing her eyes and willing herself to sleep.

CHAPTER 8

SEEKER RYTHIN BATONBURY

At the end of the week, the Seeker arrived.

Eager to glimpse this prestigious person, Faye clambered up one of the tall evergreens bordering the village centre. It was fun to watch the ridiculous pomp and splendour that the village Elders deemed necessary to receive the great Seeker in Grydin Village – without being screamed at and ridiculed by the villagers and their nasty children like Hannah.

High above the world, safe in the tree, Faye could see the vast mountain range rolling away in all directions, the myriad shades of green creating a complex tapestry. Along the horizon were the scourges that marked the outlying villages of Peakhurst and Thrisden. It was freeing, perhaps a tad isolating... and lonely.

"Chin up, Faye. Here he comes!" Zen whispered in her ear, its cool body wrapped around her neck, hidden beneath her cloud of blonde curls.

Faye grinned and peered carefully down through the branches, noting the tall, straight frame of the spindly Seeker, wondering at the flowing black gown with gold cuffs that billowed out around him, revealing glimpses of his very-average travel outfit. He wore brown breeches, white cotton shirt, thick black leather belt, brown dusty boots... His long salt-and-pepper hair was tied back from his angular face by a plain hair tie.

However, the most fascinating part of his visage were his dark brown eyes, glinting with yellow power. Faye let out an amazed breath. She could feel the energy emanating from him and the impact his boots had on the ground, almost as though each step thudded into her chest. As he crested the last rise and made his way into Grydin proper, it was almost as though this highly magical Seeker trod on her skin rather than the soil.

"Why is that happening?" Faye whispered, rubbing her chest as she sensed the small sparks of the Seeker's power flowing into the ground.

"You're tied to the land, Faye. You always have been," Zen whispered back before clicking in its throat.

The odd sound seemed to echo in her bones briefly, dulling the effect of the Seeker's magical presence.

"There, now it won't be so strong," Zen buzzed contentedly.

"What do you mean, I'm tied to the land?" Faye frowned, peering down at the soil far below their perch.

"Well, it's because you were born here. It's in your blood. Now, don't fret any more about it," the lizard crooned. "Look! I wonder what they're saying?"

The Elders strode forward to meet the Seeker on the path into Grydin, shaking hands and sharing greetings. Then, they immediately swept the man away for the official welcome at the Rikton's Boarding House – the only place big enough to house a formal occasion.

Faye was quite sure Jeremy and Jimmy would be invited to the big to-do, and the Rikton girls would be waiting on the Seeker himself with those simpering manners reserved for elite guests.

Tomorrow the formal selection would take place beneath these very trees, which stood in a half circle around the central green and represented Grydin's community 'hall'. It was tradition for the selection process to be witnessed by many people to ensure that there was nothing corrupt going on. The Elders made even more pomp and dash about the ceremony by issuing invitations to everyone in the village, exclusively calling them to the gathering shortly after daybreak.

Everyone, that is, except for Thayrille Hogansvort and the child called Faye.

"Come on, dear one. Let's get back home before Thayrille wonders where we are," Zen kneaded her shoulder, offering her silent comfort.

Faye nodded and began laboriously making her way down the tree.

Thayrille said she didn't care much about their not receiving an invitation. It meant nothing, as Pendalin Laws stipulated that *anyone* could go, invitation or not... and Faye intended to put that Law to good use.

Faye impatiently scrubbed at the old copper pot, keenly aware of the time ticking away. The stern-faced Healer stood nearby, concocting some cough serum for another summer cold plaguing the village. Faye wished that she could plead for Thayrille to release her from her duties early — she had already wrangled an agreement that she could postpone her lessons until after the Seeker's Selection.

The only thing that remained between herself and freedom were these damned chores – particularly these last few pots that were stubbornly clinging to their grime. The harder Faye scrubbed, the more obstinate the muck seemed to become.

Faye was becoming flustered, a lank blonde lock sticking to her sweaty forehead, her eyes glancing towards the infernally ticking clock above the door lintel.

"Allow me," whispered Zen, perched in its usual position around her neck.

The lizard puffed up and whistled an unusual trilling note. The grime slowly dissolved from half the pan! Thayrille glanced up from her work, those fly-away frizzes bouncing around her ears. Faye continued scrubbing as though nothing had happened. After a few moments, the Healer returned her attention to the serum.

Zen trilled again, a little more softly. The rest of the grime vanished from the pot, and it sparkled with renewed life.

Squelching a grin, Faye grabbed the next pot and continued her pretend scrubbing. On the random occasion, Zen trilled that note, the pots becoming shiny and clean. Thayrille, more than once, wedged a finger in her ear and wriggled it around as though trying to dislodge some wax.

By the end of a half hour, the last pot gleamed.

"Alright, Thayrille. My chores are done. I shall return straight after the Selection," Faye promptly stood back from the sink, releasing the stained rag so it splashed back down into the gritty dishwater.

Thayrille looked up in surprise, then carefully examined the pots with a frown. She didn't appear pleased that the chores had been done so soon. The girl suspected that the Healer had deliberately set difficult tasks this morning to make Faye late to the Selection.

The woman did not want confrontation between the villagers and her young ward. Thayrille knew things may turn ugly. While Faye did appreciate her concern, she was determined not to be steered off course. The Law said she could go. And go, she would!

Finally, the Healer seemed to accept this and nodded once before returning to her work. No words of caution or worry were uttered. Thayrille knew that Faye would be careful and didn't wish to waste unnecessary breath.

The spry girl raced out the front door and down the path towards the village. She was already late, she knew, but hopefully not *too* late. When Faye reached the edge of town near the tall trees, she saw that the entire population of Grydin had turned up and surrounded the clearing.

There wasn't a single gap in the crowd, and it ran at least four people deep. There was no way she could slip in there and watch. The girl would be shunned, elbowed, and perhaps forcibly removed. And there, at the crest of the slight hill, was a tall man in a long robe, speaking in low tones to a shorter figure.

The Selection had begun!

Panicked, Faye slunk around to a spot behind the trees, but they blocked her view, and other small children had gathered there in the limited space between the thick trunks.

"Up the tree. Like yesterday," whispered Zen, its little claws digging into her shoulder anxiously.

Seeing the solution almost at the same time, Faye quickly scrambled up an evergreen. She crept across its branches to the next tree until she managed to perch herself almost right above the Selection. Faye strained her ears and could just make out the voices murmuring below.

Jimmy was being spoken to at that moment. He was being asked numerous questions about school lessons and was struggling to come up with adequate answers. This was because he had spent most of his lesson time sneaking off into the orchard, stealing apples, Faye knew.

She'd seen him and that Archie-lad at a distance, always the two of them getting into mischief. Curiously, the bigger boy, Jeremy, had stopped hanging around the two troublemakers after that fisty-cuffs episode years ago. Nowadays, more often than not, Faye saw Jeremy learning the woodsman's trade from his father.

"I'm sorry, lad, but I cannot accept you into the Academy," the Seeker said finally, his craggy face frowning harshly while his stern brown eyes glowered down a long, hooked nose.

And there, just as Faye expected, was that gleam of yellow magic tinged with green. She could feel the tickle of power and that pressure in her chest, although it was much reduced after whatever spell Zen had cast on her yesterday.

She saw Jimmy back away from the Seeker, flushed and angry, before pushing out of the crowd, running. Faye was vaguely sorry for the boy but also vindictively pleased – which she knew was wrong. It *was* his own fault, though, failing the Selection like that.

Should have stayed in school, the girl thought as she silently shook her head and pursed her lips primly.

The Seeker seemed annoyed and raked his stern gaze over the crowd.

"Is there anyone else?" he demanded, standing tall and proud, his brown travel robe billowing around his lanky frame to reveal the same non-descript white linen shirt and brown canvas trousers he had worn yesterday.

His boots looked quite dilapidated up close and were laced with thick leather straps rather than fine silver thread. He was clearly a working man and not afraid to show it.

No one said anything. Disappointed, Faye realised she had missed the other selections. Jimmy's must have been the last.

Blast Thayrille's interfering chores!

The girl loved her foster mother dearly, but there were times when she wished the woman cared less about her.

"I ask again, is there no one else that would come forth?" Seeker Rythin reiterated, his voice booming. "A Seeker may not pass this way for many years. It does not matter your age, or whether you believe you have the capacity. If anyone here has the slightest desire to join the Academy, let them come forth now."

No one moved.

The man appeared to sigh tiredly as though he his expectations had been dashed. Then, the most inexplicable thing happened. The sturdy branch upon which Faye had perched started to wobble and bend like a rubber noodle beneath her hands!

With a shriek, Faye felt herself slip forward precariously. She clutched at the branch, the twigs and leaves scraping at the sensitive flesh between her fingers. Her upper body toppled forward. Then, she was falling, falling, falling, and the distant ground was racing up to meet her.

With an "oomph!", Faye landed hard against the Seeker, saved from an injured limb only by his quick reflexes and a flash of yellow-green magic. Quickly scrambling to her feet, to her horror, Faye found herself surrounded by a crowd of stunned, puzzled, and even outraged faces.

"Well, then, who do we have here?" the spindly Seeker asked in surprise, his black brows arching up to join his hairline as he brushed himself free of fallen leaves.

Faye spun in a hasty circle, then hesitated as she looked upon the angry faces of the Elders and villagers.

She shouldn't be here! Thayrille would be livid when she found out!

"Your name, child?" the Seeker prompted when the girl gazed up at him in mute terror.

"My name is Faye," she whispered, barely loud enough to be heard.

"And do you wish to join the Academy, Faye?" He glanced between her and the people of Grydin with a shrewd look. Their stony, disapproving faces told a whole new story - one that cast a dark shadow over their town.

"No, Seeker! Hear us! This child is an uneducated whelp – an orphaned demon-brat that has no place in our Village. She is unworthy of a place at the Academy." One particularly vindictive old Elder continued querulously, "She will suck the souls of unborn children. You cannot take her to an esteemed city such as Tryssdale!"

The Seeker looked calmly at the Elder, but Faye could see the brewing anger in the way small blips of yellow energy raced long his arms between his chest and fingertips.

"Really? And here I thought that *I* was the Seeker. Are you trying to usurp my job, old man?" Rythin asked, goaded into a cold rage.

The Elder seemed horrified by the idea, and began to babble nonsense, until the Seeker held up one glowing hand. The display of power quelled whatever other accusations or excuses the people of Grydin were about to throw at him.

"Answer my question, girl, and answer honestly. Have you a wish to join the Academy?" Rythin repeated the question, his whiplash tone demanding the truth.

Unable to lie, Faye nodded.

"Well, it seems that a Testing is in order," Rythin said, a dangerous look on his face as others in the audience found their voices and began to protest.

Curses flew to them, such as 'daughter of a whore', 'evil demon' and other horrible insults. Jack, standing near the back of the audience, roughly pushed his way forward.

"Shame on all of ye!" he bellowed, the flesh above his beard ruddy with rage. "Faye is just a young, innocent girl! I was there the night she was born, and there was nothing demonic about her or her mother! I buried the poor woman, for goodness' sake! The only evil was her poor health, shabby clothes, and the obvious mistreatment she received before coming here."

His outburst was a long time coming, for it was passionate and heart felt. It did nothing to silence the villagers, however.

"The woman shouldn't have come! She died and left the whelp parentless. Now *our* Healer is forsaken by this brat, to rear and raise it, and take time away from *our* health!" one Elder spat, his grey hair hanging in tangled ropes around an unshaven face.

"What of the boy that wintered with her that year? He saw the woman with his own eyes! He said she was a monster! Not Human! A demon!" declared another Elder.

Jack's eyes narrowed dangerously, and he seemed about to give the old man a piece of his mind – and possibly his fist.

"No, Master Jack, it isn't worth it!" Faye exclaimed, clasping the Forrester's hand.

She didn't want him getting in trouble for her sake! All she wanted was to slip away, to return to her attic room and start this day all over again. The poor girl bitterly regretted her desire to come to see the Selections in the first place.

"See! See how she uses her demonic wiles to sway strong men! A strumpet, just like her mother!" yet another Elder shouted.

"ENOUGH!" the Seeker roared, his face apoplectic with rage. "I've heard enough! As a Seeker, I revoke the Elder's right to Council! There is something seriously wrong with all of you people, and I'll let the Constabulary at Wythmarch know! I'll have a new Council established here before the next week is out, believe me! And that will be but small justice for what you have put this poor child through all her life! I have never heard such drivel and abuse aimed at a child!"

The Elders and villagers looked askance and about to protest once more, but one searing glare from the Seeker shut every opposing mouth. A ring of yellow-green fire had erupted from the man's boots and was chasing its way around the ring of protesters, keeping them back from the central green so they would be unable to physically remove Faye from her position before the Seeker. It also helped that the Seeker was ensconced in a cloud of magical light that whipped sparks of energy around his body.

The sight was powerful. Terrifying. Breathtaking.

Satisfied that there would be no further interruption, the Seeker began to question Faye as though there was nothing out of the ordinary about the situation.

"What is the Capital of Pendalin?" the Seeker asked, more quietly now, his tone so forbidding that it never occurred to Faye to avoid answering him.

"R-R-Rixondale," Faye stammered.

Rythin nodded, and continued his geography questioning, then grammar, spelling, arithmetic, scientific principles, healing, and much more.

Faye answered every question, and as she saw the satisfaction bloom in the Seeker's eyes, her voice became steadier, her answers more confident. She forgot that Jack stood protectively close, and that the villagers and Elders were there, glaring at her in affront from across the threatening ring of magical fire.

How on earth had the child learnt so much?! The outraged thought was apparent on each face. How did a child of twelve know more than any adult in Grydin? She could imagine the thoughts flying through the villager's minds. They had forbidden her schooling.

Gradually, the questions grew harder, and Faye's voice became husky. Eventually, on a tough arithmetic question regarding the nautical distances of the Talmeraic Isles, Faye was forced to admit defeat.

"I don't know, sir," she admitted, wrung out and ashamed.

This was it. She was doomed! Never to attend the Academy *ever* in her whole life. Stealing herself for rejection, Faye raised her head slowly and peered up into the Seeker's glinting eyes.

The Seeker looked down at Faye sternly, his weathered face craggy with lines and puckered scars that bore evidence of a long, well-lived life.

Surprisingly, instead of ridiculing her for not knowing the answer, the Seeker merely chuckled and said, "I should hope not."

The glow had dissipated, and the fire had faded, leaving the old man looking as Human as any other Elder the girl had seen. She looked at him questioningly, then glanced at those who remained in the circle. She was surprised to find Jack standing right next to her, and the village Elders were nearby, too, white-lipped and silent.

Faye also noted that not one of them attempted to step over the black, burnt line that marked the path of the insidious green-yellow mage fire.

"Only someone that grew up in the Isles and is a competent sailor would have been able to answer such a question," Seeker Rythin said with an encouraging smile and wink. "Now, finally, there is but one thing to do."

Clasping his hands he created a ball of glimmering yellow-green light. Slowly, that ball descended on Faye and gently touched the crown of her head. Her entire body tingled, and a zap like lightning touched her. She gasped and choked, stumbling a step before steadying herself by gripping Jack's sturdy hand. She couldn't see what was happening, but there was a gasp from the remaining crowd, those that hadn't stalked off with disgust at the proceedings.

"So, it is determined," the Seeker murmured, pleased as punch. "You are to come with us to the Academy."

Shocked, Faye said the only thing that she could think of, torn between excitement and dread. "But I'm only twelve!"

The Sorcerer laughed, his white teeth straight and even.

"We've had younger than that, my dear!" Rythin exclaimed, his dark eyes no longer so stern or angry.

"Like Thayrille?" Faye asked without thinking.

The Seeker paused for a moment, as though piecing a few facts together to make a whole story.

"Yes. Exactly like Thayrille," he murmured, a strange expression flitting across his face. "Please tell Mistress Hogansvort that I'll be by to see her this evening, after the dinner hour."

Realising she had now been dismissed, Faye raced off like a jackrabbit. As she ran, she tried to ignore the fading tones of the Seeker's voice, ironically commenting how an uneducated demon could pass both the test of knowledge *and* the test of honour – far better than the Edlers own children had.

CHAPTER 9

ASHES AND BURNT WOOD

When Faye returned to the Healer's Cottage, she found Thayrille bottling serum. Faye could see that her shoulders were tense, her motions angry. A stranger would assume the woman was furious over her ward getting her own way and attending the Selection, but the girl knew it was just how Thayrille was all the time. The Healer was forever stressing and worried that things that could go wrong, would go wrong.

Usually, Faye would have gone straight to her studies without a word, leaving the grouchy woman to her thoughts – but this time, she had to tell Thayrille that Rythin was coming. Having a Seeker come to the house was something Thayrille would certainly want to know. Her foster mother would *not* be pleased.

Faye dithered in the doorway, unsure how to breach the routine.

"What is it, Faye?" Thayrille asked in her usual stern voice, impatiently blowing a strand of hair away from her face as she continued in her task.

"I was selected," Faye said quietly, the words unintentionally slipping. She hadn't intended to be so blunt but was at a loss how else to tell her the news.

Thayrille's head jerked up, and a myriad of expressions crossed her face. Annoyance, sadness, ironic acceptance... Then, her features returned neutral once more, with only her lips pressing together.

"Indeed." the Healer muttered before returning to her serum as though Faye's admission was of no consequence.

Faye hesitated; she could sense the swirl of pent-up emotions in the woman. It was so odd. It was almost as though sensing Rythin's immense power up close had suddenly made the girl sensitive to all sorts of unlikely things. Thayrille, Faye knew, could summon a small amount of yellow energy when the occasion called for it. And right now, with such intense anguish flavouring her thoughts, a spark of power seemed to run wild through the room.

Faye really didn't want to find out what would happen if the Healer's precarious control was broken. It finally dawned on the girl that this was precisely the reason why Thayrille hadn't wanted her to attend the Selection in the first place. She hadn't wanted her ward to cross paths with the old Seeker.

But *why* would Thayrille be worried about Rythin discovering Faye?

"Seeker Rythin is coming after the dinner hour to discuss things with you," Faye informed her nervously, shifting from foot to foot.

Thayrille nodded silently.

Faye knew this was her dismissal, so she quietly left the room. She sat at her desk in the Healer's study and stared at the plethora of books and scrolls with aching eyes. The girl knew she was meant to be pursuing an in-depth analysis of some archaic treatment for ringworm, but she couldn't concentrate. Nor did she really believe that learning this information would do her any good. She was no longer Thayrille's student, but a pupil of the Academy. Faye sat there and stared into nothingness. Even Zen was quiet at its place around her neck.

Just as the Seeker had promised there was a knock on the door after the dinner hour as Faye and Thayrille were finishing up their silent and tense meal. The Healer nodded at the slim, golden-haired child from her place at the dining table, indicating that Faye should answer the door. The girl sprang to her feet and ran down the hall, pausing before the vast wooden panel. Slowly, she opened the door, revealing both the Seeker and Jack on the narrow stoop.

"Please, come in," Faye said shyly and led them to the kitchen.

Thayrille was serving tea, and she promptly set a mug before each man without asking if that was their preference. It was an unspoken rule within the Healer's residence - you get what you were given... and Gods help you if dared ask for anything different!

"So, you'll take her, then?" Thayrille said without emotion, sipping her own tea.

The woman's brown locks had been retied at the base of her neck, the flyaway strands for once tamed. Evidently, Thayrille respected the old Seeker and wanted to look her best.

"Yes. She'll have a place at the Academy — as you did as a child," Rythin said, taking hold of one of Thayrille's hands, a warm smile on his lined face.

Faye didn't know what to think. A million questions buzzed around her brain.

Rythin *knew* Thayrille! And more than just a passing acquaintance... almost like they were... friends!

And he was old, Faye realised - far older than she had first thought. His lined face appeared to belong to a man beyond sixty or seventy, without that yellow-green glow smoothing his features.

Thayrille nodded, not quite looking Rythin in the eye.

"We'll look after her, Thayrille. It won't be so bad, not like it was when you were a girl," he soothed, drawing the Healer into a hug. "It's a different world now. Not that it was all that terrible back then, either. I think your bad experiences here may have marred the memories."

The Healer took a shuddering breath and nodded. Her eyes gleamed with unshed tears. It was as close to crying as Faye had ever seen her.

"Perhaps you should leave us, Faye. Go and start organising your things, decide what to take with you when you leave," Jack said quietly, his hazel eyes tender as he gazed at the despondent Healer.

Faye nodded reluctantly and took herself upstairs. Zen, she noticed, decided to remain by the stove's warmth.

The little snoop!

After an hour of sitting on her bed, lost in thought, Zen finally joined her.

"And?" she demanded when the robust little reptile scuttled into her room.

"You leave next Weeksend, in the company of the other Selected. Rythin is needed elsewhere, so another, junior Seeker will come and escort the three of you," Zen informed her.

"And Thayrille?" Faye whispered.

"She's afraid that you won't ever come back," Zen replied heavily, its sturdy rainbow body heaving its way up her bedcovers and onto the springy mattress.

Faye frowned in confusion. "Well, I can't really, can I? Once I'm at the Academy, then that's it. Right?" The girl twiddled the tassels from one of her plush pillows.

"Well, no, apparently not," Zen replied as it padded around in circles to find that perfect, comfy spot, like a cat. "Students are allowed some time over summer to visit relatives... or, in your case, to visit Thayrille. If you wish to."

The girl's brows drew closer together, puckering in consternation.

"Well, of course I'll come back to visit. If she'll have me..." Faye wondered absently if perhaps the Healer was simply done with her.

As far as Faye was aware, Thayrille hadn't been like the other mothers' in the village. She hadn't been overly affectionate, frustrated, angry, or domineering like other women around Grydin. The two of them had always shared a cordial, if somewhat cold, relationship built on mutual respect and understanding and *lots* of personal space. Perhaps the Healer was happy to be rid of her, now that Faye had a place at the Academy. After all, she was just an orphan and had no real ties or kinship to anyone here. Zen clucked its tongue, snuggling down.

"That's just the thing. Thayrille *wants* you to return, but she's afraid you won't. She hasn't exactly been motherly over the years, and she is full of recriminations. So Rythin has come to an agreement with her. You'll return each summer to continue your education – namely Healing work, as Thayrille is the foremost Healer of this era. And, of course, to continue your combat work with Jack," Zen informed the girl.

Faye did a double take, her stomach dropping down to her knees.

"Jack *told* them about that?" Faye whispered, aghast.

"Oh, yes," Zen said with a satisfied chuckle. "Thayrille was fit to have kittens. Rythin calmed her down enough to listen to reason though."

Faye nodded slowly, some of the panicky doubt that skittered beneath her skin finally leaving her. She'd have to thank them both. And Thayrille. The woman may not have been *motherly*, but she was the only mother the girl knew. Thayrille had always taken care of Faye, in her own stilted way.

"It looks like everything is changing, Zen," Faye whispered as she crawled into bed next to the lizard.

"Yes, and for the better, I'm sure."

The days passed quickly, with her usual chores suspended and all sorts of preparations to be completed. Faye mended her knapsack and clothes; she shined her boots and belt. In case of emergencies on her journey, she assisted Thayrille in making a small Healer's box that included willow bark serum, cough syrup, salve, bandages, pins, and more.

Jack visited every afternoon, much to the Healer's dismay, and continued their weapon's practice. They had been working more on the stick lately, and Faye was becoming quite adept. The first afternoon, the burly Forrester gave her a new, thick wooden sparring stick, which looked more like a staff. The head of the stick was widened, and had many intricate patterns carved into it.

It would seem that Jack was quite the whittler...

"Ye can use this as a walking staff, during your journey. On the way to Austin Academy, it's rather hilly, so no one will question ye having it," he told her in his deceptively quiet voice.

"Wouldn't it be better to have a sword? I'm adept enough now with the practice swords..." Faye mused as she hefted the stick and admired its weight.

The Forrester was already shaking his head.

"No weapons are to be brought to the Academy," he intoned, a cross look on his face. "And ye're not to admit to my informal tutoring of ye. That's all hush-hush, because those Academy folk are rather stern about the 'proper' way to do things. At least it was beneath Old Ythmun Harbringer. From what I hear, though, his Assistant, Sorwell, stepped up as Weaponry Master not long after I left there. So, the rule might not be as strictly applied. They'll be wanting to teach ye from the start, regardless, once ye get there."

Faye nodded, though she really didn't understand. Surely it would make more sense for her to show them what she knew, and to pick up where she had left off with Jack?

"Now, the stick... It looks just like an ordinary walking staff, but you're a demon when you fight with it. Ye'll give any bandits a run for their money. And, they don't teach this weapon at the Academy," he grinned without real humour. "Much to their own detriment."

A few days later, Faye was in the back garden working through a warmup drill with the stick while waiting for Jack. Faye practiced with her new staff, quickly adjusting to the added length and weight. From what she heard, bandits abounded on the road between here and Tryssdale. It paid to be prepared for anything.

She paused after several fluid motions, nodding to herself as she felt the excellent balance of the polished staff. A small flutter of pleasure slipped through her chest as she reflected on the enormity of such a simple-seeming gift. Jack never did things by halves. When he gave her an item, he ensured it was of the best quality.

I'm going to miss him. Faye felt the moment of her imminent departure like a lead clamp around her heart.

The miserable feeling was dispelled when the breeze shifted, bringing with it a trace of an acrid stench. Faye sniffed in confusion, valiantly trying to identify the strange scent. She detected the faint trace of woodsmoke, but it differed from the Healer's fire. The caustic smell singed her sinuses and made her eyes sting.

Moving with a sense of curiosity, Faye followed the smell around to the front of the house and saw the sight of devastation. The Forrester's cottage, Jack's *home*, was blazing!

Faye's heart stopped, horror blotting out every other thought and emotion. She was frozen, staring at the climbing flames as they licked over the worn wooden walls of the cottage, black smoke billowing into the air.

Zen buzzed harshly around her neck, snapping her out of her horrified daze.

"*Thayrille*!" Faye screamed shrilly, finally finding her voice. "Thayrille! *Fire*!"

The Healer burst out the front of her cottage, uttering a string of profanities that had the young girl's jaw sagging open.

"*Quickly*!" the woman hollered, racing past Faye in a flash of blue skirts. "Jack's inside, collecting his gear for practice! I saw him but ten minutes ago!"

Faye bolted after Thayrille, tucking away those colourful phrases into the back of her mind to consider later. The two reached the burning cottage simultaneously. The place was well alight, the thatched roof a roaring furnace and the source of the billowing black smoke. Every shattered window was gushing orange flames.

"Jack!" Thayrille screamed, peering through the choking smoke and blistering flames.

A muffled shout came from inside the cottage. A large hunk of wood leant against the front door. Someone had trapped him inside!

Scandalised and fearful, Faye couldn't think. What to do? Helpless tears fell from her eyes. The Healer was panicked, and Faye couldn't help but feel hopeless. That block of wood was enormous!

Who would save Jack? The other Woodsmen would be off doing their regular duties, and the Smithy was on the other side of the town... There was no one else close by that she could think of with the brawn to help shift that log!

"Stay sharp, Faye," Zen murmured from her neck before scuttling down her shoulder and dropping to the ground.

The glistening lizard scuttled into the burning building through a shattered window, as Thayrille circled the cottage, looking for a way in. The Healer's face was deathly pale, her freckles stark against her white skin.

Suddenly, as though by magic, the front door fell inwards, flames blowing out. The Healer instantly leapt at this fortuitous opportunity and darted in, with Faye close behind. Jack lay unconscious near the fallen door. Thayrille and Faye pulled him quickly from the wreckage. The fresh air from the open door began to feed the flames, and the house was engulfed in seconds.

Zen, Faye noted, was sitting on Jack's back, its scales changed to a muddy brown to blend with the soot-lined shirt. The lizard clicked and buzzed a moment, and Faye saw that Jack began to breathe again.

He had been dead!?

Work done, the lizard scampered invisibly up Faye's arm and draped itself around her neck. Once clear of the building and smoke, the Forrester began to groan.

He was *alive*, and awake!

Thayrille carefully lowered the burly man to the ground, unable to carry him further. One arm appeared badly burnt where his sleeve had caught on fire, and he was having trouble breathing – probably from smoke inhalation. The heat from the roaring inferno that his house had become seared the flesh on one side of Faye's face. They couldn't stay here! They had to get further away.

"Thay..." Jack whispered, bleary-eyed as he peered groggily up at the woman.

The Healer shushed him, hurriedly making a stretcher from a skinning rack that dangled empty from a nearby tree. Faye helped roll Jack onto the thing. He passed out again – the pain from his burns too much. Silently, the pair pulled Jack up the hill to the cottage, leaving the Forrester's home to burn unhindered. They managed to get him up the stoop and into the primary healing room with a concerted effort.

Once there, Thayrille was in her element. She only spoke to give Faye explicit directions. It wasn't the first time the girl had assisted in a healing, but it was the first time it had been one this severe... And the first time it had been someone she cared about.

Calming herself with deep breaths, Faye helped in any way she could, instantly obeying each of the Healer's instructions. By the end of an hour, Jack was sleeping comfortably, drugged into oblivion, his wounds cleaned and dressed. His shoulder had been severely damaged, most likely from trying to charge his way out the front door. His foot had also suffered, hanging limply at a strange angle, presumably injured from when he had followed the shoulder charge with a kick. Thayrille had used a little Sorcerous healing to realign the bones before setting the whole lower leg, from knee to toe, in a cast.

Faye had studied this bit of rare magic with avid attention. Thayrille hardly used her power, and the sparkle of warm yellow light fascinated her.

Afterwards, the two sat in the kitchen, sipping their own mugs of medicated tea. It was hushed in the old house. Not a single villager had come to check on Jack, nor to tend to the blazing inferno of his cottage. Even the Healer's regular patrons seemed to have found reasons to avoid dropping by for their usual prescriptions or treatments.

"Who do you think did it?" Faye asked, staring into her brew.

The only other sound was the ticking clock above the doorway and the clink of their clay mugs against the rough wooden tabletop.

Thayrille shrugged dejectedly, her nose reddened and her eyes bloodshot. Faye couldn't tell if it was simply a reaction to the burning house's acrid smoke or the suppressed need to cry.

"Could have been anyone. Probably some young hot heads, feeling that Jack had betrayed their ideals of manly men by standing up for you at the Selection Ceremony," Thayrille said hoarsely, sipping her tea.

Faye shivered in foreboding. What a terrible reason to attack the Forrester! He was a state-appointed representative of the Pendalin government. Surely, they realised that attacking him would bring the wrath of the Constabulary down upon their heads?

"Why not try to get us? Why attack Jack?" she asked, the thought troubling her greatly.

Was it her fault that the poor man had died such a terrible death, before Zen brought him back to the realm of the living? Jack was a kind, dependable, fair kind of fellow. Strict, yes, but that made him such a great Forrester. He dealt out a fair punishment to all and sundry, never taking sides nor showing favouritism...

"Forrester's are a dime a dozen in these parts, but Healers...? It could take them another decade to get a new Healer." Thayrille replied scornfully, her lip curled with abject disgust.

"Perhaps it's best that I'm going," Faye whispered, tears slipping down her face, cutting a track through smeared ash. "It might make things easier for you now."

Her foster mother snorted into her mug before setting it down with a thud, spilling tea everywhere, and looked at Faye with hard eyes. It shocked the girl that the warm liquid was left unattended, and she fought the urge to leap to her feet for a rag to clean up the mess. Whatever happened to the fussy woman who panicked that the wooden table would become stained?

"Now, you listen to me, child." Thayrille said. "You are *not* to blame! Even before you were born, before your mother was ever known of, these *people* treated me badly." She spat the word 'people' as though it were a curse. "They abused me, cheated me, and tried to harm me on many occasions. Things would've only gotten worse if it wasn't for Jack helping to protect us. When your mother came to me, I knew the Elders would disapprove, but despite their imminent curses and slander, I chose to help her. When she died, I made the choice to keep you. Bedamned the Elders and their backward ways! Their choices have been the bad ones. *Their* actions have been base and inhumane – *not* mine! And certainly *not* yours. You and I will *never* be creatures like that! So *do not* blame yourself."

This impassioned speech ended as suddenly as it began.

Flushed, Thayrille turned away to snatch up a kitchen towel and began scrubbing at the puddle of tea as though suddenly returning to reality. Faye felt that the woman probably needed privacy to get a hold of her unusually rampant emotions.

"I'm going to go lay down," Faye said quietly, loathe to disturb the awkward silence. "Just call if you need me."

The Healer nodded, shoulders stiff and angry, hair coming free of its tie and bobbing wildly hither and thither. The girl slipped away, but just before she left the room, she saw those straight shoulders slump, and heard a soft sob.

Jack woke the following day, after sleeping almost fifteen hours straight. Faye happened to be sitting by him, for Thayrille had an enraged Rythin to deal with.

With sorcerous aid, Seeker Rythin had returned from Wythmarch in just over three days. When he had found the still smoking wreckage of Jack's cottage, and had heard some garbled events of 'fate' causing the blaze in punishment of Jack's defence of the demon-child, he had marched straight to the Healer's Cottage in fury.

Thayrille tried to calm the Seeker down, undoubtedly with a medical concoction mixed with his tea.

Faye could only imagine how angry the man would be once he learnt the truth of the situation. She could hear the rumble of his voice through the walls, occasionally punctuated by the Healer's lighter tone.

"...thought I was dead." Jack rasped, making Faye jump.

Quickly, she moved to feed him a spoonful of syrup. Jack tried to dodge the spoon, muttering, "No more sleep."

"No, Jack, this will help you wake and soothe your throat," Faye crooned reassuringly, offering the spoon again.

Reluctantly, Jack stilled and opened his mouth and accepted the trickle of honeyed syrup. After a moment, he sighed and opened reddened eyes.

"Rythin?" he asked, puzzled.

"He's here, in the kitchen. You must have heard him yelling before," Faye said, now offering a cold drink of water through a narrow bamboo straw.

When Jack continued to look puzzled, she supposed she had better explain.

"He's returned from Wythmarch. And the villagers told him their version of what happened, which he's seen through like glass, and he is *not* happy," Faye said softly, unsure if Jack's ears could stand loud noises. She knew hers couldn't!

"WHAT DO YOU MEAN THE DOOR WAS BLOCKED BY A LOG?" Rythin's yell carried down the hall.

Thayrille could be heard shushing the enraged man.

"*That's* why it wouldn't open," Jack muttered fuzzily, trying to blink his scratchy eyes.

His voice seemed to gradually strengthen, which meant the serum was doing its job.

"Wait, I have drops," Faye whispered and applied the soothing serum from a dropper bottle to his eyes.

Jack groaned slightly with pleasure as his aching eyes cleared.

"Thanks," he slurred as he tried to focus on various objects around the room. "They almost did me in, those damned villagers."

"I think they did, but when we got you outside, you... somehow... revived," Faye answered with a slight hesitation.

Zen had brought him back to life, she was sure. When she had questioned the lizard, however, it had changed the subject.

"Fresh air," was all Jack offered by way of explanation. Faye nodded again, her blonde curls bouncing around her narrow face, though she knew it wasn't true. They sat in companionable silence for some time before Jack spoke again.

"My cottage?" he asked, his voice sounding stronger still.

Faye fed him another teaspoon of the honeyed serum and placed another round of drops in his reddened eyes.

"Nothing but ashes and burnt wood," she sighed, then flinched as she realised how harsh that had sounded. Perhaps she should have been a bit more tactful...

Jack nodded, unoffended.

"Get a new one, now," he said, looking on the bright side, then added after a moment of consideration, "One with a back door."

Faye let slip a giggle.. Then she was laughing helplessly, her sides cramping from the effort. Jack joined her, his own laughter raspy and difficult. Soon they were both crying, holding on to each other in comfort.

"I know, lass, I know. Tis not the end of the world," the burly man crooned as he held the sobbing girl, his own eyes filled with tears.

He looked up to see Thayrille standing in the doorway, who was close to tears herself. She cleared her throat, which caused Faye to jump up and hurriedly scrub her face.

"So, you're awake," the Healer said softly, her dark eyes filled with some indecipherable emotion.

Jack nodded once, then grimaced in pain. Rythin followed the Healer into the room, and the two joined Faye, sitting around the bed. Thayrille checked Jack's temperature, her small pale hands caressing his forehead with perhaps a little too much tenderness. She abruptly turned away, blinking rapidly as she retrieved another serum bottle. This one was a tincture for muscle aches, probably to help loosen the tight knots in the Forrester's neck.

"Can you tell us what happened?" Rythin asked, his temper brought down to a simmer.

Jack frowned as if trying to remember. Faye added more drops to his red eyes.

"I was getting my sparring stick so I could come here for Faye's lesson. They were waiting in the woods just outside. When I was inside, I heard something bang against the door, and then it sounded as though all the windows were smashing. Every room was on fire and began to fill with smoke. I couldn't get out from the windows. There was only the front door. I kicked it." He frowned now, looking dubiously at his encased leg. "It hurt."

Rythin nodded, his eyes beginning to blaze with his yellow-green power again.

"Yes, I examined your cottage. It seems that all the windows were smashed to allow ventilation. And thrown into every room were firebombs. Crude ones. They were made from small bottles of whisky, with a lit wick coming from the neck." The Seeker said severely. "The Constabulary should be here in a day or so, anyway. They certainly won't be happy with this turn of events. Some people will be imprisoned, possibly hanged."

Faye grimaced and touched her own throat. By all accounts, hanging was not an easy death.

"Faye, perhaps you can make Jack a tea? With willow-bark and curacous leaf?" Thayrille said, cutting Rythin short with a pointed look.

The Seeker nodded apologetically – he had forgotten the child was in the room. The girl took the hint and slipped away, grateful for some space.

CHAPTER 10

THE PIPE

The remaining time before Faye needed to leave sped by in a blur of endless tasks. Firsday was gone in a blink, Secday barely a wink, Midwok and Forday combined in a haze of sleep deprivation as Jack had developed a nasty infection in one of his burns that needed cleansing every two hours overnight. Yet finally, despite all efforts to avoid this moment, it was now Fifday, and Weeksend was glaring at her from the other side of one last sleep in her little attic room.

Faye was nervous despite being as prepared as she could possibly be. Her knapsack was repaired and packed with essential items, although she might unpack and repack the thing one more time, just to be safe. Her new stick, gleaming with one last coat of beeswax, leaned against the side of her stout wardrobe. Zen lay snoring on her bed, its colourful hide gleaming from the gentle polish she had provided earlier.

As for the debacle of the burning Forrester's cottage... The Constabulary had arrived the previous day, and the Councillorship upheld by the village Elders had been formally revoked. There had been such a commotion, such screaming and tantrums from those elderly meddlesome men, that Thayrille was summoned to administer sedatives. Meanwhile, the villagers had been interviewed, and the identity of the arsonists was found.

It was Jimmy O'Locklynn and his cronies. With the local thugs cooling their heels in a makeshift stockade, the Elders under house arrest, and the villagers staying close to their dwellings while things cooled down, the small cluster of villages had become quite a pleasant place. Things in the Grydin Triad appeared to be changing for the better.

Faye was almost sad she couldn't stay and watch the events play out. Members of the Constabulary were staying on, firstly to oversee the rebuilding of the Forrester's cabin, and secondly to make sure there were no more dangerous retaliations. The Captain of the squadron that had been interviewing Jack and working closely with Seeker Rythin had also been making interesting doe-eyes at Thayrille, much to Jack's evident disgruntlement.

Thankfully, the Healer was her usual stern self and didn't encourage any of that *romantic nonsense*.

Furthermore, the Constabulary had forcibly retired or transferred anyone employed by the Pendalin Democracy – the government that ruled the lands in place of a King or Queen. Aside from Jack and the Bloomsbry's, who hadn't involved themselves in any of the shenanigans, the villagers who were removed included the three woodsmen and their families, the two finance clerks, the messenger clerk, and the carpenter, along with his two sons. Jack had been offered a transfer but steadfastly declined, wishing to stay in Grydin for his own reasons.

That left many job vacancies in the village, and with the removal of those families and their dependants from Grydin and it being a small place, that was very much a lot of people gone.

Faye wondered who the Constabulary would find to replace them. Good people, she hoped. People who would lead Grydin out of its backward slump.

Sighing, Faye rechecked her room, looking last-minute for any forgotten items. Her sparse room held a narrow single bed, a deep window-seat, a plump armchair, and a single dresser against the wall opposite the door. There was also her wardrobe that held all her worldly possessions. The furnishings were second hand items, as was nearly everything in the Healer's Cottage, not that Faye minded. They added charm.

Now that she had packed everything away, the room looked almost... desolate. Her drawings, stones, feathers, pillows, and other decorations were neatly stored. Her clothing was packed...

A quiet tap sounded on her open doorframe, immediately followed by Thayrille. In her usual no-nonsense way, the woman walked across the room and began to sort out a few freshly laundered shirts for Faye to pack into her knapsack. Those stern eyes noted the difference in the room, and her brows puckered as though she were displeased in some way. Perhaps Faye had forgotten to dust behind the dresser? Or maybe the grim Healer had wanted her to wash the window while there was still light?

Faye decided to wait to see if her foster mother would speak first. The woman was never shy in pointing out the tasks that Faye had forgotten or had left incomplete. After a few moments of awkward silence, Faye couldn't keep quiet any longer.

"Thank you Thayrille, for everything you've done for me," she blurted, staring fixedly at her knapsack as she fiddled with the straps.

The Healer started, then gave a brusque nod. After a few more minutes of silence, when Faye was almost certain she wouldn't say anything, Thayrille abruptly turned and sat beside her foster daughter, hands clasped tensely in her lap.

"I wish I could have been a better mother to you," the woman said haltingly, staring stone-faced at the wall.

The tension melted inside Faye. She now saw how difficult this imminent parting was for the woman.

"You were great, Thayrille. I mean, you're not my birth mother, and I always understood that. You did the best you could," Faye murmured placing a hand on top of her foster mother's.

To her surprise, Thayrille turned her hand and clasped Faye's in return, instead of pulling away as she thought she would. This was the first affectionate contact the girl ever shared with the woman-at least that she could remember. No hugs, no kisses, no pats. She hadn't realised how empty she had felt until now, when her heart swelled with affection.

"I've never spoken about your mother, I always found it too difficult," Thayrille began, then overrode the slight noise of protest Faye made. "No, no. I must tell you now. You're old enough to know. You have the right to know."

Thayrille sighed as though organising unruly thoughts. Her frizzy brown hair had escaped its confines again, the soft strands dangling around her face like very fine, coiled springs.

"I was an orphan too, you know. I was given as a babe to the Girls' Home in Rixondale. It was a slum pit, and the children of the orphanage were sold into labour at an early age. Those who were too young or unfit for labour worked the streets instead – thieving, pickpocketing, and the like. That was how Rythin found me. He was a junior Seeker back then, fresh from the Academy. You wouldn't know it, as he was a grown man of forty at the time, but as you'll come to find, there are many different people, from many different walks of life, at the Academy." She paused for a moment, lost in memories of those wretched early years.

"He could see that despite my experiences, despite all odds, I had remained innocent of many of the vices that children like me indulged in. I was very intelligent and quick, too, or so he told me. He paid a sum to the orphanage and took me with him – I had no real choice. I didn't really mind, though. Rythin was kind to me. When I got to Tryssdale, he gave me over to a very stern woman; she was the head housekeeper of the Academy. She set me to chores, as a way to make me 'honest' and purge my thieving ways. When I wasn't running errands or scrubbing something, I did my lessons with others of my age. I quickly accelerated through the classes at the Academy. By the time I was fourteen, I was ready to graduate. However, they deemed me too young."

Thayrille paused again, an annoyed look crossing her face. Her eyes were narrowed, and her lips pursed back into her usual forbidding expression.

"I wasn't too young, and I proved that to them. There was a wasting disease plaguing Pendalin. Many were dying, young, old – everyone. After a year of studying the disease, I finally developed a vaccine. They had no choice but to let me graduate when I was fifteen. I was then given two choices. Become an intern – just another face in the crowd in Tryssdale or another large city. Or I could come here and be *the* Healing expert in the Grydin Triad. I accepted the placement here and this cottage. I still wanted to prove myself. This quiet way of life gave me time to conduct research and develop my own medications. The villagers were very critical because I was so young. Who ever heard of a county Healer being fifteen years old? They continually tried to underpay me or undermine my authority. Well, you know some of it."

The woman flushed uncomfortably but then continued. "Seeker Rythin checked on me after three months and saw how things were. He exploded at the villagers. He told them there was another placement for me, a place where no-one would care about my age or experience because the need for a Healer was that desperate. He said he'd take me there and leave them without a Healer at all if that was their wish. I guess the Elders were worried – they really did need a Healer, after all." Thayrille clenched her unoccupied hand, her face taught with displeasure, "Their scheming eased for a while, but slowly built back up. I sometimes wonder if I should have taken that offer and left this place. But no. Unfortunately, I burnt my bridges that day. I was angry with Rythin for interfering and threatening to remove me, as though I was still a child. So, I shouted at him and told him never to return here. To leave me be. And being just as stubborn as me, the man took me at my word. I guess it took twelve years for his temper to finally simmer down enough for him to return to Grydin."

Again, she was silent for a moment, mulling over the idea. "But then you came, and Jack... Well. Jack is... You know Jack, he's just so... I mean, I want to say..."

Thayrille shook her head, and a tired, drawn look came to her face. It wasn't like the stern Healer to struggle to find words. Whatever she was trying to express about the burly Forrester must have some real emotional weight to it to have the woman stuttering and stopping like that!

"Jack means a lot to me. He has been so kind, for over twelve years now, since the day you were born, even though I haven't... That I didn't... I mean to say that I want... Oh, never mind! What's between me and Jack shouldn't worry you at all. And it really was a good thing that I didn't run away. During the heavy winter of that year, that's when your mother came to me. She fell on my doorstep, destitute and half-starved. I knew she could not pay my fee, but I helped her regardless. Sometimes I wonder if *that* was another cause of the Elders displeasure with me. I always charged the villagers the full rate..."

"That's sinful! Hating you because you assisted a dying woman for no fee!" Faye burst out, angry and sad all at once.

Her mother was not some *inconvenience*! Faye herself had still been in the womb and would have died if the Healer hadn't helped them both!

Thayrille shook her head sadly.

"I've no proof, and other incidences caused their dislike of me to deepen in those early years. My temper for one, and my blunt speech for another. You may have noticed I don't tolerate idiots lightly. My age, helping your mother, keeping you..." she trailed off for a moment then cleared her throat. "Your mother never told me her name. She wasn't... What the villagers have told you is correct to a very small extent. This will be hard to hear..." Thayrille paused and looked at Faye's pensive face.

"Your mother wasn't Human. I don't know what species she was; I've never encountered anyone that looked like her and I have never been able to find any creature in the history of Pendalin that fits her description. Her hair was rough and white, almost like coarse cow hair but longer. Her face was pointed and delicate, insect-like. Her eyes were incredibly pale and glassy grey. You look Human, though, far more than she did, so I assume whoever fathered you was Human."

"She *wasn't Human*?" Faye repeated, some of the tension leaving her face. "That's it? She wasn't any of the other things, then?"

Thayrille smiled sorrowfully and shook her head, laying to rest the worst of the girls' fears. That smile, as sad as it was, changed the Healer's face to something close to pretty. The girl imagined that a true smile would probably make the woman an absolute beauty... It was a startling thought.

She wondered briefly if Thayrille had ever smiled at Jack. Maybe *that's* why he hung around so much...

"No, not as far as I knew. She looked like a poor waif that had been hard done by, but definitely *not* a harlot," the Healer said briskly. "She birthed you within minutes of entering the cottage, then she slipped away. She had haemorrhaged and there was nothing I could do to stop the bleeding. She left me nothing but your name. I have no idea who your father is. She was already weakened by hunger and cold. It had been snowing that night. The birth was too much." She sighed. "I found myself in a predicament. I had a newborn baby to care for and a funeral for some mysterious woman to arrange. At the time, there was a young village boy, named Perry. He stayed with me during that winter to assist when needed, in return for shelter and food. His mother couldn't afford to feed him, and his father treated him badly, so it was an ideal arrangement. You may remember him a little, he only stayed two years before he was apprenticed as a bricklayer in another town. I'm afraid that most of the misinformation the Villagers received about your mother came from Perry."

Faye nodded, vaguely recalling a boy's freckled face and a shock of red hair. He had seemed nice.

"I sent him to call upon the Forrester that night. Back then, it was a grumpy, grizzly old man called Broc. To my surprise, when the boy returned, he brought Jack with him instead. Broc had died from heart failure while visiting his sister in Rixondale, it turned out, and Jack was his replacement. I was so isolated from the town's doings that I didn't know any of this. No one had told me." Thayrille's face took on a grim look. "Jack took stock of the situation, then helped me bury your mother so no one from the village would see... I used what small magic I could muster to soften the dirt as he dug. We did the best we could. Her grave... Her grave is beneath the great oak just yonder, past Shepherd's Lane where no one from the village would easily stumble across it. Meanwhile, I did what I could with herbs, medicines, and cow's milk to nurse you. You seemed to thrive despite the sparse nature of your care."

The Healer smiled slightly at the memory. Faye returned the smile, squashing a spurt of discomfort. The great oak that her mother was buried beneath sounded as though it were the same one that the girl now used as a secret playhouse. She had no idea how she felt about having such a happy place above the sad remains of a desolate woman. But Thayrille continued her story, not leaving Faye much time to ponder.

"I was but a girl, only just sixteen, with no memory of my own mother and no knowledge or instinct to care for a baby. You took it in your stride, though, never complained, always so well-behaved. We got along well, you and me. The villagers, whenever they came for treatment, let me know how much they disapproved of my helping the woman and keeping you. But I was proud and stubborn. So, I ignored their mutterings. Then the Elders called upon an Orphanage sponsor that spring. He came and demanded that I hand you over. I kicked him out and refused to give you up! Your mother had come to me and had placed you in my care. And that's all there was to it. I mayn't have been the best foster mother, but your home here was far better than an orphanage. And now, you're off to the Academy!" The woman took a shaky breath, rearranging her thoughts once more.

"I'll say this to you before you go," she continued quietly, intensely, as though afraid to be interrupted. "You are beholden to no one. You will meet people, just like those from the village, who will tell you that you can't achieve anything, that you don't belong at the Academy due to your bloodlines, finances, or any number of things. I say once more, you are beholden to no one, for they would all see you fail or die than to achieve greatness. Just like I found, and just like your mother found."

She reached into her apron pocket at that point and pulled out a delicate metal instrument – a pipe or flute, perhaps. Faye had never seen anything like it. However, she saw, with a shiver, that the pipe had those same strange carvings that she herself had drawn and painted all her life. Many were hidden in her secret treehouse, lining the walls and floor. More were carved into her practice swords and sparring sticks over the years, and still, another set glistened on her latest staff that now leant against her wardrobe.

What were those symbols? What did they mean?

"This was the only thing your mother carried. It was tied around her neck with a leather thong. I had to cut the strap to remove it," she said, handing the pipe to Faye.

Thayrille stayed quiet for a long time after, simply holding the girl's hand, their shoulders butted up against one another in silent comfort.

"I'm very grateful for the home you gave me, and that you didn't give me up to an orphanage. You always did right by me," Faye murmured, finally breaking the silence.

Thayrille gave a small, watery smile, then stood up quickly.

"Well, make sure everything's packed. And get a good night's sleep, the trek is long and arduous," the Healer said briskly, swiping at her eyes as she left the room.

Faye felt her shoulders slump. For the first time in her life, she had finally been shown the deep, caring side of Thayrille's nature – and now, the glimpse was over, and everything was back to the way it always was.

"Oooh, a pipe!" exclaimed Zen, crawling out from its place beneath the covers.

The little reptile had probably been eavesdropping the entire time!

"Yes, I suppose. I've never seen a pipe like this, though." Faye sighed, packing her linen shirts into her knapsack.

"Neither have I. It's unusual. Perhaps a panpipe. They were common amongst the Elves," Zen said, examining the instrument.

"What has that got to do with anything?" the girl asked in confusion as she checked over her possessions to make sure she had everything she needed.

"Uh? Oh, nothing, I suppose," the lizard replied absently, scenting along the pipe as a cat would.

After her knapsack was completely packed, Faye picked up the slim pipe. She admired the beautiful patterns as they shimmered in the afternoon light.

"Fey'Rhain," she read, instinctively knowing the symbols.

Another shiver worked down her spine. Perhaps it was just her imagination playing tricks on her, she decided. Filled with doubt and uncertainty, Faye placed the pipe inside her knapsack.

Chapter 11

Journey

The following morning, Faye crept down early to say goodbye to Jack. He was mending well, but between the burns and his leg, it would be months before he was fully recovered. The Forrester rested comfortably against his pillows, a book propped open next to him. A lantern was lit, allowing him to read even though the sun had not yet risen. His tangle of chestnut hair was held securely back with a leather cue. His shoulder was still heavily bandaged, his arm in a sling. He looked so broken; it brought another tear to Faye's eye.

"You're meant to be sleeping!" Faye whispered forcefully as she entered the room.

The man started guiltily, closing his book with a snap, then relaxed when he saw it was her.

"Goodness, lass, that tone was identical to Thayrille's!" he joked, giving her a warm smile. "So, yer off, then?"

Faye nodded and pulled herself together, swiping at the dampness that had gathered at the corners of her eyes. She whispered, "I can only stay a minute; I just came to say goodbye."

She briefly hugged the man and stepped back, feeling like another piece of her heart was breaking. If Thayrille was like a mother, then Jack was like a father. He had taught her so much and protected her like a lion protecting his cub... Why was it so hard to say goodbye?

"You'll be alright?" she asked, concerned about his injuries and lack of a house.

Jack nodded quickly, not looking the least upset by his current situation.

"Thayrille's letting me stay here until all the injuries are fully healed and the new cottage is finished," he said, very pleased by the idea. "She'll look after me... or kill me through trying."

Faye grinned; that was very likely true. She gave him one final hug and a kiss on the cheek and left the room. Dew had dampened the stone steps that led down from the cottage's front door and darkened the pavers that created a meandering path down the hill to the village proper. The girl stepped carefully, frequently casting forlorn looks behind her as the brightening sky highlighted the outline of her home. It felt strange to be leaving the place, and to realise that she may not see its sturdy stone walls and stout chimneys for nigh on a year.

Faye blinked rapidly and drew in several deep breaths as she stomped her way down the hill, around the ashen remains of the Forrester's burnt cottage and past the village main. She waited on the outskirts of the village at the predetermined meeting place, sitting atop the broad stone boundary marker that held the worn wooden sign *Welcome to Grydin Village*. She gazed out across the dense forests of pine and oak pockmarked by deciduous trees that wore a crown of lime-green summer leaves. In the autumn, they would change to yellow and orange, then fade to a burnt brown as winter overtook the land. The leaves would drop, and their skeletal branches would appear like ghostly monsters rising from the snow. Faye wouldn't see those changes this year, and it caused a bittersweet pang in her heart. She hoped that nothing would change too much between now and next summer, when she was due to return.

Zen's small body vibrated comfortingly against her neck, concealed by her shirt collar and loosely bound hair. The two had agreed that the reptile would remain hidden as much as possible, just in case animals were forbidden at the Academy.

As ever, only Faye was to know of Zen's magical powers, and most importantly, its ability to talk. To an outsider, Zen would be nothing more than a colourful, exotic pet.

Soon after dawn, once the faintest pink lined the horizon, a young man materialised from the mist, leading another two children. It was the mysterious junior Seeker, Jeremy Bloomsbry and the loathsome Hannah Rikton.

"Hullo! You must be Faye," the Seeker called cheerily as he approached.

He was a young man, perhaps in his mid-twenties, with tousled sandy blond hair and bright green eyes. His ready smile and jaunty tone immediately soothed the Faye's worries. As long as *he* was with the group, she doubted there'd be much trouble with the other village children.

Hannah gave her a scathing look, an expression that Faye had become somewhat familiar with over the years. Hannah's cornflower blue eyes were derisive and her perfectly groomed blonde hair had been braided back from her face. She wore a warm calico dress with silver trim, those lethal sturdy walking boots she favoured, and a trim fur jacket.

As the three approached, Hannah deliberately turned her face away to rudely ignore Faye.

Jeremy, at least, managed to mumble an embarrassed 'Hello'. His brown eyes were fixed on the ground about ten meters away from Faye, his short brown hair as unkempt as always. Clearly, he was remembering the time he had joined Jimmy in beating her up, thinking she was a boy. That unfortunate incident lay heavy between them, and Faye figured it might take some time for those sharp memories to fade.

Thankfully, for reasons that weren't entirely clear, the Constabulary had allowed the Bloomsbry family to remain in Grydin Village, even though Jeremy's father was one of the government-employed Woodsmen.

Faye wondered if it had something to do with Jack. Perhaps the Forrester had put in a good word, seeing how Jeremy had changed and the fact that Mister Bloomsbry was quite a reliable Woodsman.

Faye nodded but didn't say anything. The Seeker noted the tension but decided to ignore it.

"Alright, let's go." They began walking down one of the many narrow tracks that led away from the village of Grydin.

Soon, the trees had swallowed them up, the shadows shrouded them in gloom as the sun struggled to ascend, and the path was treacherous - as Jack had predicted. The trail had been fairly smooth at first, but before long, they turned onto yet another track and the way became clogged with ferns and debris. Faye's staff was coming in very useful. No one, not even the Seeker, commented on Faye's staff.

"Master Seeker?" Hannah began hesitantly, her blonde tresses appearing far from glossy in the current climate. "Is there no other, more civil path for us to follow?"

"Why, yes, there is. However, that path is well known to bandits and the like. I've heard of a particularly vile group that is yet to be caught by the Constabulary, and they are pillaging travellers right at the moment. I thought to save us heartache by travelling this less-than-well-known path," the Seeker replied, never hesitating a step.

Faye and Jeremy were having no trouble keeping up with the Seeker, and each was secretly glad to avoid bandits.

"Oh," was all Hannah could say, her prim mouth twisted in a displeased pout.

The girl was a spoilt princess, by all accounts. Faye had never known her personally, having only had the barest contact with the girl. But she had paid attention when various villagers came to receive treatment at the Healer's Cottage. What she knew of Hannah was that the girl was given her every want and desire, if her performance at school was maintained. She was self-centred, mean, and frankly vile with a murderous streak.

For example, the first time they had come in contact, Hannah had tried to brain her with a rock. All the other times they had met around Grydin, Hannah and her sisters would screech abuse at her from a safe distance.

All of her nastiness was hidden behind a pretty face and simpering manners.

Though, Faye had to grin at the moment, for Hannah's manners had almost vanished and the pretty face had faded behind a very sour demeanour. Even Jeremy seemed to tire of her vapid charm after a few hours.

"How long until we arrive at the Academy, Master Seeker?" Jeremy asked sometime later as he attempted to put some distance between himself and Hannah.

"Oh, about a week or so, as long as the weather stays fine." The sandy-haired man replied. "And please, call me Tyrone."

The day wore on with very little other talk before finally Seeker Tyrone called for the lunch break as the sun peaked.

"Just a half hour, then we must be off. This track is rather winding and will add a little time to our journey," he said, still cheerful as he traipsed around the next bend to find a dry place to sit and eat lunch.

Once the Seeker was out of earshot, Hannah collapsed onto a damp log with a frustrated groan.

"Why on earth should we be trudging along this forsaken path? I'm certain that no bandits would dare to attack *us*! Why, two grown men, myself, and a small child! Hardly likely at all," Hannah grumped, digging roughly through her knapsack, her eyes casting a flirtatious look at Jeremy.

Faye could have said a few choice things about the lack of morals that bandits would likely have, but held her tongue. Zen buzzed reassuringly at its place around her neck, offering quiet comfort to help her keep her words in check. Jeremy appeared to be in a similar predicament, obviously uncomfortable with Hannah referring to him as a *grown man* and batting her eye lashes at him like some floosy.

"I don't know, Hannah. Tyrone seemed certain. You know how those Seekers are – they each seem to be gifted with foresight. They can sometimes *sense* things, you know," Jeremy offered wisely, eating a chunk of bread and meat from his pack.

He was a straightforward sort of boy, Jeremy. After the initial awkwardness he and Faye had shared, he treated his two female companions about the same. Not too much chatter, but a polite diplomatic response to any question. No doubt the boy had learnt a lot from working with his father.

Hannah merely pouted, not willing to argue but certainly not willing to agree, either. Faye finished her lunch and went to find Tyrone to see when they were leaving. He was not so far away, having a private rest just beyond a few trees.

"So, young Hannah isn't all that happy with my leadership, hmmm?" Tyrone asked with an amused gleam in his green eyes as he munched on an apple.

Faye shrugged non-committedly, setting her knapsack down near a low tree bough before perching on the branch.

"Don't you talk?" Tyrone pressed, raising an eyebrow.

"Only when it matters," Faye said after a moment, with a small smile.

The Seeker laughed in his merry way.

"Excellent! A girl after my own heart, I see," he said with a hint of irony.

Faye secretly doubted that Tyrone would ever stop talking, especially to people he was fond of – regardless of if the topic was essential or not. He reminded her of Zen in that regard.

"Alright, let's make a move." Tyrone jumped to his feet and let out a sharp, commanding whistle.

A moment later, Jeremy and a flustered Hannah scampered around the bend in the path. The look on the girl's face was not a pleasant one and spoke volumes about her feelings at being summoned in such a manner.

The Seeker ignored the glower and strode off down the track, Jeremy following close behind. Faye made to move into place directly behind the boy, but she got no further than a step when she fell to the ground with a muffled *oof.*

Blinking in confusion, the girl raised herself to her knees before a heavy weight smacked her in the middle of the back, pinning her to the damp ground.

"You listen, and listen carefully, demon-spawned whelp," Hannah hissed at her.

The older girl had tripped her up with a stick! Now, Hannah pinned Faye down with one of her abhorrent murderous walking boots, using her greater weight and height to her advantage.

Faye made to call after the Seeker and alert him to the attack, but Hannah jabbed her sharply in the ribs with the stick driving the breath right out of her lungs. Faye gave a pained groan.

"None of that!" the girl snapped. "Now, if I had my way, I'd slit your throat and dump you in a gully somewhere along this wretched track! *No one* would ever find your corpse, nor recognise it, once the forests beasts had their fill. *But*, unfortunately, that Seeker has the gift of magic, which means you're safe. For now. Now, I'm warning you, you soul-sucking whore! I will look for an opportunity to make your life miserable. So, stay right away from me from this moment on. And no cosying up to Jeremy or the Seeker. They are both off-limits, especially to an orphaned trollop like you! Are we clear?"

Faye grunted in agreement, her lungs aching from her inability to breathe fully while Hannah stood on her spine.

"Excellent. One more thing. You tell the Seeker about our little *chat*, and I will find a way to end you. Sorcery or no sorcery. Kapish?" The girl shoved Faye one more time as she removed her booted foot. Hannah left Faye sprawled in the dirt, gasping for breath, while she hurried along the path to catch up with Tyrone and Jeremy.

"I can bite her." Zen offered, buzzing angrily from its place beneath Faye's hair. "And we can shove *her* body into a gully somewhere."

"No. There'd be too many questions." Faye coughed as she picked herself up and grimaced at the smears of mud and slime covering her clothes. "We'll let this slide. For now. People like Hannah often get what's coming to them."

The lizard emitted a harsh vibration before settling again.

"Fine. But if she tries that stunt again, all bets are off!" the reptile grumbled in a threatening tone.

Faye silently agreed as she hobbled along to catch up with their small travel group.

By late afternoon, they reached the foot of the mountains and set up camp in a peaceful meadow. Faye noted with some amusement that Jeremy chose a spot quite deliberately, placing the Seeker between himself and Hannah, exactly as Faye had done. It would seem the boy would rather be in closer proximity to the *demon-spawned whore* than the supposed upstanding Grydin village-girl.

Faye kept her observations to herself as she expertly pitched her bivvy and unrolled her light but warm blanket. They had also been gifted to her by Jack. The Forrester always assumed people camped when travelling, just as Woodsmen did.

Hannah, by this stage experiencing the worst day of her life, was almost in tears and squalling.

"What do you mean, camping in the open? Where's the Inn?! Where's the Hotel?! Surely, we can afford better accommodation than *this*?"

Unintentionally, Jeremy rolled his eyes at the same time Faye did, and they shared a look of amused contempt. They each started a little and dropped their gaze – uncertain if it was appropriate for them to communicate privately, even in this small way.

Tyrone finally got Hannah settled beneath a spare tarp and blanket. The four of them built up a toasty campfire, roasting nuts, bread, and a tasty legume that Faye showed them how to identify and dig up. She hadn't lived the past twelve years in a Healer's cottage for nothing! Thayrille's tutelage had included all manner of practical knowledge, from cooking and baking to growing and harvesting their own food.

The girl also ensured she gave Hannah a wide berth, not allowing any part of her person to come into touching distance of the nasty bully.

After the small meal had been cleared up, everyone retired to their blankets, exhausted from the days gruelling trek. Before long, rhythmic breathing and light snores filled the clearing, indicating that the other three had finally fallen asleep. Faye, secure in her ability to navigate any habitat in the dark, decided to slip away from camp to spend some time alone, the comforting weight of Zen still nestled against her neck. She wasn't used to travelling closely with strangers. Especially that horrible beast disguised as a girl.

Her chest still ached from that confrontation earlier in the day, and Faye needed some space to unwind before she could go to sleep herself.

Once she was well away from the others, she sat upon a large rock that bordered a small stream and took out her mother's pipe from within her coat pocket. It seemed to gleam in the moonlight, shining in shades of blue, red, yellow, and green.

The name Fey'Rhain glowed eerily along its surface.

"How come I know these symbols here? What does Fey'Rhain mean?" Faye whispered curiously.

"Oh, the script has power, as it comes from the Elves. I dare say Fey'Rhain is the name of the pipe's original owner, and you can read it because of your own Fey blood," Zen offered quietly in her ear, its voice nothing more than a whisper in the darkness. "Go on. Let's see what it sounds like."

"What if it wakes the others?" Faye hissed, nervous about the idea of playing the unfamiliar instrument.

It was clearly magical in nature, given the way it glimmered in the moonlight, and the fact that the symbols seemed to shift and change like liquid water. Zen had just said the script was a magical construct created by the Elves! It meant this pipe was very, *very* special.

Who knew what might happen if she played the dang thing?

"I doubt it. They were all snoring like warthogs back there. And we're far enough away not to disturb anyone. Just try it!" the lizard pressed impatiently.

Experimentally, Faye put the flute to her lips and blew one note. It came out swift and clear, echoing through the trees. Faye paused, scared for a moment that it may have woken the others.

No sound of alarm or query came from the direction of the camp, so Faye returned her attention to her pipe. She frowned at the instrument, locating the holes along its length. Placing her fingers awkwardly along them, Faye tried again, more softly this time, testing the different notes. She paused and cocked her head, almost certain she could hear the echo of those notes in the forest. The ground seemed to hum expectantly, as though waiting for more music.

Faye hesitated, the pipe at her lips, unsure what to do. She didn't know how to play. Then, from deep in the forest around her, notes seemed to shimmer and skate to her ears. Notes of an ancient, beautiful song of homecoming and safety.

Concentrating on those ghostly notes, Faye matched them to the holes in the pipe and began to copy the music. Before long, the ethereal music seemed to absorb into her soul, and she played loud and strong, as though she had known it all her life. As she finished, Faye noticed the trees and stars glowed with ephemeral power.

"Beautiful," Zen whispered. "However, I must suggest that you not play in front of anyone else. It would be difficult to explain."

"Why? How do I know this music?" Faye asked softly, confused and feeling inexplicably lonely now that the glow was fading and the music had gone.

"Oh, it's the magic of the pipe. Strangers may decide to take it from you, if they know you have it," Zen said, but something in the lizard's tone made her think it wasn't telling the truth.

Faye knew more than to try and push for a better answer. The lizard was far more stubborn than Thayrille or any Human she knew, when it came to keeping information to itself.

"We should get some sleep," she sighed and returned to camp.

The journey was predictable after that. Up at dawn for a brief breakfast, trudge along the track for a couple of hours before morning tea break. Then, off again for a couple of hours before lunch. More walking, afternoon tea, walk a bit further, then make camp. All the while actively avoiding Hannah. It took some careful manoeuvring, but Faye managed to keep Tyrone between them for most of the trip.

The track became steep, and Faye was so very glad of her staff. She had no idea how many times she would have fallen or tripped, without that supportive stick. Hannah bore testimony to this, for she was covered in dirt before long, as was Jeremy. The only difference was that Jeremy wasn't so vocal about it.

Faye would be lying if she said she *hadn't* experienced some level of vindictive pleasure at seeing Hannah so discomforted every time the older girl slipped and fell in the mud.

On their fourth night of camping, Hannah decided to grace them with her sullen conversation to alleviate some of her misery. Their small, rosy fire suddenly felt significantly less cheerful that night.

"So, Jeremy," Hannah began, the brightness of her voice somewhat brittle. "What do *you* hope to achieve from the Academy?"

After four days of near silence, Jeremy appeared startled at being targeted for conversation. "Oh! Um, probably a Forrester, like Master Jack," he said, flushing slightly.

"Oh, that's perfect for you!" Hannah gushed, then turned to Faye, her tone shifting from sweet to sardonic in seconds "And what about you, child? What would you do?"

"Child?" Faye retorted archly before she could stop herself, mimicking Thayrille's stern tone. "You're a mere two years older than me, *girl*."

Jeremy stifled a snort as he sharpened his hunting knife, and Tyrone cleared his throat a few times and gave both girls a warning look. Hannah purposely turned her face away from Tyrone, ignoring his silent censure, and glared at Faye silently for almost a minute, inarticulate with rage. Faye clearly recalled the feeling of being pinned under the older girl's painful boot but wasn't fearful enough to back down. If Hannah wanted to start something with her right in front of Tyrone, she was more than welcome!

"You dare address me so, bastard brat?! You heathen, unclaimed, unwanted, *reject*!" Hannah exclaimed, her voice almost a high-pitched whistle.

"MISS RIKTON!" Tyrone thundered, leaping to his feet in outrage, towering over the three of them.

Hannah jerked back a little, scared by the violence in the Seeker's normally cheery voice.

"Never!" he now rumbled in a low growl, far scarier than his bellow. "Never, in my company, dare to insult an orphan for being an orphan."

His eyes glinted dangerously in the firelight, and yellow magic blazed from his hands like lightening. Hannah didn't dare say another word, staring at Tyrone in terror. The torrent of power sent a corresponding ripple of energy through Faye, making her feel as though her skin was being peeled from her body. Zen clicked rapidly from its place around her neck, dulling the painful sensation.

Would she *always* respond to another's power this way?

"It's alright, Master Tyrone," Faye said, her voice trembling in reaction. "She's only repeating what her elders have said. It's nothing I haven't heard before."

Faye felt saddened by that fact.

The anger faded from Tyrone's face, and he breathed deeply. The lightning magic also vanished, pulled back inside where it wouldn't harm anyone. The quiet sounds of the night began to permeate the air once more.

"Hear me, both of you," the Seeker said, his still angry eyes encompassing both Jeremy and Hannah. "The Academy, where you intend to spend the next few years, is home to people from all walks of life. Some people that are from rich families, from poor families – and then there are those with no family. Like *myself*."

Hannah flinched; Jeremy nodded thoughtfully.

"You will also find," Tyrone continued, "people who aren't entirely Human. Some have ancestors of other races – Goblin, Centaur, Faerie, Sprite. There are even rare ones with dual bloodlines, half-and-half. And an even scarcer few... aren't Human *at all*."

He waited a moment while the children, including Faye, absorbed this.

"We are a multicultural, multiracial Academy. We honour acceptance and tolerance for *every* being from *every* background. And if you cannot adhere to that, you have no place there. Understood?" he asked sternly.

Jeremy nodded rapidly, while Hannah nodded just once and never made eye contact.

The camp was silent after that, apart from the crackle of the fire.

Later in the evening, as the others drifted off to sleep, Faye once more felt the need to escape from the oppressive presence of people. The episode by the fire had upset her more than she realised at the time. The land seemed to be whispering to her, singing to her as it had four nights previously, as though wishing to soothe away her worries and fears.

Taking her pipe, the girl slowly slipped away amongst the trees until she came to a clearing. This open space had a surface that was scattered with broken bits of ancient stone and was surrounded by equally ancient trees. The eroded stones seemed to murmur and sigh.

Heart beating rapidly, Faye perched on a branch near the far edge of the clearing. She raised the pipe to her lips and then listened carefully.

Yes, there it was! The tune Faye had thought she heard back at the camp. It was a song of sadness, loss, death, and remembrance.

Slowly, she caught the pattern of the tune and began to play. The notes spiralled around the forest, and the grass glowed softly under the moon, as did the flowers and leaves. Then, the ruins began to glow with a silver light. The magic started to creep and glide up into the air, creating an illusion of the various buildings in their complete state. More ghostly towers and buildings rose out of the forest, filling the gaps where no trees grew.

By the time Faye had finished the song, the entire area, for at least a kilometre all around, shone dully, a vision appearing ...

It was a city!

As Faye faltered, the illusion began to fade.

"What is it, Seeker Tyrone?" Jeremy's voice asked in awe from the rim of trees opposite Faye's hiding place.

The girl froze, uncertain if they had seen her. Tyrone and Jeremy stood in the shadows near where Faye had entered the clearing. They were staring in awe at the fading ghost city, their eyes hopefully now night-blind from the dazzling display of lights. The last thing Faye wanted was to be spotted lurking in the woods with a mystical pipe!

"The ancient city of Galleymai!" Tyrone's voice was low and excited. "I would recognise those guard towers anywhere!"

"Galleymai?" Jeremy asked.

"An ancient Fey city. It was built by Humans and Elves but inhabited by many magical and non-magical creatures... In ancient times, there was a great war. The city was demolished, and thousands died. That was one of the many battles that ended the relationships between Fey and Human almost two hundred years ago. Slowly, in more modern times, we've rebuilt that relationship – at the Academy anyway," he paused for a moment, as though reliving old memories. "Seekers have been searching for these ruins for years. We hadn't realised that they lay so far from civilisation."

"How did it light up like that?" Jeremy asked, the clearing now dark once more.

"Who knows? Perhaps it was the magic of a full moon, or the alignment of the earth and stars. Just count yourself lucky we happened to be here to see it," the Seeker replied. "Let's get back to camp."

Silently, they crept back into the shadows.

Faye waited for ten minutes before silently following. She managed to slip into her blankets without notice, her mind awhirl.

CHAPTER 12

CONFRONTATION

The next day passed in silence, as did the day after that. Hannah had made the tactical decision not to attempt conversation with anyone again, and Jeremy appeared to prefer his own company. Faye was too nervous and wary of Tyrone now to ask many questions, despite her agile brain being filled with comments and queries.

As the afternoon of their eighth day drew to a close, the four travellers were footsore and cranky. Tyrone's mood had improved, but he was still short with Hannah. Hannah, in turn, was piously snooty – as though Tyrone had been in the wrong.

Around midday, they finally joined the main road leading to the Academy and so were no longer hampered by dense forest and narrow, forgotten tracks. Unfortunately, they were also now exposed to a predator's greedy eye.

"Right, you lot. We just have to make it to Wythmarch, and then the roads will become safe again. I wish there was another route we could take, but there isn't." Tyrone told them as he hoisted his pack more comfortably onto his shoulder and set off down the graded road. "With any luck, we've left the bandits behind us."

Faye scrambled to catch up to the Seeker, determined to keep as far away from the sullen Hannah as she could. All seemed well until an hour before sunset, when their monotonous, silent trudge was suddenly interrupted.

A man wearing a dark cloak was blocking the road. As the small group drew closer and slowed, another figure joined the first. Tyrone indicated that his three wards should stand behind him. Jeremy carefully loosened his hunting knife hanging from his belt and stood beside the Seeker. Hannah held back a little but refused to cower. Her expression became even more snooty than usual.

Faye, a feeling of foreboding stealing into her belly, slowly turned to eye their backtrail. They had passed a dense thicket not too long ago. At the front of the party, one of the two strangers hailed Tyrone.

"Hello, there. There's nothing to be concerned about, mate. Just strip ye'selves of ye valuables, and we won't harm ye. Tha's a good lad," the bandit said, his voice gleefully menacing.

At the sound of the man's voice, Faye noticed that another two men crept out from beneath the cover of the thicket at their rear, surrounding them.

"Tyrone, there's two more at our back," Faye said in a low voice. They were trapped!

The Seeker flicked a finger, indicating he had heard her.

Tightening her grip on her staff, Faye slowed her breathing. She ran through the meditation drills Jack had taught her to do before entering a sparring session.

Slow the breathing. Check.

Relax each muscle, one by one. Check.

Clear the mind. Check – sort of.

"Our apologies, friend, but I am a mere Seeker, travelling with students from the Academy. We are poor and have nothing of value," Tyrone responded casually as the two men approached him.

The two behind also closed in.

"Me thinks otherwise, *friend*. That girly right there seems to be clutchin' her necklace rather tightly. Must have some value," leered the lead bandit.

Faye silently cursed Hannah – the greedy swine! She had no doubt that the girl had many valuable things on her – such as jewels and gold.

Faye only had her staff, knapsack... and her mother's pipe. It wouldn't take a genius to realise that the pipe, a shimmering magical creation, would fetch a decent amount of gold at any city market. She was loath to lose it, especially to these unkempt common criminals.

A calm settled over the girl as she thought this.

Hannah or no Hannah, these men would have stopped them and searched them. They had deliberately lain in wait along the only stretch of road to join the southern mountain pass to the valley below. All travellers would have to pass this way, and these bandits took advantage of that fact!

The only thing their small group could do now was to try and protect themselves as best they could.

"Stay behind me, girls. This could get ugly," murmured Tyrone.

Faye noticed with disdain that only now did Hannah obey the order, slinking behind the Seeker's larger form. Tyrone added in a low voice, "Jeremy, hold off the two behind."

Jeremy joined Faye, facing the two men who were now closing in rapidly, blocking any retreat. A shimmering heat prickled at Faye's back, the feeling of magic being conjured. That odd sensation filled her chest, informing her that the land was responding to the power Tyrone had conjured.

These criminals obviously don't realise what a Seeker is capable of, Faye thought cynically. Or, if they did, they simply didn't believe that their intended victim *was* a Seeker, despite his claim. *Fools.*

"You should get behind me," Jeremy said nervously, knife in hand.

Faye stubbornly replied. "I can handle myself," refusing to move an inch.

Jeremy glanced at her, then shrugged. Clearly, there was much about the girl which wasn't as he had expected. She certainly was no wilting flower, that was for sure.

"Take the one on the right, and I'll nab the guy on the left," the boy said instead, renewed confidence in his voice.

Faye nodded once, then focused on her target, Zen's body warming against her neck – another sign of magic brewing.

"I'll help the boy," whispered the lizard into her ear, readying itself to pounce.

Faye nodded again, surprised by Zen's faith in her ability. But then, she had been trained by Jack and could almost knock him flat with the stick – something few could boast of.

They were as ready as they were ever going to be.

The four men attacked simultaneously. The two men in front flew at Tyrone, both bearing long knives. Faye didn't see much more than that from the corner of her eye before the other two were upon her and Jeremy.

Zen leapt from her shoulder the moment the boy clashed, knife on knife, with the left bandit. The right bandit approached Faye with a more confident swagger.

"Now, laddie, just hand the stick over, and ye needn't be hurt," he said confidently, walking straight up to the small figure.

Big. Mistake.

"I am *NOT* a *BOY*!" Faye snarled, as she side-stepped gracefully and whacked the man across the head.

His arms went up instinctively and caught the blow before it did too much damage. Faye took the opportunity to swing the stick around her body, using her momentum to quickly drive the heavy staff head into the man's ribs. Something crunched, and he grunted, his arms coming down to clutch his middle.

The world appeared to glow yellow as Faye changed direction once more and successfully pummelled the staff into her attacker's right temple. He crumpled to the ground without a sound.

Meanwhile, Jeremy stood gazing bewilderedly at his own attacker, also unconscious with a viciously hissing lizard on his chest. A thin gash had been opened along the boy's forearm, testimony to the bandit's determination to strike.

"Zen, enough," Faye said absently, looking over her shoulder.

Zen fell silent, then sheepishly climbed up the girl's body to drape itself once more around her neck. Behind her, the first two men were unconscious, slumped before Tyrone, who still sparkled with that yellow power he had conjured.

"What on earth just happened?" Jeremy asked, dumbfounded. "Is that *your* lizard?"

"Yes," Faye replied shortly as she carefully approached Tyrone.

That was when she noticed that Hannah sat hunched on the ground, hands over her head, screaming non-stop. And had been screaming non-stop since the attack began.

"Hannah, shut up!" Faye said firmly.

Hannah's squeal faded abruptly.

Tyrone turned to them, that feral energy sparking from his hands to the ground, from the ground to his chest, and along his chest to his head. Faye could feel the echo of that power along her bones.

"Tyrone, they're done in. There's no more," she said in that same firm voice.

After what seemed an age, the Seeker nodded once. The sparkling yellow magic faded.

"Let's begone from this place. It will be a while before they wake," the Seeker murmured, nudging the two inert men that had attacked Faye and Jeremy.

He frowned slightly as he noticed the large lump rising along one man's face.

"What happened to these two?" he asked.

"Oh... Faye hit that one with her staff, knocked him clean out! And her lizard attacked this one," Jeremy said, his confusion apparent over the whole situation.

"Lizard?" Tyrone asked, baffled.

Faye and Zen had agreed to keep the small reptile a secret. Neither was certain if students were allowed to keep pets or magical companions. Judging by Thayrille's reaction to Fey and Human bonding, Faye really didn't want to find out. There wasn't much for it, however. Zen had shown itself now.

Reluctantly, Faye nudged Zen. The lizard slowly poked its head out from beneath her collar to glare balefully at the curious Humans.

"I see," was all Tyrone said, examining the small, colourful, scaly head with a raised eyebrow.

The lizard hissed in warning, then disappeared beneath her hair once more. The sandy-haired man looked about before gathering his gear up from the ground, clearly dismissing the small reptile as interesting but unimportant.

"Let me cleanse and bandage that arm, Jeremy," Faye offered. "You never know what nasty grime might be on that knife."

The boy sat heavily on the ground while Faye retrieved her emergency medical kit. With practiced motions, the young girl cleaned the wound and had it dressed efficiently.

"Come along, then," Tyrone said to them all in a cheerier tone once Faye had repacked her kit. "We best notify the Wythmarch Constabulary, so they can come collect this bunch. It shouldn't cost us too much extra time if we hurry. Then, we can sleep in a *real* bed tonight! Won't that be a treat?"

Even Hannah didn't argue as they set off at a much brisker pace than they had travelled to date.

That night was a sombre affair as the group sat silently around a large wooden table at the Inn Tyrone had rented rooms for the night. They usually didn't talk, anyway, but this particular evening, their joint experience seemed to weigh heavy between them.

Their table was close to the central hearth, some distance away from the other patrons, which afforded the small group a little privacy. Tyrone seemed distant and stoic, now that he had displayed the extent of his powers. Jeremy seemed embarrassed that he had been saved by a lizard. Even Hannah seemed keenly aware that out of all of them, she had done nothing to try and save them – only screamed like a ninny and hid behind everyone else. At least, Faye *hoped* that's how she felt. Knowing Hannah, though, the nasty git was probably just feeling hard done by. The girl was certainly back to being snootily pious as she picked fussily at the house stew that Tyrone had ordered for them all.

"You know, Master Seeker, I don't think I'm rather partial to this stew. Is there anything else on their menu?" Hannah muttered, a distinct whine in her tone.

"I'm sure there is, if you have the coin to pay for it," Tyrone told her with equanimity before sliding her still-full bowl right out from beneath her spoon and promptly splitting its contents between himself, Jeremy, and Faye.

The other two children ducked their heads, eyes wide with ill-disguised glee as they quickly shovelled their extra helping of the delicious stew into their mouths. After over a week of trail rations, neither of them would turn their noses up at perfectly delightful food!

Hannah's jaw sagged in shock, clearly outraged that her food had been taken from her and that she now had to pay for her own meal. She mulishly glared at the Seeker, to no avail. Finally, realising that she would either have to organise another meal or starve, Hannah slid huffily off her seat. She stomped her way over to the wooden counter at the rear of the Inn's main room.

"Sorry if that seemed unfair," Tyrone sighed, pinching the bridge of his nose. "Dredging up that amount of power, as I did today, makes me tired and grouchy, and absolutely *starving*. I have no patience for that sort of nonsense, quibbling over perfectly good food. Not tonight."

Faye peered up at the Seeker in concern.

"Is it always like that?" she asked tentatively.

"Aye, more often than not. For a person who can conjure sorcery, the power comes from within and there is often a heavy price to pay. Every Sorcerer has a unique capacity for power, and when the power inside oneself is drained... Let's just say it's not a pretty sight," Tyrone replied softly.

"Can't they draw on the lands power?" Faye pressed, keen to gain as much knowledge as possible now that Tyrone seemed in the mood for talking and Hannah was otherwise occupied.

"No. No one in Pendalin can do that. Only the ancient Elves were reputed to access the power of the earth. Everyone else either uses gems, their own innate core magic, or a combination of both. Each method takes its toll on the conjurer," he elaborated as he polished off the last of his stew with a hunk of fresh-baked bread. "If a body isn't careful, the power conjured can sap their life force and leave behind a frail empty husk. I think they have a whole Ward set aside at Tryssdale Medic Centre for those foolish enough to tamper with power beyond their capabilities."

Faye nodded thoughtfully, recalling the power she had conjured with her mother's pipe. The slim metal instrument appeared to be magic in origin and could raise dormant energy from the land itself – all without Faye making a single contribution of her own power – not that she had any. At least, she *thought* she didn't have any power. Maybe... Maybe it was different power than the normal type of sorcery.

It made Faye wonder if she *did* have latent magical abilities herself. She *was* half Fey, after all, even though Thayrille could never work out what Clan her mother had come from. *All* Fey had magical powers. Didn't they? What if, despite being half Fey, she never actually developed a talent for magic? What if she were just an ordinary Human, like Thayrille, or Jack, or Jeremy?

Not that it matters, Faye chastised herself. *I have other talents!*

Faye wondered briefly if Jeremy had seen her accuracy with the stick, or had he only seen that final whack when the attacker had been felled? She wasn't brave enough to ask, in case he hadn't seen, and the inquiry just raised awkward questions.

The Seeker finally broke the strained silence that followed his last gruesome answer when Hannah rejoined them with another annoyed huff.

"Some day, huh?" he commented quietly, sipping carefully at his hot mug of cocoa.

"Yeah," Jeremy grunted, now carefully sharpening his knife with a small whetstone; his body turned towards the fire so he wouldn't have to look directly at Hannah. Jeremy had become increasingly distant towards Hannah, the longer they travelled together.

"What was that piece of magic you did, Tyrone? Was it sorcery that they teach at the Academy?" Faye asked, intensely curious as some of her earlier reticence left her.

She couldn't shake the desire to talk about magic, particularly to someone that was able to conjure it.

"Yes. I apprenticed as a Sorcerer for a while, before I decided to become a Seeker. I'm still studying part time, but I wanted to get out and travel a bit more," Tyrone replied, some inner tension fading as he gave Faye a wan smile.

"You can do that?" Faye gasped, her eyes widening in discovery. "Study part-time while Seeking? And you don't have to be a fully qualified Sorcerer to be granted Seekership?"

"Of course not! Only satisfactory results in Intermediary Sorcery are required to Seek, and the Academy is quite flexible about study hours," he replied, some of the awkwardness easing from his demeanour as his weak smile changed to a good-natured grin.

Perhaps, Faye thought, she had been approaching this strange, powerful man all wrong. Instead of waiting for him to make all the overtures, maybe what she should have been doing was asking all those hundreds of questions brimming silently in her mind. She was so used to waiting for Thayrille to instigate conversation that it didn't occur to her that Tyrone might be just as nervous amongst strangers as she was. It seemed he was more like Jack – ready to listen and talk, if only she could get the confidence to ask.

"What good would it do *you* to be a Seeker?" Hannah spat at Faye, her tone bordering on rudeness.

"To Seek," Faye replied shortly, Hannah's tone reminding her why it was sometimes easier just to keep quiet.

Hannah sighed then tempered her voice, so it was more huffy than snide, as she stirred her hot cocoa. Funnily, the older girl sat hunched over her mug, as though genuinely worried that it, too, would be snatched away from her.

"I didn't mean it like that. You appear to have many talents – weapons, forestry, music..." Hannah vaguely waved her hand, indicating the pipe that Faye was absently twiddling between her hands. "There are many higher paying forms of employment than a government gofer."

Faye shrugged, mollified a little by Hannah's effort to be civil and amused at Tyrone's pained expression. Was Hannah just stupid, or did she honestly not realise how offensive her comments were to a man like Tyrone? Afterall, he *was* a 'government-paid *gofer*', as Hannah put it.

The Seeker rolled his eyes behind his cocoa mug and let the barbed comment slide.

"It's always just been a dream of mine," Faye said, returning the pipe to her pocket before anyone could request a tune.

They didn't know she could play; it was a secret just between herself and Zen, and nor did she feel like trying it out in a public space like this Inn! The land felt devoid of power here, anyway, as though the multitude of people and their dwellings had culled the lands magic.

"And a fine dream, too," Tyrone said hurriedly before Hannah could push the issue. "Just keep yourself open to change, Faye. I wanted to be a Clerk when I first joined the Academy. Then it was discovered that I had latent magical powers. Although I fully intend to become a Sorcerer one day, I'm quite happy with Seeking for the moment."

Faye nodded in response, then claimed exhaustion before too many more revealing questions could be asked.

"Yep, I'm for bed, too." Jeremy leapt to his feet with alacrity, following the younger girl up the stairs to their rented rooms above.

Thankfully, Tyrone had been thoughtful enough to organise a room for each of them, so Faye wouldn't have to share with Hannah. The other girl, now stuck downstairs awaiting her belated dinner in the sole company of Seeker Tyrone, did not appear to be in any sort of gentle mood.

Finally, ten and a half days after leaving Grydin, they came to Tryssdale, home to Austin Academy. As they descended the final escarpment to the fabled city, the chilly mist that had shrouded their final days dispersed and the roads became clear. Tryssdale was a large place, mostly made of stone with narrow paved alleys that separated the tall buildings.

Faye gawked as they entered the first of many winding streets, trying to take in the myriad of sights and sounds.

Innumerable people swarmed and by the sheer number of windows gleaming from every soaring stone wall, reflecting slices of the crystal blue sky, it was evident that this was only a portion of the cities total population. Heart thudding, palms clammy, and nervous sweat gathering along her upper lip, Faye felt she was about to have a full-blown panic attack.

Zen buzzed reassuringly, its little claws kneading her shoulder firmly as the girl stumbled along in Tyrone's wake. Faye now understood Jack's concern over whether she was ready for this experience.

The city was immense and a child such as Faye could easily drown here, swallowed up by the winding streets and towering stone buildings. The child felt as though she were just one ant in a riotous colony. Miniscule. Unidentified. Unimportant.

As they rounded a bend in the road, a magnificent palace rose from amongst the close-packed buildings, surrounded by emerald-green grass and a picturesque copse of trees.

The vast complex took up approximately half the valley, residing on a hill over the sprawling city like a benevolent benefactor.

"*That* is Austin Academy," Tyrone called over his shoulder, indicating the massive building.

"It looks like a King's castle," Jeremy said in some surprise.

"Well, that's because it *was*," Tyrone said with a wry smile. "It was built by King Germaine, as a Winter Palace. He resided here when things down south got too cold. It also allowed him to strengthen his bond with the northern lands and pander to the Barons in these parts."

"Why is it now a university?" Faye asked with a frown. "The Summer Palace in Rixondale has remained preserved."

She was sure she knew the answer, but it escaped her for now.

"Very true, Faye," Tyrone said with approval. "That's because the Summer Palace is the original, and only, location of the Throne of Pendalin. If the King or Queen of Pendalin is to ever be restored, then they need that throne – just as it is – as well as the Sceptre and the Crown."

Faye nodded. She had read that somewhere.

"I suppose it would make sense to turn the Winter Palace into something useful. The future king or queen surely wouldn't mind," she mused aloud as they trudged up the cobbled street.

"Exactly," Tyrone replied.

The girl focused on the distant structure, determined to block out the overwhelming complexity of Tryssdale itself.

They passed through the bustling streets in silence, admiring the ancient buildings and eyeing the merchandise displayed in windows. Faye continued to feel distinctly uneasy whenever she lost sight of the massive palace. If it hadn't been for the weighty lizard at her neck, vibrating comfortingly against her skin, she would have fallen to the ground by now and huddled up in the foetal position. She had never been in a crowd before, and this was the first time she had ever been in a group larger than four people, barring her Selection back in Grydin. It was a scary realisation.

Intellectually, Faye realised that she could attend classes with up to thirty other students – but the reality of the sheer volume of Human presence was daunting.

"I'll be with you," whispered Zen, as the lizard's head rubbed against her ear.

The girl nodded, unable to speak through her constricted throat.

"I couldn't do it without you, dear one," Faye muttered, hunching her shoulders and ducking her head uncomfortably as she scurried after Tyrone.

CHAPTER 13

REGIMENTAL ROUTINES

The four weary travellers finally emerged from the warren of streets onto a clear cobbled path that switch-backed up the hill towards the vast stone building. The Academy was surrounded by a crumbling stone wall, reminiscent of the ghostly apparition of Galleymai that Faye had unwittingly called up with her pipe.

Faye wondered if perhaps Elves had helped design this palace, too.

They entered through the towering metal-plated gateway and continued to follow the broad cobbled road straight to the main entrance. On either side were vast green fields studded with trees which ended in the nearby distance against looming, craggy mountains. The entire valley was ensconced in those protective natural walls. From a tactical perspective, the palace had been built in a defensible position.

When they finally arrived at the massive front doors, the small group was accepted into a large room off the immense entry hall. As soon as Faye crossed the threshold, the cool tingle of old power washed over her, welcoming her like she was a child who had finally come home. It was an unsettling sensation and reminded Faye of the feeling gleaned from her favourite oak tree. Perhaps the land here recognised something inside of her, just as it did back home...

"Hi ho, we have some new recruits!" the Clerk exclaimed in greeting as they entered the airy room. He opened a thick ledger that sat squarely on his desk with a sense of pomp and fuss. "All right, details, details, please, children."

Jeremy and Faye exchanged an uncertain look before the boy stepped forward with far more confidence than she.

"Jeremy Bloomsbry, sir," he said promptly. "From Grydin Village."

"Good, good. Father's employ? And mother's?" the Clerk asked absently.

Jeremy responded promptly, "Woodsmen and Seamstress, sir."

"Age?"

"I'll be fifteen come spring next."

"Brothers or sisters already attending?"

"No, sir. I'm the first," Jeremy declared proudly.

"Excellent, lad! That should do it. Next!" the Clerk peered shrewdly at Hannah as the girl stepped belligerently in front of Faye.

"Hannah Rikton, sir. Also, from Grydin Village. Father is a Clerk. Mother is a Boarding House Mistress. And I'll be fifteen at summer's end. I'm the first of *my* siblings to attend, too," she said in a rush, fluttering her eyelashes prettily.

"I see," was all the Clerk said, with a rather sour nod.

Faye suppressed a smirk. It was surely good for Hannah to be knocked down a few pegs, she mused. Although, the blank look in the girl's eyes didn't bode well.

Faye wondered if the older girl had plans to knock the Clerk down and whack him with a stick, too. Perhaps the man was thinking along the same lines, because he met the girl's wooden stare calmly, allowing a small *zing* of azure power to alight in his dark eyes.

Faye raised her eyebrows at this silent contest of wills and was thrilled when Hannah lowered her gaze and backed down imperceptibly.

"Right, now you, young one," the Clerk turned his stern gaze onto Faye, causing her to shuffle her feet nervously.

That spark of power was still shining forbiddingly deep in his eyes.

"Faye," was all the girl could manage through her constricted throat.

"Family name?" the Clerk queried, back to his professional demeanour.

"I... I haven't one," Faye whispered, eyes prickling a little.

She wondered if she should have declared herself Hogansvort, like Thayrille, but decided not to. Her foster mother had made it clear that Faye was to pave her own way from this point forward. The last thing the girl wanted to do was use her foster mother's reputation for some sort of underserved gain.

Hannah snorted, causing an embarrassed flush to race up Faye's face at the sound. Zen vibrated silently against her neck in comfort.

"Oh, you must be the special case Rythin mentioned," the Clerk said with a sympathetic smile, the warning spark of power fading from his eyes. "I already have your details right here, my dear."

The Clerk jotted down a few things in his ledger, then once he had finished, the book glowed gently with a smidgeon of that azure energy. When the Clerk saw Faye's curious look, he gave her a smile.

"Magic. Just a simple replication spell," he explained. "This way, the instructors will be able to view your details and place you in classes while we get you settled."

Two other adults appeared in the doorway as though summoned by a silent bell. One was a small, fussy-looking man with smooth black hair tied in a short tail. He persistently straightened his jacket and cleared his throat as he peered sternly at the three children, his many begemmed rings on his slim fingers glinting with an array of colours. The other was an overly tall and solid, serene woman with sun-kissed skin and dark brown hair done up in a tight bun.

Jeremy was asked to accompany the man, Mister Drayck, while the girls were to follow the woman, Mistress Tryllia. Tyrone was left to report the details of their trip to the benevolent Clerk.

Their separation happened so suddenly and efficiently; Faye's head was reeling. The girls and Jeremy parted ways in the dim entrance hall, with the Ettiquette Master, Mister Drayck leading the way to the boy's dormitory and the Housekeeper Mistress Tryllia, the girls.

Faye climbed first one set of stairs, then another, right behind the no-nonsense clack of the giant woman's sturdy heels, determined not to walk alongside Hannah and risk the girl trying to bodily throw her down the stone steps.

"Right – how old are you, girl?" Mistress Tryllia turned and asked of Hannah, her tone brusque but kind.

Faye doubted that it even occurred to Hannah to be offended by the woman's use of the term 'girl'.

"Fourteen," Hannah said promptly, aiming to appear innocent and sweet.

"Excellent, we have a few others of that age. You'll do rightly with them," the woman said serenely.

Tryllia led them along the third floor, twisting and turning through halls and corridors as they went deeper into the palace. Finally, they found another corridor, lined with plain wooden doors. Mistress Tryllia paused outside one of these and opened it briskly. Inside, there were four tidy beds lining one wall, four tidy desks lining the other, and four tidy closets standing between the desks.

"There should be two empty closets. Choose one to place your things into," the Housekeeper instructed Hannah.

"I'm to *share* a room?" Hannah asked incredulously.

Faye recalled a tidbit of gossip that Mistress Brianey, the Baker's wife, had divulged during one of her many visits to the Healer's cottage. Hannah had come from a crowded household, but even there, she had been given her own room, so she could 'study' in private. Apparently, the other Rikton girls were unlikely to attend the Academy and had to share a room. It seemed Hannah expected that same special treatment here, too.

"Yes, girly, and you'll like it, too," Mistress Tryllia said sternly. "I'll give you a half hour to settle and then I'm to collect you for lunch."

With that, the stout woman smartly closed the door behind Hannah and continued down the hall. Faye, a sort of amazed amusement welling in her chest, silently followed and fought down a grin. This was *not* how she imagined her first day at the Academy to play out!

Faye had harboured the secret fear that Hannah would have the instructors wrapped around her little finger from the first and that it would be *herself* that was treated harshly through the other girl's machinations. It would seem, however, that Hannah's attitude was not appreciated nor tolerated in the vast stone palace.

"Now, dear, how old would you be?" Mistress Tryllia asked in a gentler tone, her dark eyes softening as she peered down at the little blonde thing happily skipping along in her wake.

"Twelve, Mistress," Faye replied politely.

She asked off-handedly, "No brothers or sisters here, then?"

Faye flushed and shook her head. She clearly remembered the slurs she had heard over her lack of family.

"Ahh, never mind that, my dear. You'll make friends soon enough." Mistress Tryllia smiled warmly. "You'll have to have a room to yourself for now. We don't have any around your age, and I'll be be'jiggered if I leave you in that sly serpent's company. Tyrone had a thing or two to say about that girl in the letter he sent ahead from Wythmarch."

Faye found herself smiling in appreciation. So, this was one woman Hannah could not fool. And if Tyrone *had* reported much of what Hannah had done or said during their journey, then *none* of the instructors would be giving her leeway. She hoped.

Mistress Tryllia guided Faye up two more flights of stairs, down a hall that looked identical to every other, round another corner and into a quiet dead-end space. The alcove contained just one door and would be easily missed as a storage cupboard to the unacquainted.

Mistress Tryllia opened the stout wooden door with a flourish and ushered the girl inside ahead of her. This room was smaller than the other, barely bigger than her attic room back in the Healer's cottage, and contained only one bed, a desk, and a closet. It was heaven.

"Ye be lucky, a very private room you'll have," she said with satisfaction.

"Thank you," Faye said simply, smiling at the Housekeeper with profound relief. "It's perfect!"

Mistress Tryllia nodded once, clearly pleased that such a small thing made the young one so happy.

"See you in half an hour," Tryllia closed the door softly behind her.

Zen wriggled free of Faye's collar as soon as the door clicked shut.

"Part Fey, that one," the lizard enthused. "Only a little, though, far back in her history. Can't even tell which creature."

"Gorgon, perhaps," Faye mused, reflecting on the Housekeeper's stern, strong face upon her solid frame.

"Quite possibly," Zen said in agreement and clambered down Faye's arm to the bed. "She senses you're like her. That's why she's so kind."

"I just wish I knew *which* Fey Clan I'm from," Faye sighed heavily.

Unfortunately, at that moment, Faye was unpacking her things and so missed the uncomfortable wince that crossed the lizard's face.

After the girl had unloaded her knapsack, she went to the single window and peered out. Below was a great green field, studded by small and large groups of trees, and bordered by those craggy grey mountains. From this vantage point, Faye could see that her room was far above the ground, higher even than her snug cubby within the branches of her favourite oak. Heights had never bothered the girl, so she leant out the window to examine the land to the left and right of her room.

It was a stark landscape, entirely opposite to her view back in the Healer's cottage, but still very beautiful. Faye felt tears prick her eyes as a wave of homesickness washed over her. She desperately wanted to sit by Thayrille right now and have the Healer give her that no-nonsense, stern advice she had come to rely on. It had never occurred to Faye that missing Thayrille and the cottage would be one of the situations she would have to deal with, especially so soon. She had thought the excitement of her arrival here would wash away any *paltry emotions*, as Thayrille called them.

The Academy was going to be an entirely different, alien experience and Faye wasn't sure she was ready for it.

"Chin up, dear one! This will be the adventure of a lifetime!" the lizard crooned, butting its head against her jaw before it scampered down her arm to explore the room.

The lizard, it seemed, had the zoomies and was darting hither and thither around the confined space. Faye smiled helplessly, figuring that the poor reptile had been cooped up beneath her hair for long enough. No wonder the creature had so much energy bottled up!

Faye spent her remaining time enjoying simply being alone. Zen had finally worked through its pent-up energy and settled onto the bed, snuggling beneath the pillow so it was completely invisible. The lizard was probably exhausted – she doubted Zen had gotten much sleep on the trip. She felt that it had been staying up late, watching over the camp for danger, especially in the form of that murderous wasp, Hannah.

For Faye, this was her first time alone in almost two weeks. She could feel the strain slowly fade away as she sorted her knick-knacks into her desk drawer. Her clean clothes were hung carefully in the closet, and her dirty items were placed in the wicker basket marked *laundry*. Her staff was propped neatly against the wardrobe, just as it had been back home in Grydin. She exchanged her sturdy walking boots for loafers, sighing in relief as the aches in her feet eased against the soft leather.

The minutes slipped by and before long Tryllia was tapping on her door. Faye opened the heavy panel cautiously, peering out and identifying the knocker before allowing the door to swing all the way open.

"Come along," Tryllia said, smiling in satisfaction as she noted the tidy room and the empty knapsack that hung from a hook by the wardrobe.

Faye immediately fell into step just behind the woman, awkwardly glancing behind her as she closed the door. Zen hadn't offered to accompany her, and the girl felt bereft by the lizard's absence. She was so used to the little creature nestling against her neck that a pang of separation anxiety struck her.

Ignoring the urge to snatch the reptile up, reminding herself that the little thing deserved an uninterrupted sleep, Faye hurriedly caught up with the stout woman.

"Excuse me, Mistress Tryllia?" Faye asked curiously, eager to take her mind off Zen's absence. "How many students attend the Academy?"

"Oh, nigh on eight hundred," Tryllia replied, seeming even more pleased at being addressed so politely.

Faye blanched. That was twice as many people than the Grydin Triad, including all the outlying villages! In just *one* building!

The chance for further conversation stopped once they went back down the stairs and reached Hannah's room. When Tryllia opened the door, the older girl was only halfway through unpacking.

"Just a moment," Hannah said sulkily. "I'm not finished yet."

Tryllia noticed the rumpled bed opposite the chosen wardrobe. It appeared that Hannah had not unpacked straight away, as bidden, but had flung herself in a huff on the bed instead.

"Now, see here, girly. Lunch is just about ready. So, you have a choice – leave what you're doing or find your own way to the mess hall," Tryllia told Hannah sternly. "And gods help you if you take a wrong turning and end up somewhere you shouldn't."

Hannah appeared about to retort in kind but changed her mind when she saw the ill-humoured expression on the woman's face and a glint of rose-lavender power in her dark eyes. It appeared that the primping princess wasn't confident in her navigation skills, nor in taking on yet another adult who appeared to have sorcerous powers. Faye watched as Hannah quickly stuffed her things into the base of the closet opposite her bed and closed its door firmly.

"Where's the lock?" Hannah demanded, realising there was nothing other than the handle to keep the wardrobe closed.

Tryllia said impatiently, "We do not condone locks at the Academy. It breeds secrecy and greed." She gestured for Hannah to join them. Hannah hesitated until Mistress Tryllia turned on her heel abruptly and started to walk down the hall, Faye close on her heels.

"Stay or come as you please," The Housekeeper called over her shoulder.

Hurriedly, Hannah sped out of the dormitory and caught up with the two of them about halfway down the hall. Faye determinedly looked straight ahead and walked a mere step behind Tryllia to avoid getting caught in any backlash that Hannah might decide was appropriate. She didn't have Zen's soothing vibration at her neck nor her own sparring staff to defend herself.

Thankfully, Hannah walked a few steps behind, her pretty face scrunched in an unhappy scowl.

The two girls were taken down the hallway and past the broad corridor they had arrived through. At the end of this narrow passage was an open area with many chairs and lounges.

"The common room," Tryllia said. "There is one on each level of the dormitories. You are to use the common room on your own level only, unless specifically invited by a friend. If you make a nuisance of yourself in a place that you have no business being, and have no one to veto your presence there, then your admission may be revoked."

Mistress Tryllia glanced back sternly at Hannah.

"You will both be watched closely. So I highly recommend you do not stray from your designated areas. For you, Miss Rikton, that will be your dormitory room and the common room on this level," Tryllia announced sternly, casting the lagging girl a pointed look.

Hannah appeared to be chewing on her tongue, on the verge of saying something unpragmatic, before she kept her silence and simply nodded her understanding.

Satisfied, the stout Housekeeper continued on. She led them to the far side of the room, where a narrow stairwell spiralled back down into the depths of the Academy. They scaled down another two flights of stairs, passing a common room like the one above as predicted, before alighting on the ground floor, inside a massive dining hall.

At one end was an open kitchen where people of all ages served copious amounts of food. Along the left side of the combined kitchen and dining room were vast doors that opened onto the green grounds beyond the palace, allowing a late summer breeze to freshen the room.

"Now, each student must do kitchen duty while they're here. You'll be slotted into the roster and informed of your times," Tryllia said, ushering them over to the line of students awaiting their lunch. "If you fail to complete these duties, your admission will be revoked."

Faye raised an eyebrow at the brusque tone and made a mental note never to argue with the woman. It seems one *toe* out of line could see her sent back to Grydin in shame!

Jeremy stood down the line, looking rather perplexed as he was served a large plate of pasta and sauce along with a small loaf of steaming bread. Faye could just imagine Jeremy was wondering how he could be expected to cook anything. He was notorious for lacking ability, as evident during their recent travels.

"First, I have to share a room, and now I'm expected to *cook*?!" Hannah sputtered in indignation.

She was far away from her family's strange ways and rules. It seemed Hannah was discovering she didn't much like a life that didn't revolve around herself.

On the other hand, Faye enjoyed cooking and preferred to keep busy with chores. It was how Thayrille had raised her, and she suspected this routine would maintain a sense of normality in her strange new life.

"Yes, indeed! *If* you're lucky. Thankfully there are other chores to be done if you have no experience cooking. We always require another dishwasher." Tryllia nodded serenely before she turned around and left the mess hall through one of the many internal archways.

Faye managed not to laugh at the affronted look on Hannah's face, making sure to place several strangers between them in the lunch line, just to be on the safe side.

After several minutes of ordered shuffling along the line of students, Faye was finally able to step up to the serving counter and was dished up a plate of pasta. She lifted the plate to her nose and sniffed curiously.

"It's not poison, kiddo!" exclaimed the youth who had served her, an amused grin lighting up a freckled good-humoured face.

"No, but it could use a tad less salt and perhaps a sprig of basil, a clove of garlic, and a pinch of marjoram," Faye responded with a nervous smile.

The server looked rather dumbfounded, but the next student in line demanded their food before he could reply. The girl quickly found a seat, far away from everyone, particularly Hannah. Faye watched as the older girl peered around herself, looking suitably lost. When no one deigned to pay her any attention, Hannah sat down huffily and picked at her food.

Faye, never one to turn her nose up at a hearty meal, gobbled her pasta with relish.

Bland but perfectly edible, she thought.

Somewhere above, a loud bell tolled, and within minutes, the mess hall was filled with calling, chatting, and bickering students. The line grew to epic proportions as the remainder of the school body entered the mess hall, fresh from their lessons. The noise was intolerable to Faye's sensitive ears. She was used to the peaceful silence and measured pace of Thayrille's cottage.

As soon as she finished the last strand of pasta, Faye returned her plate to the counter, where other dirty dishes were stacked. Another server pressed a large blueberry muffin into her hands as she crept along with plans to escape the bustle and noise through the gaping outer doors. Faye blinked in surprise and managed to stutter a thank you, completely taken aback. The matronly-looking woman gave her a wink before vanishing into the depths of the kitchen, as though plying food on unsuspecting people was an everyday occurrence. Perhaps it was.

The Academy was offering surprise after surprise. Faye shook her head, that sense of panic and the general notion of being utterly overwhelmed filling her chest again. Or was that the power she could feel simmering beneath the stones?

She wished Zen were here!

Faye leant against the architrave of the outer doorway, valiantly trying to get a handle on the panic building inside of her. Her chest was tightening, she was finding it hard to breathe.

Sharp claws pricked at her leg and Faye's eyes snapped down. Her lizard, camouflaged the same colour as the stone walls around them, had inexplicably appeared at her foot. Its sturdy little body scampered up her side, its sharp claws gripping her linen shirt as it obtained its usual position.

"And *breathe*," Zen whispered in her ear, vibrating subtly at her neck, its entire form deftly hidden beneath her cloud of hair. "And another."

Faye drew three deep, calming lungfuls of air before slipping out the giant archway into the sunshine, away from the hustle and bustle of the rapidly filling mess hall. The grounds were empty and quiet, allowing the tension of the past hour to drain away.

"Where did *you* come from?" Faye whispered to Zen as she found a quiet patch of ground well away from the noisy mess hall.

"I have my ways, you know! Sorry, I fell asleep. I didn't intend to leave you alone on your first day, dear one," the lizard apologised as it continued that unrelenting vibration that soothed away her anxiety.

"Oh. Right. I didn't want to wake you. I figured you deserved a good sleep," Faye murmured.

She flopped onto the grass, nibbling on the too-sweet muffin as she examined the grounds. They were sparse, with monotonous swathes of green grass taking up most of the valley, broken only in the distance by patches of wildflowers. Her eyes alighted on the group of trees she had seen from her dormitory window. Why leave a notch of untouched woods in the middle of a strategically cleared lawn? Faye peered closer. Now she was on ground level, the girl noticed that hidden beneath the spreading branches was a low stone building. What could it possibly be? A gardening shed, perhaps? She thought she could smell a waft of manure and sweet hay. Perhaps a stable?

"What do you think so far, dear one?" Zen asked, its vibration lessening in intensity as the girl relaxed and breathed easily.

"Oh, umm, it's surely *something*, isn't it?" Faye sighed heavily as she made a sweeping gesture to encompass the vast stone building behind them and the landscaped grounds. "I just... The amount of *people*..."

"I'll be with you, any time you need me," Zen assured her, nuzzling her neck.

After a time, another deep bell sounded in the palace causing Faye to whip her head around to peer curiously through the gaping doors to see what would happen now. She wasn't disappointed.

The students leapt from their chairs, benches scraping, dishes clattering into dirty piles in a streamlined production. No one bumped into each other, nor was there any mess left on the tables. Students, young and old, began to file out, climbing stairs, or exiting from numerous doors.

Once most students had vanished, Tryllia appeared in the archway and beckoned the young girl back into the vast hall. Faye approached slowly, reluctant to end her solitude, although she felt much better now that she had the lizard's familiar weight on her shoulders.

Inside, Tryllia led Faye, Hannah and Jeremy to a freshly scrubbed table. Several servers meandered about the other empty tables to wipe down the various surfaces before returning to the kitchen for the inevitable clean-up. Faye nervously watched them, relieved that no one seemed interested enough to approach them.

"Now, you three, induction," Tryllia said and had the three sit down at the same bench.

Faye elected to sit on the very far end, a good half meter away from Jeremy who sat in the middle, and as far away from Hannah as she could physically be without sitting at the next table over. Once settled, the girl gave Tryllia her undivided attention.

The first thing the woman did was to give them each a piece of thick parchment with a generic daily plan. Faye glanced down at the set of instructions printed neatly and clearly on the one side, and her eyes bugged a little at the highly detailed structure.

For a moment, the girl wondered if Thayrille had a hand in writing it. It certainly seemed like the sort of finicky detail the Healer adhered to!

Jeepers, Faye thought, *that's a* lot *of lessons! Surely we aren't going to have our noses in books that whole time? I think even* my *head would explode!*

The thought must have been apparent on her face, because Tryllia smiled softly and took pity on her charges by offering reassurance.

"I know this seems like an intensive schedule, but you will soon get used to it. Many classes are often a 'double', where two hours are taken together for one class. There is also an excellent balance between theory lessons and practical lessons."

The woman demonstrated her point by showing the three of them another sheet of paper with a colour-coded example timetable.

"Here. The first column of the table represents Firsday. The first two boxes in the column are shaded green and represent first and second class, which in this case is Agricultural Studies. Most often, students are out on the grounds tending to the gardens. We grow most of our own food here to supply the meals everyone eats. The third class in pink is History for one hour only, while fourth and fifth class shown here in blue are combined to give students two hours of Practical Science. Sixth and seventh class are shaded yellow and represent double Art Studies. Does that make sense?"

The three children nodded, and Faye felt the tightness in her chest ease. Well, she supposed that didn't sound so bad!

<u>*Weekly Schedule*</u>

<u>*Weekdays:*</u>
7am— First morning bell. Dress and have breakfast.
8.30am— Second morning bell. First class.
9.30am— Third morning bell. Second class.
10.30am— Fourth morning bell. Morning tea break.
11am— Fifth morning bell. Third class.
12pm. First afternoon bell. Lunch break.
1pm— Second afternoon bell. Fourth class.
2pm— Third afternoon bell. Fifth class.
3pm— Fourth afternoon bell. Afternoon tea.
3.30pm— Fifth afternoon bell. Sixth class.
4.30pm— Sixth afternoon bell. Seventh class.
5.30pm— First evening bell. End of classes.
6pm— Second evening bell. Dinner
9pm— Third evening bell. Lights out.

<u>*Weeksends:*</u>
7am— First morning bell. Dress and have breakfast.
8.30am— Second morning bell. First class.
9.30am—Third morning bell. Second class.
10.30am— Fourth morning bell. Morning tea break.
11am— Fifth morning bell. Third class.
12pm. First afternoon bell. End of classes. Lunch break.

"You will each receive your own copy of your individualised timetable from your Mentors. Your Mentor is a Senior Professor to whom you will be assigned as you settle into Academy life. They, in essence, serve in place of a parent or guardian for young ones such as yourselves. Any problems you are experiencing can be discussed with your Mentor. If any discipline is required, that also falls under the responsibility of your Mentor," Tryllia continued, then paused to study each of them, as though assessing their level of comprehension.

"What, exactly, is meant by *discipline*?" Hannah was naturally the first to ask the pointy question, clearly not liking the idea.

Faye wondered if the girl had ever been disciplined in her life.

"Well, Miss Rikton, while you are a student of the Academy, there are certain expectations. For example, you will always behave respectfully and respectably. Your instructors will likely set you additional theory tasks to complete in any free time you have, normally in the afternoons and evenings. It is expected that these will be completed by the appointed time. Otherwise, you risk failing your classes." Tryllia blinked at her meaningfully. "If you fail to meet the expectations of your Professors, your Mentor will determine what discipline is required. If you continue to fail your classes after that, first counselling will be provided, and if there is no improvement, your scholarship will be withdrawn."

Jeremy and Faye exchanged a brief glance. Hannah groaned slightly as though this day could get no worse. Even once accepted by the Academy, the challenges kept rearing their ugly heads.

Expulsion was a very genuine threat.

"Now, between these schedules, you will also have a kitchen duty roster. You will rotate between duties for cooking and dishes for either breakfast, lunch, or dinner. You will normally have a duty once every week which coincides with an empty slot in your timetable. If you don't maintain these duties and refuse to contribute to the Academy, then your..." the woman paused expectantly.

"Scholarship will be withdrawn," chorused Faye and Jeremy, instinctively knowing Tryllia's next words.

"Exactly," she responded with a pleased expression.

Hannah looked even more upset.

Faye couldn't help having cynical thoughts about Hannah's work ethic. The snide girl had recently been a big fish in a small pond – but now it seemed she was a small fish in a very *gigantic* pond. It left Faye with rather a deep sense of satisfaction.

"Now, I will give you a tour of the parts of the Academy you will frequent. Then I will take you to each of your mentors, where your classes and schedules will be allocated." Tryllia rose from the bench abruptly, and the three scrambled to follow.

Upstairs, downstairs, along this corridor, through that archway... Faye gazed in awe as they explored the first five levels from the ground level up. The tour lasted a good hour and gave each of the three but a glimpse of each main area, from the kitchens and mess hall to the dormitories and communal bathrooms.

The brisk pace had Faye's heart thrumming, and before long, her legs were aching. After the past ten days of intense travel, the girl longed for a hot bath and a good night's sleep! She was just wondering when this infernal *marathon* would end, when Tryllia finally stopped along a quiet corridor. Lined on either side by sturdy wooden doors, they were on the sixth, and final, floor of the Academy.

The occasional stained-glass window threw splashes of colour over the flagstone floor as the afternoon sun shone through, causing dust motes to dance delicately through the air with a golden shimmer.

"These rooms belong to our professors. You will only come here if you are summoned or have made an appointment. Appointments can be made through me at my office in the Student Storeroom on the ground floor, just off the entry hall," Tryllia informed them as she paced quietly down the corridor, beckoning the three to follow.

Each door bore an enamelled nameplate with the professor's name and position within the Academy.

Hannah was left at one door, stating *Hanly: Sorcerer* which opened after a brief knock. A kindly old man ushered her inside, and the sullen blonde girl looked like she had finally struck gold. Tryllia sternly shook her head at the old man's kind, inquiring look. He ever-so-slightly rolled his eyes to the ceiling in response as he deliberately left the door propped open and resumed his seat behind his broad desk.

The other two weren't allowed to linger and were ushered further down the line of doors. The next stop was Faye's. The door was large and looming with another plaque saying *Academy Vice Administrator*. There was no name, and Faye could feel her heart thud with uncertainty. The Vice Administrator sounded important.

Why would Faye be the one to be landed with such an authority? Was it because of her history in Grydin?

When the massive wooden panel creaked open, Faye felt her hands grow sweaty, and her dry throat made it hard to swallow. Then, to her utmost surprise, Seeker Rythin was standing there! He was as imposing as ever, dressed in comfortable-looking trousers, a button-up maroon shirt, and a loose forest-green academic robe.

"Come in, Faye. Come in, child!" he said, a twinkle in his eye as he saw her surprise and relief.

Tryllia smiled and left with a reassuring wink, taking Jeremy down the hall to a third door.

"So, how were your travels? Quite adventurous, I hear," the old Seeker commented drily.

Faye half shrugged. Rythin had obviously been told the whole story by Tyrone, probably in that mysterious letter he had sent from Wythmarch. She had nothing more to add.

The girl examined the elderly man, noting the white streaks in his grey-black hair. His face was lined, and he walked with a slight limp as though his hip pained him. She had to admire the old man's resilience; other than the minor hobble, he seemed completely at ease after the events of recent weeks.

The Seeker led her to a seat, then resumed his place behind the large, broad desk. It was very similar in design to Hanly's, indicating that much of the furniture in the room was standard issue. The room itself was an airy, comfortable study, its stone walls shrouded with tapestries and other wall hangings. There was another door, half concealed behind one of those decorative tapestries, that was securely closed. Faye assumed that this was where Rythin's bed chamber was located.

"So, Faye," Rythin mused, peering at two sheets of paper on his desk. "Here is your duty list – we operate on a fortnightly cycle. Your 'A' week is Midwok lunch duty, and 'B' week is Resday breakfast, although I'm sure the kitchen duty manager won't say no if you want to pitch in every Resday, if that's your preference."

Resday was the day that fell between Weeksend and Firsday. Designed as a national rest day, Faye often felt it was a waste of perfectly good time to sleep in or laze about. Therefore, she had no qualm about having an early duty when all the other students would be still abed.

"Oh, yes, Resday will be fine," she assured her mentor and was pleased when the man scratched out her Midwok lunch duty before adding her name to Resday A.

"Umm, what do I do instead of the Midwok duty? Is there another class I should attend?" Faye asked curiously as Rythin handed her the roster.

On each side of the paper was a seven-day timetable, broken into the three main meals of the day, breakfast, lunch and dinner. One side was labelled *A Week* and the other was labelled *B Week*.

"No, of course not! That will be relabelled as 'PS' for private study," the man smiled with equanimity. "It will give you the opportunity to complete all those study tasks your instructors will set."

Faye frowned more closely at the kitchen roster, tallying up the name's underneath each of the twenty one scheduled duties.

"I thought there were over eight hundred students...?" Faye asked, doing a quick tally and coming up short. "There's only roughly half of that here!"

Rythin grinned, appreciating her mental agility.

"Very good," he laughed. "Yes, we have over eight hundred students. Not all are full time, and not all are adolescents. I'm sure Tyrone and perhaps Mistress Tryllia would have told you a bit about the Academy's diversity..." he explained with a small smile. "Anywho, the newest perform kitchen duty. When you are placed on the roster, you are given a number. There are four hundred and twenty duty positions. You currently occupy position four hundred and seventeen. As new students are added to the list, your number reduces. Once you hit zero, then you're left off the roster. We're constantly enrolling new students, thanks to our diligent Seekers. So, by that stage, you should have been here a few years, but not for your entire education. It's the benefits of success at the Academy."

Faye nodded, feeling this system was just.

"Now, as for your lessons..." Rythin murmured, perusing the second piece of paper.

"We normally begin our new admissions with a six-month bridging course to allow all students to catch up on missing knowledge and skills. It enables our new recruits to start with the same prerequisite knowledge. But to be frank, you are far too advanced for those. Unfortunately, they *must* be completed before your true classes can begin," he sighed, but there was a devious twinkle in his dark eyes. "As such, I have certified that you have completed the course."

Faye gaped at him.

"But, sir, shouldn't I do things properly?" she asked uncertainly, not liking this special treatment.

If all new students were meant to do the bridging course, then surely there shouldn't be an exception. Was her so-called mentor just giving her a leg-up in the Academy because of their joint association with Thayrille? Would he show her favouritism simply because he was acquainted with her foster mother?

Thayrille had drilled into her that there was no such thing as shortcuts. Only those that were lazy, deceptive, and of poor character did such things, and accepting a hand-out from a family friend because it made Faye's own life more comfortable seemed so ... *Hannah.*

Rythin shrugged, his bushy brows pulling over his eyes in a thoughtful frown as he noted her reticence.

"Sure, if you wish to endure an entire semester of basic arithmetic, grammar, geography, science, history, language and physical fitness." He spread his hands expansively and seemed a bit annoyed that there was still hesitation on the girl's face. "Look, recall the lessons that Thayrille taught you about three years ago."

He waited until the girl nodded cautiously.

"That's what you would be doing," he said, smacking the table for emphasis.

Faye flinched, both at the unexpected noise and the knowledge of how boring such a course would be.

"Exactly. I've passed you on every topic because I've already assessed you. On that day, in Grydin," Rythin explained matter-of-factly. "So, this is your timetable. The classes you will attend are as follows: Level Two Agricultural Studies, Level Two Language, Level Two History, Level Two Geography, Level Two

Mathematical Applications... I've skipped you over the first Levels for all those, as you are quite knowledgeable." he murmured, perusing the list.

"Yes, now let's see... Level One Sorcery, Level One Healing, Level One Weaponry, yes, yes, I know, you're no novice to either of those last two, but it can't be helped. These are very practical subjects, and their instructors refuse to skip *anyone* – unless they've demonstrated their talent directly to them. And, as has been pointed out to me, I must place you in at least some beginner classes so that you can meet students your own age."

The Seeker seemed somewhat ruffled by this fact, causing Faye to wonder who had dared to dictate anything to the wily old man. About the only person she could imagine doing so was Mistress Tryllia.

It occurred to the girl that perhaps that's precisely what had happened. Faye wondered what the role of *Housekeeper* meant. It seemed the large woman was a person of authority, perhaps even above Rythin in the Academy hierarchy.

Now that she appeared resigned to her lot, the spindly man passed over the sheet with a graceful flourish.

"Excellent! That should keep you busy," he said with a pleased smile. "Any questions? Concerns? No? Good! Now, off you go! I'd suggest taking an hour or so this afternoon to orient yourself with your classroom locations. You'll need to know how to get down to the training grounds for Weaponry. Ask Tryllia if you see her. She's taken a liking to you, I see."

With another smile and a wink, Rythin ushered her out the door. Faye found herself staring at the firmly closed wooden panel, alone in the middle of the corridor amidst the dancing dust motes. The name plate gleamed dully in the early afternoon light, and accompanying silence weighed heavy on her ears.

I wasn't even given a chance to ask anything! Faye thought crossly.

She was almost tempted to stamp her foot in frustration or smash her fist on that door until the complacent old man opened again. Zen buzzed in amusement at her neck but wisely kept its opinions to itself.

Faint noises from further down the hall caught the girl's attention. Having just finished a detailed tour, Faye recalled in that direction lay the classrooms and the multitude of students currently completing their Fourth Class. Momentarily distracted from her consternation, Faye wandered towards the sound, feeling oddly adrift. She did as suggested and matched the classroom doors, engraved with their own unique symbols and colours, to those neatly printed on her schedule. After she had found all her theoretical and practical classrooms, Faye ventured down four flights of stairs to locate the training grounds. A helpful passer-by pointed her toward the copse of trees at the edge of the grounds, and the low stone building she had noticed earlier.

The squat cottage was known as the Weaponry Shed and was home to Master Sorwell. Within its stout walls were various weapons, horses, and other gear that would assist in the training of budding recruits. There was also a sandy oval on the opposite side where sparring took place, an extensive range for archery, and various obstacle courses for fitness.

Curious, Faye sat in the shade of a nearby tree and studied her timetable in more detail.

With a sinking feeling, Faye noted that Level One Weaponry commenced at an odd time – before breakfast, four days each week, and right after breakfast another two days. It seemed she was expected to attend dawn practices regularly.

Feeling a tad overwhelmed, and bone *tired*, Faye navigated her way back up the never-ending stairwells and through several corridors until she located her out-of-the-way private little room. Now, she thought with some relief, it was time for a nap!

Chapter 14

WEAPONRY

Faye's first day wasn't as bad as she had thought it would be. It was tough, no doubt, but hardly impossible. Dawn Weaponry had been the first major obstacle. Pupils were responsible for their own early rising – without any bell!

Luckily, Zen offered to wake her at a quarter to six. Faye wondered about the other students – they didn't have a magical lizard to assist them.

Zen nipped Faye's nose lightly, at the agreed time, startling her from a sound sleep. Faye was instantly wide awake, heart thumping and nerves zinging with energy. She rolled out of bed, pulled on leather trousers and a linen shirt and ensured her personal belongings were stowed safely. She also pulled on her light sparring moccasins, knowing that her regular boots would only weigh her down.

"Hey, Zen, are you coming?" Faye whispered, gently poking the snoozing lizard on his exposed rump, wondering why the creature had burrowed further under her coverlet rather than clambering up to her shoulder as it usually would.

"Grfff-ng-umph," the reptile replied, pulling its rearend away from her poking finger.

Faye rolled her eyes and left the thing where it had chosen to nest, figuring it was better to leave it here anyway. There was no lock on the door, and Faye couldn't be sure someone wouldn't come in and poke around through her things. Her mother's pipe was stowed carefully in the cavity beneath her wardrobe, along with her most favourite semi-precious gems she had found down in Grydin Grotto.

She and Zen had figured it was best to keep them there, out of harm's way and only accessible to a body that knew *exactly* where to look. Zen, at least, would keep an eye on things here while she hopped down to her very first lesson.

As soon as she shrugged into her light coat, the girl silently sped down the hall, navigating three flights of stairs in near darkness, slipping through a partially opened external door in the mess hall, before crossing the dew-damp grounds. She found her way through the copse of trees to the cleared grounds opposite. The early morning moisture attempted to cling to her moccasins, but thankfully they were waterproofed, so the water beaded along their surface before running back onto the grass.

She was five minutes early, but already students were present and lining up in the sandy arena that bordered the low stone shed. Uncertain, Faye joined the straight line, trying to match their military posture. A few other stragglers arrived after Faye. She tried to memorise a few faces, but this proved difficult in the predawn gloom. Faye was relieved to find that there were both girls and boys in the line-up, despite males being the dominant gender.

As the sun finally crested the nearby mountains, six o'clock chimed softly from a clock in the low stone building.

A tall, broad man stalked out into the brightening grounds. He was a wild-looking giant! Towering almost seven foot tall, his tan arms bulging with muscles and his bushy copper hair glinting orange beneath the rising sun. His eyes were a bright piercing gold that raked over his platoon with a discerning gaze.

Without a doubt, her Weaponry Instructor, Master Sorwell, was *not* entirely Human. The girl wondered which Fey clan the man belonged to...

Sorwell stopped at one end of the line, closest to Faye, and began barking insults and criticisms at the students, his voice thundering against her eardrums like a voracious waterfall. Faye gazed up, up, up into the man's stern face, almost losing her balance as her head tilted a little too far off-centre. She snapped her gaze back down to the giant's chest and straightened her posture as he neared her.

"Blaire – lazy! On time, on time! Fresh shirt, Louin! I can still see last night's gravy slopped on that rag! Goreman, what do you call those laces? Disgraceful, tie them again!" roared the instructor.

Faye's eardrums vibrated sickeningly under the cacophony of sound, sending her empty stomach flipping and flopping while her brain sloshed left and right.

By all the Gods in all the Realms! *How* could so much noise come out of one set of lungs?!

As Goreman dropped to one knee and scrabbled to retie his laces, the instructor paused in front of Faye and looked at her, clearly puzzled. He crouched down so he was on eye level with the tiny girl, frowning over her cloud of curly blonde hair and frightened sky-blue eyes, before standing again on legs as thick as tree trunks.

"Who are you?" he demanded rudely, pointing a thick, stubby digit straight at Faye, not quite touching her face.

The girl swallowed against her now-dry throat, staring at the massive blunt finger that pointed to a spot between her eyes. The man was surly and intimidating, towering over her like a fierce avalanche on the verge of crashing down. Faye now profoundly regretted the decision to leave the comforting form of Zen back in her room. She could really use a friend right now!

"F-F-Faye," the girl stuttered in a dry whisper, then repeated her name more loudly. "Faye."

"Surname?" he rumbled, eyeing her over critically.

Faye flushed and shook her head. His unusual golden eyes raked over her tiny form, noting the small muscles and thin limbs.

"New recruit?!" barked the instructor, glaring at her with those piercing eyes.

Still unable to speak, Faye merely nodded.

"That's 'Yes, Sir', recruit!" bellowed the instructor right in her face, the force of his roar pushing a few straggling strands of hair around her ears.

Goaded by uncertainty and fear, Faye automatically bellowed back with all her might, right in the instructors' face.

"SIR, YES, SIR!" her voice rang out across the grounds.

For a moment, she thought for sure she would be disgraced and kicked out of Weaponry for yelling at her instructor. But to her surprise, the beast of a man just nodded approvingly.

"Good set of lungs," he said, his voice backing down to his usual bark. "Bit small – but those are the ones a person has to be careful of. You be the one Tyrone told me about, that felled a bandit with that stick?"

"Yes, sir," Faye responded, not so loudly this time, standing as straight as possible, blue eyes staring directly ahead.

Tyrone had *told* Sorwell about that? Did these Academy people have nothing better to do than gossip? The girl suppressed a petulant frown, instinctively knowing that any type of sass would be dealt with harshly and decisively. With effort, she kept her expression blank, waiting for further instructions or comments from the golden giant.

The instructor nodded briskly, pleased by what he saw, then moved on down the line. Faye's heart still hammered, and she couldn't believe a single insult hadn't been thrown her way during the confrontation. Every other student had copped some sort of reprimand!

Her thundering heart continued to slow as she drew in several deep, calming breaths, just as Zen had schooled her to do throughout yesterday.

Perhaps the instructor reserved that mean treatment for seasoned recruits, she mused.

After roll call, the recruits were led on a brisk jog around the grounds. Faye was quite used to this form of exercise and kept up easily with the lead joggers. After their jog, the students had to perform sit-ups and push-ups. Once more, this came easily, for she had done many such exercises with Jack.

Then came the sparring. Faye was partnered with another young recruit, a boy that was unsurprisingly bigger than her. The boy had been the smallest of the recruits until now and his expression clearly showed that he felt somewhat awkward having to fence with this tiny child.

"Sir, this one's only a kid!" he exclaimed in exasperation as he was made to stand facing Faye.

Faye, on the other hand, narrowed her eyes in concentration and sized up her opponent.

Let's see who is just *a kid!* she thought vindictively.

The instructor had an odd look on his face as he examined her ready stance and confident grip on her practice weapon. The wax-wood baton was perfectly balanced and heavily scarred by endless bouts of smashing and clashing.

"What say you, lass?" Sorwell rumbled, one golden brow raised in question.

Faye glanced nervously between the two, twirling the baton by its handle a time or two, testing its precise balance and comforting weight. The giants' eyes followed the move with a glint of approval.

"Ready, sir," Faye answered with a nod, some of her nervousness easing.

She *knew* how to spar, and this boy was nowhere near as big nor as experienced as Jack!

"Recruit Shamson, did you not hear what I said before?" Sorwell barked. "It's the small ones you need to watch out for!"

"Yes, sir!" shouted the boy reluctantly.

Shamson had been so busy watching the instructor that he hadn't noticed his opponents' familiarity with the practice weapon.

"GO!" Master Sorwell hollered, and there was a clash of timber swords around the sandy arena.

With a rough sigh, the boy half-heartedly struck out at Faye with his wooden baton. The girl responded instantly and, within a few lightning-fast moves, had disarmed her opponent. The copper-haired giant laughed uproariously as he watched from the sidelines.

"Gotta do better than that, Shamson!" he barked, still laughing like a rumbling earthquake.

Faye felt her face flush, and it felt for a moment as though her ears were about to combust. The girl wondered if they were as crimson as Jack's on that day he'd flirted with Thayrille... How embarrassing!

Other recruits had stopped to watch, too, grinning in appreciation. The boy, Shamson, had turned a deeper shade of red and retrieved his sword. He had a more determined look on his face now.

He wouldn't make that mistake again.

"What're ye all gawping at! I dinna tell ye to stop!" Sorwell roared, causing a flurry of movement as all the recruits leapt towards each other with a *clack* of wood on wood.

Faye and Shamson began to circle each other, assessing the way the other moved. When the attack came this time, Faye met the blows in a measured way – matching herself to the boy's skill so neither would fall. The last thing she wanted was to give Sorwell another belly laugh or another reason to attract his attention again. She didn't want to stand out on her very first day!

The sparring session ended ten minutes later, with neither Faye nor Shamson getting the better of the other due to Faye's careful manoeuvring.

"TIME!!" bellowed Master Sorwell.

He clapped both Faye and Shamson heavily on the back. The boy managed to brace against it, but Faye – who had not experienced this kind of affection before – stumbled and landed on her knees in the sand.

Oh, Blessed Mother! Faye let out a near-silent groan as she staggered back to her feet.

"Very good, recruits, very good!" the giant called, seeming quite pleased. "Now, *rotate*!"

Perhaps Sorwell had suspected that Faye had held back; perhaps he was keen to test her limits because when the recruits changed partners rapidly, Faye found herself facing a tall girl with a stern expression.

Her chocolate skin, ebony eyes and tightly braided black hair made her look like a slice of midnight. She was absolutely stunning. Yet, the fine scars that marred her smooth skin made her appear particularly forbidding, as did the cool, confident, controlled look in her eyes. It was difficult to pick her age. Fifteen, perhaps? Maybe sixteen?

This girl, Faye realised, wasn't so green.

"I apologise in advance if I injure you," the dark girl said simply, her voice almost musical in tone.

She seemed aware that her larger size and experience could easily lead to misery. The girl attacked without hesitation the moment Sorwell hollered. "GO!"

She was definitely good!

The only thing the girl hadn't considered was that Faye had trained with Jack – a man twice the dark girl's weight and a fair bit taller, too, with ten times the girl's probable experience.

Once more, Faye managed to keep her feet until the end, although she worked for it this time. She had to use every trick and skill that the burly Forrester had taught her over the last four years to maintain her own. The bigger girl looked scandalised. She hadn't expected that!

"Rotate!" bellowed Sorwell.

Faye found herself now facing a medium-height boy... No... Young *man*, really.

How he held himself indicated that he was another seasoned fighter, probably closer to eighteen years old.

Faye was starting to tire now and wondered if she could stand against this new challenger. He was about a head shorter than Jack but nearly as broad. His sandy blonde hair was held back from his face by a thick cotton band, and his light grey eyes glittered with amusement as he peered down at the delicate little girl.

Their wooden swords clashed as they circled and swiped at each other, testing one another's defences. Sweat began dripping from Faye's brow, and she wondered where she could source herself one of the bands the young man wore, noting that it easily absorbed any invasive moisture to keep it from his eyes. She decided that at the first opportunity, she would find herself one of those.

As though sensing her distraction, the youth increased the speed of his strokes. But Faye managed to maintain her own. Breathing hard, she countered every rapid blow – but it seemed it wasn't enough. It was as though she were training with Jack all over again!

As the final seconds trickled by, just moments before Sorwell yelled, "TIME!" the sandy-haired young man leaned in with his sword, then unexpectedly whipped one foot around and knocked Faye's feet right out from under her.

Flat on her back, Faye found herself panting in the dust.

"Well fought, Krins!" Sorwell shouted, clapping the youth on the shoulder.

Faye was pleased to see that Krins looked just as tired as she felt and that he stumbled beneath Sorwell's heavy hand. To her surprise, Krins offered his hand to help her from the ground. Faye accepted and was hauled to her feet in short order.

"Good show, kid!" he laughed at the dazed expression on the girl's face, standing close in case the poor thing keeled over again.

"RECRUITS! STRETCHING ROUTINES!" Sorwell hollered from next to them, almost bursting Faye's sensitive eardrums again.

Her stomach heaved in response, but Faye kept herself together by sheer force of will.

Feeling weak, the girl stumbled after the other recruits as they paired up and began to stretch. Krins partnered with her again and guided her through the routine, offering a supporting hand when she overbalanced or stumbled from exhaustion.

Arms, legs, waist, arms again, back, legs again... The routine was invigorating and eased the tightness Faye was beginning to feel. After several minutes she felt revived and could step away from

Krins to continue on her own. In the distance, they heard the first morning bell.

"Recruits, to the showers!" Sorwell barked as soon as the bell fell silent.

Obediently, the recruits filed into the low stone building, boys and girls separating into their own gender-assigned bathing rooms.

"Faye, here a moment," the golden giant thundered before she could tiredly shuffle after the small group of girls.

Faye hung back, now eyeing over the copper giant nervously. She felt she had managed to stand out despite her efforts not to.

"That was some fine fighting, recruit. Who taught you those moves?" he asked, softening his tone now that it was a one-on-one conversation.

Instead of a thundering roar, his voice was merely a deep, bone-trembling rumble. Faye winced, knowing she had to lie – she had promised Jack.

"Natural talent, sir?" Faye asked hopefully, then flinched as she saw Sorwell's eyes narrow in displeasure.

"Humph, I see."

He didn't seem *too* angry, but Faye was sure that he suspected a Sword Master had unofficially trained her and wished to remain anonymous. The girl knew it wasn't the proper way to do things, but there wasn't a lot she could do to change that.

The real question would be *would* her Weaponry instructor press her for a more truthful answer? Or would he allow her mysterious past to slide?

Sorwell nodded once. "To the showers with you," he said, then turned away to pack up the practice swords.

Faye let out a gusty sigh of relief once his back was turned. For today, it would seem, she would be allowed to keep her secrets!

The array of thirty-odd batons were already stacked and strapped into one bundle, which must have weighed a good hundred kilos, but the man simply hauled them up single-handedly over one shoulder and strode off around the building with them, whistling a jaunty tune.

Faye shook her head, dazed, before hurrying into the building. She could hear the voices of the other students towards the back and figured these must be the gender-specific bathrooms she had noted earlier. Only once Faye reached the two large doors imbedded into the back wall of the building, did she realise that she had no idea which one was which! Listening carefully, Faye recognised the familiar voice of the girl she had fought, echoing from behind the left-hand door.

Shrugging Faye went in and was relieved to find she had entered the female bathroom. It was a large stone room with one wall lined with nozzles. Steaming water was streaming from the metal spouts, and the half dozen girls of Weaponry were all naked, soaping themselves up under the spray without shame.

Flushing, Faye wasn't sure what to do. She couldn't even remember the last time Thayrille had to bathe her; she had been independent for so long...

Where did she look? There were naked limbs *everywhere*!

"New girl! Faye, right?" one of the girls called, her brown hair appearing black beneath the spray.

Faye nodded shyly, averting her eyes, her face flushing pink.

"Don't look so worried! We're all girls in here. Dump your dirty clothes in that basket, then come get cleaned up," the girl said cheerily, grinning at Faye's obvious discomfort.

Taking a deep breath, Faye did as she was told.

"I'm Trish, by the way," the friendly brunette offered, once Faye had hastily plunged beneath her own torrent of hot spray.

"Britt," said a redhead nearby.

"Rory," another girl offered.

"Rita."

"Belle," declared yet another.

The girls introduced themselves too quickly for Faye to really memorise faces and names.

She was at least a full head shorter than the shortest girl there. She felt more like a child than ever! Slowly, Faye began to accept the obvious. Each of these girls was at least fourteen, or older than that, and had all the expected attributes of a woman grown. Faye was only twelve and looked like a skinny pale wraith compared with these buxom girls. She really *was* a child.

Faye found a sponge, soap, and a gel for cleansing hair on the shelf recessed into the stone wall. Once she scrubbed every inch of her body, Faye collected one of the large fluffy towels stored on a nearby shelf. She dried quickly and then looked around in confusion. She had no fresh clothes!

Seeing her puzzlement, the friendly brunette who had spoken to her handed her a large robe.

"Here, kiddo. You're meant to bring your fresh clothes down with you, so you can get changed. Who's your Mentor? They're meant to explain the routine to you any time you begin a new class," Trish said kindly, her brown eyes sympathetic.

Feeling even more embarrassed, Faye quickly wrapped the robe around herself and became lost in its voluminous folds.

"Seeker Rythin," she replied softly, feeling her face grow red again.

The older girls emitted a low whistle, clearly impressed by this admission.

"Wow, you must have some talent! Old Rythin normally doesn't bother himself over new students, other than Selecting them. No wonder you didn't know to bring fresh clothes," Trish said in awe. "Why, I don't think he's actually mentored anyone in *decades*!"

"Of course, she has talent! Didn't you see the way she held her own against *me*?" exclaimed the tallest of the girls, the well-muscled warrior that Faye had sparred with.

The others giggled and murmured.

"*Varsity* prides herself on being the only unbeatable girl in Weaponry – at all three levels," Britt commented archly with a sassy lift of her auburn eyebrow and a twinkle in her eye.

"Now, Faye, you should race up to your room and dress so you can still make it to breakfast. Don't go through the mess hall, though; creep around to the back stairs so no-one will see you dressed in just a robe. Other recruits – the boys, mainly – have had to race through there before, and their robes have been... confiscated," Trish continued, matter-of-factly, offering her friend a withering look.

Faye nodded wide-eyed.

"Quickly now, before the mess hall fills up!" Britt carolled cheerily as she towelled herself dry.

Faye waved at the group of girls vaguely, her mind full of the next steps she needed to take to prepare for the day. Back stairs, no dawdling, work out how to navigate the different pathway back to her room... Tell Zen *everything*. And then she still had to dress and get down three flights of stairs to breakfast!

Feeling the first pangs of panic, Faye hurriedly raced back through the building towards the castle, clasping the robe tightly around her small frame.

Managing not to trip on the robe, Faye found the back stairs easily and crept up them. Her muscles protested weakly, so it took far longer than Faye expected. Once she reached the third landing, she thanked her innate sense of direction and found her way through the twisting corridors without incident. Several other girls were also returning to their rooms clad in their bathrobes, so the small girl blended in nicely.

Once in her room, Faye was tired, sore, and out of breath. Zen looked at her curiously.

"Apparently, Rythin forgot to explain a few things to me — like the fact that I needed fresh clothes to change into after Weaponry!" she said with a trace of annoyance. "It didn't occur to me to take a second set!"

Faye quickly scrambled through her closet and pulled on a fresh pair of trousers and a shirt. It was the only other clean set she owned, as the filthy outfits she had worn on her trip from Grydin had vanished from her room and had yet to be returned.

Slowly, with worry squirming in her belly, Faye realised she would quickly run out of clothes. The other set she had left at the Weaponry building, and she had no idea when or if she'd get them back.

"Relax," the colourful lizard yawned, shaking itself fully awake. "I'll figure out something for you. In the meantime, Tryllia came by to give you something. She saw your schedule, too. She didn't realise you'd begin your proper classes so soon."

Faye looked over at her desk, where Zen indicated.

Her two schedules lay there, undisturbed, but next to them was a stack of books tied with a ribbon. Faye examined them and was pleased to find that the books were, in fact, notebooks for her classwork. There were seven in total, one for each class.

"I'll need to find a way to thank her," murmured Faye, touching the smooth leather bindings.

She opened the top book and found that it had a removable pad of paper, so she could replace it when necessary. Each cover also held a slim ink-filled pen.

"Told you Tryllia liked you," Zen said with satisfaction as it examined the implements.

"Zen, when you find me more clothes, could you possibly source a small gift for Tryllia?" the girl asked hesitantly. "I wish I had coin so we could purchase things."

The lizard scratched its head ponderously.

"The clothes will be easy — they will surely have a fund for struggling students and will provide you with the necessities. I think that's where Tryllia would have come across the notebooks," Zen mused. "As for Tryllia, I think we could make her a charm using one of your colourful stones from the Grotto - you packed most of the small ones, didn't you? I think something unique and handmade would appeal to her motherly nature."

With a grateful smile, Faye finished dressing, then scooped up Zen and her new books.

There was *no way* she would leave her only friend behind a second time!

CHAPTER 15

FRIENDS HAPPEN

Breakfast was the same rambunctious, noisy affair as dinner and lunch the previous day. Faye accepted a warm roll, a small tub of soft cheese, and some fruit from the servers.

Not wanting to sit amongst the hubbub, she ventured outside and sat on the open grounds. The air was now pleasantly warm, the sun had dried up the dew, and a light breeze played amongst the blades of grass. Faye found it very soothing.

Before long, Trish joined her, her brown hair now dried and bundled up into an elegant chignon atop her head. Her curvaceous form was emphasised by a figure-hugging green dress clasped tightly around her waist by a broad leather belt.

"What an idea! Wish I'd thought of this," Trish said cheerily, tucking into her own ample breakfast.

Faye smiled briefly before continuing to eat without speaking, unable to help notice just how pretty her unexpected companion was. It seemed odd for a competent warrior-in-training to get around with elegant hairdos and pretty dresses... although, unlike

Hannah, Trish didn't seem to have any problem getting her lovely clothes mussed from sitting on the grassy ground.

Faye frowned at herself, wishing she could get that *other* girl out of her head! It wasn't Trish's fault that the few teenage females Faye had any knowledge of were the nasty gits from Grydin. Surely there were at least a *few* sensible females attending the Academy?

But what if this seeming overture of friendship wasn't so innocent?

Zen buzzed reassuringly around her neck, causing Faye's jittery nerves to settle and the tension to sop off her shoulders.

"So – the routine," Trish said after a few minutes of awkward silence. "We rise at five-thirty on dawn Weaponry days. I'd recommend finding a small alarm clock, one of those wind-up ones, to set the time. It's easiest to wear your outfit for the day down to the Shed, then change into your training clothes in the showers. Once you have completed the training, shower, change back into your outfit, then it's time for breakfast. Your training clothes will be laundered then placed on your shelf. Every recruit has a shelf to store their clothes, towels, and robes."

Faye nodded, relieved. That made far more sense. She glanced once more at Trish's flowing skirt, examining the delicate brocade that lined the hem. The young woman evidently came from a wealthy family, able to provide her with a quality wardrobe. Noticing her look, the older girl grinned.

"Yes, you can wear dresses, even though you're a skilled killing machine! You can wear whatever you like – although I must say that those breeches and shirt make you look like a boy," Trish teased.

"It's all I have," Faye said with a shrug, hiding a flush of anger by turning her face away.

She was *NOT* a *BOY*!

The brunette frowned at that, her groomed brows slanting down delicately.

"I don't suppose Old Rythin told you about the Storeroom?" she asked tentatively, then shook her head before Faye could answer. "No, of course he didn't."

Faye sighed and rubbed her neck absently, careful not to shift Zen out of its hiding place beneath her hair. She didn't like the heavy feeling settling in her gut, especially when Trish criticised Rythin. Even if the wily old Seeker *hadn't* told her about this mysterious Storeroom, or the Weaponry routine, or every other crucial aspect of starting Academy life! Rythin had given her a chance. He believed in her. He loved and respected Thayrille. That made him as good as family.

Faye glowered down at her plate, refusing to meet the older girl's compassionate gaze.

"Students that don't have much and are pre-approved by the Academy are allowed to take things from the Storeroom. Mistress Tryllia will tell you if you're approved or not. They have everything you'll need there. Books, pens, clothes, shoes..." she trailed off as she noticed the stack of standard issue books sitting beside Faye. "Have you already been?"

Faye shook her head. "No, Mistress Tryllia dropped these off this morning, she must have realised I wouldn't have time to collect them before class."

Somehow, Faye managed to keep her tone neutral rather than aggressive, but it was a near thing! If it hadn't been for the soporific effect of Zen's persistent buzzing...

"Well, if she's giving you books personally, you must be on the list! You can go this evening, after dinner," Trish said, the confusion clearing from her face. "I can show you the way if you like."

"Why?" Faye demanded, finally peering up Trish with distrustful, narrowed eyes.

"So... So you can find the way more easily, as you've not been yet?" The older girl offered in confusion.

"No, I mean... *Why* are you being so nice to me?"

"Why wouldn't I be?" Trish huffed a very unladylike snort through her nose. "You really expect people to treat you poorly on your first day? You have trust issues, my dear!"

"Growing up where I did, we called them *survival instincts.*" Faye spat in return, her face flushing with temper. She clearly remembered the feel of Hannah's boot between her shoulder blades the first day they had left Grydin. What if the girl's here were just as bad, if not worse, than that odious Hannah Rikton?

Trish froze halfway through getting to her feet, her lower lip caught between her perfectly straight teeth as she studied Faye with those deep, impenetrable brown eyes. Instead of storming off in an offended huff as Faye thought she would, Trish settled back down on the grass.

"Why am I nice to you? Well, it's rather simple." The brunette shrugged on elegant shoulder. "You remind me of my sister. You're of an age. And she has that same world-weary look in her eyes sometimes. She's the reason I'm here, you know. She's sick, and no-one can figure out what's wrong. So, I'm training to become a Healer. I want to help her, and anyone else I can along the way."

Faye's shoulders slumped heavily. She normally had a good instinct about people, and her heart was telling her that Trish spoke the truth.

"I'm sorry." Faye whispered around a tight throat.

"Don't be. You've not had an easy life, I can tell. And so can some of the others, so don't be so prickly with them if they decide to make friends. Like Britt, and especially Varsity. They've done it tough, too. Only, if you turn that acid tongue on them, you might not get a second chance. Me, though? I'm pretty impervious to insult and injury. I'd still like for us to be friends, if you want to." Trish offered another of her beautiful smiles.

Faye tried on a tentative smile in return and nodded, willing to trust this stranger for now. Zen buzzed its agreement silently against her ear, clearly pleased by the offer.

Trust. For now. The lizard seemed to agree.

The raucous sound of the second morning bell clanging out over the grounds broke the peace. Sighing tiredly, Faye got to her feet. She returned her plate and began laboriously climbing the stairs to her first double lesson – Level Two Agricultural Studies. Faye wondered what she was meant to learn. She and Thayrille had maintained their own garden that had combined a slew of vegetables, fruits and healing herbs. Tryllia had mentioned that the students would look after the gardens here as a contribution to their supplied meals, in addition to kitchen duty once a week.

No sooner had she arrived at the allocated Agriculture classroom, she was herded back *down* the stairs, through the mess hall, and along a twisting path that led to the side of the Academy opposite the Weaponry Shed.

Their instructor for this morning was a frail-looking old man with stooped shoulders, flyaway white hair, and bulbous grey eyes blinking owlishly from behind a pair of heavy spectacles. His name was Professor Rambert, although Faye distinctly heard a student or two refer to him as Professor *Ramble*. It didn't take long to work out why!

The old man clearly was a bit vacant, his mind having gone the way of many Elders, jumping from topic to topic and becoming distracted relating a fascinating story or two from his misspent youth. Needless to say, Faye was fascinated and stuck close to the old man in case he needed any assistance with lifting and carrying.

None of the Elders from Grydin had ever allowed her within ten meters of them and never had any one of them a kind word to say.

Thankfully, her own knowledge was adequate enough to manage this particular walled garden. The class was to weed, water and fertilise this section. As Faye easily recognised the range of summer plants, she was able to readily point out any pest species to the other students in her class. Left to his own devices, Professor Rambert wouldn't have realised that his wayward students were plucking out the broad bean seedlings right alongside the wild daisies.

By the end of the two hours, Faye was satisfied to see the garden set to rights. She readily accompanied her instructor back through the mess hall and up the many stairs to the classrooms above, asking him pointed questions about the history of the Academy and his experiences working here over the past sixty years. Faye was quite disappointed when the fourth morning bell clanged through the building and indicated it was time for her third lesson of the day. Language.

Carefully, Faye checked her timetable and matched the symbol on her schedule to the plaque on the door. Upon entering the room, Faye was surprised to find Britt and Trish from Weaponry seated near the front of the room and the shadowed form of Varsity lolling against the back wall, clearly ready for the lesson to begin.

"Come sit with us, Faye!" Trish called with a bright smile, indicating an empty seat beside her.

For some reason, the young girl's first instinct was to brush past the bubbly, vivacious Trish and join the dark and silent Varsity instead. Faye had a feeling that a warrior like Varsity wouldn't pester her with endless questions or inane conversation. She had that no-nonsense aura about her, quite similar to Thayrille, and Faye found that comforting.

Just as she was about to walk on by the empty seat, Zen buzzed softly at her neck, stopping her in her tracks.

"Make friends!" it hissed softly in her ear. "You said you would!"

Faye managed to prevent a roll of her eyes as she reluctantly plopped herself down in the empty seat and gave Trish and Britt a wan smile. She supposed the interfering lizard was right. If she wanted to learn more about the Academy, she should probably sit with people willing to speak with her.

"Hi," Faye muttered before busying herself with her notebooks and pens, studiously avoiding eye contact.

She could vividly recall seeing these girls naked mere hours ago, and the fact was causing her some discomfort.

"Hi, yourself! I saw you were down with the Agriculture students this morning. I sort of miss that class these days," Trish sighed longingly. "All that time outside, listening to the old man ramble on and on about irrelevant stuff."

"You don't study Ag? What were you doing this morning, then?" Faye asked, perplexed.

Hadn't Tryllia said *all* students contributed to food production at the Academy?

"Hospitality," Trish replied promptly, hurriedly retrieving her notebooks and pens as their instructor entered the room. "I'm part of the group that harvests the produce and actually *makes* something out of it! I thought it would be more interesting than digging in the dirt."

"I thought we did that on our kitchen duty?" Faye was puzzled.

"Gods no!" Trish laughed lightly. "There wouldn't be enough time! Kitchen duty is when you heat up the food, clean the kitchen, wash dishes, and serve, serve, serve. Your role as a Kitchen Hand is to get rid of as much food as possible, make sure every student that passes by you has plenty to eat, and then clean it all up again!"

"So, Hospitality is where you *make* the food?" Faye repeated tentatively. "And Agriculture is where you *grow* the food?"

"Yep. We mostly bake food stuff, like cakes and muffins, and prepare bread dough for baking, staple meals for heating up, and so forth. It's not too difficult, as we normally just follow a recipe card given to us by the Kitchen's Duty Manager. Ross is the boss and normally decides what we make on any given day," Britt chimed in. "Old Harvey, the *actual* Kitchen Manager, can't be bothered to do a lot these days, so he leaves it all to his second in charge."

At that point, the instructor, a stern-looking woman with tan skin and nutbrown hair, cleared her throat to gain their attention.

"Right, you lot, settle down and let's begin," she announced.

There was a rustle of pens and papers as each student flipped to a new page and wrote the date on the upper right corner before copying the notes their instructor scrawled across the chalkboard. The front wall was almost completely covered in the black slate, the white stick of chalk squeaking irritatingly across its smooth surface.

Faye gritted her teeth and attempted to ignore the insufferable sound.

That first lesson wasn't so difficult. The class was a more in-depth form of grammar than Faye had learnt from Thayrille and encompassed both the Common Tongue and the Ancient Tongue of Pendalin. Faye found each language as easy as the other, so she glided through the content without too much trouble.

"Wow, you're pretty smart, then?" Britt asked candidly at the end of the lesson, noting the tiny, neat writing filling the first five pages of Faye's notebook and all the correctly answered questions she had ticked in green ink.

Faye shrugged, unwilling to comment. Was she smart? She supposed she must be relatively intelligent. After all, Rythin himself had skipped her over all the beginning material with nary a bat of an eyelash.

"Of course she is! A brand-new student, only what? Ten years old? And skipping first Levels? Of course she's smart!" Trish linked her arm companionably through Faye's and smiled kindly down at the petite girl as they left the room at the end of their allocated hour.

The three were making their way back down the stairs to the mess hall, eager for a top-up of food provided by morning tea. Dawn Weaponry was hungry work!

"Um, I'm actually twelve," Faye corrected her shyly, a little offended that these older students would assume she was *that* young.

But then, given her physical looks, it was little wonder!

Zen buzzed in amusement at her neck, and Faye knew she wouldn't hear the last of that comment! Her wayward companion would likely make plenty of jokes about her tender years once they had some privacy.

"I've been wondering..." Faye began awkwardly as they navigated the stairs amongst a stream of bodies, careful not to bump into anyone, before plunging forward with the question. "Why are you two enrolled in Level One Weaponry, but are completing Level Two Language?"

The two girls glanced at her oddly and Trish replied, "For the same reason you are. Everyone's at different levels for different subjects here. Somehow, the instructors fit it together, so people aren't far ahead or falling behind. Many people must also repeat subjects or continue the same one on a different strand. That's how someone like Krins, for example, can be doing all three levels at once," she explained with a kind smile. "Also, some people want to do every subject but can only do up to nine at a time, so they complete all three levels in one area before beginning another."

Faye felt slightly embarrassed, for it was obvious when she thought about it. On the other hand, just speaking with someone on friendly terms about the Academy made her feel a little less overwhelmed.

The girls enjoyed platters of fruits, cheese and crackers for their morning treat, along with some preserved meats and more cakes. Trish told Faye all about the process used to make each item, and how tray after tray was stored down in the industrial-sized cellar to keep it cool and fresh for the day. Faye absorbed the information like a dry sponge, pelting the girl's with so many questions she was surprised that she hadn't been whacked upside the head yet and told to shut up.

Much too soon, the next bell sounded. Faye was beginning to get used to the jarring clang and barely flinched when it echoed around the mess hall, signalling the end of their break. The girls sighed, grabbed their knapsacks, and headed back up the stairs.

The hardest part of her day so far was navigating the multiple flights of stairs needed to reach the plethora of theory classrooms. Faye heartily wished that the classes were located *downstairs*. It would save a lot of time travelling between the mess hall and class!

Their fourth lesson of the day was History. Faye began learning about the ancient Humans and their arrival in Almanaic in far more detail than the simple tome she had read as a small child. Most things she knew, some was all new.

Thayrille hadn't kept much literature on the subject as the past held little to no interest to her. Most of her books were about healing and herblore, veterinary practices and Human biology.

Varsity had melted away during break time and now appeared to be attending a different class altogether. She wasn't in her usual space in the back row. Faye was disappointed that she had missed the opportunity to spend more time with the mysterious girl. Britt and Trish, however, sat with her again and continued helping with the unfamiliar things in the lesson. At the same time, Faye corrected them when she knew something they didn't.

Another hour passed, and she moved on to Geography where, to her delight, Varsity lolled against the back wall. Faye was keen to go sit with her, but Britt and Trish once again monopolised her person, dragging her to the front row so they had the best view of the chalkboard and their next instructor. Master Bailey was a middle-aged warrior and an expert in stratigraphic mapping.

Faye began learning about the layout of Pendalin in greater detail. From the towering Orathwyn Mountains to the north were perpetually capped in snow, to the artesian bowl in the centre of the continent that had become a drought-stricken desert when the river had dried up some thousand years ago. Faye was surprised to find that some of the sandy-bottomed canyons that she and Jack had practiced in over the years were, in fact, the dried out remains of the once vast river system that bisected Pendalin – the ancient Gordyan River.

This class also hosted nearly half the Weaponry recruits from that morning. As well as Britt, Trish and Varsity, Faye recognised Rory, Belle, Goreman, Krins and Shamson by name, and a few more by sight. It seemed that Geography went hand in hand with Weaponry, which made sense, she supposed.

Faye was relieved when the lunch bell rang, for her stomach was rumbling painfully loud. The fruit and crackers from morning tea seemed a lifetime ago!

During lunch, Faye once more sat out on the open grounds and was joined by Britt, Trish, Belle, Rita and Rory. In the distance, nearer the Weaponry Shed, Faye could see the silhouette of Varsity and inwardly cursed her entourage. She doubted these girls would want to join the midnight warrior. She also doubted

Varsity would appreciate the company of a gaggle of gossiping girls, either. The female Weaponry cohort had a distinct split, and the young girl was torn.

As Faye sat heavily on the grass with her overloaded plate of food, Zen, who had been snoozing all morning around her neck, decided to make an appearance.

Britt stifled a shriek as she saw the rainbow lizard slide out from beneath Faye's hair and help itself to some of the grapes on her plate. After the first startled exclamation, all the girls stared in fascination as the lizard steadfastly ate its body weight in fruit.

"Oh, this is Zen, my lizard," Faye said awkwardly, wishing that the colourful reptile had given her some sort of warning.

The girls exclaimed in wonder at the lizard's colourful scales, seeming less afraid when they noticed how it ate the fruit rather than wanting the meat hidden in the pasta sauce.

"Yes, it's vegetarian – mostly," Faye replied to their enquiring look. "And no, it doesn't bite."

Just threatens to, on a regular basis! Faye thought to herself in some amusement.

"Is it a boy or girl?" Trish asked curiously, picking Zen up and cradling it in her arms once it had finished its feast.

The lizard began to make that vibrating, clicking noise that it often used to soothe Faye. As Thayrille had frequently commented, it was very much like the purr of a cat.

"No idea. I think it might be both – you know, self-procreating," Faye said uncertainly, suppressing a jealous pang as she watched the lizard bask in the sun in the other girl's lap.

The small group 'ooh-ed' and 'ahh-ed' over Zen, taking turns stroking and petting the lizard's hide. The little reptile enjoyed itself immensely – never in its whole life had it received such attention as this!

The girls chatted and giggled over their lunch while Faye just listened. She wondered why these girls were constantly following her about and sitting near her. Faye had never had a friend, other than Zen and Jack, so it took her almost half an hour of pondering before she realised that the girls were trying to befriend her. She felt a warm glow in her chest when she worked it out, although the feeling was tempered by her disappointment that Varsity obviously did not have the same interest.

Faye wondered why she was obsessing so much over the dark warrior. There was just something about her, something Faye sensed was special. Different. Important. Yet, she couldn't quite put her finger on it.

The first afternoon bell rang, and the girls all groaned as one. Their muscles were stiff and sore after the morning's vigorous workout. They rose slowly to their feet and returned their plates to the kitchen.

"What lesson have you now, Faye?" Trish asked, briefly checking her own timetable.

"Double Sorcery," Faye replied, glancing down at her timetable to see that she had the right day and week.

The girls did a double take and goggled at her. Their eyes told their own story. Sorcery, it would seem, was something *else* that was unusual about her.

Faye wondered if she would ever make friends or if all the other students would make it a habit of staring at her like some sort of.... Freak?

"Really? Wow, it's very rare that one so young is taken into *that* class," Trish whispered, stunned.

The girls seemed to be caught between wariness and being impressed. Faye shrugged helplessly. She hadn't realised that Sorcery was something reserved for older students – even *she* didn't know why Rythin had enrolled her in that course to begin with. She hadn't ever demonstrated any magical abilities to date. Except for her pipe playing, which was secret, she had never shown a single iota of magical energy. Although...

Faye placed a hand surreptitiously on her chest. Ever since that day in Grydin when she first saw Rythin, the girl had been oddly aware of magical energy. Zen had said she was tied to the land. Maybe that was how it started?

Or perhaps Thayrille had told Rythin about her mother and the fact that she hadn't been Human? The thought of anyone knowing about this *other* heritage made Faye feel distinctly uneasy. It certainly wasn't a piece of information she was prepared to share with anyone herself. The girls parted ways at the top of the stairs, with Faye hurrying down the corridor searching for the correct room and the weaponry students staring after her with a considering expression.

CHAPTER 16

SORCERY AND HEALING

Faye entered the sorcery classroom a little later than the others. Their instructor hadn't arrived yet, so Faye figured she was safe from reprimand. It also gave her a chance to take in the unusual room.

The other classrooms had five rows of six single desks, with a broader space through the middle to serve as an aisle. This room was unlike those. On each side of the centre aisle were tall, large work desks with stools rather than chairs and a small cauldron perched beside them. Faye noticed that the desks could double as workbenches, if the occupant chose to stand rather than sit on the stool. Each row was set along its own tier, so every student could view the instructor's desk uninterrupted. The three rows curved around in a semicircle, with four desks on each side of the aisle. The aisle was a series of small steps, leading to the bottom of the room.

A large, empty cauldron and workbench stood at their base, along with a massive slate board, facing the students' desks. This was the instructor's desk, most likely belonging to the congenial old Sorcerer called Hanly, whom she had glimpsed the day before. She would bet her staff on it.

The hairs on the back of her neck rose and her ears prickled. Glancing around warily, Faye realised that every student was staring at her silently. There was no babble, no whispers – just silence.

"Sorry, child, you must have the wrong class," a bored voice drawled from nearby.

The boy who had spoken was a lot older than Faye, at least sixteen. His oily, smooth black hair created a widow's peak in the centre of his tan forehead. His dark, almost black eyes glittered oddly with ruddy-purple power deep within their pupils.

This boy was definitely *not* completely Human, although he appeared more so than Master Sorwell. He also seemed to be the youngest here.

Faye clutched her timetable, reminding herself that Seeker Rythin had placed her in this class – for whatever reason.

"It's on my schedule," Faye replied, keeping her tone polite.

The boy frowned, then held out his hand imperiously for the schedule. Faye reluctantly handed it over. The instructor *still* hadn't arrived, and she was at a loss on what else to do. With none of her new Weaponry friends here, and the rest of the students watching quietly, Faye figured if she just went along with him, for now, then she could ride out the next few minutes until the Sorcerer made his appearance.

The boy sneered at the paper before he frowned in annoyance.

"What is this crap?" he snapped, flipping over the paper to look at B Week, his ruddy-purple eyes following the Level One Sorcery lessons marked in red.

Faye kept silent, hoping that the boy wouldn't tear up her paper in a fit of spite, as someone like Hannah would do. She was acutely aware she had no idea of what her next class was. The boy thankfully thrust the paper back at her and sneered once more.

"Sorry, kid. No-names are not welcome in *this* class," the boy leered, his eyes hateful.

Faye was puzzled over this seeming insult, until she noted that her schedule listed just her first name – her only name. It must list both names for other students.

Faye flushed in shame.

Then she recalled Thayrille's stern face and how that woman had claimed her, kept and raised her. She may not have a surname, but she had the best education possible! Rythin himself had skipped her over much of the beginner content!

Faye straightened, a spark of defiance in her heart.

You are beholden to no one! Thayrille's impassioned words floated up from the depths of her memory. *There will be others that would see you fail, rather than achieve greatness...*

This boy couldn't tell her what to do! He was only another student, *and* a new one to Sorcery, too. They were both in the first level, after all.

Faye eyed the dark-haired boy over, noticing he was shorter than the other males of the class, and more solidly built. But his hands were carefully manicured, his skin free from scars and callouses. Faye had no doubt she could take him on.

"Sorry, Butch, but my aim in life isn't to please you. I'm here because I want to be, not because *you* say I can be," Faye said, matching the snide attitude.

She knew it was a mistake the moment the words came out. The boy's face hardened, and his eyes began sparking with that ruddy-purple energy, his latent power blooming from those dank, dead pupils.

The girl saw that his power was strong in its own way – not Weaponry style, but in Sorcery. The girl refused to back down from this argument, however, and stood unflinchingly. She doubted he had enough know-how to kill her, and Zen would surely be able to prevent any significant damage. She could feel the lizard vibrating soothingly against her neck, offering silent support in this inexplicable confrontation.

"Styrran Isthmus," rasped a stern, deep voice from behind her. "Class is about to begin and you're in my way."

The boy, Styrran it would seem, quickly backed down, the purple energy retreating into his eyes. He shrugged negligently, as though the situation didn't matter, and resumed his seat, thankfully unblocking the way down the aisle.

The new person, a boy who looked about the same age as Styrran, had just entered the room. He was tall and elegant, dressed in sleek black clothes. His hair was also black, cut short and swept rakishly away from his face. On his right hand was a large blue stone ring, readily visible as his long fingers cupped his chin thoughtfully. Warningly.

His eyes were a deep green, shimmering with a black, misty power that somehow captivated and entranced her.

Warlock. The word shivered through Faye's mind as she stood bewitched.

No wonder Styrran backed down so quickly!

Warlocks were renowned as highly magical, very powerful creatures. They were part Human, part Fey. They were raised in Clans, far from major Human civilisation in the Highlands territory bordering the Orathwyn Mountains. They were also trained from a young age in combat magic.

It should be unusual to see a Warlock here, at the Academy, Faye thought, puzzled. *They usually keep to themselves and have their own schools. Don't they?*

Faye examined him, wondering why a boy such as him would be here at the Academy in the first place. After Faye finished analysing his sturdy polished boots, her eyes wandered back up his trim black attire to his emerald eyes. She raised an eyebrow when she noticed he hadn't moved.

The Warlock returned her piercing stare for what seemed a long time before seeming to come to some sort of decision about her. He gestured for her to follow him down the aisle, practically gliding down the stairs with a distinctly feline grace. His manner was so commanding that Faye didn't even consider disobeying.

The Warlock chose a desk near the front and to the right side, where the view of the Sorcerer's table was excellent. He said nothing as he placed his notebooks on his desk. Faye did the same on the one next to him, resisting the urge to look back at Styrran Isthmus. She was sure he was glaring holes in her back.

Zen continued to vibrate reassuringly against her neck.

"I'll bite him for you," the lizard whispered, and only through long practice did Faye resist the urge to shush it.

She feared that the Warlock, or perhaps one of the other nearby students, might just hear the disembodied voice, the room was so quiet!

Thankfully, at that moment, the Sorcerer entered the room, and all attention turned to him.

He *was* that same short, friendly-looking man assigned to mentor Hannah! Sorcerer Hanly. For one so cheerful, Faye would have expected the class to be laid back and relaxed, but it wasn't so. The students sat in stony silence, staring avidly at the man before them, waiting for their first assignment.

"Welcome," Hanly called, then, with a flick of his hand and a spark of cheery yellow-gold power, the large slate board behind him filled with notes.

The silence in the room was suddenly broken by the scratching of pens on paper. Faye glanced at the Warlock, and noticed he was copying the notes into his own book.

Hurriedly, she did the same.

The notes on the board explained the origins of magic and how every creature was a part of an intricate web that spanned the lands of Pendalin. Some creatures, the notes read, could tap into the magic web and perform sorcery. Faye absorbed the lesson as she wrote it. Then, no sooner had she finished, the Sorcerer flicked his hand. The board went blank.

The class sat back as one, closing notebooks, and silently awaited the Sorcerer's next task. Faye found the whole thing rather creepy.

"Now, who can name me the three primary ways to access the power of Pendalin?" he asked.

A range of hands shot into the air.

"Ahh, Duncan," the Sorcerer said, nodding at the Warlock besides Faye.

"A magical charm," the boy said, his voice bored and measured.

Faye also noticed that he twirled the ring around his finger. She frowned at the glittering blue gem, wondering why he would need such a thing when he was of Fey blood. All the Fey were natural magicians...

Rather than seeming pleased by the correct answer, the Sorcerer appeared somewhat exasperated, as though Duncan had been continuing a long-standing argument. "Yes, yes, of course. Now you." The portly man pointed at another young man sitting on the opposite side of the room.

Faye noticed that Hanly flicked his hand again, and more writing appeared on the slate board, providing a more detailed explanation of magical charms and their ability to summon power and convert it into a usable form.

Faye scrambled to copy it down before it vanished.

"Meditation," the student answered quietly, his voice slow and deep.

"Excellent!" Another flick and the word *meditation* scrawled itself over the board along with a few informative sentences. "And you?"

A girl, or young woman, answered this time as the Sorcerer pointed in her direction, her voice almost disdainful.

"Blood," she purred. "Some of us just have raw talent passed down from our Fey ancestors."

The Sorcerer was nodding briskly.

"Very good, very good! Now, everyone in this room is either magical by blood, possesses a charm, or otherwise has the potential to access magic through meditation. Some of you will have a combination of these three. As such, *everyone* has the right to be here and practice Sorcery, *regardless* of their background," Hanly stated in a most serious tone.

Faye had the idea that the old man had somehow heard the argument between her and Styrran. However, he hadn't been in the room, which made Faye uneasy. What else was the Sorcerer privy to?

The lesson continued from there, as Sorcerer Hanly had the class copy notes on the different ways to access magic, the various forms of magic, and the locations of the most magical places in Pendalin. Faye was surprised to learn that Grydin was considered an epicentre for the magical ley-lines deep beneath the ground.

She had never considered her hometown anything special, yet a learned professional was now telling her that Grydin and its surroundings were noteworthy. At the end of the two hours, Faye felt as though her hand was about to drop off. She had managed to copy every note, regardless.

This class had been her most challenging so far – she had never been taught so much about Sorcery in all her life! Thayrille had felt it wasn't an appropriate lesson for a child, and the Healer harboured the barest knowledge herself. With only a small spark of yellow power, the Healer didn't have the talent, ability, or desire to become adept at the art of Sorcery. This, naturally, had impacted Faye's own learning on the subject.

As the bell tolled for afternoon tea, Faye slowly got to her feet, every muscle twinging and aching. Sorcerer Hanly vanished through a small side door, strategically avoiding any deliberate laggers that might have a question or two.

Faye began packing her things, wondering if Duncan would speak to her, but the Warlock simply grabbed his own pack and rapidly climbed the steps. The mysterious young man appeared to be in no mood to talk and seemed satisfied that the girl wouldn't encounter any more trouble from Styrran.

Tired, Faye hobbled up the numerous steps much more slowly and was the last student to exit the room.

Afternoon tea was a quieter affair. Zen had another feast, but Faye felt too tired to do more than pick. Her Weaponry friends were nowhere to be seen, and even the mysterious Varsity wasn't sitting in the shade of the Weaponry Shed.

In general, there weren't as many students attending the break, and Faye surmised it was because they didn't wish to climb the *million* flights of stairs *again*. It would soon become her favourite time of day.

The third afternoon bell rang, and it was time for the last lesson – double Healing. Faye already knew much about healing, but as Rythin had indicated, sometimes you had to do things in their proper order, which meant starting from the bottom.

With a tired sigh Faye dragged her sorry self back up the stairs and searched along the classroom corridor until she reached the correct door.

Faye found that the Healing room was set out differently yet again from Sorcery and her earlier theory lessons. This room was all of one level, but the benches were arranged in a 'u' shape around the instructor's desk. There were three benches per row, and only two rows. Each bench could seat up to four students and were at capacity once Faye joined the chatting group. The girl was relieved to see three familiar faces sitting at the one bench that held an empty seat. Trish, Britt and Rory were in the class, too!

The instructor was already in position at her designated workbench. She was a middle-aged woman with fly-away caramel hair sprinkled with grey and piercing blue eyes. She wore a practical pale green day dress beneath a sturdy canvas apron, similar to what Thayrille often wore. Almost as though it were some sort of Healer's uniform. She barely noted Faye as the girl slid into her seat, as she was busy writing a set of notes on the board. Faye could have cried, her aching hand protesting as she gripped her slim pen and began laboriously writing again.

The three Weaponry girls kept glancing at her and each other warily, as though unsure what to do about the young girl joining them this time around. Faye kept her eyes down and blinked away the prick of tears. Well, it would seem making new friends was a short-lived event! Perhaps it was like that for all Sorcery students. Perhaps that was why Duncan hadn't been sociable at all and that Styrran had been so vile...

The class launched straight into the most common cure-alls, beginning with a discussion regarding the uses of various herbs, their names, and their application. All of which Faye knew. The Healer then decided it would be a fun lesson to place two muddled-up lists on the board – one a list of herb names and the other a list of their properties, each completely in the wrong order.

The class was meant to use their textbooks to copy the lists in their correct sequence, matching the herb with its properties in alphabetical order. Faye had finished within ten minutes, and it only took that long because she had to write much slower due to the cramps in her poor hands.

The Healer was surprised.

"How do you know all of this, child?" she asked in wonder as she passed by their worktable, noting that the small girl was the only one no longer scrambling to complete the task.

"My foster mother is a Healer," Faye said uncertainly.

"Oh, who is that, my dear?" the Healer queried, excitement on her face at potentially teaching the ward of a colleague and perhaps an ex-student.

"Thayrille Hogansvort," Faye replied reluctantly. She didn't know if she should tell people of her life before the Academy. Some parts were rather sensitive.

The pleased expression died from the Healer's face, and her eyes narrowed. Faye felt that her honesty had been a mistake.

"Indeed." The Healer sniffed and vaguely gestured to the other students. "Since you seem to know *everything*, you can help the others."

Faye found herself staring at the Healer, open-mouthed. Trish and Britt stifled a snicker while Rory raised a shocked eyebrow. The awkwardness that had enveloped their group suddenly dissipated as they each looked at Faye anew, their wariness receding beneath another wave of reluctant admiration.

"Don't look so disheartened," Britt said with a grin. "Healer Merkin is always being compared to Healer Hogansvort. They went to school together – and Thayrille's an absolute legend at the Academy."

Faye looked at the girls, puzzled. "Why?"

"What? She never told you!" they asked, aghast.

"She's an amazing Healer, graduated at fifteen – AND she cured the Dark Plague that ravished the country over a decade ago!" whispered Trish, her eyes sparkling.

"Oh. *That*," was all Faye could manage.

Thayrille had told her of her achievements, but not in those terms. It sounded ordinary, run-of-the-mill, when Thayrille had relayed the story. Just another day in the busy hubbub of Tryssdale Medical Centre.

"So, you were raised by the great Healer," Britt said, really impressed, her auburn hair in a tangled mess around her face from the number of times she had shoved a hand through her locks. "Why didn't you say so earlier?"

"I didn't realise it was important." Faye shrugged, dropping her gaze down to her worksheet, cheeks reddening.

Would all budding friendships be this tenuous? Blooming one moment, then withering the next, as yet another piece of Faye's past was revealed, only to bloom once more? It was exhausting!

"Of course you didn't!" Trish exclaimed, elbowing an astounded Britt in the ribs. "It's only your first day. And it totally makes sense! You are an incredible person, just like Hogansvort. I can tell."

The girls worked quietly for a while, with Faye correcting any mistakes, mulling over their words. Was she really that special? She supposed, from the outside, it seemed that way.

A highly intelligent, gifted orphaned raised by the greatest Healer of their time, already adept at Weaponry, Healing, and any other number of subjects – and a budding Sorceress. Faye was starting to feel quite overwhelmed by her growing reputation.

"You'll surely pass this course in a heartbeat, Faye," sighed Britt, after crossing out her fifth mistake.

Faye shrugged. She probably would, but she didn't feel right boasting about it.

"So, how was Sorcery?" Trish asked in a whisper, her brown eyes gleaming with curiosity.

Before Faye could answer, Healer Merkin called for attention.

"Now, boys and girls, you should have a complete table of herbs and their properties. I have boxes filled with these herbs. You must identify them! Carefully place each specimen in your book on a fresh page, using a little glue to hold them in place. Be sure to label each one clearly, then press your book closed tight – we wish to preserve them," Healer Merkin explained, her shrewd blue eyes sweeping over the room, lingering on Faye with a considering look.

The students nodded dutifully and went to collect their sample box. When it was Faye's turn to approach, the woman's eyes narrowed. It wasn't exactly a mean look, but Faye felt whatever the Healer had in mind wouldn't be pleasant.

"Now, Faye, you'll have to identify and label these herbs as the other students do. But, in *your* box, I've placed a few extras. Don't disappoint me," the Healer said in a level voice.

Faye gulped; blue eyes bugging with nerves. Even though she was sure she could identify nearly every herb in Pendalin, she began to doubt her ability to complete the task. Taking a deep breath to steady herself, Faye returned to the workbench where her three friends were already sifting through their samples.

"What's wrong?" Trish asked, noticing the girl's pale face and Merkin's cheery one.

"She decided to test me with a few extra samples." Faye muttered, then got straight to work.

She steadily identified and labelled the first twenty plants before Britt and Trish had even completed five. Rory was having slightly more success, but still struggled with the final four specimens. After that it got a little more difficult.

Faye came across similar cousins and whatnot that were harder to remember. She cleared her mind and breathed deeply, absorbing the unique scent of the herbs, imagining that she was back in Thayrille's kitchen, and it was just another relaxed and informal lesson.

Thayrille would get Faye to close her eyes and breathe in the scent. After a moment of consideration, the girl had needed to identify the herb to Thayrille. If Faye was wrong, she would have to examine the herb and try again. If she was *still* wrong, then she had to tear a tiny bit of leaf and taste the herb – which were often bitter and disgusting. Faye had found that the last test was perhaps the best teacher, for she never wanted to taste the herb again!

"Carpicous," mumbled Faye, inhaling the herbal scent again.

She could already feel nerves and muscles relaxing. It was one of the herb's most famous properties, to relieve muscle tension and knots. She deftly glued it into her book and printed a neat, clear label beside the stem before picking a few leaves off. These Faye held beneath her tongue, so the sap dissolved into her saliva, and she valiantly managed not to gag on the awful taste. To be thorough, Faye jotted down a few properties she knew of next to the label. The remaining plants took her a while, and she had only just finished when the last bell tolled.

"Excellent, everyone! Please place any scraps back into the box and return the box to my desk," Healer Merkin called as the room exploded in a flurry of movement.

Everyone was in a rush to get a good seat for dinner.

Sensing that she wouldn't be able to leave until Merkin had checked her work, Faye took her time clearing up and told the girls she'd meet them downstairs. Britt and Trish exchanged concerned looks before ushering Rory from the room once their bench was tidy.

Exactly as predicted, Healer Merkin swooped down on Faye once the last student left the room.

"Finished?" she asked briskly, her blue eyes snapping.

Faye nodded as Merkin started flicking carefully through her book.

"First twenty, perfect, as I expected," Merkin murmured, as she checked each specimen in order.

She slowed down as she reached the last ten. The Healer spent almost a minute on each one, checking and double-checking. Finally, Merkin nodded.

"Perfect, again," she said reluctantly. "Why are you in this class? You're obviously far and beyond the standard we teach at the Academy."

Faye shrugged helplessly.

"Seeker Rythin wanted me to start at the beginning, most likely to experience healing from a different person," Faye answered hesitantly, her voice barely above a whisper.

Her heart thudded in her chest, and she found herself concealing her sweaty hands by shoving them deep into her pockets, much like Thayrille was apt to do.

Healer Merkin nodded and sighed slowly, tapping a pencil thoughtfully against her thinly pursed lips.

"I see. Sometimes, it is best to have multiple teachers, so you do not find yourself stranded in a rut. I apologise for my earlier attitude, child. Thayrille and I are competitors of old," Merkin murmured, sitting on the stool that Britt had recently vacated. "But that's hardly anything to do with you."

Faye nodded, unsure what to say. She was very much glad that the lesson was over, and that hopefully there wouldn't be another one like it!

"Now, the question is, what are we to do with you?" Merkin asked, more to herself than to Faye.

The two pondered the question for a while before the middle-aged Healer nodded as though she had come to an answer. Faye waited pensively for the final decision.

"Each lesson I teach has a theme," Healer Merkin explained briefly. "Today, as you realise, was identifying fresh herbs. The next lesson will be identifying herbs in their range of forms – fresh, powdered, paste, and serum. As I did today, you'll be given extras to test your knowledge. I will even provide you with samples of herbs from other lands if you like?"

Faye perked up with interest. She hadn't seen herbs from other lands yet. Thayrille had always scorned their use, claiming that herbs from Pendalin were more than enough for every ailment.

Noting the expression on Faye's face, Merkin finally appeared satisfied and genuinely friendly.

"I see Thayrille hasn't changed," she clucked, shaking her head and causing little wisps of hair to escape her ponytail. It was so similar to how Thayrille's hair constantly came loose it caused a sharp ache to bloom beneath Faye's ribs.

"Even as a girl she used to turn her nose up at non-Pendalin plants. She'd be surprised, I'm sure, to learn that some of these plants are stronger and more effective than the ones native to our homeland," the Healer muttered with a slightly caustic inflection. Faye nodded in agreement, not daring to argue. She well knew Thayrille's prejudice and given the pugnacious personality of the woman before her, she didn't wish to quibble for quibbling's' sake.

"Alright, off to dinner with you, my girl," the Healer said, kinder than she had previously been.

Faye thanked her politely for her time and ran down the steps to dinner. It was so strange! That hectic lesson had almost felt like home... In fact, now that she was heading down to the busy mess hall for her next meal, she felt inexplicably depressed. Perhaps even homesick.

"Never mind, dear one," Zen murmured in her ear as she stumped down the stairs. "You'll be back in Grydin this summer, and the time between now and then will pass in the blink of an eye."

Faye doubted that but she was too tired to come up with a suitably pithy retort.

As promised earlier that day, Trish led Faye to the storeroom on the ground floor after dinner.

"I can't stay. I have a paper due for Basic Chemistry tomorrow and need to check a few facts in the library to finish it," Trish excused herself with a cheery smile and a wave. "See you in the morning, kiddo!"

Faye waved forlornly at the retreating back, watching as the girl's skirts swished as she strode past a group of boys chatting together on one side of the entrance hall. The boys stopped and stared after the curvaceous figure, their expressions a study in admiration.

Ahhh, so that's why Trish likes dresses, Faye surmised with an amused shake of her head.

Well, that definitely *wasn't* something *she* was after! Faye would be happy if any boy just saw her as a friend and nothing more.

Straightening her shoulders, Faye entered the vast storeroom. The place was piled high with bric-a-brac, shelves and racks of clothing, and a plethora of things Faye struggled to name. She found Mistress Tryllia perusing a set of important-looking documents at a large desk at the back of the room. Gracing the top of the broad wooden surface was a plaque declaring *Mistress Tryllia Hosrowan, Housekeeper and Head Administrator of Austin Academy.* Faye blinked in surprise at the lengthy title.

Well, that certainly explained a lot! she thought, bemused.

When Faye approached Tryllia, the Housekeeper looked up and beamed, the epitome of a matronly lady rather than an authority figure.

"Why, hello, Miss Faye! How was your first day? Did you get your notebooks?" she asked pleasantly, her dark eyes gleaming and her sun-kissed skin appearing almost yellow beneath the lantern glow.

Faye gave Mistress Tryllia a genuine smile as she eased her aching buttocks onto a nearby stool and prepared to tell Tryllia all about her classes. It seemed only fitting that she should answer the Academy Headmistress's questions in suitable detail.

"Yes, thank you! The professors are very kind, and the classes were certainly interesting! And thank you for those notebooks. I didn't realise that I'd need so many things. My foster mother never thought to mention it," Faye answered a tad grumpily, feeling a bit of her stress over the situation escape her control.

Zen felt warm around her neck and vibrated softly. It seemed the lizard was very pleased to be back in Tryllia's presence.

"Och, Mistress Hogansvort probably thought it would all be sorted as soon as you arrived. And it would have been, too! But both Seekers Rythin and Tyrone forgot to mention!" Tryllia exclaimed, bustling out from behind her desk to assess the towering shelves that covered one storeroom wall.

Deftly, the Housekeeper began to pluck various objects from shelves, racks, and drawers.

"Here is a new pack to store your books for each class," she chattered happily, placing a small, sturdy knapsack on the bench.

It was made of thick canvas and leather and was far superior in quality to Faye's second hand – and heavily patched – knapsack that she had used for years.

Tryllia filled the pack with extra bits and pieces. Pens, pencils, rubbers, notepads, ruler, drawing compass, sketchpad… The list went on. Before Faye knew it, the knapsack was bulging and wouldn't close properly.

"Och, never mind, you'll be fine carrying it up the stairs. You can store all this in your desk. Now – clothes! I've heard-tell that you'll be needing a few outfits, as you've only two pairs of trousers and shirts!" she said, whipping out a tape measure with a small sparkle of rosy-lavender power.

Faye wondered who had told her that, as Tryllia set about taking the girls measurements. Zen chuckled smugly, and Faye grew suspicious. What had that sneaky reptile been up to? And *when*? The lizard had been wrapped around her neck nearly all day!

Within minutes, Faye was being loaded with nightgowns, trousers, shirts, robes, dresses, socks, shoes, and hair accessories. Tryllia frowned as she realised that the small girl would never be able to carry the massive load up all those steps, so she exchanged the towering mound of clothing for the bulging bag.

Faye led the way up to her room, with Tryllia close behind, staggering a little as her quivering muscles struggled. Today had been perhaps the longest day of the girl's short life, and these cursed stairs were sure to be the instrument of her undoing! How was she meant to navigate them *every* day when she felt like her bones were turning to liquid and her muscles were atrophying?

Once they arrived back in Faye's room, Mistress Tryllia began sorting through the array of items. In a brisk, motherly fashion, the Housekeeper helped Faye pack her new belongings away while chattering the entire time. She told Faye many things, from bits of gossip about Faye's instructors, to the history of the Academy, and much else.

Tryllia, after all, ran the entire facility and kept everyone in line, as had her mother before her, and her mother before her. The role, it turned out, was hereditary and dated back to the time of King Brandon.

Faye listened politely, storing away various bits of interesting information. Finally, as the girl began to unintentionally yawn, the towering woman embarrassedly excused herself and apologised for keeping her from her rest.

"Thank you so much, Mistress Tryllia. For everything!" Faye said whole-heartedly, her eyes stinging slightly.

This was the first time anyone had taken such good care of her. Just for a moment, Faye imagined this would be what a proper mother was like.

Zen quietly cleared its throat from its position around Faye's neck. The girl stiffened, worried that Tryllia would notice, but the woman was busily stacking the last of the stationary items on the small desk on her way out the door. The girl still wasn't sure what her instructors would say about this secret companion of hers and wasn't all that keen to find out at the moment.

Faye startled a second time when she felt something heavy slither down her shoulder and into her right hand. Puzzled, the girl glanced down to find that Zen had sneakily dangled a leather chord over her shoulder, a beautiful purple amethyst tied to its middle. The girl recognised the stone as one she had found back in Grydin during one of her forays down into the Grotto hot springs.

She blinked several times, wondering when Zen had found the time to make a necklace out of the thing. The lizard had been with her *all* day. Hadn't it?

The necklace was simple but gorgeous and quite the appropriate gift. Exactly what Faye had in mind this morning when she had asked her colourful companion to find a present for Tryllia.

Faye shyly held out the necklace to the stout woman.

"I made this for you to say thanks," the girl shrugged self-consciously.

Tryllia's face lit up with a radiant smile that turned her serene face from pleasant to timelessly beautiful and she gave the tiny girl a big, warm hug.

"You're welcome, child," she murmured as she promptly tied the necklace around her neck. "If you need anything at all, come by my office and just ask. Now, get some sleep."

The woman quietly closed the door behind her as she left the room.

"Thanks, Zen," Faye said fervently.

The lizard merely chuckled in that mysterious, smug way again. Zen, it appeared, liked Academy life way too much.

CHAPTER 17

SETTLING IN

After that exhausting first day, everything became more routine. Faye could locate every class on time, every hour of every day. Britt and Trish continued to make an effort to include their young companion in all sorts of activities, both in class and in their free time. They often passed notes to each other, making plans to traipse down to Tryssdale city on Resday, or to meet up in the mess hall or grounds after class.

It was through their easy manner and genuine kindness that Faye began to feel somewhat less overwhelmed and ceased experiencing those occasional panic attacks that constricted her chest and made it hard to breathe. In addition, her very private little room became a sanctuary for herself and Zen to talk in depth about their experiences and thoughts on Academy life.

The little lizard was the most important aspect that helped Faye through the first weeks of unexpected homesickness. It constantly curled around her neck, whispering the odd comment or piece of advice that assisted Faye in understanding the people around her. As always, if Faye ever encountered a particularly unpleasant person, Zen would offer to bite them.

She often pondered how this small reptile had become so wise in so few years. They had shared all the same experiences since she had found Zen as a hatchling, yet the creature seemed to know so much about the world! It was another unsolved mystery surrounding her companion and something the little lizard refused to discuss or explain.

"When you're ready," Zen would assure her whenever she asked the pointy questions.

"But *when* will that be?" Faye would demand cantankerously, beyond frustrated by the little lizard's evasiveness.

At that point, the reptile would often buzz, click, or vibrate against her neck, causing her angst to slough straight off her heart. Then it would change the subject, and the day would go on.

Zen often advised her to draft letters to Thayrille, encouraging her to valiantly try and express her feelings regarding the Healer. But the girl was never satisfied enough with her scrawled notes to send the letter to their quaint cottage, which would forever be considered *home*.

Faye surmised that she could wait until Thayrille wrote first. A *reply* letter was perhaps a lot less *needy* sounding, Faye was sure. And she knew how Thayrille felt about 'paltry emotion', as she would often call it. The bundle of unsent letters grew, each one tenderly tucked away in the back of her desk drawer.

Dawn Weaponry was still the most significant physical challenge, as Faye had to continue to wake well before dawn before being promptly pushed to the limits of her abilities in swordplay, fitness tasks, and coordination.

By the end of the week, Faye found that her muscles had become accustomed to the additional activity and didn't cramp and ache as much as they had that first day.

On Weeksend morning, she was up again at dawn, this time for her first-ever kitchen duty. Faye shyly presented herself in the mess hall just after five thirty, where Ross, the Assistant Kitchen Duty Manager, asked her a series of rapid-fire questions.

"Do you know your way around a kitchen? Know how to wash? To scrub? To serve up a meal? To cook? Know how to collect dishes? Or follow an order without argument?" he barked, reminding Faye of Master Sorwell.

Faye instinctively knew that this boy, Ross, was a Weaponry student, most likely a Level Three by the looks of him. As a Duty Manager, it was understandable that he was one of the few older volunteers she hadn't met yet at Dawn Weaponry, given that he had this incredibly vital task instead.

"Yes, yes, yes, yes, yes, yes, and yes, Sir," Faye responded sharply, standing to attention just as she did in Weaponry every morning.

A funny look passed the youth's face before he grinned slyly.

"So, you can *cook*, you say?" he inquired with an air of innocence, seemingly sure that she had mistakenly answered yes to that question. "How many hours have you clocked?"

"Three evenings a week, for the past four years, Sir," Faye responded truthfully.

Cooking was yet another skill Thayrille had taught her thoroughly. The Healer had often told her that good cooking was essential for a good recovery. Ross looked surprised by that admission, but this time pleasantly so.

"Ho-ho!" he exclaimed, clapping his hands together. "We haven't had a bona fide chef in the Academy since Greyson left two years back."

Faye felt uncertainty grip her as she was nabbed and dragged into the kitchen. She had no idea if *chef* was an accurate term for her abilities. She had only ever cooked a meal for four, at the most, and only under Thayrille's strict instruction.

Shrugging mentally, Faye dubiously recalled the Healer's pleased opinion that her Ward had a way with herbs and spices. After all, true success was in the tasting and Faye had made many a meal that Thayrille and Jack had enjoyed immensely.

By the end of that first kitchen duty, Faye was deemed a more than acceptable cook and placed in charge of spices and whatnot for nearly every meal. Since Resday was a quiet day with many students lying abed or adventuring away from the Academy, Faye was asked to spend the three hours of her duty experimenting with the lunch pasta sauce, the dinner gravy, and a few other specialties. Once she had perfected an item, she was to jot it down exactly, in proper measurements, for the other cooks to follow. These were the recipe cards that Trish and the other Hospitality students would follow each morning, preparing the array of food served in the Mess Hall.

Faye did her best, spicing up the red sauce with basil, garlic, and oregano, and the white sauce with sun-dried tomatoes, chicken bits, and a mixture of herbs and a little chilli. Thankfully, due to her Agricultural Studies class, the girl was quite familiar with the fresh ingredients that grew in abundance in the Academy gardens. It was quite a fulfilling pastime, and her efforts became widely appreciated by the other students as the first wave of edited recipes appeared at the lunch buffet.

The only true difficulty Faye was having was in Sorcery. This lesson maintained its level of difficulty throughout. It also became increasingly apparent that, despite her Fey heritage, she didn't possess a single bit of magical talent outside her ability to play her mother's silver pipe.

Each lesson, Faye would arrive amid the derisive stares of Styrran and several other Sorcery students who shared his prejudice. She would pass them by without a glance, ignoring their silent attempts at bullying, and sit at her place in the front row next to Duncan. She often thought, considering many of them were almost actual *adults*, that these beginning Sorcerers would find harassing a twelve-year-old distasteful and quite beneath them.

She even said this aloud once, on her way down the stairs, keeping her voice level and disdainful. Many of the Sorcerers had the grace to look shamed at their behaviour, and from that day forth, they ceased their censure.

Styrran, however, kept at it regardless.

The Warlock Duncan spoke only to answer questions, remaining as mysterious yet charismatic as their first meeting. Since he didn't invite conversation, Faye was determined not to pester him with any either. It reminded her of her days at the Healer's Cottage with Thayrille. Words were not wasted there, either, yet there appeared to be a mutual affection and understanding between them.

Their lessons in Sorcery also varied in their nature, like Weaponry. When Faye arrived at her midmorning lesson on Fifday, she discovered that the workbenches had vanished and large, comfy mats had taken their place.

"Today," Sorcerer Hanly told them cheerily, "we are practicing the art of Meditation."

Someone groaned quietly, clearly displeased by the announcement. At first, Faye was rather pious and thought how that unknown groaner should perhaps choose a different course if they felt that way. But then she undertook her first ever session in the mystical practice.

The following two hours were spent listening to nothing but silence. The students were meant to find their 'inner power' — whatever that meant.

Time ticked away painfully slowly and by the end of the session, Faye fully understood and appreciated the feeling underlying that groan. Although she kept that to herself.

All Faye did for that two-hour block was spend the time introspectively wondering if she had merely imagined her musical bond with the land and the ephemeral power that saturated its soil.

"Tonight," Zen hissed in her ear. "We'll try the pipe again."

Faye twitched her shoulder in simultaneous agreement and indication that the lizard should shut its mouth. Duncan was sitting so close and might hear even the softest of whispers in the dead silent room!

At the end of the fruitless lesson, Hanly announced that every Fifday would be devoted to meditation. Faye balked at the idea – she had been driven so hard for the past few days that she thought she would fall asleep! If she were made to do it every Fifday, after already having endured five consecutive dawn sessions of Weaponry, she didn't know how she would manage it.

As was her habit, though, Faye said nothing.

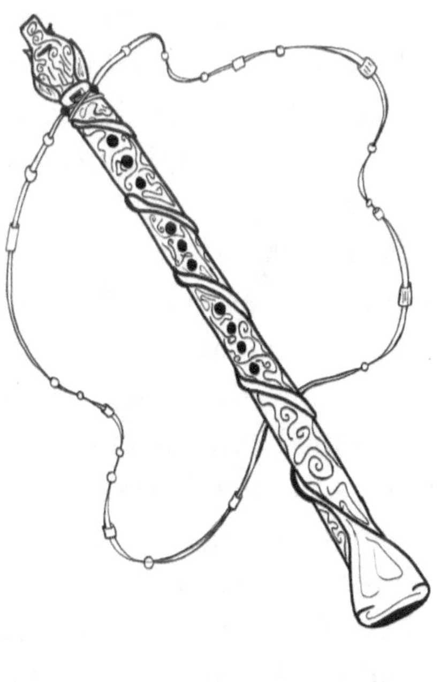

239

Faye and Zen intended to slip away to the very boundary of the Academy grounds as soon as dinner was over. Much to Faye's surprise, the trickiest part was working out how to dodge the invitations to study or play card games with her new friends.

"Oh, um, I have to ask Ross something in the kitchens. How about I meet you in the library afterwards? I'll probably be a little while," Faye lied glibly, aiming for a nonchalant expression.

Trish crossed her arms and glowered at her suspiciously.

"Are you *sure* you're not just avoiding another round of Prude Poker? Britt kicked your butt last time, and you weren't very forthcoming in answering our questions!" the older girl demanded.

Prude Poker, as it was called, was a particular version of regular Poker but with additional rules and exceptions that were unfamiliar to the young girl. There was often no rhyme or reason to them, and when a wild card was played, suddenly, a winning hand became a fistful of rubbish. The loser was then asked a tonne of personal questions by the playing group. The questions were often designed to be pointy, causing the loser significant discomfort. And Faye *always* lost!

Faye flushed at the memory of being given the third degree about her life to date, particularly all the inane questions the girls asked about Thayrille and Jack! It was such an awkward experience, having to talk about herself and explain the nitty-gritty details of her relationships, thoughts and feelings.

Faye had come to realise just how much she *hated* girl talk!

"No! I'm not avoiding it! I just have something I must do for a bit, but I *promise* that I'll come to the common room and play afterward," Faye groaned.

"Fine. I'll hold you to that, kiddo!" Trish grinned at her young friend before bounding away towards the stairs that would take her to the dormitory above. "You've got an hour before I come hunting you down!"

"Close one!" Zen whispered in her ear.

Faye had to agree. As much as she *loathed* Prude Poker, she would have hated revealing her true plans for this evening more than losing yet another round.

With a harsh huff, Faye impatiently entered the kitchen, actively avoided eye contact with any of the servers and exited straight through the back door into the first of the kitchen gardens. The waxing moon was bright enough to light her way, and the stars glittered in the navy sky. The air was beginning to take on that crisp edge of early autumn, and Faye shivered slightly, drawing up her thin canvas jacket. She would have to revisit the storeroom soon to browse the winter clothing selection, she decided.

Faye navigated the pebbled pathways until she found the other entrance that the Agricultural Studies classes used during the day. Once through the stone archway, she scooted along the exterior wall of the gardens to the distant boundary fence. The ancient, cobbled wall was a mere token that did little to keep anyone out or in. Still, it appeared more as a courtesy marker to indicate what was and wasn't Academy land. Faye could see the sandstone cliffs rising against the night sky, a darker black swatch that surrounded the entire valley.

Examining the lay of the land, Faye noted an enormous oak tree that stood sentinel nearby and instinctively headed for the massive trunk. The girl frowned in confusion as this tree seemed almost *devoid* of life. There was no comforting sensation as she lay her hands on its bark, nor was there any welcoming gleam in the leaves. The tree was dark and dank. Alive, yes, but missing that special *something* that made her secret cubby tree back in Grydin her most favourite of places.

"What do you think, Zen? Safe enough to climb?" Faye whispered.

"Eh? Oh yes, by all means. Go ahead, dear one," The lizard poked its colourful snout from beneath her collar, scenting the air. "This is as good a place as any."

Faye confidently scaled the trunk and branches until she found a comfortable fork to plug her bottom into before sliding her mother's pipe out of her pocket. She was relieved that the slim metal object hadn't fallen out during the climb.

"Zen, Thayrille said that my mother wore this around her neck. Perhaps we could make a cord for it? Then I wouldn't be afraid of losing it all the time! I could keep it with me. It might be safer," the girl suggested tentatively, thinking about the secret hidey-hole where she often stashed the instrument while she was out and about.

"Hmmm, leave it with me. I'll find something appropriate. Just don't wear it to Weaponry! The girls will want to know all about it," the lizard cautioned.

Faye grimaced as she realised the truth of that.

Drawing a deep breath, she placed the slim pipe to her lips and played the haunting tune that seemed to echo from the surrounding rocks and trees. Instead of glowing in ghostly grandeur as the ruins of Galleymai had that fateful night, Tryssdale Academy merely glittered eerily in the near distance. The walls were still the original stones of the Winter Palace, and there hadn't been any significant changes in centuries. However, the power beneath the foundations felt disjointed, as though it were all bunched up and knotted from centuries of neglect. Once the pipe music sounded, the webs of energy shivered and stretched, reaching out to every corner of the valley until they became an even network of invisible threads. A mysterious ache within her bones, one that Faye hadn't even been aware she was experiencing, finally eased and allowed her to take a full, unimpeded breath. She shook her head experimentally, wondering at the sudden absence of that peculiar sensation of pressure that had lurked there since her arrival.

"Well, it would seem I have *some* magic, Zen. Just not the type that lets me perform Sorcery like the other students here," Faye sighed, disappointed.

What was she meant to do about that?!

"Never mind, dear one. It will come to you eventually. Besides, I think you already have enough on your plate without dealing with any latent powers! Be patient, and they'll surface when you're ready," the lizard chided gently, buzzing contentedly around her neck.

The vibration had a soporific effect, and the girl felt her worries melt away and a sense of complacency steal through her chest.

"I suppose you're right," the girl huffed, noticing that her breath was beginning to make small plumes of mist in the growing chill of night. "Alright, I suppose we'd best tuck into bed. We have Weaponry in the morning."

"Aren't you forgetting something?" the lizard chuffed in amusement, pricking her shoulder pointedly with one sharp claw.

"Oh! Dang it! Why did you have to *say* something? I *could* have just forgotten about that blasted poker game, you know," Faye grumped as she scrambled back down the tree.

"How else do you plan to make friends, dear one?" Zen countered reasonably.

"Who needs friends, anyway?" she grumbled, heading back to the kitchens and the girls awaiting her in the common room above.

The lizard didn't answer, and Faye figured she would just have to resign herself to the next hour of girl talk. She wondered briefly where Varsity got to in these evening hours. Faye *still* had the odd desire to track the older girl down and spend time with her. There was something about her, some instinct Faye had that told her Varsity was unique and worth becoming acquainted with.

She would bet her sparring stick that the mysterious warrior disliked girl talk just as much as Faye did!

CHAPTER 18

WHAT IT MEANS TO BE FEY

Weaponry became easier as her muscles adjusted to the more vigorous pace of sword sparring with various partners. Each of her four dawn Weaponry sessions had the same routine – warm-up, sword-sparring, then stretching. Each week varied in content. There was archery, equestrian studies, knife-throwing, and hand-to-hand combat drills.

Faye was an old hand at combat, of course, but the new weapons of bow, arrows and knives of different shapes and sizes was an unexpected delight. It didn't take long for her to become accustomed to the varied skills needed to operate them and soon she could hold her own amongst the more experienced students.

Faye also discovered, to her dismay, that every B week there was an extra two-hour theory session on Firsday. It reminded her of the tactical lectures that Jack had indulged in during the winter months, being that the session was more about theoretical tactics than actual combat. The Weaponry group also were able to spend more time grooming and feeding the horses, so at least that was *something* the girl enjoyed.

As the days turned to weeks, Faye realised that she hadn't practiced once with her sparring staff – it had remained stowed safely beneath her bed. She was also keenly aware that she hadn't seen Jeremy or Hannah in the past fortnight. It was as though they had vanished into the stream of Academy students.

Faye wasn't too upset about that fact.

On her fourth Resday at the Academy, Faye slipped away and retrieved her staff instead of joining the Weaponry girls for their weekly lunch trip down to the city. She found a quiet place near the Shed and began her drills. Thankfully, the grounds were empty as there were no scheduled classes and many students were either still abed or heading out of the Academy grounds for the day. No one else appeared to be lurking around the copse of trees, giving the small girl peace and privacy.

After almost two hours, she stopped, feeling ragged and drained. It had felt good to go through the familiar routine, stretching muscles that had spent the past few weeks suffering under her neglect. Faye let herself into the Shed – that low stone Weaponry building that housed all the resources used by the Academy's budding warriors – and showered quickly, changing out of her spare set of training clothes.

Faye had to admit that undertaking the Weaponry class was well worth the rewards. They had a bathroom, so they didn't have to share the commons with hundreds of other students. They also rose before dawn on most days, which she now liked, *and* they received the equivalent of those four lessons off every week, so she could easily complete the study tasks owing from her theory classes. So, essentially, a Weaponry student had more free time than other students.

Not everyone could hack Weaponry though, for it was a gruelling and physically demanding course.

Faye also now owned an entirely new wardrobe, thanks to the Student Storeroom, and indulged in the luxury of leaving two sets of training clothes down here in the Shed; that way, she could fit in extra sparring with her staff whenever she liked. Faye was still uncertain where her grubby, worn clothes she had travelled in had gone, not that she minded too much.

After getting cleaned up and dressed back in her day clothes, the girl slipped from the Shed, quietly closing and locking the heavy door behind her. Faye squealed in fright as she turned and almost ran straight into an imposing figure standing right behind her.

Automatically Faye's staff came up in a defensive block, the heavy end impacting the flat hand of her opponent as they pushed it away before it could do any harm.

"Well, aren't *you* full of surprises?" chuckled a deep, melodic voice.

Faye blinked up at Varsity, stunned that after spending every day of the past few weeks looking for the mysterious older girl, she suddenly appeared right when the younger girl wished she hadn't.

"Um, Varsity! Hello," Faye said nervously, clasping her staff as her brain raced through a million and one excuses for being here at the Shed unsupervised ... on Resday no less! *And* attacking the other girl with a heavy, blunt stick.

"I was watching you earlier. That's not any sort of fighting that Sorwell teaches," Varsity commented as she negligently leaned against the Shed's stone wall, arms crossed casually over her chest, her dark eyes steady and inquiring.

"Oh... Yeah... That... Um," Faye was at a loss for words, and Zen was no help, crouching silently beneath her shower-dampened hair.

The girl felt her stomach drop. If Varsity *told*... Just how much trouble was she likely to get in? Jack had preferred she not say anything about his informal tutoring, and this would be a lot to explain! It was certainly *not* something that Sorwell would just let slide.

"Teach me," the older girl demanded, determination in her square jaw.

Faye did a double take. *Teach* Varsity the stick? She wanted to *learn* from Faye?

"Uhhh, sure. I mean, I guess I could try. I've never taught anyone a weapon before..." Faye muttered uncertainly, wondering how she would find a stick of the right length and weight for the taller, imposing girl.

"Excellent. Same time, same place. See you next week." Varsity gave Faye a small salute, just two fingers held casually to her brow, before swaggering off towards the mess hall.

Faye stood there in the shadows, trying to work out what had just happened.

"Ooooh, this will be fun!" Zen crooned, delighted by the prospect of spending time with the tall warrior girl. "She's going to be a natural! I can *feel* it!"

"Do you think she'll tell?" Faye asked uncertainly, her palms sweaty against the smooth wood of her staff.

"Nah, I think Varsity knows how to keep things to herself," the lizard responded thoughtfully. "Come, dear one, the day wanes while we stand here gawping!"

Faye reluctantly left the seclusion of the Shed and returned to her room, intending to finish off the variety of written tasks she owed to her instructors for that week. She was battling with the Sorcery essay when she decided she needed far more than her own knowledge and scribbly notebooks.

Leaving Zen snoozing quietly in the bed, Faye left her room. She made her way to the library, which was situated inside one of the corner towers of the palace and had many levels of its own. The library levels were comprised of a combination of desks, lounges, and shelves upon shelves of books. Each level focused on a specific theme or topic. The entire sub-establishment was ruled by a stern, mousy-haired Sorceress named Mistress Lilly. Her shrewd blue eyes analysed all visitors to her domain as though memorising their faces as she entered their details into her glossy thick ledger, noting the time of arrival, time of departure, and any books accessed or borrowed.

Faye had a feeling that this strict woman would remember every iota of information, particularly whatever they had borrowed, and *exactly* when it was due back. For such a sweet-looking woman, she was unnervingly intimidating.

Once passing the Librarian's intense scrutiny, Faye crept up to the fifth floor, where books on sorcery were located. The girl had just sat down with a particularly thick tome on the basic principles of meditation when a dark shadow slunk into the seat opposite.

It was Duncan.

"Busy day?" he asked casually after almost a full minute of expectant silence.

Faye nodded once, uncertain where this was leading.

Had he seen her down at the training grounds, like Varsity had? Or was he making idle chit-chat? He had never spoken directly to her before. The whole day was turning into one unnerving experience after another!

Duncan seemed to take the nod as an invitation and settled himself more firmly in his chair, pulling out his books. His deep green eyes swirled with black mist as they focused on the paper before him. It appeared he was also here to work on his Sorcery essay.

Faye hesitantly continued her own work but found she couldn't concentrate. She was being eaten alive by curiosity. Thayrille, she had known all her life and knew what her silent company meant. Trish and Britt made it clear they were after another friend to join their 'Girls Are Warriors' group, and even Varsity was pursuing time with her due to her knowledge of a foreign fighting technique. This Warlock, however, she couldn't read. It annoyed her.

So, she stared at him until he finally looked up and met her inquiring gaze. The youth sighed and pushed away his essay – which hadn't been expanded on in the least these past twenty minutes.

"Look – you're an orphan, I'm an orphan. You're half Fey, I'm half Fey. We've got more in common than many of the other students in this place," he said, his voice low, the usual bored quality replaced by something intense.

His eyes lost that aloof, measured look and shimmered softly as the swirling black mist intensified. He was pleading for acceptance.

"How'd you know?" Faye asked, surprised.

He rolled his eyes.

"Hard not to. You practically glow with nature energy. And I heard what Styrran said to you about being a 'no-name'," Duncan said, now looking a little awkward.

Faye nodded slowly and offered a shy smile.

"It's true – I've no knowledge of my mother or father. I don't even know which Fey Clan I belong to. But don't tell anyone," Faye said, panic causing her stormy blue eyes to widen.

The Warlock grinned faintly and shook his head.

"Never. I know what it's like to be targeted, because you're not entirely Human," he said softly, his rumbling voice managing to sooth her fears.

"Is that why you're here, because you've lost your Clan?" Faye asked sympathetically.

The boy's face clouded, and he nodded.

"I was found as a babe, abandoned. I was given to an orphanage, then received a place here when I was five. It was pretty obvious what I was," he said, his face darkening, his voice deepening to a feral growl. "I don't know which Clan, if any, I belong to. Plan to find out one day. They'll have something to answer for."

Duncan drew his work back towards himself, avoiding her gaze as though he had revealed too much, and began earnestly working on his essay. His sapphire ring glinted strangely, almost like the crystalline stone had absorbed the maelstrom of power the boy had just conjured.

Faye blinked in surprise. Perhaps that ring was more important than she had realised. She had previously wondered about its significance and recalled the odd interaction between Sorcerer Hanly and Duncan that first lesson.

Perhaps the ring housed spells to curb his natural Warlock powers? Maybe that was how the Academy could keep him here comfortably, even though it was a common assumption that Warlocks and Humans wouldn't, or couldn't, mix.

The girl watched her unexpected companion a little longer, feeling a spurt of compassion. *He was like a younger, male version of Thayrille*, she thought sadly, and continued with her own essay.

Faye knew that despite making no effort whatsoever, she had made another friend. She puzzled over the phenomenon, wishing desperately that Zen were here so it could offer her its usual sage wisdom to help her navigate this new and unexpected development.

Another fortnight slinked by and Faye found herself in a predicament. She was due to meet Varsity soon down at the Weaponry Shed yet found herself hovering uncertainly before the Student Storeroom door.

The entry hall was a vast, quiet space filled with the odd whisper of sound as a distant door closed or laughter and conversation echoed through the ventilation shafts. Most students were off doing whatever they tended to do on Resday, so the usual rabble was absent.

Faye had just completed her usual rotation in the kitchens and realised somewhat belatedly that she *still* hadn't sourced her warrior friend her own sparring stick.

The week previously, Faye and Varsity had attempted to search the grounds for a sturdy, straight branch of the right girth and weight for the taller girl. Still, every stick they encountered was either too brittle or too willowy. The aged, brittle sticks simply shattered on impact, while the willowy sticks whipped like an elastic rod, almost taking out someone's eye.

After much contemplation, Faye had suggested Mistress Tryllia and her resources as a solution, but Varsity had been reluctant. Apparently, the older girl didn't like to be under the stout Housekeeper's stern gaze. Faye had offered to come here and sort something out. Mistress Tryllia seemed to like her, after all. Only, the week had trickled by with nary an opportunity to come down here!

A strange sensation struck the small girl as she dithered before the stout door, wondering if she dared to ask the Housekeeper for a non-approved weapon. It was almost as though her life force was being sucked forcefully into a whirling vortex. Faye stumbled a step and caught herself up against a nearby stone pillar. Shaking her head, feeling her ears were filled with water, the girl searched the empty hall.

Nothing. No one.

No, wait! A voice. Two voices. Three!

Faye followed the sound, noting that the strange sensation strengthened. The girl stopped in front of the small antechamber where newly enrolled students registered at the Academy. The same Clerk she had met several weeks before was frowning over his ledger, tapping it furiously while glaring suspiciously at the robed Seeker and an overly large boy that stood before him.

The boy, Faye noted, was rather ugly. He had pock-marked skin, yellowed blunt teeth, dead-looking moss-coloured eyes, and short, bristly hair similar to a brindled dog's.

Peeking around the doorway, Faye's eyes widened in alarm as she felt the force the boy exuded. Usually, she could detect a faint musical jingle or a trace of warmth that zipped beneath her skin whenever she came upon someone with a talent for magic and sorcery. *This* boy, however, was the exact opposite. He was *absorbing* the magic from his surroundings, rather than emitting the tell-tale signs.

"No. No, I don't think so, Seeker Galliger. We will refer his case to Seeker Rythin, as Housekeeper Tryllia and I told you yesterday, but this type of talent will *not* be conducive to our students' learning! How can we operate here, inside the Academy walls, if all the magic of the place is sucked down into this vortex? Can you not just switch it off, boy?" the Clerk demanded irritably, his azure power sputtering as he attempted to activate the spells on his ledger.

Clearly, the fact that his power was being siphoned negatively impacted the man's ordinarily cheery disposition.

"No," the boy answered sullenly, his voice little more than a cantankerous growl.

"No, I suppose not. I'll summon Rythin, then. He arrived back late last night. You can take this... I'm sorry, lad, what did you say your name was?" The Clerk paused, perusing his register and frowning over the pages.

"Cronuel," the boy answered in that same short, clipped tone.

"Right. Take Cronuel out onto the front grounds where he can't do any more damage. I'll speak with Seeker Rythin immediately," the Clerk assured the two.

Faye scampered back, returning to the Storeroom, eager to get away from the magic-leeching boy. She paused momentarily to peer back over her shoulder, rather uneasy to find the strange boy, Cronuel, staring straight at her, an unsettling hunger on his face as they locked gazes.

"Come along, lad. Exit's this way." Seeker Galliger motioned impatiently, seeming at the end of his tether.

Faye wondered why the Seeker thought the *Academy* was the right place for the magic-leeching brute. Surely it wasn't a good idea to stick the boy in amongst a heap of junior and trainee sorcerers?

The girl decided not to linger.

She broke eye contact with the strange boy and hastily pushed the Storeroom door open before slamming it closed behind her. Breathing hard, she leaned against the door as the power of the insidious vortex gradually faded. Seeker Galliger, it seemed, had finally convinced the boy to follow him outside.

"Faye! What an entrance! Is everything alright?" Mistress Tryllia looked up from her paperwork, positioned behind the broad desk at the back of the large room.

"Oh. Yes. Um. There's a new student. Maybe. Rythin is going to be consulted," Faye babbled uneasily.

Apparently, she was more affected by the boy's strange power than she had first realised.

"Oh?" The woman raised an eyebrow and then peered at the closed door with a rose-lavender glint of power in her dark eyes.

"Oh, yes! I see. Yes, it would be best if Rythin dealt with that special case. Now, what can I do for you, young Faye?"

Tryllia turned her attention away from the door and peered at Faye, her eyes still filled with motherly concern.

"Oh, well. Alright. Um. I was wondering if the storeroom had any sort of, well, sticks?" she gabbled, clutching her sparring stick in both hands.

Having been disconcerted by that Cronuel fellow, Faye was having a hard time recalling her practiced speech. She had planned to convince Tryllia that a sturdy walking staff was a completely reasonable item for a student to need. She had even brought the stick Jack had gifted her to show the woman exactly what she was after.

Tryllia raised both eyebrows in curiosity, peering at the wooden staff the girl clasped nervously in her hands as she rounded her desk.

"Hmmm, a sparring stick we're after, is it?" the Housekeeper asked. "I suppose you know a few tricks with that bit of timber, then? I recall Tyrone telling me about your interaction with that nasty bandit on the way here..."

The question was innocuous, yet Faye felt there was a deeper meaning under the gentle inquiry. She nodded hesitantly, wondering if Mistress Tryllia would report her to her Weaponry instructor for having a non-approved weapon at the Academy.

"Right. Yes, I suppose it would be... I mean, depending on how things pan out with the other... Yes. It would probably be best..." Tryllia failed to finish any of her thoughts, trailing off as she tapped her chin. "Come along, child. There isn't any in here, but I could probably source you something in the Armoury."

"We have an *armoury?*" Faye's eyes widened in glee, eagerly following the Housekeeper from the Storeroom.

The entry hall, thankfully, was empty of all other people. Cronuel was presumably still waiting out on the grounds as instructed. Tryllia briskly led the way to the other side of the entry hall and down a short set of stone steps. They were met by a solid timber door that was bolted and padlocked shut. With a mutter and a fiddle of keys, the stout woman found the right one and opened the heavy door.

Inside was a small antechamber with a desk, a ledger and an inkwell. On the opposite wall was yet another door, this one constructed of steel decorated with copper inlay. The patterns were intricate and probably centuries old.

Faye examined them closely, while Tryllia found the correct key that unlocked this door too. Beyond was another set of stone steps that led into a black, cavernous space. Tryllia clapped her hands sharply, causing a series of mage lights to illuminate their surroundings. Wall to wall, floor to ceiling, were an array of weapons. Swords, knives, bows, arrows, trebuchets, catapults... The space was crammed full of all sorts of war machines and devices.

"Now, where did I last see those things...?" Tryllia bustled over to a stout armoire against the left-hand wall and opened its doors.

Inside were a range of throwing stars, nun-chucks and bladed sticks.

"No, not that one." Tryllia shook her head in annoyance, then bustled to the next armoire along the wall.

There, held in place by a set of iron manacles, were a range of sparring sticks of different sizes and weights.

"Did you know which size you were after, my dear?" she asked, turning an inquiring eye on the small girl.

"Oh, umm, yes. May I choose?"

"You may," Tryllia smiled.

Faye stepped forward and examined the range of staffs. They were old, a little dusty, and in serious need of a good wax coating. But they were tempered hardwood, ideal for sparring. They also had the leather grip positioned in the middle, just like her staff.

The girl held her stick against the most likely candidates, comparing the thickness and length, until she found two she thought might do.

"May I hold these two to check their balance?" Faye requested.

Tryllia unlocked the manacles and pulled the two indicated sticks free of the bundle, holding first one and then the other out to the small girl. Faye gripped them, hefted each, then twirled them around her hands, careful not to clip anything with the whizzing ends.

"I'm thinking this one." Faye held up the darker timber.

The staff was the perfect height and was about as heavy as the staff that Jack practiced with. Varsity would be able to handle it easily, given a bit of practice. Tryllia nodded gracefully and returned the rejected stick before closing the manacle again and shutting the armoire firmly.

"Now, in case I haven't made it obvious, I must emphasise that you mustn't tell anyone where you got that stick. The armoury is off-limits to students, and it would cause quite the stir if anyone found out I supplied a student with a weapon." Tryllia said sternly, eyeing Faye with glittering lavender eyes. "Particularly one that is *not* taught by our Weaponry Master."

"Oh, yes, understood!" Faye assured the Housekeeper, wondering why the woman had decided to grant her request in the first place.

Surely Tryllia should have just mouthed empty apologies and denied having the ability to help her? Why had she randomly agreed to provide her with a second sparring staff?

As the two exited the armoury, Faye caught the very edge of the magic-leeching vortex and peered warily out the open front doors of the entry hall. She could just hear Rythin's voice on the other side, evidently speaking with Seeker Galliger and his charge, Cronuel.

"Right, my dear. Train well. I best go assist Seeker Rythin in this matter." Mistress Tryllia strode off towards the front doors, her lavender power swirling a little as she was ensconced by the vortex Cronuel produced.

"Oh, I most definitely will," the girl muttered, poking the crouching lizard in its usual place around her neck. "What do you think that Cronuel is about, Zen?"

The lizard was stiff as a statue, its little claws nestled into the collar of Faye's shirt.

"Oh, nothing good, dear one," the reptile croaked, nuzzling its head into the crook of her neck. "Let's get away, Faye! I don't like it."

Faye frowned in concern and picked up the pace through the winding corridors at the back of the entry hall until she came out near the rear exit. They were far enough away that she could no longer feel the suctioning pull of the leech's anti-power. There was no one about, so Faye reached up and dragged the lizard out of its hiding place so she could look at it. Its scales were devoid of the glittering array of colours that normally appeared and were instead now a strange bronze. The lizard was panting and looked as though it were about to faint.

"Are you alright, Zen?" Faye asked in concern, stroking the lizard gently.

Slowly, the usual rainbow hue returned, and the reptile breathed easier.

"Yes, quite alright, now, dear one. Let's just avoid that magic leeching creature from now on! That vortex is much too strong for me in my current state." The lizard shuddered, reaching once more for Faye's shoulder. "Let me back on. It's time for your session with Varsity. I think we can safely assume that Tryllia is allowing you to unofficially train with the stick due to that *thing's* presence here. I dare say the Academy will have no choice but to let the brute stay. I mean, where else can they put the thing?"

Faye allowed the lizard to burrow back under her tumult of blonde curls where it could safely conceal itself from any casual observer.

"I suppose you might be right," she sighed, made thoroughly uneasy by the thought. "It's going to make things more interesting around here. If that's even possible!"

Faye continued her journey down to the Weaponry Shed, unsurprised to find Varsity already changed and waiting for her in the sandy sparring circle just beyond the stone building.

"Here!" Faye called and tossed the newly acquired sparring stick towards the other girl, causing it to spin horizontally end over end through the air.

Varsity's hand shot out and snatched the weapon as it reached her, whipping it end over end as she tested its balance.

"Nice! Figures that the Housekeeper would have one of these lying about!" Varsity grinned at the younger girl. "I won't even ask how you managed to convince the old fogey! She's not known for doing a student any kindnesses. Now hurry up and change, little Phoenix. It's time to teach me proper."

Faye grinned, delighted by the surprise nickname. A phoenix was a magical creature of immense power that could rise again and again, never dying, forever immortal. It made the girl feel... Powerful. Confident. Capable.

Excitement thrumming through her veins, Faye darted through the Shed's open door, eager to get her training gear on.

Yes. It was certainly time to practice stick sparring in earnest!

CHAPTER 19

THE POWER WITHIN

Weeks slipped easily into months. The weather became steadily cooler, and the leaves turned to gold. Varsity was making excellent progress with the stick and easily managed the heavy wooden pole. As Zen had predicted, the girl was a natural!

Trish had become a fast friend and encouraged Faye to join in all manner of fun with the rest of the Weaponry cohort, particularly Britt and Rory. The Weaponry girls had created their own little exclusive club that provided each member with caring and support. Faye found a new confidence in herself through their influence and pragmatic encouragement. She was learning much about what it meant to be a teenage girl.

Then, there was the sullen Warlock Duncan and his primarily silent company. The boy was an enigma that Faye itched to solve. However, until he felt more comfortable with her, she could only guess his mood and feelings. Having been raised under the strict rule of Thayrille, Faye knew better than to pry.

The girl sighed heavily as her mind meandered along those familiar paths one Midwok morning. She sat at one of the large kitchen counters, perusing the stack of menu cards that Ross had stored in the cabinet beneath.

She was *meant* to have this block free, as Rythin had rescheduled her duty to Resday, but the girl still found herself roped into *just one more recipe*.

"Why so glum, chum?" Ross called as he approached, his brow creased in concern.

Even though the young man was often too busy to notice the usual moods of his kitchen staff, even he had cottoned on that Faye was feeling rather... blue.

"Oh, I don't know. I just feel..." Faye shrugged, trying to pinpoint the source of her disquiet.

"Oh, I think I have a notion," the Assistant Duty Manager nodded knowingly.

Faye flushed slightly, then paled with anger as her agile brain leapt to the most common reason boys often thought girls were glum or moody. As her eyes snapped up to his, she realised that his significant look wasn't aimed at her, but over her shoulder. Frowning, Faye turned in her seat and instantly noticed the presence of a detestable figure out in the mess hall. It was obvious that *no one* else wanted to be near him, because his was the only table in sight that still had empty spaces.

Faye had seen the strange magic-leeching boy, Cronuel, here and there around the Academy, normally under the stern eye of one instructor or another. They had yet to meet face to face formally, and the girl was determined to delay that as long as possible! She glowered in Cronuel's direction, unhappy by the fact that Zen had been right about Tryllia and Rythin allowing the boy to stay.

The force of his anti-power felt more... *muted*... at the moment, which was probably why Faye hadn't noticed the boy's presence out in the dining hall. She wondered if the Sorcerer's had found some sort of functional spell that helped to minimise the intensity of his magic-leeching curse.

"So, you feel it too, huh?" Faye asked softly, loathing clear in her young voice.

"Yup. Many do. We're all wondering what on earth the profs were thinking, allowing that thing to stay here," Ross agreed. Sighing heavily he rubbed the back of his neck. "It's like an itch that can't be scratched, or an angry ache that can't be soothed."

Faye nodded. Yes. The vortex that Cronuel produced was particularly unsettling. It seemed to affect the older students or those that had some level of magical gift, the most.

"Well, where else could they put him? With a power like that, the Seeker's and Sorcerer's probably want to keep an eye on him," Faye shrugged dejectedly.

"Yeah, you're probably ri... Hello?! What's this? Why would *they* sit with the great lummox?"

Faye turned again to peer at Cronuel and noticed that his near empty table had two more occupants. The girl was less than thrilled to see that Styrran, of all people, seemed to have struck up a friendship with the odd beast. The Gorgon-boy was chuckling at something the other said and was passing his new *friend* a book. They appeared quite cordial, as though this wasn't the first time they had spent break together.

Faye's gaze slid to the girl sitting next to Styrran and felt her stomach roil with a mixture of feelings. Hannah was sitting there, blonde curls carefully coiffed and vapid blue eyes gazing up at Styrran with something akin to admiration and possibly... *devotion*. The girl was crushing on him!

Faye had not directly crossed paths with Hannah since their admission to the Academy, and she now wondered if that was due to her own clever manoeuvring, or because Hannah was also avoiding *her*. The fact that Hannah was cosying up to Styrran had her deeply uneasy. Faye didn't like the idea of the enemy from her past joining forces with the enemy of her present, let alone if they were both in cahoots with a creature like Cronuel.

"That does *not* bode well," Faye murmured.

"I'll say. That girl is a right piece of work! And Styrran Isthmus isn't much better. I even asked for the two of them to be removed from my kitchen, but old Rythin won't hear of it." Ross shook his head in disgust. "Mooching layabouts, the both of them."

A clatter of dishes distracted the young man, and he hurried off into the kitchen, leaving Faye at the metal counter with her stack of recipe cards and a worried frown.

"Those three will bear watching," Zen murmured in her ear as it peeked out from beneath her hair, cautiously watching from between the glistening strands.

She noticed that his little claw was beginning to turn bronze in response to the distant whorl of anti-magic.

"I'll say!" Faye agreed whole-heartedly, wondering precisely what she was meant to do about this unexpected and unwelcome development. "Let's take these cards out into the kitchen gardens. We can put some distance between us and that *thing*."

The girl slid from her stool and scurried out the kitchens back door.

Classes were winding up as the first semester drew to a close, and mid-year examinations were completed. As far as she knew, Faye had aced every class. She'd even been given advanced standing in some subjects, so she could skip straight to the Level Two or Level

Three course the next semester, depending on her demonstrated ability.

Each course offered by the Academy consisted of set modules. Therefore, it didn't matter if you started at the beginning or halfway through the year – you simply continued the course until each module was complete. Some students even attended for just the one module each year, such as Tyrone and the Sorcery course. The girl remembered that the young Seeker had mentioned his study arrangement during their arduous trek through the Arythmun Mountains some months previously.

Faye would begin Level Two Healing, Level Three Language, Level Three History, and Level Three Mathematical Applications in the spring. All her other classes remained the same.

Weaponry had been, by far, her best subject this semester. Unfortunately, Master Sorwell refused to allow *any* recruit to skip stages. Those who studied the art of war were a rather methodical bunch.

Faye's worst subject, by far, was Sorcery. Her performance was adequate, but far below her ordinary standards. Of all the class, she had the best grasp of the theory part of the subject, but the practical side...

Faye took a deep breath as she plonked herself down on her stool in the front row of the Sorcery classroom during the final Charms lesson of the semester. Hanly had provided all of his students with a rhombic gem, its properties lending itself to magical spells. Faye glared at the inconspicuous translucent stone, feeling like a complete failure. She was only just mustering enough powers with magical charms to pass... If she concentrated *really* hard, then she could make the damned thing glow. But that was it!

Duncan could make illusions prance across his desk, and other students could create a tower of fire! All she could do was conjure a little fairy light! How useless!

"Chin up, young Faye!" Hanly encouraged, noting her sour expression while bustling about readying himself for the coming lesson. "Seeing as you can make even that small light in the first place means you *must* be magical by blood! And you're only young. Twelve is still an early age to master the conjuring of magic, particularly as this is your first experience with the subject! You've passed this semester, and that in itself is an accomplishment!"

Faye glanced up and frowned at the jovial Sorcerer, wondering how much he actually *knew* about her. Why was he being so encouraging and passing her based on this abysmal little flicker of power? She couldn't recall telling him anything about her lack of Sorcery knowledge and experience. Still, she supposed he might have an idea after observing her lack-lustre accomplishments this semester! Faye wondered if Thayrille *had* told Seeker Rythin about her non-Human mother. *If* she had, then it wasn't hard to imagine the next step was Rythin telling *all* her instructors that tidbit of information.

Faye didn't like being the subject of other people's conversations. It made her feel... Violated.

"Is there anything else, anything at all, that you think might aid your magics?" Hanly pressed, his light blue eyes piercing as though waiting for some big revelation.

Faye was loath to tell him about the pipe and its strange connection to the land's power, so mutely shook her head. Hanly sighed in disappointment before giving her another encouraging smile.

"Just keep doing what you're doing, then, young Faye. You'll get there eventually,"

He began the lesson as per usual, flicking one pudgy finger at the slate board so the notes for the lesson were transcribed rapidly across its surface in eerily glowing light. Faye set the glowing stone aside and hastily scribbled into her notebook, Zen buzzing soothingly at her neck.

Duncan cast her a sympathetic look before sending a shadowy outline of a blooming rose in her direction, his own rhombic crystal glittering with a cool black mist. Faye slapped her hand down onto her desk, instantly dissipating the smoky illusion and gave the youth a frosty glare. The Warlock snickered in amusement before returning to his own work, his lips kicked up in a small smile.

Faye rolled her eyes and paid extra close attention to the instructions on Charm Magic today, just as she did *every* practical lesson. It *still* didn't help her performance in Sorcery, though.

Fifday crept around and Faye sat in the mess hall at the end of one of the long battered wooden tables during the lunch hour. She was only half listening to Trish and Britt as they gossiped with Rory, most of her mind stewing over the coming lesson. She had double Sorcery next, and she was not looking forward to it. She had been drilled to the bone in Weaponry all week, mainly because it had been exam week and Sorwell had been testing all the recruits to within an inch of their lives. AND she had also been staying up late finishing final study tasks for all her subjects.

She was so bone-tired she could barely lift her fork to her mouth. Even Zen's warm vibration against her neck barely perked her up.

The vivacious, red-headed Britt stopped her inane chatter for a moment as she sipped her drink, then noticed Faye's despondent look. She petted the younger girl's arm consolingly.

"You could always beg off sick and nap in the medic ward. You truly do look ill," Britt suggested sympathetically.

Faye shook her head. As tempting as the idea sounded, she simply couldn't do it.

She had always attended every class to date. It was one of the things that allowed her to pass Sorcery – her supposed 'enthusiasm'. If Sorcerer Hanly even suspected that her illness was not genuine and concluded that she wasn't honestly trying her hardest, she would fail. And with Sorcery, there were no second chances.

If she failed, she risked having her scholarship withdrawn, and there was no way that she or Thayrille could afford the hefty fees associated with a non-scholarship enrolment at the Academy! The Healer was barely making ends meet as it was due to the sordid-minded Elders and villagers that kept short-changing her.

The general hubbub of the mess hall was interrupted by the clanging crash of the bell, tolling the end of their break and summoning students to their next lesson. It seemed incredibly loud, even with the surrounding din of the lunch meal. Groaning, Faye stiffly got to her feet and vaguely waved goodbye to her friends before lumbering back up the stairs. She was so relieved to reach the top she almost cried.

When she entered the Sorcery classroom, she stumped down to her usual place, her feet heavy with exhaustion. Duncan was already there, poised elegantly in the expected meditation pose on the mat next to hers. He cast her his usual silent, bored look – but by now, Faye knew him well enough to see the concern in his emerald eyes. She minutely shook her head and collapsed onto her cushy mat.

Sorcerer Hanly arrived soon after and hastily beckoned the latecomers to take their usual position. With great effort, Faye managed to fold her legs one over the other and rest her hands, palming them up on her knees – her thumb and forefinger lightly touching. She then straightened her spine. It was rather painful due to her aching ribs and their associated muscles, but she didn't complain – hoping the discomfort would keep her awake for the next two hours.

The room fell into a profound hush. Every rustle, every whisper ceased, replaced by an absolute silence that felt like being wrapped in a thick, suffocating blanket. Faye could feel her heart thrumming in her chest and could hear the pounding of her pulse in her ears.

Now, the real challenge would begin.

Stay awake, she chided herself sternly.

Faye tried to keep her mind focused, she truly did! She felt herself fall inwards, her sense of physical-self floating away into the oppressive silence of the room as she searched for that ephemeral place where her soul connected to the magical web of Pendalin. The heaviness of her limbs faded, and the muscle aches vanished. The sensation was similar to when a body were falling asleep at night, then jerked themselves awake as that weightless feeling caused a deep-seated panic. Only Faye was unable to jerk awake. The tether to her physical self was thin and precarious, leaving the girl adrift in this strange dream-like state. Zen was still warmly vibrating against her neck, making the softest of rhythmic clicking sounds in the back of its throat, and soon her mind was wandering strange paths.

In her mind's eye, she turned a corner and was ensconced by grey mist, surrounded by that vibrating clicking noise. Through the grey mist, she thought she heard a bird warble. She followed the sound curiously. The grey mist slowly turned a silvery green as she twisted and turned along the imagined path.

Suddenly her vision changed, and she had entered the clearing of the ruins of Galleymai, or somewhere very like it. Birds were singing, the sun was bright, and the entire world shimmered under a bright, silver sun.

And beneath it all was the music!

Sharp, soft, shrill, deep, soughing through the boughs of trees, tinkling through the creek bed. It was all around her, as if she could drink it through her skin, absorbing it into her soul. She felt so uplifted, so enlightened. The world made sense. She *understood* the magic and her place amongst it. She could feel her mother's pipe warming against her skin, eager to sound its ephemeral music once again.

Faye... a voice whispered, sounding close but far at the same time.

Faye! louder now.

Faye opened her eyes and looked about her with a slight frown. She was still at the Academy, and not in the meadow at all. The other students, including Duncan, had stopped their meditations and looked at her with either awe, disbelief, or fear. Sorcerer Hanly stood before her, a strange look in his eyes that she couldn't decipher.

That's enough, Faye. You're doing too much. Let it go.

She could see the Sorcerer's lips moving, but the words were distant, as though they were echoing down a vast tunnel. His eyes were no longer blue but that cheerful golden yellow particular to his power. But instead of appearing pleased that Faye had finally conjured what felt like a torrent of energy, he seemed genuinely worried and anxious.

Faye wondered why – she felt fantastic!

In her mind's eye, she could still see the meadow, the birds and the trees. In the distance, she could even see the grey, craggy mountains that surrounded Tryssdale. She could feel Zen's heartbeat and gentle clicking in both places, real and extrasensory. The lizard spoke directly into her mind.

The old man's right, Faye. Best not to overdo it, the sibilant voice whispered.

And, just like that, the mist began to fade and that other-worldly feel evaporated.

Faye's frown deepened. All the niggling aches and pains were gone from her body, and there was a slight buzzing in her head. She almost felt like she was going to faint!

"What happened?" she slurred, trying to focus on Hanly.

"You finally conjured your powers, but just a little more than I expected for your first time," Hanly replied softly, placing a steadying hand on her arm. "Perhaps you should lie down for a while and rest."

Faye nodded agreement, but even this was too much.

As her vision spiralled and her head raced, she felt herself fall back onto the mat and knew no more.

CHAPTER 20

FRIENDS ARE GREATER THAN FOES

With a start, Faye awoke. Darkness pressed in from all sides, and heavily starched sheets pinned her down to a firm bed. As her eyes adjusted, the girl noted the curtain-shrouded windows and the dull gleam of metallic furniture in a spacious room. Puzzled and panicking, she finally recognised a nearby medic trolley belonging to the day nurse. She had seen that very contraption during her Healing course, when she and the rest of the students had taken a tour and learned more about identifying and bandaging breaks, strains, and burns.

She knew where she was! The Infirmary!

Exhaling a shaky sigh, Faye rolled her head around in the opposite direction as a soft snort sounded nearby.

Mistress Tryllia!

The stout woman was sleeping soundly in the chair beside her bed. Groggy, Faye pushed herself up, shaking her head doggedly to clear the fog from her mind.

How on earth had she gotten here?

As she gained an upright position, a warm object slid from beneath her hair and slumped limply onto her lap. Faye felt a rush of relief as she recognised Zen's chunky form.

"About time you woke up!" the lizard grumbled softly.

"What happened?" Faye whispered, careful to keep her voice low so Tryllia wouldn't wake.

"You finally found your core – the place you can go to conjure magic. Only thing is, you immersed yourself right into the centre. It overwhelmed your physical self. You've been unconscious for over fifteen hours. They had to carry you here when they couldn't revive you in class. Well, I suppose passing out could have been due to your physical and mental exhaustion as well," Zen said reflectively, raising its rump into the air and stretching in a very cat-like fashion.

The lizard was nothing if not fair. Faye sighed, and then another thought occurred to her. She had conjured magic!

"What colour did I turn?" she asked, intensely curious.

The one thing she had noticed at the Academy these past months was that the various people of magical heritage had energy of specific colours, nominally representing their Fey clan. She knew Duncan's energy was purest black when he conjured. She supposed that was typical of a Warlock. Tryllia had glints of rose-lavender, which likely meant a Gorgon heritage. Hanly turned a Human-yellow and even Rythin, Faye reflected, had elements of green in his yellow power, indicating a Faerie heritage.

Zen snorted in amusement.

"What colour do you think? You turned silver. Same colour as your mist," the lizard replied.

Faye's excitement faded, replaced with a sense of foreboding.

"What does it mean then? What Fey clan turns *silver?*" she whispered in consternation, then paused as dread pooled in her stomach. "They know I'm half-Fey now."

Again, Zen snorted, this time in derision.

"Hardly. The Warlock already knew you were Fey. Hanly suspected but definitely knows now. The others? Pfft, they're ill-educated whelps who can't tell the time of day, let alone what it means to be Fey. They don't even know about colour significance!" Zen scathed.

"Oh," was all Faye could think to say. "So... What does silver mean, then?"

Seeing the look on Faye's face, Zen hurriedly cuddled up to the girl, nibbling affectionately on her fingers.

"Oh – I'm not too sure about that. No one at the academy has ever seen silver before," the lizard babbled, before changing the subject. "Now, colour conversion. I should have told you about the colours long ago but never found the time. You've always suspected that colours were important, though."

Faye nodded, slightly mollified.

"So, tell me now," she hissed.

"Well, any shade of black to pewter grey are those Warlocks, their shade dependent on the amount of Human in them. Pure white power belongs to the Elves. Violets are normally Gorgons in some capacity. Blues are Sprites. Greens are Faeries, Nyrads, and the like, spring green is Molvern. And yellows are Human Sorcerers," Zen informed her, confirming Faye's earlier assumptions.

"That would explain Styrran; he tends to turn a muddy purple colour. He probably has Gorgon blood in him. What about oranges and reds?" Faye asked, feeling as though it was significant that Zen hadn't told her about *those.*

"Oh, that's magical reptile colours. No chance of mingling with Humans, completely incompatible," Zen assured her, dismissing it instantly.

"I guess I should try to rest some more. Things'll be pretty hectic in the morning," Faye said after a few minutes of companionable silence as another wave of exhaustion rolled over her.

She had more questions, but she wanted to be more awake and aware when she got around to asking them. Even when Faye was settled in her covers and the lizard was curled up comfortably against her chest, sleep was still long in coming. It wasn't until the first rays of dawn lightened the room that Faye finally slipped into an uneasy slumber.

Faye woke again at midday, feeling thoroughly addled. Zen had vanished, and Tryllia was still doing her bedside vigil, though this time wide awake.

"How do you feel?" Tryllia asked kindly when Faye sat up, the worry fading from her face.

"Like I've been thrown by a horse," murmured Faye, rubbing her temples.

Tryllia made sympathetic noises as she rubbed Faye's back with an enormous yet elegant hand. Her nails were carefully manicured, and her long fingers were decorated with a various begemmed rings. Many glinted with stored power, making Faye wonder over the woman's magical skill. Was she an adept Sorceress as well as Academy Administrator? How had the girl not sensed this before?

"Here, drink this. Healer Merkin said it'll help," Tryllia murmured, handing Faye a steaming mug.

Faye gratefully sipped on the brew, noting the variety of herbs. It was the same stuff Thayrille had often made for her but spiced up with a sprig of spearmint. That painful pang of homesickness entered her chest again, causing her throat to tighten.

After she had drained the mug, Faye felt almost like her old self. With a bit of motherly assistance from Tryllia, Faye managed to dress and comb her hair. Then she was provided with a small plate of fruit, cheese, and biscuits. Famished, she polished off the entire thing, keenly aware of Zen's absence as she slowly ate the grapes. They were usually the lizard's favourite fruit!

"You must be feeling better, indeed!" Tryllia exclaimed with a smile, taking the empty plate.

Feeling far more balanced than she had in a while, Faye experimentally hopped off the bed and shuffled forward a few steps. Her muscles felt a little like jelly, but her balance was steady, and she no longer felt dizzy. She gave the hovering woman a confident smile.

"I'm alright, Mistress Tryllia. Promise,"

"Excellent. If you're feeling up to it, Seeker Rythin is wanting a word," Tryllia replied, indicating the Infirmary exit.

Faye took in another shaky breath, feeling nervous. Rythin wanting a word was tantamount to facing a firing squad! The girl wondered just how much trouble she was in. Was she to be expelled? Hidden away? Tortured and examined and experimented on to find out more about her mysterious unforeseen powers?

Faye had to stop her rambling mind from conjuring the most horrid of outcomes, figuring that *if* anything untoward was intended, then *surely* the Seekers and Sorcerers of the Academy wouldn't have left her in the Infirmary of all places, under the watchful eye of Tryllia?

The Housekeeper led Faye through the many corridors to Seeker Rythin's office, keeping a sedate pace that the girl could easily match. Before long, the pair entered the quiet corridor of the staff's private rooms. Rythin's heavy wooden door swung open as Faye approached and, much to her confusion, she was greeted by Sorcerer Hanly.

Puzzled, Faye entered the spacious study to find every chair filled. Rythin sat behind his desk, Hanly resumed his perch on a plush armchair, and Merkin was seated in another. Sorwell was even there, standing broodingly by the window, his towering form filling almost half the room, or at least it felt like it.

Uh-oh, was all Faye could think. Surely it wasn't a good sign when nearly *all* her instructors wished to meet with her? She suddenly wished Zen were here, vibrating comfortingly against her neck. But the lizard hadn't returned.

"Faye! Report!" barked Sorwell as he saw her, his relief evident on his face.

Automatically snapping to attention, Faye detailed her state of wellbeing in short terms.

"Well, Sir! No broken bones, no burns, cuts, or scrapes. Fit as a fiddle," Faye returned.

"Perhaps we can save the military tactics for the parade grounds, hmm?" commented Rythin with a rueful smile.

Faye managed a weak grin and sat in the proffered seat before the expansive desk.

"The brew worked well, I see," Merkin commented with one of her rare, faint smiles.

Faye nodded. She couldn't relax, though, despite their kindness and obvious concern. She felt that there was more to this meeting, which drove her to distraction.

"Alright, people, let's end the poor child's misery," Hanly interrupted, before Rythin could add another inane comment. "You're not in trouble, Faye. We just need to clarify events and come to some sort of arrangement."

Faye felt the tension inside her increase.

"So, it's finally been revealed that you are, in fact, half-Fey," Hanly continued with a measured, dark look at Rythin. "That means you are one powerful being and need to be trained correctly in a number of things."

Faye nodded hesitantly, unsure if she agreed with the 'powerful' part. To date, the best she could do was cause a crystal to flicker with light. And glowing silver, while impressive, was hardly evidence of some unfathomable magical energy... Was it?

"As such, Sorwell will be teaching you combative magic. Merkin will begin teaching you a Sorcerer's Healing. And as for Sorcery itself, I've decided to move you straight to Level Three," the portly man informed her cheerily.

"But what about Second Levels? Surely there are important things I still need to learn before I get to the Third?" Faye protested weakly.

Here she thought she'd either be kicked out, completely smothered and hidden away, or paraded about. It seemed life could go on as normal, even for a half-Fey.

"Not really, no. You see, Second Level is more for Sorcerers that aren't magic by blood. You know, the ones that need to work to draw their magical energies from Pendalin through meditation or jewels and such. Once they become adept at sourcing their own power, only *then* will they be allowed into the Level Three course. I have spent the first semester getting to know your cohort and what latent powers you all have. You, and a select few in your class that are magical by blood, will skip ahead because we don't need to teach you how to draw your power," Hanly explained.

"Well, there you have it, Faye. It's for your own good, child, so you don't hurt yourself. Your power is already inside you," Rythin added gently, his dark eyes kind. "Magic is often linked with emotion, which is why when some of us get scared or angry, we appear to shimmer with our inner energy. The stronger our powers, the more violent our reaction. That's why we must teach you how to control your powers, especially now that the dam has been breached. Your instructors will help you achieve that control. And don't try anything on your own; it could prove fatal."

Uneasy silence greeted this statement, and the girl understood how serious the advice was.

"So, do you know who your mother or father was?" Hanly asked expectantly, breaking the silence.

Faye shook her head. "None, sir. Thayrille only met my mother and said she had never seen anything like her before. And she never found any historical record indicating which Fey clan my mother came from," Faye explained heavily. "My mother didn't get a chance to tell her anything, except for my name, before she died."

After a moment of consideration, she reached inside her shirt and pulled out the pipe. With Zen's assistance, she had attached the slim instrument onto a plain leather thong, decorated with colourful beads so she could keep it with her always. It had become a comforting weight against her chest these past months, reminding her of her right to be here in this wonderous place despite the continued heckling of Styrran and those like him.

"My mother had this around her neck... that night," she whispered, hesitantly holding out the slim metal pipe, her eyes flicking watchfully from adult to adult.

Hanly examined the pipe closely and used a little magic to make the thing glow brightly. He nodded for a few moments, muttering to himself. Then he returned the pipe, and Faye found she could relax once more. The Sorcerer didn't seem that interested in keeping it.

"Fascinating," he frowned. "The carvings are slightly different from what we know. I don't speak Elvish fluently, but from what I know of the language, the script seems to be telling a story of some kind. Or providing a list of instructions."

"*Elvish*?!" Faye exclaimed, clutching the pipe to her chest in shock.

"Oh-ho, child! That doesn't mean you *are* Elven. Why, Elves haven't been seen in centuries. Many believe that they are extinct! It just means, in all likelihood, that your mother was pure Fey and had been gifted the pipe by someone of Elvish descent," Hanly said reassuringly.

Faye wondered if that were true. It couldn't explain how the pipe and land sung to her, or how she could read some of the carvings on the pipe. Uncertain, the girl decided to keep quiet about these latent talents. She was still unsure just exactly *how much* she could trust. Or *should* trust.

"Well, it's unlikely we will ever find out exactly what class of Fey you are, child. Or that your pipe will be deciphered," Rythin sighed sadly. "No-one in the known world still speaks Elvish."

Hanly reluctantly agreed.

"Alright, Faye. Attend classes as normal until the end of semester. I'll draw up a new timetable for you for the spring. Now, off with you," Rythin said briskly.

Faye sprung up from her chair, nodded politely at all her instructors, and then fled the room. There was no way she was waiting around for a second invitation.

Feeling drained and exhausted once more, Faye finally reached the sanctity of her room. The events of the past two days had depleted all her reserves – and Zen had still not returned! She had to admit worrying now. This was the longest they had ever been separated.

As the girl pushed open her bedroom door, Faye froze.

Sitting on her bed was Hannah. This was the *last* person Faye expected to see, sitting comfortably in her private room tucked away in the hidden alcove. Not for the first time, Faye cursed the meddlesome absence of locks on the dormitory doors!

Old emotions welled up at the sight of the arrogant face and snide blue eyes framed by blonde, artfully curled locks. Faye clearly remembered the sly snake tripping her up with that stick and squashing her into the ground with those hard booted feet. She also recalled the way Hannah squealed and screamed like a ninny when those bandits attacked them.

The girl could certainly dish it out, but she couldn't take it, Faye thought pugnaciously.

Renewed confidence flooded her veins, and Faye decided it was time to stand her ground. What could Hannah really *do* to her, anyway? Faye wasn't the same shy, uncertain waif as last summer.

"*There* you are!" Hannah gushed, a fake, dimpled smile stealing over her repugnant face.

Faye slowly entered the room but stayed near the door, still feeling distinctly uneasy. It was an unspoken code amongst the Academy students that one didn't enter another's room without permission. If you shared a room, it was expected that you cleared it with your dorm mates before inviting someone new. People often just saved each other angst and heartache by meeting their friends in the common rooms.

This was an essential part of Academy life, as there were no locks and so students relied on trust. No one, as far as Faye knew, had ever broken that trust.

It figured that Hannah would be the first.

When Faye remained silent, Hannah's fake smile faded a little.

"So, I heard you were called into a rather big meeting – Seekers, Sorcerers, Healers and the like," Hannah began, fishing for information.

Faye remained resolutely silent. She had an idea where Hannah had heard such a juicy tidbit of gossip. But why would *Styrran* care enough about her Sorcery mishap to tell *Hannah* about it? Why, for that matter, did Styrran think it mattered that Hannah knew *anything*? Hannah had no magical powers and was just another silly first year student in the scheme of things. How had the two even become friends in the first place, if that's even what they were?

Faye had the overwhelming instinct that it had to do with *her*. Hannah knew about Faye as they had both been raised in Grydin Village, and perhaps for his own reasons Styrran felt that Hannah's association with the small girl was interesting enough to make her acquaintance. It was a disturbing thought, and Faye wondered for a moment if she were placing too much emphasis on her own importance. Other than the continual heckling and unkind words, the Gorgon-boy had pretty much left her alone all year.

'A bully never does anything without careful thought and consideration.' Jack's words came back to her. *'Once someone has it in for ye, ye can never trust their actions or intentions. They plan for vengeance more oft' than not and are in it for the long haul.'*

Faye recalled the many conversations she had with the Forrester while growing up, valiantly trying to understand why Hannah and her sisters treated her the way they did, and why Jimmy perpetually, unrelentingly targeted her. Perhaps, just as Jack had said, Styrran was another bully who felt Faye had wronged him somehow by merely existing.

Suddenly, the girl wondered if Styrran's friendship with Cronuel was something morbid in the making. Having a partnership with such a beast would serve a bully well, particularly if the key to controlling those magic-leeching powers was ever mastered...

"Something to do with the kerfuffle you caused yesterday... an explosion, I heard!" Hannah pressed when the girl didn't answer.

"I didn't invite you in here," Faye responded, stealing her courage as she glanced pointedly at the open door, indicating that the other girl should leave.

Hannah's efforts at smiling altogether died at that point, and her normal derisive sneer reasserted itself.

"I don't *need* an invitation, brat. So, I'm guessing they've expelled you, then?" Hannah spat, some satisfaction in her voice.

Faye said nothing, just pushed the door open a little wider.

"Answer me, you parentless, demon-spawned harlot!" Hannah hissed when Faye was not forthcoming. Hannah stepped closer to Faye and grabbed the candlestick that sat on the small desk.

Faye had a flashback, recalling the time Hannah had been so overcome by rage she had reefed a rock out of a creek bed and attempted to brain her with it. Faye felt her mouth turn dry as she wondered if Hannah actually intended on beating her with that candlestick... This time Faye would have no choice but to defend herself. And that really *would* get her expelled!

"Better watch your words, whelp, before I knock them straight from your mouth!" snarled a voice from just outside the door, breaking the mounting tension.

Surprised, Faye glanced over her shoulder to find Varsity's familiar scarred face peering through the doorway, followed closely by Britt, Trish, Rory, Goreman and Krins. With his usual bored elegance, even Duncan was leaning against the corridor wall, casual except for the black misty power simmering around his emerald eyes.

Hannah just stared at them as her face went completely blank.

Faye swallowed a giggle. "Now, Hannah, it would be best if you left," Faye said, her voice serene but brokering no argument.

Faye was delighted to note that Hannah surreptitiously returned the candlestick to its place as though using the polished metal as a weapon had been the furthest thing from her mind. For the moment, at least, they had reached a stalemate.

The menacing crowd created a path, ominously silent as they waited for Hannah's decision. The girl cleared her throat but didn't say anything. Flushed and wary, she quickly walked out of the room, careful not to get too close to anyone. After she had vanished down the corridor, Trish let out an explosive breath.

"What a piece of work!" Trish exclaimed angrily, casting a disparaging look over her shoulder at Hannah's retreating back.

Varsity clenched her fists. Her ebony eyes held a perilous look. "Perhaps I should have knocked her one just to teach her a lesson," she growled.

"I'm glad you didn't. She's a bit of a spoilt princess and is only spouting that trash because she knows no better. The Elders from our village have said worse about me. And to me," Faye said quietly, an inexplicable spurt of sadness dampening her mood. "Hannah Rikton isn't worth being expelled over."

There were a chorus of protests as everyone crowded into her room, consoling her, and denying all possible insults to her person. Faye had to smile at them all, warmed right to the core by their friendship. She noticed one person who remained outside the room.

Duncan still leant against the corridor wall.

Their eyes met, and a silent communication passed between them. He had needed to see for himself that she was alright. Now, it seemed, he was satisfied, and Duncan once again retreated behind that aloof exterior. With an elegant nod, the boy pushed away from the wall and slipped down the empty hall, disappearing from view.

"What an odd fellow," Trish commented curiously, noticing Faye's line of sight.

Faye shrugged.

"Warlocks are like that," was all she said, keen to dismiss the idea of Duncan before Trish or Britt found the boy noteworthy enough to ask about him in their next game of Prude Poker. Faye, for a variety of reasons, was just not ready for that!

CHAPTER 21

RISE ABOVE A BULLY

Faye's friends stayed for a short while that evening, seeking reassurance that their smallest friend was alright and not actually expelled or injured. The girl gave that reassurance and told them a doctored version of her Sorcery lesson, and how she would now be enrolled into the Advanced class. They were mightily impressed and bid her goodnight when they noticed she was swaying on her feet.

As Faye lay in bed, drifting off, she felt the slight weight of Zen slip onto her chest. Faye was so relieved, and because she expected only evasive answers to any and all of her questions, she didn't bother to ask where the reptile had been all this time.

The lizard paused briefly during its nighttime ritual of circling until it found just the right spot to curl up on. Its tongue flicked in and out in agitation.

"That *girl* was here," the lizard hissed, clearly in a sour mood.

"Hannah? Yes. But Varsity and the others scared her off," Faye said sleepily.

"What did she want?" Zen demanded.

It sounded so defensive Faye was sure that if it were a cat, its fur would be standing on end.

"Oh, wild rumours are flying around about what happened in Sorcery. Seems that she thought I was expelled, and she wanted to make sure," the girl replied, stifling a yawn. "I'm pretty sure she's reporting everything she knows to Styrran. Although I really can't fathom why *he* even cares about me or my life."

"I could bite her for you. My fangs are poisonous, after all," Zen offered, menace lacing its voice. "Him, too, for that matter."

Faye snorted softly in amusement.

"Nay, lizard, you'd just get us both in trouble. Nearly everyone knows about you, and they would assume I set you on them if they were to wind up dead from some venomous bite," she chuckled. "That might be a bit of a giveaway, if you start acting like a magical familiar rather than a typical pet!"

As Faye seemed entirely good humoured about Hannah's visit, Zen had no choice but to let the matter go – reluctantly.

"You've grown up, Faye," Zen said after a minute of silence. "Hannah doesn't intimidate you anymore."

Faye smiled drowsily.

"She can't get at me without dire consequence, Zen," Faye mumbled as she drifted off to sleep. "You and all my friends... You'll all protect me."

Zen grinned at the truth in the statement.

"Zen?" Faye asked, just as she was falling asleep.

"Yes, dear one?" the lizard responded quietly, buzzing soothingly against her chest once more, some of its dark mood easing as its cool-scaled body warmed against her heart.

"Was my mother Elvish?" Faye asked. "They think her pipe is Elvish. But she didn't look anything like the pictures or descriptions in the history books, did she?"

"No, dear one, she didn't look like anything from a book. Who knows how she came by that pipe? Put it from your mind for now," the lizard said.

If Faye had bothered to open her eyes, she would have seen the look of chagrin on the lizard's face.

Faye enjoyed her last week of classes as exams were done and all study tasks were completed. The lessons themselves were more interesting discussions on more esoteric aspects of each course designed to help students think outside the box.

The only dampener to the experience was some of the stares and whispers that followed her. The rumours had begun about her being some sort of *natural sorceress*, whatever that meant.

The last Midwok of term saw Faye finishing up later than usual in her Healing class. With a grumble beneath her breath, the girl decided to stop by her room briefly to return her gear before heading down to a late dinner. As she navigated the spiralling steps and entered the dormitory common room, Faye frowned at the small crowd of cackling students filling up the space.

She usually would ignore their antics, but on this occasion, their many bodies were blocking her way to the corridor and her room beyond. Faye was about to squeeze through the first gap when the gale of laughter subsided, and she could hear a most unwelcome sound.

Hannah's voice was soaring above the heads of the other students, clearly reading something aloud that the gaggle of adolescent girls found hilarious.

"Oh, and there's this one, girls! *Dear Thayrille, I have to ask an awkward question, and I don't feel comfortable doing so with anyone here. My menses have yet to begin. Do you think the delay is normal? All the other girls have theirs already...*"

The next gale of laughter drowned out the rest of the sentence.

Faye froze, her cheeks flaming in humiliation. Hannah was reading *her private letters*! Aloud! To this group of unknown girls!

Why, in all blazing glory, did they even think it was *funny*?

Faye pushed through the crowd, silver power sparkling on her skin as she stomped to Hannah. The older girl was perched on an armchair, ruffling through all the draft letters Faye had written, but never sent. She was sorting through the neat script in order to find the most embarrassing details.

"Oh, and another... And this one is about a *boy*! Oh dear, the poor little poppet has so many *feelings*... Oh, Faye! Why, hello, poppet," Hannah's lips curled into a vindictive smile as she fanned herself with several sheets of paper.

The pilfered pages were stacked on a nearby lamp stand, the envelopes in shreds on the floor around Hannah's feet. The wilful damage inflamed Faye's anger.

"You've gone too far, Hannah Rikton," Faye hissed, stepping right up to the other girl so they were almost nose to nose, her eyes glinting silver.

"And what do you plan to do about it?" Hannah's chin set at a belligerent angle, despite the fear deep in her eyes.

The girl was trying to bait her! To get a reaction! And Faye could think of only *one* person devious enough to use a twit like Hannah, to illicit a violent response from a newly anointed so-called *natural sorceress*.

Cool it! Zen's voice hissed through her brain, the unfamiliar sensation of their telepathic connection startling the girl enough that she was able to slip away from the sharpest edge of her rage.

The little lizard had its claws dug hard into her shoulder, and undoubtedly the girl would have bleeding puncture wounds as a result!

Faye's mind raced and whirled as it simultaneously tried to think clearly, despite the anger simmering in her veins, while adjusting to the sensation of Zen in her brain. Faye recalled how the two of them had been joined like this once before, that day she had unexpectedly tapped into her silver power. The lizard had somehow linked its consciousness with hers, assisting the girl to let go of her magic and return to her physical body before passing out. Now that bridge had formed, it seemed, it was relatively easy to reactivate this link between them. What a handy trick...

If you snap and attack another student with your powers, no matter the provocation, then there will be serious consequences. Potentially even expulsion. Or worse! Zen warned her urgently as it vibrated harshly against her neck.

Yes. That was very much a disastrous *Styrran*-type plan. To have Faye attack Hannah in a fit of rage, leading either to her expulsion or imprisonment... The girl was beginning to understand the long-term game plan that Styrran was playing at. His association with Hannah had always seemed inexplicable, but now...

Faye blinked rapidly as she fought for control, then snatched the remaining papers from Hannah's hand. With deliberate motions, Faye gathered up the stack that had already been rifled through, clutching the precious messages to her chest. Writing letters to Thayrille had been cathartic for the young, homesick child. Having her worst enemy *read* the things aloud for the entertainment of other sordid minded *cretins* was beyond humiliating.

"I'm reporting you to Rythin. You've snuck into my room without permission and *stolen* my personal property. These envelopes were clearly *not* addressed to *you*," Faye snapped, grateful that her little lizard companion was vibrating against her neck and preventing her from launching into a full-blown rage.

Panicked, Hannah reached out to snatch at her arm, desperately trying to elicit a physical confrontation one way or another. Only, she jerked her hand back with a pained shriek on contact.

"You burned me! She *burned* me! Did you see? With her powers, she *deliberately* burned me!" The girl wailed, cradling her right hand to her chest.

Faye glanced back at Hannah and saw the raw blisters forming on her hand.

"Good. A lesson to you to *never* touch me!" Faye snapped with zero sympathy. "Not ever again, Hannah Rikton."

With that, Faye stalked back to the stairs and took herself straight up to Rythin's study. He was her Mentor, and he would surely do *something* about this gross breach of privacy!

Faye really had to work out a better way to safeguard her room!

When she arrived to Rythin's office, he listened earnestly to her report on Hannah's actions and assured the upset young girl that the situation would be dealt with seriously during Midwinter break.

And that, Faye tried to convince herself, *would have to be good enough*.

The last week of semester sped by, and soon Faye was on a month's holiday. The days were easy, with no classes scheduled or study tasks to complete. Sorwell still expected his Weaponry students to show but relented enough to allow them a sleep-in

— roll call postponed until seven. The days became frosty, yet this northern land didn't experience snow like the Arythmun Mountains.

Faye missed the deep drifts, snow sculptures and other fun she could partake in back home in Grydin. Specifically, she missed the surreal beauty of the Grotto and the opportunity to swim for hours to escape the winter chill. Most of all, she missed the lazy winter days learning with Jack and Thayrille. The quiet cottage and forests of Grydin seemed like an entire world away.

Nevertheless, Faye enjoyed this time immensely, for she and her friends had races on horseback, they played tag, relay, and many other fitness games. She was able to meet Duncan regularly in the library, and they often wiled away an hour or two discussing some text or other they had each read. He was an intelligent companion with a sharp sense of humour and dry wit. Faye was pleased to find he was also filled with all sorts of fantastic knowledge about the Academy, its history, and the Fey Clans of Pendalin. Sadly, the youth didn't know much about silver power... only that it wasn't of Warlock origin.

Faye was shocked to discover that Midwinter was suddenly upon them, as was her thirteenth birthday. The girl felt no different yet somehow had graduated into that mysterious category known as *adolescence*.

"What do you think, Zen? Do I look any different?" Faye peered at her reflection in the small bedroom mirror. Her hair was as riotous and blonde as always, those same stormy blue eyes staring back. Her face was pixie-like and pale, just as it had been at the beginning of the school year. She didn't *look* any older, she was sure.

"You look lovely, dear one. Just as you should," Zen replied lazily from its position on the bed.

"I've always thought that once I was thirteen... I don't know... I'd grow quite a bit? Or maybe fill out? I'm still as skinny as I've always been," she sighed in disappointment. "And I *still* don't have my menses! You'd think turning thirteen would do *something*, wouldn't you?"

"What's that, Faye? When did you turn thirteen?" a voice demanded from her doorway.

Faye's eyes jerked around to peer at the voluptuous young woman filling the archway. The door had obviously been left ajar for the older girl to sneak up on her like that!

Faye's eyes trailed compulsively over Trish's robust figure, a feeling of dull resignation filling her chest. Trish had already turned sixteen and was far and beyond what one would term a *womanly* figure. Faye doubted she would *ever* look like that!

"Oh, umm, today, as a matter of fact," Faye mumbled, flushing pink as she realised she was staring.

She hadn't revealed her birthday to any of her friends, wanting to avoid the riotous celebrations that seemed to accompany such an event.

"And you never *told* us?!" Britt chimed in over Trish's shoulder.

Oh, great! There was *more* of them!

It seemed the Weaponry girls had wandered over to Faye's room, probably curious as to why the girl hadn't appeared at breakfast yet.

"I didn't want to make a big deal out of it," Faye shrugged self-consciously.

Thayrille had never made a big to-do on any of her previous birthdays, and the girl felt it would be... *unfaithful*... to celebrate herself heartily now that she was in another place.

"Oh, I don't think so, kiddo! It's your birthday, and we're going to celebrate! Grab the lizard, and let's get going! To Tryssdale!"

Trish hustled Faye to her closet and snatched up a winter jacket and her leather boots.

"Oooh, shopping trip!" Britt enthused. "I'll go get my things!"

Before Faye knew it, the three of them and several other Weaponry girls were bundled up against the bitter cold and trudging down the icy cobbled path to Tryssdale City. Their group was laughing heartily, swapping jokes and friendly insults as they swarmed down the twisting narrow streets.

"You know I don't have any money," Faye tried to feebly protest, still trying to find a way out of this predicament.

"Oh, puh-*lease*!" Britt exclaimed, her cheeks rosy in the cold air and her eyes snapping excitedly. "It's your *birthday*! *You* don't spend a *dime*."

And so it proved. Faye was hustled into shop after shop, forced into that dress, or this top, tried on that necklace and this ring, and ended up flaring silver in protest of getting her ears pierced. Trish and Britt reluctantly relented, only because the Alchemist stared bug-eyed at the silver girl.

By the end of the trip, Faye had a completely new formal outfit and matching shoes gifted to her by her overtly cheerful friends.

"What, exactly, is the *point* of them?" Faye asked doubtfully as she carried the variety of bags back up to the Academy after having shared lunch and a hot cocoa with the girls.

"Well, now that you actually own a dress, you have something to wear to the Midwinter Graduation Ball!" Trish said brightly, causing Faye to blanch in horror.

"You expect me to *wear* this thing? To a ball?"

"Of course! You weren't planning on wearing those leather breeches and cotton shirt, were you?" Britt rolled her eyes, clearly thinking she was being funny.

Faye clenched her teeth shut against a caustic reply. The young girl hadn't planned on *going* to the ball in the first place!

Yet, two nights later, her hair was brushed and tied up in a bun, and Britt even knotted a pretty bow around it. Faye wriggled her way into the nonsensical blue gingham gown the girls had chosen and scowled at her reflection.

She felt that she had never looked so much like a *girl*!

Zen snickered from the bed, its rainbow form sparkling with amusement.

"Shut up, you! Or I'll tie a matching bow around *your* neck!" Faye threatened.

Zen quickly fell silent, gazing at her reproachfully.

"You've never worn a dress," The lizard said critically. "And that one suits you quite well."

"I wear nightgowns all the time," Faye retorted, fussing with her neckline.

The dress was a pearlescent blue that complemented her pale skin and blue-grey eyes, with a boxed neckline that highlighted her defined collarbones. The skirt flared out in several layers, some of which sported *frills*. The dress was sweet, innocent, *girly*...

"I suppose it is only once a year," Faye mused, flopping down onto the bed next to Zen.

The lizard scampered up her arm and nested around her neck. It looked strange, in the mirror, because Zen was usually hidden beneath her tangle of blonde hair.

"There's the summer graduation, though," the lizard reminded her with an evil smirk.

Faye groaned despairingly.

"I'm having Tryllia find me a decorative vest and black trousers – that should be good enough!"

Zen laughed softly as Faye shrugged its cool body off her shoulders, stood up and stalked out the door, impatient to have the evening over with. The lizard chose to remain in their room, content to spend the hours doing goodness-knows-what. Once more, Faye wondered about what Zen got up to when they weren't together. Surely the little lizard didn't just *sleep* all the time?

Faye already knew that Zen could camouflage itself and scurry around the Academy as it wished, just like it had the first day when it had found her during that panic attack in the mess hall. She also wondered why these pointed questions only ever gained clarity in her mind when they were apart. The moment Zen was back around her neck, vibrating in that soporific way it had, all these pertinent queries just seemed to *melt* away.

Faye dismissed the nagging unease as she stomped into the common room at the end of the hall. Some of her friends were already waiting there, chatting and laughing. They crowed and wolf-whistled when they saw the petite, delicate girl dressed up so prettily.

"You look like a candy wrapper!" Goreman said loudly, grinning wickedly.

Faye snarled. "I can still take you, Goreman!"

The boy burst out laughing, as did many others.

"You look hilariously cute, all angry in that outfit!" Britt cackled, her red hair done in an elegant twist and her trim form clad in a lovely green gown.

Faye was about to turn tail and march straight back to her room when Trish grabbed her arm.

"Come now, just this once wear a dress. I promise next graduation, you won't have to," Trish pleaded, looking extremely pretty herself in a wispy pink layered skirt and matching blouse. "You really do look beautiful, Faye. Quite elegant, in fact."

Faye looked up into her friend's warm eyes, accepting the compliment with the minimum churlishness. Drawing a deep, calming breath, Faye relented. Trish had been her first friend and had steadfastly supported her since her arrival at the Academy.

For no one else but Trish would Faye suffer the indignity of wearing this ridiculous dress!

Despite her self-consciousness, the evening was highly enjoyable, and Faye was asked to dance by a variety of boys. Ross, Krins, Goreman and Shamson came again and again. They found it hilarious to lift and twirl the tiny child around so easily.

Some of the first-year boys even attempted some bad flirting, finally seeing her in a different light. Needless to say, Faye shot them down with a few well-placed, acrid comments, determined not to let them become romantic ninnies! They were friends, and she wanted nothing more!

Faye often joined in gales of laughter and animated discussions with some of her other acquaintances across her various subjects and was delighted to spend time with her various instructors outside of the classroom setting. Professor Rambert was in fine form, sharing his classical rambling stories with anyone who would listen.

Faye was also decidedly thankful that she saw neither Styrran nor Hannah in attendance. The girl didn't know *what* she would do if confronted by either of them! Especially without Zen's soothing vibration keeping her calm.

Faye had a wonderful time despite the confining outfit, and she felt safe for the first time in her short life. Accepted. *Normal.*

Reflecting back on her childhood in Grydin, Faye realised that until this moment she had only ever felt out of place – an outcast. But now, surrounded as she was by her diverse group of friends, the girl finally felt like she belonged.

It was a fabulous feeling.

At the end of the evening, Faye was saddened to realise that Duncan had been the only one that had not appeared. She wondered if he even attended these things – she couldn't imagine his aloof, haughty figure swinging around the dance floor or clapping raucously as the graduates were presented with their diplomas.

The final surprise of the evening was the sudden appearance of a large quiet-spoken boy she had last seen several months before.

"Hullo, Faye," Jeremy smiled shyly, approaching her by the drinks table. The girl had taken a break from the festivities to grab a goblet full of punch.

Faye's head jerked up, astounded to see the smartly dressed youth peering down at her with a sheepish gaze.

"Jeremy Bloomsbry!" she gasped in surprise, overcome by uncertainty as she stood facing him. "Um, how are you?"

Why was he talking to her? Was he after information, just like Hannah? Had Styrran befriended him, too? Her wariness felt justified, yet Faye decided it was misplaced as she noted the boy's awkward shuffle from foot to foot and how his cheeks were tinted pink in embarrassment.

"Oh, I'm good, I guess. Been busy. You've been busy, too, I suspect. I haven't seen you in my classes and I kinda missed... I mean, it was okay travelling with you on the way here. You're alright by me. You know?" Jeremy offered shyly, struggling to express himself. "What I meant to say is... I've been wanting to tell you for *ages*..." Jeremy sighed heavily and ran one large hand through his short bristly hair. "I'm sorry." Talking about emotions and feelings was just as awkward for Jeremy as it was for Faye it seemed!

Faye blinked owlishly up at him, wondering if he was apologising for his stuttering speech or saying *sorry* for a different reason.

"I... Umm... Okay," Faye managed awkwardly.

The boy's face lit up in a relieved grin. Apparently, he was under the mistaken impression that she automatically had understood his bumbling speech and had accepted his stilted apology.

"I really didn't know you were a girl, that day. And I'm sorry I laid into you. And I'm sorry I didn't try harder to be friends after. You always seemed to never be around whenever I had a moment. I used to pop by the Healer's cottage every now and then to see if you were free after your lessons, but you were never there. Master Jack would tell me to look for you in your tree house, but I could never quite find the courage. And I'm none too good with heights, so I couldn't exactly climb up after you, anyway," the boy shrugged self-consciously as he found his words.

"Anyway, what I'm trying to say, is if it's alright by you, I thought we could be friends. I spent that whole trip here trying to work up the nerve to say that, but never could. Then we were in different classes, and I haven't seen you since..."

Faye felt a slow grin break out over her face as the boy trailed off and shrugged, finally running out of things to say.

"Of course we can, Jeremy! I'd like that," she beamed at him, her heart thrilled by this sudden development.

She was stunned to think that if she had only stopped running off to hide in the forest, she could have had a friend in Grydin! All this time! She had never known that he had so awkwardly been trying to make friends. Jack had certainly never mentioned that the boy had tried to seek her out a time or two!

Well, the girl thought to herself, *better late than never*!

"You're not... You're not too worried about what Hannah will think?" Faye asked hesitantly as they stood side by side companionably sipping their goblets of punch.

"Pfft, no! I avoid that self-centred bi... Uh, *brat*, as much as possible," Jeremy returned, flushing when he almost let a swear slip out.

"Good. She's bad news, as I'm sure you've realised."

Jeremy nodded. "That I do! I've known it since we were all in diapers. She's been expelled, you know. Her admission was withdrawn, and the professors packed her up and sent her back home." There was a note of satisfaction in Jeremy's voice as he revealed this most juicy piece of gossip. "Serves her right, really. I heard there was a bit of blow up when her father had to come collect her."

Faye stared at Jeremy, stunned. She couldn't believe it!

She was satisfied by this news. Hannah had it coming, and just as Jeremy said, it served her right!

Faye spent a little longer talking with the stolid boy before Trish appeared at her elbow, her dark eyes raking him over with a particular light.

"Faye, why, who is *this* handsome fellow?" the older girl asked.

Jeremy flushed pink and muttered a vague *hello* beneath his breath, awkwardly tugging at the collar of his dress shirt.

"Oh, right. Trish, Jeremy. Jeremy, Trish," Faye offered, curiously eyeing her friend.

The older girl hadn't really shown an interest in getting to know any of the boys outside of weaponry, and it seemed odd that Trish would make the deliberate attempt to introduce herself just because Faye was talking to the boy now.

"I don't suppose you know how to dance, Jeremy?" Trish asked with an expectant gleam still in her dark eyes.

"Oh, umm, yes, actually. I can turn a step or two." Jeremy had turned from pink to brick red, but to Faye's surprise he readily took the older girl's arm and led her onto the dance floor.

He instantly caught the beat of the music and began to twirl Trish in time, elegantly gliding around the centre of the room.

Since when did Jeremy know how to *dance*? Faye wondered in amazement. It would seem there was much she didn't know about this boy.

Faye clapped along with the others rimming the dance floor before she was scooped up, yet again, by Krins for another dance.

The evening ended later than Faye normally stayed up, and she fell into bed afterwards, completely exhausted. Even Zen didn't try to make conversation, but curled up beside her, instantly snoring softly.

CHAPTER 22

LITTLE PHOENIX

Before Faye knew it, the holiday had passed, and it was time to resume classes. Once more, the girl had a meeting with Seeker Rythin. The day before the spring semester began, Faye sat before his desk, studiously examining her timetable.

She frowned. It was far more confusing than her first timetable had been. She had Weaponry at virtually the same time each day. However, her other classes seemed to be all over the place, with almost half the theory ones notated with a small 'PS'. There were also many more blank spaces where no classes fell.

"What does this mean, again?" Faye asked Rythin, pointing at the small notation.

She had a feeling he had told her previously, in an off-handed way, but she couldn't quite recall...

"Private Study," Rythin replied succinctly. "Now that you're doing a combination of courses at three different Levels, there are bound to be some clashes. Your practical courses, Healing, Sorcery, and Weaponry have been given preference. The others though, will need to be caught up on in those private study blocks. As your instructors will inform you, you will only be able to complete some of the Modules due to the sheer number of clashes."

Faye frowned, trying to get her head around it.

"Never fear, child. It just means you'll take the course over a longer period, perhaps two or three years instead of one. You'll still have finished everything by the time you're fifteen. It's quite an achievement, in fact," he said with an encouraging grin. "Very much like somebody else we both know!"

Faye sighed, nodding. She could deal with that. After all, Thayrille had managed it back in her day, and Faye had often looked up to the Healer as an educational role model.

Her first Third Level Sorcery lesson was a revelation, though. As was the fact that this particular stage of education extended over three years.

When she arrived in class and resumed her usual place in the front row, Faye was surprised to discover that Duncan was already there. The girl glanced at him, momentarily thinking she had mixed up her schedule and had come to the wrong class. The amused look in Duncan's eye told her that he knew what she was thinking, and that she was wrong.

She raised one eyebrow as if to say, *'Oh really?'*

The brief incline of his head said, *'Oh, yes indeed madam, you be not the only talented one here.'*

Her slight toss of hair replied, *'Humph, we shall see.'*

Then, his lips tilted slightly, and the smallest crinkle appeared around his eyes, which told her he was internally cracking up laughing. Their silent conversations were very strange indeed and indecipherable to any other person, but the two understood each other perfectly.

Sorcerer Hanly entered the room soon after, his jovial face beaming at them.

"Gather around, all!" he called cheerily. "No need for anyone to lurk up the back. Plenty of space down here!"

Faye glanced up and noticed the two students lurking along the back row. The shadowed two reluctantly gathered their things, trudged down to the first and second rows, and sat unhappily in the only two remaining seats.

Faye was dismayed to see Styrran was one of them, but she kept her expression neutral. No need for the boy to realise how much his presence discomfited her!

"Ahh, better! Now, class, let's welcome our new arrivals – Duncan, Faye, Styrran, and Gerty," the Sorcerer announced.

The rest of the class nodded their heads in greeting.

As the lesson proceeded, it seemed that unlike First Level Sorcery, these people were able to laugh at themselves and enjoy good humour. It was a far more relaxed atmosphere, exactly as Faye had always felt Hanly's classes should be. It could also have something to do with the average age of the class. Most others here were at least eighteen years or older!

"Now, forgive me as I briefly explain things to our new members," Hanly said graciously, nodding at his old – and older – students. "You are about to embark on a three-year course in advanced Sorcery that requires complete dedication."

Faye noticed that Styrran started at this news. No one had told him either, and he didn't look very happy by the news.

"Your performance will depend on your natural talent and your ingenuity," Hanly continued. "The content will be presented as individual modules, and you must master each skill before moving on to the next. You all have natural talent and can access the magical energies of Pendalin. As such, your performance will depend on your commitment and creativity. As young Faye here discovered, not so long ago, if you persevere long and hard enough, you often come out with the results you need."

Faye felt herself flush. It would be common knowledge by now of her Fey heritage. She still felt shy and uncomfortable about strangers knowing.

The lessons from then on were just as tricky as those from the previous semester. The difference was that each lesson was highly detailed about one element of Sorcery. Faye had to learn to channel small wisps of her energy and incorporate that power into set spells, which was far more challenging than simply plunging into the torrent of silver magic.

The first module they undertook for the semester was 'illusion weaving', which drew on her ability to conjure magic through meditation and feed it through a lens, such as a rhombic crystal – akin to their lesson last semester. Faye was unsure of how her performance would be affected, considering the previous foray into her 'inner soul', but Hanly had every confidence she could control it this time. As it turned out, he was absolutely right.

Since the barrier was breached, Faye could easily find the well of magic inside of her. It was a bubbling silver stream, chuckling gently deep within her chest. As she wasn't dead tired, and knew the dangers, Faye was able to tease out a small strand and carefully channel the power as needed. It was exhausting work but worthwhile.

All in all, Sorcery soon became her best, and favourite, subject.

Faye's first Weaponry class of the semester also stored one small surprise – Jeremy had been accepted into Weaponry!

During their warm-up, which consisted of one of the many obstacle courses that circled the training grounds, Faye managed to find a few moments to speak with him. She hadn't seen much of him since the Midwinter Graduation Ball but was determined to take him up on his offer of friendship.

"So, you're going to be a Forrester?" Faye asked with a friendly smile.

Jeremy nodded, as they swung together over a set of monkey bars, then scrabbled swiftly down the opposite support pole.

"Yeah!" Jeremy panted in reply, his breath creating white blooms in the chill air. "Master Sorwell approved me after an interview and a small test."

Faye was silent for a moment, thinking how *she* had never been tested by Sorwell – she had just turned up! The girl easily clambered over the next obstacle from long practice.

"How... how can you... keep up... with the... pace?" Jeremy panted, noticing Faye's lack of sweat and steady breath.

"I've been doing Weaponry since the beginning of the year, so I'm used to it," she replied casually.

Jeremy startled and missed the next hand hold on the wooden wall they were scaling. He almost fell, but Faye's hand snatched out and caught his shirt with surprising strength. After a moment, Jeremy regained his grip.

"So *that's* why you weren't in the beginner classes!" Jeremy exclaimed, pausing in surprise. "Hannah and me, we thought it was because you had to attend a more junior school first, because you're so little." Jeremy was red faced as he began to climb once more. "Sorry. I know that seems stupid. I saw Rythin test you back home in Grydin. You knew things I had no idea about! *And* you took out that bandit by yourself. Of course you wouldn't have had to do beginner classes. I really don't know why I thought you did."

"Is that why Hannah left me alone all that time? Even though I kicked your butts in Selection, she honestly thought I was in some junior school, and she felt oh-so-superior again?" Faye asked with a frown, her voice stern.

Jeremy flushed further beneath his already red face.

"I... maybe... I suppose... I don't know," the boy stuttered, looking upset.

Jeremy had assured her that he didn't give any credence to Hannah or her vile opinions, yet here was a prime example of his being led by the girl's backward views. Again!

Faye shook her head ruefully.

"I'm not angry with *you*, Jeremy," Faye sighed. "Hannah and I have never gotten along. It just explains a lot. Like why she hadn't approached me until the very end of last semester when she heard that I was actually enrolled in Sorcery – due to that... mishap."

Jeremy nodded.

"Um, yeah. I heard about that. I thought, you know, maybe you just did Sorcery because you *do* have some sort of strange magical powers – which would explain why everyone back in Grydin thinks..." he trailed off, face now permanently splotched shades of red and purple in embarrassment.

"What? Think that I'm a hell-spawned demon set on sucking the souls out of newborn children?" Faye quipped, rolling her eyes.

Jeremy shrugged shamefacedly, unwilling to continue digging the hole he'd suddenly found himself in.

"Enough conversation and more action!" bellowed Sorwell from nearby, his towering copper form gleaming in the early light.

Faye leapt into action automatically and chuckled as Jeremy gave an exhausted groan.

Maybe a few more lessons being ground into the dirt would help the boy recover his common sense!

The lesson progressed and Faye found, to her confusion, that Sorwell began to explicitly teach moves in swordplay – unlike the all-in sparring Faye had done the previous semester. As students paired up for practice, Faye noticed that not all the old faces were present. There were some more fresh faces, too, besides Jeremy's.

Varsity paired her, so that they could each get a workout without having to practice the moves with the newer students.

"What's going on? Why is Sorwell taking things so slow?" Faye asked the older girl in confusion. "Where are the other girls?"

She and Varsity had gotten to know each other quite well these past months, as they continued to meet up every Resday for a good two-hour sparring session out beyond the Weaponry Shed. Faye noticed that Varsity was conspicuously the only female recruit from their last semester cohort present today!

"Yeah, I know," the tall girl answered Faye's question moments before Sorwell called 'go'. "It's like this every spring session. You were kind of enrolled backwards, but you're not the only one to do so. See, Autumn Semester is when new recruits are usually doing their beginner classes, so the Weaponry course starts now, in Spring Semester. The other girls weren't asked to volunteer in the mornings. They'll be doing their second Levels later today..."

Sorwell's command boomed over the training grounds, cutting short the conversation. Faye and Varsity circled each other warily, no longer so sure of themselves that they would blindly attack. Faye, not known for her incautious actions, leapt at Varsity suddenly hoping to surprise her.

No such luck!

The fight was on, and for the next ten minutes, the girls whirled and twirled, slashing, stabbing and slicing at each other with their wooden swords. The new recruits stopped their own hesitant sparring to watch, jaws open. They had never seen such a lethal, elegant dance!

Sorwell noticed his new recruit's lack of attention but decided to allow them to watch. Some of the cockier young men would then understand that girls really could fight. A valuable life lesson, particularly if those boys grew to become Seekers, Forresters, Guardsmen, or Constables.

At the end of ten minutes, Sorwell bellowed "TIME!" and the girls parted swiftly, while the new recruits jumped in shock. Varsity grinned at Faye, and they clapped hands companionably.

"Rotate!" Sorwell now boomed, alternating partners swiftly.

Faye was paired with a new boy, who was one half a head taller than she was. He looked nervous and was sweating lightly, his damp brown hair clinging to his forehead.

Faye felt a spurt of compassion.

"Don't worry, I'll go easy," she said kindly, giving him a reassuring smile.

The boy nodded briefly but still looked worried.

When Sorwell yelled "Go!" the panicked boy sprang into action and began slashing his sword all over the place without rhyme or reason. He had already forgotten the drills he'd been taught. Faye caught his sword with her own, disarming him instantly. The boy looked like he was about to cry. She retrieved the wooden sword quickly, handing it back to him.

"Okay, follow my lead," Faye murmured, holding the boy's eyes calmly.

He nodded, meeting the delicate girl's steady look, and calmed down with several deep shuddering breaths.

"Forward thrust, high arc, right side thrust, low arc, left side thrust..." Faye began to intone, repeating the sequence of moves they had been taught that morning.

The boy calmed down further, concentrating on Faye's rhythmic voice. Within moments, they were sparring carefully, circling slowly the entire time.

"TIME!" Sorwell bellowed.

Faye found she had even broken a sweat, due to the repetitive motions of sequence-work. She had forgotten how demanding it could be!

The recruits rotated on Sorwell's signal, and Faye partnered with another nervous new male recruit and briefly wondered about the fact that few girls opted for Weaponry. Before their next sparring session began, Faye informed the boy of the sequence she intended to practice with him. The boy nodded, gripping his sword tighter with sweaty hands.

Then they began. This boy was a bit more talented than the other, so Faye diced up the routine, adding a few more challenging moves. The boy adapted readily, and Faye continued adding moves until they were almost sparring.

Before she knew it, time was called again, and Faye was breathing hard and sweating. After stretching, Faye went to hit the showers when Sorwell called her over.

"Nice work, Recruit! You seem to have a knack for teaching the new students," Sorwell said, his voice still slightly booming, his golden eyes sizing her up with an approving look.

"Thank you, Sir!" Faye replied. "It's actually a better work-out than I realised, Sir."

Sorwell laughed in his uproarious way. "It is at that, recruit! Now, hit the showers!" he thundered.

Faye nodded and jogged towards the Shed.

Sorwell was often sparing in his praise, so Faye felt incredibly proud of her performance that day. The copper-haired giant seemed proud of it too, because from then on, Faye was only allowed one good practice session with the senior volunteers like Varsity, Krins or Goreman before she was put to work tutoring new recruits.

Faye didn't mind — it helped her recall some simpler techniques. She felt it even helped improve her own fighting skills.

Every Resday, as agreed upon, Faye met Varsity at the Shed and continued to practice with the staff. It was getting trickier, however, to slip away from any number of her other friends, especially when they did their best to waylay her on those mornings. Trish, in particular, began the habit of haunting the mess hall so she could catch Faye at the very end of her Kitchen Duty.

On this particular Resday, it was Varsity who found her, a disgruntled look on her face.

"Sorry, Faye, I have to skip out on training today," the older girl grumbled in aggravation. "I've an appointment in town. I'll see you later."

With that, Varsity disappeared, leaving Faye behind to blink after her in confusion. She wondered briefly what sort of appointment Varsity might have that couldn't wait? It was Resday, after all. Who made appointments on Resday, anyway? By tradition, most places were closed except those catering to tourists.

The girl had little time to ponder, though, as Ross came about and engaged her in a debate on whether to add coriander to a spicy beef salad or not. Once Faye was able to escape the kitchens, she collected her sparring staff and headed down to the Shed, despite having no Varsity to partner with.

If nothing else, she could run through the drills to work out the kinks in her own muscles.

With a change of clothes, hair tied back, and Zen happily snoozing in the recesses of the Weaponry Shed, Faye let herself out into the sandy area on the far side. Its surface reminded the girl of the deep canyons she and Jack used to practice in.

For a moment, Faye closed her eyes to fight back tears, deeply missing the burly man. Perhaps she should send *him* a letter. There were so many things she felt far more comfortable telling the kind Forrester than her foster mother. But no. She *had* to send a letter to Thayrille *before* sending one to Jack.

It was only right.

Faye pushed those nuisance thoughts and feelings out of her head and heart, determined to continue with her usual routine. She was part way through her first round of warmup drills with her staff when she was rudely interrupted.

"What on *earth* are you *doing*?" Britt's voice burst out.

"Britt! Shut up, for the Gods' Sake, woman!" Goreman hissed from nearby.

"Oh, great! You just had to blow our cover, didn't you!" Trish groaned in aggravation.

Faye whirled around and to her utter shock found her Weaponry friends all staring back at her, equally agog. It appeared Britt, Trish, Rory, Krins, and Goreman had been observing her for several minutes from within the concealment of the trees that bordered the Shed.

Faye froze.

She was standing in the middle of the sandy sparring arena, midway through a move, gaping at them like a fish out of water. No doubt, the gentle motions she had been performing with her staff looked a sight to her friends.

Faye sighed as she noted the curious, highly interested faces. They had snuck around the back way to take her by surprise! Resigned, Faye beckoned them over to the edge of the arena.

"Fine. Watch," she said simply, her blonde locks bundled tightly above her head and her blue eyes narrowed in concentration.

In for a penny, in for a pound, she thought to herself, quoting one of Jack's favourite sayings.

Faye began twirling her staff in an increasingly complex series of patterns. Then, she began her proper exercise routine, combining stick-play with 'hand-to-hand' combat moves. She kicked, swung with her stick, punched, twirled the stick through the air, made it whip and whistle, then stuck it hard in the ground and used it as leverage to complete a lightning-fast adult-height head kick.

Her friends watched open-mouthed as Faye continued for almost ten minutes straight, before standing still again. She wasn't even out of breath.

The stunned silence shattered as Britt let out a loud 'whoop' of delight.

"Did you see that?!" the redhead crowed, laughing with delight. "You're an absolute demon!"

They all gathered around, examining the staff they had often seen propped up against Faye's closet and began asking questions.

Finally, Krins shrewdly demanded, "Can you teach us?"

Faye hesitated as she looked into the young man's steady grey eyes.

"Sure, I mean, I can try," she replied with a shrug. "Um, I'm kind of already teaching Varsity. But she's got something else on today. The only thing is, you'll need to get yourself one of these sparring sticks. Regular branches don't work, they aren't strong enough."

Goreman and Krins exchanged a disgruntled look.

"Nice of Varsity to tell us!" the boys muttered.

"I asked her not to tell *anyone*. I'm not too sure if we're allowed to train with this." Faye lifted her staff helplessly, the desire to defend Varsity battling with the knowledge that the older girl didn't *need* anyone to defend her. She was fully capable of taking care of herself.

"You know what the Profs are like, particularly with *unapproved* teaching." Faye said.

"Right. Now, where can we get one of those staffs?" Goreman muttered, rubbing the back of his neck thoughtfully.

"Armoury," Krins replied, grinning at Faye's guilty start. "Oh, yes, young Faye. You aren't the only student to have visited *that* treasure trove! I'll have a word with Old Tryllia. She's good friends with my mum, so she won't mind my asking."

"Well, if you can convince Mistress Tryllia to give everyone here a staff, then I can teach you all," Faye relented, giving in to the inevitable and trying not to think too hard about what Varsity might say about these people crashing their party every Resday.

From that day onwards, Faye arranged regular training hours – including one or two during the week when it happened that she and her friends shared a timetabled *private study* session. As the Weaponry recruits had more free blocks than other students, it made it easier for the small group of friends to practice unseen. Although, finding a secret location was perhaps the trickiest part.

Thankfully, Varsity took the additional sparring partners in stride – especially as she was more knowledgeable than Krins and Goreman in the art of stick fighting and, therefore, became more of an assistant to Faye. In the end, after having several near misses, it was Varsity herself that came up with a solution.

"The battlements," the tall warrior girl suggested. "No one ever goes up there; the door is normally locked. It just so happens that I have a special key that gets me into most places. Which, if you were to tell *anyone* about, would *not* have a pleasant ending."

The group looked at her with some surprise before grinning in appreciation and promising not to tell a soul.

Yes. Of all the people attending Austin Academy, it would naturally be Varsity that had an illegal skeleton key!

As the days passed, increasing numbers of weaponry recruits turned up, having heard whispers of this informal class from the original group. Faye felt a little uneasy as the group grew. She knew that the stick wasn't taught at the Academy, and she had no idea if it could lead her into trouble. Despite her reservations, however, every recruit was somehow able to procure their very own sparring stick. Mistress Tryllia, it seemed, had her own reasons for approving the illicit training.

Finding a convenient way to contact them all became challenging until Varsity once more used her ingenious brain to devise a solution.

Faye had just finished dressing for the day up in her room, prepared to head down for her early morning kitchen duty, when she noticed a small card had been slipped under her door. Curious, Faye picked it up. It was glossy white and small enough to fit into the palm of her hand. On one side was a stylised phoenix taking flight amidst a flame. On the other were a set of numbers and letters. One, Zero, A and M.

The girl ran a hand over the card, frowning thoughtfully. Varsity called Faye *Little Phoenix*, but it seemed so unlikely that the stoic warrior girl would slip a card under her door! And the code on the back. Faye squinted and tilted her head.

"That says ten A-M, dear one," Zen sighed with forced patience as it peeked over her shoulder to look at the little card.

"Ten A-M? As in, ten in the morning?" Faye frowned. "That's about when I finish with kitchen duty."

"Yes... And what are you normally doing every Resday *after* kitchen duty?" the lizard prompted archly.

"*Sparring*," Faye snapped, irritated by the lizard's condescending tone before she realised its meaning. "Oh! So the message *is* from Varsity! We're meeting today at ten for our next session."

Faye flushed with pleasure as she looked at the stylised phoenix again. How unexpectedly sweet for the older girl to use the pet name she had bestowed upon Faye as the symbol to represent their sparring group!

"*Now* you're awake!" The lizard grinned. "Down to the kitchen with you, my dear, and bake me some pie!"

Faye rolled her eyes, noting that the little lizard was growing a bit of a paunch.

"Hmmm, you know I think I've put on a bit of extra weight around the middle, Zen. I'm thinking we might need to go on a diet," the girl answered, tongue in cheek.

Zen gasped in horror, digging its little claws into her shoulder.

"You *wouldn't*," the lizard protested.

Faye laughed as she gathered her jacket and headed for the door.

"Faye, really? You *wouldn't*! Would you?" Zen pressed anxiously.

The girl didn't answer. Instead, she whistled a merry tune as she headed for the stairs.

CHAPTER 23

THE SAWMILL APPRENTICE

"Cross that bridge when you come to it," Zen offered its solicitous advice one evening while they were in their dormitory room, readying themselves for bed.

Faye had just confided in the lizard her concerns about her sparring group being found out, as nearly *every* Second and Third Level Weaponry student now attended! Varsity's phoenix cards were working a treat, especially as whatever ink the girl used faded within a matter of hours. That way, if the card were left lying around too long, lost, or fell into the wrong hands, the information would fade away leaving the card as a simple blank white rectangle. The girl truly was a mastermind!

"Yes, I suppose," Faye said uncertainly, brushing her hair.

It had grown longer since her arrival at the academy. Thayrille had religiously, every six weeks, trimmed her hair to keep it short and manageable, but it had long since passed her shoulders and hung midway down her back.

"Perhaps I should get a trim," Faye said critically as she examined the silky ends of her hair.

"Or you could leave it?" Zen suggested, absently scratching at its colourful, scaly side. "I like it longer."

"Of course, you do! Considering you hide beneath it all the time," Faye laughed as she efficiently plaited her hair in preparation for bed.

A knock sounded from outside her door, and Faye quickly drew her robe around her before answering. To her surprise, it was Duncan! And he looked worse for wear, with his lip bleeding and a black eye blooming.

"What happened?!" Faye exclaimed, automatically aiding the boy to sit on her bed.

He grimaced, then flinched as it caused his split lip to crack back open. Faye hurriedly retrieved her emergency medical kit that Thayrille had helped her make. She applied salve to the cracked lip, and to the bruised eye, then gave Duncan a dose of willow-bark serum to ease the pain.

"Ambushed," Duncan replied, his angry, feral voice far from his usual bored tone.

His ring, Faye noticed, was almost jet black from the sheer amount of power it was syphoning.

"But you're a Warlock!" Faye cried.

Duncan shook his head in frustration. "Styrran and his new *friend*," was all Duncan said.

"Oh," Faye sighed, shifting to sit down next to him, and examine his cut knuckles.

She applied more salve.

"Tell me," she commanded.

"I was on my way back from the mess hall," Duncan murmured, flinching uncomfortably as the small girl dressed his wounds. "I was late to dinner because I got distracted with a study task in the library. That Styrran, he blind-sided me! I was heading back upstairs, and all I saw was the stairwell filling with ruddy-purple magic and suddenly it was like the ground just vanished beneath me. Next thing I knew, I was falling backwards and hitting every stone wall like a billiard ball."

Duncan touched a gash across the top of his head and grimaced again.

"Once I was out of the purple cloud, I created a personal shield spell to prevent worse injuries. I didn't know which way was up when I fell to the bottom of the stairs. Then that *thing* hauled me to my feet and my powers just... leeched away, as though I never had any to begin with. They were just... Gone."

Faye's eyes widened. So, the unnatural beast was powerful enough to actually take *all* of someone's power. Even a half-Fey. *That* did not bode well!

"So, he grabbed you, absorbed your powers, and Styrran...?" Faye prompted when Duncan seemed to lose himself in thought.

Shaking his head, the boy continued his story.

"It was an awkward spot, and Styrran had to get close to attack me. His own powers were absorbed as well," Duncan said and touched his lip gingerly. "So, the great git decided he'd rearrange my face physically instead of magically. Would have been worse if it hadn't been for that warrior-girl you train with. She came across us, and, well, she *beat* Cronuel to a bloody pulp. Never seen anything like it!"

A smile crept across Duncan's face at the memory making the boy wince as it pulled at his cut lip.

"Styrran vanished while this was going on though, and that girl Verity or whatever, dragged Cronuel straight down to Mistress Tryllia for punishment. She told me to get up here, otherwise I'd be punished, too, for fighting." He finished his story, running one large, elegant hand through his black hair, rumbling it further. "I hardly landed a single punch! But you know Academy Policy – any violence and your scholarship can be withdrawn. Even if you're the victim in the situation!"

Faye felt anger rise in her chest. "Styrran is such a defecating chicken!" she hissed viciously.

Duncan looked at her in surprise, amusement diffusing his face once more. "I believe that's not quite the right phrase. It's meant to be 'chicken-sh...'"

"*Don't* start with me, Duncan." Faye cut him off, flushing with embarrassment. "He's a defecating chicken, and that's that!"

"Indeed," he said softly, his emerald eyes misting with soft black power. "But we've known that for a while."

Faye sighed, dabbing more salve gently to Duncan's injuries. She took the opportunity to apply a little sorcerous healing to the lip and eye now that the salve had done its job to combat infection, just as Healer Merkin had been teaching her these past weeks. The bruise faded slowly, and the cut lip knitted neatly.

Within moments, the injuries had all but vanished.

"Thanks," Duncan said, examining himself carefully in her small mirror.

Faye jumped as she heard giggling voices outside her door. "You best sneak away, before someone decides to stick their head in here." She whispered. "Boys aren't allowed."

"You're right, of course. Thanks, Faye." The boy murmured, then swooped down to place a soft kiss on her cheek before slipping away in a shadow of black mist.

The girl raised one hand and touched the place where Duncan's lips had pressed against her skin, blinking rapidly before her thoughts returned to the circumstances of the Warlock's unexpected visit. The strange giddy bubble in her stomach burst as belated anger swept through her.

That no good, cowardly bully...! Faye fumed as she angrily slammed her healing kit back into the closet.

Zen clucked gently, drawing Faye out of her red haze, tactfully ignoring the unexpected peck on the cheek that had left the girl flushed and confused.

"You'll get him, one day," the lizard said. "Then he'll think twice about picking on anyone you care for ever again."

"Thanks, Zen."

Faye crawled into bed, her cheerful mood long vanished. She lay awake for a long time that night, occasionally brushing her hand over her cheek as she thought about Duncan and the dilemma of Styrran and Cronuel.

Styrran stalked through Sorcery the following day without even looking at her or Duncan. It was as though nothing had happened.

The only outward signs that Duncan gave of his anger was when his knuckles turned white as he gripped his pen, and his eyes glowed with misty black power. The blue-gemmed ring on his finger flared as it absorbed his energy.

Zen, of course, did an unexpected thing and slid from Faye's shoulders. The lizard rarely left its position around her neck and usually only when food was involved. Today, the creature swiftly climbed up Duncan's shoulder and draped itself across his neck instead, subtly darkening its scales to blend with the boy's black attire. The action seemed to startle Duncan to within an inch of his life. Faye squelched a grin, appreciating that Zen was selflessly helping her friend in his time of need.

Within moments Duncan appeared to relax back into his chair and the misty power faded from his eyes, leaving them bright green once more. Faye could almost hear the quiet vibration and clicking of Zen as it soothed the boy. She felt a pang of jealousy but quickly dismissed it.

The lesson progressed as usual, and Faye conjured some realistic illusions across her desk, her entire being radiating a soft silver light. At the end of the two hours, when the students were dismissed, Styrran strutted past with his usual confident swagger.

The swagger faltered, however, when Styrran noticed the utterly relaxed form of Duncan – without so much as a single scrape marring his bored, elegant face. Styrran dared not delay too long, so with one swift killing glance, the Gorgon-boy stomped up the stairs.

Faye eyed him with great dislike.

"If there is *one* person in this world I actually hate..." she muttered, stuffing her books back into her pack.

Duncan made a small noise of agreement as Zen slid from around his neck and returned to its usual place on Faye.

"What a beautiful lizard, you have there, Faye!" exclaimed Sorcerer Hanly as he caught sight of the colourful creature.

"Thank you, sir," she said in surprise.

She hadn't realised that this instructor hadn't met Zen before. She almost had a sneaking suspicion that the lizard had avoided this man in particular.

"What kind is he?" Hanly asked, eyeing the rainbow lizard curiously.

"Oh, I'm not sure. They live in a small canyon near Grydin, my home village. I found this little one when it hatched, and we've been together since," she answered as she finished packing her bag.

Hanly reached for Zen, intending to pat it, but the lizard hissed warningly, puffing itself up, so the Sorcerer removed his hand quickly.

"I'm so sorry, sir!" Faye exclaimed in consternation. "It's not normally so hostile!"

"Oh, never mind, child. The poor thing can probably smell my dog on me. Lizards aren't overly fond of dogs, I understand," the man said, obviously disappointed.

Faye, not wanting to offend her instructor any more than necessary, made hurried excuses about dinner and left the room.

What was that about? Faye demanded crossly of Zen as they joined the bustling crowd in the corridor.

They had been practicing communicating using their newfound telepathic connection and Faye found it incredibly helpful rather than looking like a strange twit muttering to herself all the time.

He would have sensed my magic. Zen sighed, twitching a little in discomfort.

Faye echoed the sigh.

You could have warned me so I could better protect you! I could have told Hanly that you tend to bite strangers, she scolded gently as she joined the crowd jostling down the stairs.

Zen clucked softly in apology, body buzzing with shame.

Never mind, you silly lizard. Let's see if they have any grapes left over from afternoon tea, Faye wove her way through the crowd to the kitchen door.

As she had practically rewritten the entire menu and its recipes last semester, and continued to add to the kitchen's collection this semester, she had a standing invitation to come straight into the kitchens for her dinner. No lineups, no scummy bottom-of-the-pot servings. It was a pleasant reward for all her hard work.

"Hey-hey-hey! Here she is, my favourite girl!" Ross called with his usual wicked grin.

It made Faye wonder what he had in store for her in the way of extra kitchen tasks. Today, however, he merely slapped a plate down on the counter. He began to pile it high with the choicest pieces of roast beef atop creamy mashed potato, fresh vegetables, and gravy. He also placed a smaller plate next to it, filled with grapes, strawberries, plums and some orangey fruit that Faye didn't recognise. The fruit had been cut in half, the seed removed and the remaining flesh sliced into cubes. The skin had been pushed inside out, so the cubes stuck out invitingly.

Zen sniffed the air experimentally then scampered down her arm suddenly.

"*Mango*!" the lizard practically squealed with excitement and fell onto the plate, its earlier chagrin dissipating.

Ross hesitated, unsure if he had heard correctly over the clashing and crashing of pots and pans.

"Did he just say..." the young man began, but then shook his head dismissively, deciding it had been his imagination. "He's really excited about the mango! It's fresh in! A local crop, grown over spring and summer. Ever tried one?"

Faye shook her head, still staring at Zen, amazed at the amount of noise her lizard was making. Chomping, slurping, gulping noises that were interspersed with enthusiastic groans of pleasure. With an amused chuckle, Ross handed her a bowl of the luscious fruit cubes, and Faye sampled a small piece.

The flavour was indescribable!

"That's delicious!" she exclaimed, polishing off the whole bowl.

By this time, Zen had finished half of the mango and begged for more from Ross with a high-pitched keening whimper. Faye had *never* seen Zen act like this!

With a surprised laugh, Ross retrieved another half for the lizard, which Zen fell onto once more in heavenly stupor. After he had finished the second half of the fruit, Zen burped and lay amongst the scraps, its stomach bulging. Faye shook her head in amused disgust.

"I'm not picking you up, you little piggy," Faye said in a dire voice. "You're covered in sticky juice."

"I'll give him a scrub down, if you like, Faye. I've got a sink of warm, fresh water ready to go." Ross laughed. "You tuck in before your dinner gets cold."

Agreement made, Faye slipped out of the kitchen with her plate and onto the peaceful grounds. It was still her favourite place to eat a meal, and now that the worst of winter was over, she was keen to take up the habit again. As she finished the last bite of succulent beef and mash potato, Faye felt Zen sheepishly creep up her back.

Once it was draped around her neck again, smelling faintly of citrus, Faye eyed the lizard with an imperious stare.

"It's...well... it was *mango*!" the lizard exclaimed with a hiccup.

"Have you ever eaten mango before?" Faye asked, puzzled.

"Well... no. But I know of it! My kind love to eat it. It's a delicacy," Zen explained, smacking its jaws together in blissful satisfaction.

"So, your kind is from the north, then? From around here? How was it that your egg was all the way down near Grydin?" Faye wondered out loud and noticed that Zen became resolutely silent.

"You know, Zen, you should really start being honest...!" Her lecture was cut short by a hubbub inside the mess hall.

A panicked voice could be heard shrilly demanding... Did they say *Healer Merkin*?

Heart thrumming, Faye abandoned her plate to slip back inside, noting the small crowd that surrounded a stricken young man dressed in the leather apron of a woodworker or carpenter.

"You *don't understand*! This is an *emergency*!" The man hollered, voice cracking with the strain of grief. "At the sawmill! We need *Merkin* and we need the Healer *now*!"

A flutter of panic spread through Faye's chest as she realised several facts simultaneously. Firstly, Merkin wasn't here. The

Healer had been called away for a few days to a nearby village – the woman had informed her students just yesterday and set them a ream of theory work to occupy them while she was gone. Secondly, in order for a Carpenter to attend the Academy in addition to, Faye assumed, sending help to the Medical Centre… This meant that whatever accident had occurred was life-threatening.

Someone was dying!

Faye urgently reached into her well of power, accidently plunging a little too deeply into that silver well, immersing herself before flailing back out. The girl coughed and stumbled as she was encased in her silver power a second time, the silver energy tingling across her skin and searing her chest with raw energy.

Not again, Faye! Zen buzzed harshly at her neck, attempting to syphon off some of her energy.

No, Zen! Not enough time. Just help me! We'll deal with that after! Faye exclaimed, turning her stumble into a run as she pushed her way forward through the peering crowd towards the gasping Carpenter.

"Tell me. What happened?" Faye's voice tinkled out, her silver power lending a surreal quality to the sound.

The man gaped at her for a moment, before his innate sense of urgency overcame his shock and fear.

"A Carpenter's Apprentice. Accident at the sawmill. Healers from the Medical Centre are en route, but they don't think…" The youth trailed off as grief encompassed him once more. "Healer Merkin said that if we ever had need…"

"Show me." Faye instructed as she reached out and placed one sparkling hand on the man's shoulder.

The Carpenter blinked at her, his eyes suddenly filled with silver energy as he gaped at her like a fish out of water. Meanwhile,

Faye's consciousness momentarily merged with his, seeing the accident, and the quickest path to the sawmill, in her mind's eye.

Yes. The Apprentice was dying, potentially already dead. Faye had to go and she had to go *now*.

Faye released the man, allowing him to slump in a dazed heap to the floor, his hands clutching his temples. One of the Infirmary Interns had pushed their way through the crowd, staring at the silver girl in awe. Evidently someone had sent for the next Healer in charge at the Academy.

"Care for him. He's bound to have a headache." Faye's voice jingled across the hushed crowd.

The Intern nodded once, her eyes reflecting the odd sight of the ephemeral figure and her strange silver glow. Faye raised a few inches off the ground, the route to the sawmill firmly fixed in her mind as she sped off in a streak of light, disappearing out the mess hall doors and through the gates of the Academy.

I really hope you know what you're doing, dear one! Zen chirruped from her shoulder, its own unique power swirling around Faye's magical core as it tempered the flow of the torrential energy.

Faye didn't answer, concentrating on her destination.

Faye wasn't really sure how she had arrived at the sawmill. One moment, she had been gliding through the Academy gates, then, *bam*, she was there.

The girl blinked, taking in the scene of chaos. People were crowding around a limp figure; some were howling in fury, and others crying. There were no Healers or medics to be seen. Faye glided over to the figure, the crowd automatically parting to give way as they realised a glowing silver presence was among them. The Sawmill Master was leaning over his Apprentice with red, shocked eyes. The youth, no more than a sixteen-year-old boy, lay in a growing pool of blood. His chest was torn open by the teeth of a milling saw. It looked as though he had fallen on it by accident. The grieving man looked up when he noticed the silver mist, his eyes pools of misery.

"Please, can you help him?" he croaked, staring up at Faye.

"*I will try,*" Faye's voice tinkled.

The girl gathered the flood of silver energy that now lay at her disposal, summoning every iota she had brought up from her core to wash over the boy.

His ribs and breastbone had been sawn through, his left lung punctured, and blood gushed into his chest cavity. Bloody foam was already bubbling at the corners of his mouth as the boy wetly gasped for air.

Faye's power washed through him and the boy's eyes widened, his body stiffened and arched slightly as the icy power filled his veins. Slowly, the muscles knitted together, the bone splinters flew into place and set, and the skin – blackened and bloody – closed over the wounds. The lungs cleared, the puncture healed, and the boy's breath gave one final rattle, which ended in a coughing splutter as his body rejected the congealed blood from his repaired lungs.

The Sawmill Master turned the boy over as the black gunk spewed from his mouth, followed by a trickle of silver mist. The boy passed out, followed closely by Faye as the last of her magics left her and flowed into him.

CHAPTER 24

THE GREATER GOOD

Faye regained consciousness in a rush, a vague sense of déjà vu settling as darkness pressed in on her, the sterile scent of heavily starched sheets filling her nostrils. Had she ended up in the infirmary *again*?

No. No, this wasn't the same spacious room with its gleaming metal framed beds and ornate medic trolley. Faye could hear the chiming of bells and the murmur of many voices beyond the curtain that shielded her narrow cot from the remainder of the room.

She had been here once before, during an excursion for Second Level Healing. Faye recognised the ridiculous yellow duck images that decorated the dividing curtain.

How in blazes had she ended up in the Emergency Ward? she wondered hazily.

The girl rubbed her eyes tiredly and tried to get her bearings. Lying on a cot next to her was a familiar looking boy. Her brain was befuddled. Around her neck, Zen buzzed soothingly, its strange magic permeating her body.

"What happened?" Faye croaked, trying to sit up.

"You overdid it, *again* and fainted. Just like *last* semester," Zen informed her tartly, slipping from around her neck to her chest. "You're getting into a bad habit, passing out like this."

"Not my fault," Faye retorted grumpily, her parched throat causing her voice to crack. "Besides, twice is *not* a habit."

The concealing curtain by her bed was suddenly reefed back as a medic came rushing over, alerted by her croaking voice. Faye finally managed to sit up and throw off her blanket, and the medic grasped her arm to help steady her.

"You're awake! My goodness, what a miracle worker you are! Here, drink this," the woman said in awe, shoving a large mug of medicated tea into Faye's hands. She sipped gratefully, feeling her sore throat ease, and her mind clear.

The sawmill! Faye remembered with a sickening lurch in her gut.

"The boy?" she demanded, sliding out of bed and to her knees next to the still figure in the next cot. *That's* why he looked so familiar!

"Unconscious, but otherwise fine. In perfect health, in fact," the medic said, shoulders twitching uneasily.

Faye placed one hand on the boy's head, and another on his chest. With a gasping breath, he awoke and stared into her glowing silver eyes.

"I'm dead?" he asked, his strawberry blonde hair damp from having been cleaned by the medics.

The last Faye recalled his whole body had been smattered in drying blood and gore.

"No. I managed to heal you," Faye said with a friendly, tired smile.

The boy's pale blue eyes widened, then he felt his chest frantically. The robe the boy wore ripped under his strong hands, and he stared down at his chest. Only a fine jagged white line marked where the table saw had torn his flesh open.

He gingerly touched it.

"Have you pain?" Faye asked in concern.

She was still woozy and didn't feel confident about calling on her powers at this point. At least not until she had a square meal or two.

"No. No pain," the boy said softly. He began to laugh, then started to cry. His sobs became so violent and uncontrollable that the medic had to give him a sedative. At that moment, Healer Merkin strode into the room.

Faye was surprised to see her Instructor. Afterall, the woman wasn't expected back until the following day. Had someone managed to summon her, too?

"*What* is *this*?" she demanded, seeing Faye kneeling by the boy, her hand still on his forehead, eyes aglow with silver power. "From what I've been told, she barely survived that Healing, and already you allow her to use her power *again*?!"

The medic began stuttering, trying to explain. Faye consciously let go of her silver magic, allowing it to sink back into her core and her hair and eyes returned to their regular colour.

"To bed with you, and for goodness' sake, SOMEONE GET HER SOME FOOD!" the Healer bellowed, sending the frightened medic running from the curtained alcove.

Tryllia appeared around the curtain next and instantly strode over to Faye, her usually serene face pale with worry. Tenderly, the stout woman lifted the girl into her cot, tucking a blanket around her firmly.

"Rest, my dear," she said as she puttered around, filled a tumbler full of water and placed it within easy reach of the young girl. "I came as soon as I heard. I'll care for you, and we'll have you back in our Infirmary just as soon as we can manage it..."

"These inept idiots," Merkin muttered grumpily, leaning over the Sawmill Apprentice and doing her own Healer's assessment, both physical and magical. "I leave for two days! *Two days*! And I'm summoned back here to find a Carpenter and my own student a breath away from death! What *moron* allowed an unlicensed, undergraduate to perform such a complex healing in the first place?!"

"No one *let* me. I didn't ask permission to heal him. And I didn't use my magic again, just now," Faye managed to squeak, once she was settled. "I was only checking to see that he lived."

"Yes, indeed he lives!" Merkin said angrily, her silvery blue eyes snapping. "And it almost killed you, doing it! I know all life is precious, Faye, but in this circumstance, *your* life should be considered more valuable! With your intellect, your power, and your compassion... You have so much you can offer for another century, possibly longer given your heritage, but you can't do that if you're *dead*!"

"Nay, I wasn't at risk of dying, Healer Merkin, it just drained me more than I expected," Faye protested weakly, her limbs trembling from an innate weakness that ran through her muscles.

"Humph!" was the only reply she received from both Merkin and Tryllia.

Tryllia had found a chair and automatically took a seat for a bedside vigil, her face creased with motherly concern.

"I'm fine, really!" Faye exclaimed, voice still cracking.

"Rest now. I'll watch over you," Tryllia insisted tenderly, smoothing back Faye's unruly hair.

Every strand was sticking up on end like it was charged with static electricity. Faye supposed she did look a sight and wasn't overly comforted by Zen's silent agreement. Giving up her attempt to reassure the adults, Faye relaxed back into the cot, feeling the soft mattress beneath her and was content that time would prove her case.

The week snailed by, and Faye was finally able to return to her usual classes, although many of her instructors assured her that she could return to her room to rest if needed. She still looked ready to keel over at any moment, or so she was told with alacrity by the verbose Britt. Normally her other friends, especially Trish, would protest the outspoken red-heads comments, but even they were apt to agree.

Faye's skin was more pale than usual, and her hair still had the penchant for snapping and crackling with the occasional fizz of silver energy. She took the opportunity for rest on Fifday afternoon, having tolerated another double Sorcery lesson on Advanced Meditation only to feel completely wrung out by the end. Her silver powers were slippery and hard to control, often escaping her grasp and zinging through her body like liquid lightening.

After the midday meal, instead of attending her next class, Faye retreated to the open grounds and sent her apologies to the next instructor by way of Trish and Britt.

Once out in the open, Faye breathed deeply of the cool spring air, allowing the scent of jasmine and lily of the vale to wash over her. With any luck, the playful breeze would also carry away all her troubles, along with her feelings of stress and anxiety.

A shadow fell over her, blocking out the warmth of the sun's rays.

Faye's eyes snapped open to peer up at the young man standing over her, shifting awkwardly from foot to foot, holding a package in his broad hands.

"Samuel!" Faye exclaimed in surprise and concern, belatedly recognising the shadow as the sawmill apprentice she had saved. "Are you alright?"

"Yes, yes, Mistress Faye, just fine. No, don't get up!" The boy waved her back down as she prepared to spring to her feet.

Faye watched him as he plonked himself on the grass beside her and handed her the package he had been holding.

"Made this for you, Mistress Faye. To say thanks," the boy gave a lopsided grin, automatically rubbing his chest where the faint white scar would be visible, barring the thick calico work shirt he wore. "I'd be dead if it weren't for you."

Faye blinked owlishly as she examined the gift. It was wrapped neatly in butcher's paper that had been coloured with ink. The design was familiar, a swirling pattern that spoke of healing and peace.

"I know this pattern," she murmured, perplexed.

Where did she know it from, though?

"Really? Huh. I dare say you would," the boy nodded, slowly unbuttoning his shirt. "These came up after I was home, like some sort of talisman, or mark. I ain't shown the Medics none. Figured we'd keep it between us."

Samuel pulled aside the lapels of his shirt to show his bared chest. There, on either side of the faint scar, were the same swirling designs. Faye blinked rapidly, hovering one finger over the strange alien symbols, her power flaring silver as a spark of her magic zipped from her fingertip into the mark, causing it to glow eerily.

"Heal. Repair. Rejuvenate," Faye whispered, reading the pattern.

"Aye. I certainly did all of that and more," Samuel nodded as he rebuttoned his shirt. "Me girl, she painted the wrapper and also designed the box. I only took so long to bring it to you on account of having to make it just right. We're both real grateful for everything Faye."

Faye blinked again, snapping out of her trance as the calico shirt once more covered the symbols. Her eyes shifted embarrassedly back to the gift, noting that the painted design was the same three symbols repeated over and over.

Now that she had *felt* the text on Samuel's skin, like some magically stamped tattoo in his flesh, she could read the same symbols clearly. Exactly the same way she could recognise and read the name Fey'Rhain on her mother's pipe.

A magical language, Faye thought in awe.

Her thoughts were broken by the muscled shoulder that lightly bumped her own.

"You know," Samuel told her with another lopsided grin. "A gift is better once it's opened."

Faye glanced at him uncertainly before carefully undoing the string that tied the package closed. Once the wrapping came loose, she found a beautiful, intricate wooden trinket box carved with loving detail. The three symbols repeated amidst filigree flowers. It was an artistic piece that she would forever treasure.

Heal. Repair. Rejuvenate.

"It's perfect," Faye said in a hushed voice before turning and throwing herself into the boy's arms, tears escaping her control. "I'm so glad you're okay."

Samuel wrapped his enormous arms carefully around her, patting her head and rocking her soothingly while she cried.

"Aye, thanks to you and your magic. I owe you my life. Never forget that, Silver Lady," he spoke into her hair. "Same goes for my girl. She says to tell you the same. As does my family. Although, my dad is not overly happy with the headache you gave him."

The boy laughed lightly, his chuckle a rumble in his chest.

Faye nodded silently before hastily pushing away and swiping at the copious tears.

"Tell him sorry from me. If I had delayed even a moment…" Faye lifted one hand helplessly to bat the air rather than finishing the sentence.

"No matter. He'll keep. Chin up, little one. Life is grand," Samuel treated her to one last grin before lumbering to his feet. "I best get back. Remember what I said."

The girl nodded and waved goodbye to him. Once the boy was out of sight around the edge of the stone palace, Zen slid out from beneath her hair and spooled into her lap, scenting along the trinket box with interest.

"Oooh, now this is lovely! A perfect place to keep all your gems and precious keepsakes," the lizard enthused.

Faye frowned absently at her small companion, her brain still ticking over the idea that she could instinctively read a magical language.

"Zen? The symbols on Samuel's chest. Did I put them there?" the girl asked quietly, tracing the intricate design on the wooden box, examining the symbols intently.

"Oh, yes. Or rather, your untempered *power* did," the lizard clarified, seeming far from perturbed. "The marks are the relics of the spell you conjured, particularly since you used energy from deep within the earth of Pendalin. That sort of conjuring *always* leaves a mark."

"Is that why I've been so wrecked this week? Is it because I used the earth's power?" Faye pressed.

"Yes. Now, how about we get this lovely box back up to our room, before other people want to paw at it?"

Faye's frown deepened. Why did it feel that her little lizard was attempting to distract her from this line of questioning?

"Is that how I can read those symbols? Because I'm able to use earth magic?"

Zen blinked at her with impenetrable obsidian eyes.

"It's in your blood." The reptile finally answered after a notable hesitation.

"You're going to have to tell me sometime, Zen!" Faye snapped, exasperated by her companion's secretiveness.

"Yes, I dare say so. But not now," Zen agreed readily, scurrying its way back up her arm and under her hair as she hoisted herself tiredly to her feet. "When you're ready."

She really *hated* it when Zen turned enigmatic.

"You *always* say that," Faye grumped, stumping off towards the mess hall and her dormitory above.

Faye slowly packed the last ingredients away at the end of her Healing class later the following week. They had been learning which herbs and other plants could be used to make poultices and healing salves. Naturally, Faye spent the lesson doing her extension work – comparing foreign plants to native ones. Unsurprisingly, the girl found that Healer Merkin was absolutely right about some of the strange herbs being far stronger and more efficient than the Pendalin variety. As Faye dawdled over her clean up, Healer Merkin glanced over and then tapped her foot impatiently.

"Alright, the others are gone, so out with it," the Healer said shortly, yet warm amusement lit her pale blue eyes.

Since that episode with Samuel, and the angry admission the Healer had made regarding her thoughts on Faye being such a valuable person, their relationship had somehow extended beyond that of student-instructor. Merkin had become more like a favourable Aunt – one that didn't particularly get along with her Healer-sister, Thayrille, yet was still determined to have a positive relationship with her 'niece'.

Faye grinned sheepishly. She should have known the woman, so reminiscent of her foster-mother, would have guessed she had something on her mind.

"Well, I've been thinking... I have this natural healing ability, and I know it's been a hot topic lately amongst the Academy staff. I was thinking, perhaps I should put my power to good use, you know, by volunteering in the Medical Centre in Tryssdale..." Faye said self-consciously, avoiding Merkin's surprised stare.

"Well, yes, I quite agree that having you at the Ward would be very useful. There are many terminally ill patients that you could possibly heal and give a new lease of life," Merkin said slowly, sitting down at her desk, her eyebrows puckered thoughtfully. "However, you are still a child, only what, thirteen years old? We need to take that into account. Even now, with just your studies, you're doing far more than any other child your age would dare imagine. We don't want you to burn out or see some of the true horrors of the Medic Ward. It would scar you for life."

"You forget, Healer Merkin, that firstly I'm not entirely Human," Faye said softly, trying to put her feelings into words. "All my life, I've acted older than my years, I've felt older. Whether that's because of Thayrille's raising of me or my Fey nature, we can't be sure, but I'm more like a small adult than a child. Even now, I have more in common with the older students from Weaponry than any of the other younger students. Besides, I've dealt with death before and have seen some pretty horrific injuries and sicknesses when I lived in the Healer's Cottage. I'm pretty sure I could handle the Medic Ward. I *know* I could."

Merkin eyed Faye thoughtfully, as though considering and weighing every word. Finally, she nodded.

"Alright, you can attend with me as my Apprentice. We'll start you off easy with ordinary ailments. Then we'll see," the Healer said reluctantly.

Faye beamed at her.

"Thank you, Healer Merkin! You won't be sorry!" she said excitedly. "When do we start?"

"On Forday, after the dinner hour, I normally spend some time in the Ward. I'll meet you in the entrance hall," she sighed, a small smile playing around her lips.

"Thank you! I'll see you then," Faye replied with a brilliant smile, and finished packing her things before she skipped down to dinner.

Forday came very quickly, despite Faye's fear that time would drag on and on. Before she knew it, the girl was dressed in practical work clothes and stood waiting in the entrance hall for Healer Merkin. The older woman strode into the hall moments after Faye.

"Still determined?" Merkin asked, her flyaway caramel hair bundled back away from her face in a loose bun.

"Definitely," Faye replied without hesitation.

The two strode down the path and out the gates of Austin Academy before heading into the city of Tryssdale. It took another fifteen minutes of twisting and turning streets before they reached the Medical Centre, a three-story stone building surrounded by landscaped gardens.

As soon as they arrived at the Medical Centre, Faye and Healer Merkin were ensconced by people. Medics and Healers were running from one place to another, and the sick were gathered around the seating area or lining up to fill in paperwork. The feeling of illness and death was oppressive.

Taking a deep, calming breath, Faye reached into her silver magic, drawing the ephemeral power up and out. The girl ensured that she didn't plunge in this time and was grateful for Zen's quietly vibrating weight around her neck. The two companions had agreed ahead of time that the lizard would protect Faye from her own impulsiveness and prevent any accidental overload of silver energy.

Once enough power had been teased from her internal well, Faye allowed the silver energy to form a light mist through the emergency room, encasing every person there.

Using her physical self as a centre point, Faye cast her mind into the mist of magic, examining each patient and directing her power to heal and soothe. Faye had no idea how long she stood there, but finally, as the last person in the room returned to full health, the girl slumped to her knees, exhausted.

"Really, child, you need not resort to dramatics," Healer Merkin's tart voice was underlined by concern.

"I'm alright. Just a little tired," Faye sighed and allowed herself to be lifted to her feet by two awed medics.

"You can send these people home; they're all better now," Faye told the medics, with an absent wave at the staring people.

The medics and Healers of the Ward looked at Merkin for confirmation. She nodded in agreement then led her charge to an empty examination room.

"You need a rest, I think, something warm to drink and some food," Merkin said sternly as she helped Faye onto a cot.

"Oh, no, I'm fine. I'll be better in a few minutes, honest," Faye protested, trying to get back off the cot.

"Humph!" Healer Merkin huffed. "We'll see. Now stay right there."

Faye had no choice but to remain or risk upsetting her instructor, which put her at risk of never being allowed to return to the Centre. A few minutes later, Healer Merkin returned bearing a sandwich, fruit juice and steaming healing brew. Despite having just eaten dinner, Faye was famished and gobbled the lot. Instantly she felt much better.

"Alright, let's see some of the other wards, then," Faye said with a grin, jumping to her feet with renewed energy.

"About that, Faye. Perhaps you should focus your healing on one person at a time and only the most serious. It will cause a lot of commotion if you heal rooms full of people at once. The medics and Healers here are now wary of you, and the patients are bewildered. They can't understand why they were desperately sick one moment, and perfectly healthy the next. We don't want to cause a sensation. Besides, it's not like you can be here every waking hour, healing whoever walks through those doors. And even if you could, it would put the Ward out of business," Merkin cautioned, an odd look on her face. "You must let the medics and Healers do their jobs. Otherwise, they would be unemployed, and the whole system would crash. And then, what happens when you *do* leave? The Ward needs to function perfectly in your absence. I would have discussed this with you sooner, had I known you would instantly heal two dozen people as soon as we walked through the doors."

Faye flushed in embarrassment.

"I'm sorry, Healer Merkin. The feeling of illness and death was overpowering, and I just wanted to fix it. I really didn't consider the repercussions," she said.

"That's alright, my dear. We all learn from experience," the Healer said heavily. "We *both* learned from this, I think."

After that serious conversation, the Healer led Faye to the third story, to the section where the terminally ill patients were kept.

These people suffered from a variety of illnesses, from cancers to inherited deformities, and other incurable diseases.

"Good evening, Medic Johanson. This is my Apprentice Faye. She has some Fey blood and a knack for sorcerous healing. We'd like to see if she could help with some of the unfortunates in this Ward, if that's alright?" Healer Merkin said without preamble as they entered the room.

The medic started in surprise and nodded, his hazel eyes round with curiosity as he saw the petite, blonde little girl with her luminous blue-grey eyes. Faye examined her first patient, a man that was riddled with lung disease and needed an hourly dose of healing magic just to keep his lungs functioning.

Slowly, Faye. Zen cautioned, its voice whispering deep in her mind as she began to tease another strand of power from her core, allowing the magic to pool in her chest.

"I'm pretty sure I can completely heal him," Faye said to Merkin in a low voice, ready to do as she was bid, trusting the Healer's judgment.

"Alright, but can you do it a little at a time? In stages?" Merkin asked, voice barely a whisper so no one else would hear. "Start with the damage in the lower lobe only, so he can take a complete breath."

"Why?" Faye asked, startled.

"Because this man has been on a virtual deathbed for a year now. He's accepted that he's going to die. If you heal him in one go, then his mental health won't improve at all. His mind needs to accept the fact that he's getting better. For that, he needs time," Merkin replied reasonably.

Faye nodded her understanding. That made sense. Very few people, especially so close to death, believed in miracles.

Healer Merkin approached the man with a smile.

"Good evening, Sir. If you don't mind, my Apprentice and I would like to trial you on an experimental drug that may improve your lung capacity. Would that be okay by you?" the woman asked gently.

The man, gasping and rattling wetly, nodded his permission.

Healer Merkin made quite a fuss and bustle as she drew up a dose of luminous pink liquid into a syringe, then injected the medicine into the man's fluid line. Once the medicine was administered, the woman gave Faye a pointed look, prompting the girl to perform whatever magic would start this man on his healing journey.

Faye used a small amount of power to stop the cancerous growth in its tracks and then another dollop to heal the lower lobe of his lungs as bid, just enough so that he could breathe without magical aid. The old man coughed spasmodically, bringing up a torrent of discoloured mucous. The medic on shift leapt into action and provided the man with a shallow basin.

"There, it should take a few weeks, or possibly months, but he will eventually completely heal with the assistance of the medics here," the girl whispered to Merkin, a few beads of sweat on her brow.

It was more challenging for the girl to control her magic and only use it in tiny trickles instead of healing the person in one go with a wash of power. It required more finesse and effort.

"Excellent! How about our next patient?" Merkin asked, clearly impressed.

Faye completed a round of the section. Merkin offered each terminal patient an *experimental treatment* of varying colour, and Faye applied just enough power to jump start the healing process, but not enough to completely heal them.

Some, especially those with genetic disorders, Faye would need to visit on multiple occasions. Merkin was quite pleased with their progress. Finally, at a quarter to midnight, the pair returned to the Academy.

"That was very well done, Faye," Healer Merkin said encouragingly. "If you keep at it, especially with the terminally ill, you'll make a lot of people in Tryssdale very pleased and grateful. I dare say once word gets out, the other cities will begin to arrange for their terminally ill to be sent here, too. You are going to be one busy young woman."

Faye smiled tiredly before bidding her instructor goodnight. Once alone in the stairwell that led up to the dormitories, her eyebrows knitted together in a frown. She hadn't considered the far-reaching ramifications of her healing magic. As Merkin said, the Medic Centre had to keep functioning even in her absence. What would happen to those terminally ill patients when she finally graduated and became a Seeker?

"A problem for another day, dear one," Zen murmured in her ear as she dragged herself to bed.

The weeks passed similarly, with her usual routine accompanied by two evenings a week spent in the Medic Ward, subtly healing and helping the terminally ill. In addition, Faye also helped in the manufacture of medicines, using her training with Merkin and Thayrille to help stock the Centre for the following year. She became an all-rounder once she got a handle on healing people by degrees, rather than all in one go. The Medic Ward was happy to have her around, and often asked if she could increase her hours to three or four evenings a week. Healer Merkin put her foot down on this suggestion, claiming that Faye would end up a patient rather than a volunteer if she were pushed too hard.

Faye was grateful for this intervention, as she still wished to have the time to enjoy hanging out with her friends or completing additional stick practice with Varsity and the Weaponry squad. There was also the vast array of study tasks her instructors set that needed to be researched, drafted and published before they were submitted for marking. Unlike the first interminable semester, this period of time raced by. Faye effortlessly glided through the routine, each day was filled to capacity with friends, learning, and work.

Before she knew it, the semester was winding down and the myriad of students began prepping for their final exams. Two more weeks and the summer holidays would be upon them. This left Faye feeling rather pensive, as she would be expected to return to Grydin and continue her Healing education with Thayrille.

What would it be like to return home? Faye mused to herself as she sat on the grounds outside the mess hall one evening after dinner, picking pensively at an apple-cinnamon muffin. *Will Thayrille welcome me back, or will she feel inconvenienced by having her ward return as a temporary Apprentice? Rythin made it clear last summer that I won't just be her foster-child, anymore... Will the villagers let me treat them? Or will they abuse me on sight, just like before? As Thayrille often said, the villagers were all a bunch of unsociable gits – even at the best of times.*

Zen buzzed soothingly around her neck, offering her silent comfort. There was no real answer to her questions and only time would tell...

A chorus of shouts from inside the mess hall broke her from her thoughts, and Faye instantly felt an icy hand grip her heart. Her body flared silver as she instinctively reached for her core magic.

Easy! Zen warned as it clucked near her ear, its own unique power sliding around her core energy to prevent her from pulling up too much and overwhelming her physical self.

Turning her head to peer through the open mess hall doors and into the vast space beyond, Faye couldn't help feeling that the situation was eerily similar to that evening the Carpenter had come to the Academy for help. Only, this time, the chorus of voices held a more sinister tone...

Faye abandoned her muffin and slipped back inside warily, wondering what had happened this time.

"Fight, fight, fight!" the crowd inside was chanting.

A group of older students, aged somewhere between fifteen and eighteen, had formed a ring around the mess hall, their eyes gleaming with glee as they watched whatever scene was playing out in its centre. The youths' bulk effectively blocked the access of the older, and more mature, students that would have likely put an end to whatever altercation was taking place. Faye impatiently pushed her way between the crush of bodies, wondering who in the God's name would be fighting! Everyone here knew the penalty for physical violence...

Once she squeezed through the crowd, Faye witnessed a sight that made her cringe.

"Put him down!" A young voice screamed.

A first-year girl was wailing amidst a bunch of younger students that were clustered fearfully against a nearby table, staring in horror at the scene.

The ring of youths lusting after blood and gore were preventing the younglings from escaping the violent display.

Cronuel was in the middle of the room, a limp figure held over his head as he bellowed. He threw the figure to the ground, and there was a sickening *thunk* followed by a weak moan as the body hit the stone pavers. The beasts swirling vortex pulled at her,

causing her skin to flare silver as ribbons of energy dragged from her core.

Faye gritted her teeth against the slimy sensation, glaring at the horrid beast and his latest victim. The bloody, prone figure shifted slightly, its broken hand glinting as a large blue gem caught the light.

At that moment Faye had a horrible realisation, and her heart thudded sickly in her chest.

The brutalised figure was Duncan!

Cronuel bellowed again, hurling insults at the injured Warlock who was trying to crawl away, leaving a bloody trail behind him.

"What's the matter, Warlock — too much for you?" sneered a third boy.

Styrran!

With a casual nod, Styrran indicated for the beast-boy Cronuel to proceed in his attack on Duncan.

A rage, unlike anything Faye had ever experienced, welled up inside her. She stalked right into the middle of the clearing, her entire body shimmering with electric silver energy. Faye had slipped through Zen's firm grasp on her silver power and plunged once more into her core magic. The world turned silver and morphed around her in her mind's eye. Not the peaceful silvery meadow as it had in Sorcery last semester, but a razor sharp ice-covered realm of barren stone.

"*That's enough!*" she hollered.

Instead of her regular Weaponry boom, her words came hissing out like hail tinkling on glass. Complete silence swept over the mess hall, and even Styrran looked afraid. He hadn't seen her in this silver state, having missed those previous episodes by happen chance.

What was the game here? Had the boy knowingly attacked Duncan, setting that Cronuel beast on him like a hunting dog on a rabbit, knowing Faye was just outside? Was goading her into an explosive, uncontrollable rage really worth whatever repercussions would come?

Be afraid, Faye thought coldly, her rage encompassing her entire being.

Acting on instinct, Faye cast out two magical streams of rope with deft motions, satisfied when they wrapped themselves around Styrran and Cronuel. Both boys fought against the magical confinements, without success. Styrran glowed his ruddy-purple colour but was unable to shear through his restraints. The only thing his blast of power achieved was to cause a reem of symbols to flare to life along the silver cords.

Confine. Restrain. Encompass. Enclose. Secure.

Faye read the symbols with a flicker of satisfaction. Yes. Those would do nicely!

Styrran's eyes widened and sweat beaded his brow as he looked at her with belated understanding. Faye was powerful. Too powerful. Even for him.

Cronuel, too, concentrated with all his might, trying to absorb the electric energy into himself – but there was too much! His anti-magic vortex was simply overwhelmed.

He couldn't even make a dent in the flow.

Faye frowned consideringly at the beastial boy before casting one last jet of silver power at him.

Stopper.

The single symbol flared brightly before sinking into Cronuel's chest, nullifying the whorl of anti-magic that sucked another's power into his core. The vortex had been effectively blocked!

Satisfied, Faye clenched her fists and raised her arms imperiously. The two boys were jerked off the ground completely. They each struggled harder to no effect. Faye transferred Styrran's magical tether to her right hand, then knelt next to Duncan, who was in a bad way.

This stream of silver power gave Faye unworldly abilities. She could see every injury inside the boy, like a reddish picture shining through the silver mist. He had a fractured spine, broken ribs, and a punctured lung – amongst many other more superficial injuries. A well of sympathy rose inside the girl, complementing the rage that still held Styrran and Cronuel in check.

"Be well," whispered Faye as she gently touched Duncan on the forehead.

Unlike her healing of Samuel, the sawmill apprentice, Faye tempered her energy and directed the whisps of power into each injury. Her silver magic washed over him like a soft mist, repairing the damage, inside and out in seconds. If she were asked to repeat such a feat again without her emotions running high, she felt she could not. Everything she did, every ounce of magic she performed, was guided by some deep instinct.

The familiar symbols of *heal, repair, rejuvenate*, bloomed beneath the Warlock's skin, sealing his wounds before fading.

Once the healing was complete, Faye rose to her feet again. She glanced around and noted with appreciation that the Weaponry squad, particularly those that had joined her sparring group, had pushed their own way through the crowd and were standing at the ready. Several more were mingling one row back, keeping the heckling youths in check so they didn't simply melt away into the academy. Those fools inciting such violence would be dealt with by the instructors, along with Cronuel and Styrran.

"How can we help, Faye?" Trish asked, her eyes reflecting silver light as she stepped towards the glowing girl.

"Care for him," Faye indicated the prone boy.

Trish instantly dropped to her knees to lay a comforting hand on Duncan's shoulder. Britt closely followed, helping to ease the youth into a sitting position. The Warlock was dazed and still glinting with the occasional sparkle of silver power.

Krins and Goreman managed the crowd, their eyes wary and respectful as they glanced repeatedly at Faye's glowing form.

Faye took a step and found her feet unable to contact the ground. Her silver power had encased her body, causing her to levitate. Instead of walking, the girl glided across the mess hall towards the stairs.

I had wondered how I got to the sawmill so quickly! I don't remember flying... Faye thought in wonder as she effortlessly skated over the stone pavers.

Hovering, dear one. I don't think we could call this *flying!* Zen quipped, buzzing continually, its unique power circling her own to regulate its flow and prevent the silver energy from overwhelming her.

Spoil sport, Faye chided.

They had reached the stairwell that would take them directly up to the professors private quarters. Varsity was standing within the stone archway, an ugly bruise over half her face. She didn't appear scared or wary of Faye at all, which was only to say that she had excellent control over her facial expressions.

"The big one knocked me out when I tried to step in again, like I did last time." Varsity said in way of explanation. "I tried to stop them, little Pheonix. But the oily guy did some sort of purple hocus-pocus..."

Faye nodded once and lightly touched the bruise around Varsity's eye. The bigger girl flinched which made Faye smile sadly. Would even her closest friends become wary of her now?

More silver mist poured from her hands, and the bruise completely faded from Varsity's face. Faye continued on, her reluctant prisoners dragging along behind her. She climbed all four flights of steps and walked down the perpendicular corridor to Rythin's study.

Faye opened the door without knocking, surprising the old Seeker who sat behind his desk reading some unknown document.

"What is the meaning...?" Rythin's voice trailed off in shock at the sight that met his eyes.

Faye glowed with silver energy, dragging two boys, tied with magical silver rope, in her wake. And she was seriously annoyed.

Her voice had an ethereal quality as she said, *"These boys attempted to murder another student, Seeker Rythin."*

Rythin's expression flittered between flummoxed, impressed, astounded, wonder, and a glimmer of wariness – even fear – before his usual blasé mask snapped back into place.

Styrran began to protest almost immediately.

"Never! Just some adolescent scraping...!" he blustered, squirming in his restraints.

This had evidently not been a part of his grand plan. Faye didn't quite understand what the boy thought he could do to escape the consequences of his actions, but the girl was determined that his plan would *not* come to fruition!

"Would you call a fractured spine, broken ribs, punctured lung, and severe internal bleeding a simple adolescent scrape?" Faye demanded, the silver bonds tightening around her captives and choking off their protests.

Rythin swallowed heavily and looked pointedly at the two boys, waiting for their answers.

"*I* certainly wouldn't," Rythin answered firmly, prompting the boys to chime into the conversation at any time.

Styrran looked genuinely surprised before a flash of guilt crossed his face. Perhaps the boy *hadn't* realised the damage caused by being thrown forcibly around by an oversized bear. But Cronuel had. The larger boy's face was stony and without a single hint of remorse.

"You were just meant to rough him up, you idiot!" Styrran hissed quietly at Cronuel.

Ahh, there it is. Zen hissed angrily in her mind. *So, Cronuel is nothing more than another tool to be used and discarded, just like Hannah! Styrran will escape punishment, no doubt, and Cronuel will take the fall.*

Faye glowered at the Gorgon-boy, tempted to continue tightening his restraints until he was no longer able to draw breath. Styrran wouldn't be able to hurt *anyone* again if he suffocated until dead... And *no one* was powerful enough to stop her!

Zen buzzed sharply, breaking the girl from her dire thoughts.

As much as I agree with that sentiment, you know *that isn't the solution, dear one!* Zen exclaimed, reeling in its own temper. *What would Jack say?*

A near-silent, feral growl emanated from the back of Faye's throat as she imperceptibly tightened her captives' bonds, enjoying the way Styrran and Cronuel's pupils constricted in fear as they registered the implacable vice squeezing their ribs.

WHAT would Jack SAY?! The lizard dug his claws viciously into her shoulder, breaking the skin and causing a small rivulet of blood to drip down her back. Its unique power intensified, swirling around the silver strands and tempering her instinctive aggression.

He would say... Faye hesitated, her swell of anger dissipating beneath Zen's magical influence. *He would say... The Authority is the only body with the power and responsibility to issue as severe a punishment as Death. Leave them to the Constabulary.*

Faye minutely loosened the prisoners' bonds again, holding their gaze the entire time to ensure they understood that she was making the deliberate choice to allow them to live.

Rythin, unaware of the silent exchange, broke the tension as he exclaimed in exasperation. "Perhaps I shall take care of this, Miss Faye?" His face clouded with anger, eyes glinting with yellow-green power.

Faye hesitated, before reluctantly letting go of the desire to throttle the two boys.

"Of course. I'll leave *this one* in his restraints," she said softly, guiding both boys to the chairs before Rythin's desk.

As she turned to leave, still glowing eerily, the electric ropes around Styrran vanished in a puff of silver mist, but Cronuel's remained.

"Now, the whole story, *both* of you!" Rythin said harshly, as the door closed softly behind her.

Still encrusted with rage, Faye stalked from Rythin's office, down the main stairs and out the front doors – avoiding the mess hall crowd. Out on the open grounds, Zen started clicking softly. It took a long time for Faye to calm down as the lizard's usual soporific buzz had little to no effect.

The moon had risen, and almost every light had finally been dimmed in the Academy before the silver energy faded and she returned to her room. Unsurprisingly, she found that Duncan was waiting for her.

"That was pretty impressive," he said, in his usual calm manner, his black hair still rumpled and his emerald eyes shadowed with just a hint of black power.

The blue-gemmed ring on his finger glinted with his misty black energy which, Faye noticed, now contained the occasional spark of silver.

Faye shrugged, snatching her nightclothes out of the closet.

"I'm tired, Duncan. You should go," she said softly, not meeting his eye.

He watched her angry, stiff movements for several minutes before the Warlock pulled her into his arms. The boy had recently turned seventeen and he was tall, even for that age.

Faye felt incredibly small, even more like the child she was, as she hesitantly returned the hug. Tears sprung to her eyes and she began to sob helplessly.

All this crying was starting to become a bad habit!

Duncan soothed her, holding Faye close for a very long time. When her sobs had slowed to an occasional sniffle, Duncan politely turned his back as she dressed in her night clothes, then helped to tuck her into bed.

"Sleep now. Things will look better in the morning," Duncan said, stroking her hair. "And thanks, for saving my life."

Faye felt the boy conjure a little magic, but didn't protest. The spell swiftly wrapped around her, and she was sound asleep well before the silent, black figure slipped out the door.

CHAPTER 25

MOTIVES MAKETH MAN

The following days were awkward for Faye.

Sorcerers, Scholars and Healers systematically began to interview her to try and determine her ancestry. Some theorised she was the last Elf in Pendalin; others denied such outlandish beliefs and determined she was still half-Human. They claimed she simply must be half-Sprite or Nymph or other forest Fey, for there hadn't been a half-blood of those in centuries.

The squabbling and bickering started to drive Faye mad. To make matters worse, many students openly avoided her now, as though terrified they would provoke her into that silver glow. Only her loyal friends from Weaponry seemed to recover themselves completely.

"I hope they're both expelled!" Britt said during their routine warm-up one Resday morning up in the battlements of the academy.

The Weaponry students had gathered once more to work on their sparring skills, looking to Faye to continue to teach and guide them through their learning with the stick.

"I'm hoping imprisoned," Trish commented harshly, her brown eyes darkening in anger as she whacked her staff loudly against the quintain the group had rigged against one stone wall.

"Or executed," Varsity grumbled, touching her cheek gingerly where she had recently received that serious blow to the face from Cronuel.

The bruise was gone, and the fractured eye socket had healed neatly, leaving no physical evidence of the damage done.

"How is your eye?" Faye asked.

Varsity snorted, a pleased expression crossing her face.

"Like it never happened. You sure have some powerful healing sorcery!" she replied, practicing a neat flip while keeping hold of her staff.

It was a bit of gymnastics that the group had been keen to learn after seeing Faye effortlessly change direction when she battled two people at once.

Faye shrugged half-heartedly in agreement as she quietly corrected Gorman's stance and showed Rory how to grip her staff more effectively.

She didn't know if the Fey power that had encompassed her could really be termed 'Sorcerous Healing'. She had that much energy under her control that the silver mist she could conjure simply healed whatever she told it to... And the telling bloomed into alien symbols that resonated with her magic, seeping into the recipients flesh to complete its designated task.

Faye noticed that the series of small, mottled scars had vanished from Varsity's face, smoothing the skin out so she was *more* attractive than usual. Faye had always thought that Varsity looked like a breathtaking slice of midnight, and now, with all those knotted scars healed...

Faye sighed in envy, turning her gaze out towards the horizon before she could be accused of staring.

The young girl didn't know the other's story, as Varsity had never divulged anything about her past life, but Faye suspected it was... unpleasant. To say the least. Her chocolate skin had been marred by many puckered scars and other discoloured marks, too many for each to have appeared through accidental injury. Now, it looked as though the girl had never suffered an injury in her life.

"Don't look so worried, Faye. Things will calm down soon enough," Trish chimed in, noting the strained look on the girl's face. "It always does, in a place like Tryssdale! Just one more week of exams, then it's summer holidays. Everyone's going to be too busy panicking about the tests the instructors are throwing at us, and then they'll be packing their gear to return home. By the time we all come back next semester, it will be water under a bridge."

Trish was right, of course.

The last week of semester skated past with hardly a blip in the usual routine. Cronuel vanished without a single whisper as to where, while Styrran received community service duties around the Academy, along with several in-depth interrogations conducted by a gruff Sergeant from the Tryssdale Constabulary Sector. Tryllia was a stern taskmistress as she supervised his punishment, her eyes glinting with rosy-lavender power.

Rythin had explained to Faye when she asked why Styrran was not expelled, that the boy had too much potential to simply expel or imprison. Styrran hadn't actually *touched* Duncan, after all. And Cronuel was his own person, and even if Styrran *had* been telling the beast to commit murder, the boy had free-will and could have decided for himself to leave Duncan alone.

The Academy, therefore, had decided to keep Styrran on as long as he demonstrated due remorse over the incident.

Politics! Zen muttered in disgust whenever Faye complained about the status quo.

The end of semester exams were a breeze, mainly because Faye had undertaken a mixed bunch of classes, she was only assessed on Weaponry and Sorcery this time. Therefore, her last week at the Academy was pleasantly relaxed, enabling her to avoid most other students.

She had successfully completed two Sorcery Modules and would be welcomed back into the class the following year, Sorcerer Hanly informed her after the gruelling test. Sorwell had also approached her about continuing to attend Dawn Weaponry the following year as a volunteer, in addition to studying the Second Level course. This was the exact arrangement that had senior students such as Varsity, Krins, Gorman and a few others sparring with the junior squadron.

Faye readily agreed – she enjoyed the morning routine and her Second Level classes would now be in the blocks before lunch and dinner moving forward. Faye personally felt she was making the most of her day, if she completed an entire sparring routine before breakfast.

On the day she was due to leave Tryssdale to return to Grydin, Faye was up well before dawn checking that she had packed all her belongings. She scooped out the cavity beneath her wardrobe, sorting through the array of bric-a-brac that she had stashed there throughout the school year. In the middle of the artworks, personal journals, and semi-precious stones lay the worn, rumpled letters she had written but never sent to Thayrille. The bits of torn envelope were stashed along with the rifled pages, a reminder of Hannah's manipulative, abusive behaviour.

Throughout the whole year, Faye hadn't heard a word from her foster mother. Many students had received letters from home and had written others in return. Faye logically knew that the lack of correspondence wasn't intentionally hurtful – it was just Thayrille's way.

She hoped.

Faye figured that the woman was lost in her highly involved work, preparing and creating new medicines, or researching potential cures for common diseases. Or maybe she felt just as Faye did, that writing a letter was too *personal* or not personal enough, or that the written word just didn't convey the right meaning – or any number of other excuses the girl had used as a reason not to send her letters throughout the year.

And yet, the girl's stomach churned with nerves, and her heart thrummed with anxiety. What if things *had* changed, and the reason Thayrille hadn't written her was because she *didn't* want her to come back?

No. Rythin had assured her several times that Faye would return to the Healer's Cottage to continue her training in the healing arts. So that was a given.

But what about the changes Faye had undergone? The girl would be returning to Grydin... Different. Her Fey heritage wasn't something that could be denied or hidden now.

And then there was Hannah. The screeching banshee had probably used this past semester, having been expelled and returned to their hometown at midyear break, to spread all manner of vile rumours about Faye and her powers. What would the villager say, or do, when Faye returned?

"Zen?" Faye asked quietly in the predawn gloom.

"Yes, dear one?" the lizard responded sleepily, stretching and yawning as it slid out from beneath her pillow.

"Do you think... Do you think I've become... You know. The *demon* that the villagers always thought I was? Now that I have this silver power and everything I can do with it... I mean, I *almost* killed Styrran and Cronuel. It would have been so easy to just... *choke*... the life right out of them..." Her voice trailed off as she sat on the edge of her neatly made bed, her head resting despondently in the palms of her hands.

Her knapsack was packed and stacked neatly by the door along with her sparring staff. These last few trinkets were all that was left to be placed in one of the many pockets. Then she was ready to go. Only... Did she *want* to go? Did she want to brave the potential horror that awaited her back in Grydin? Or would it just be easier to vanish into the woodlands, to live amongst the trees and the ethereal music that emanated from deep in the Arythmun Mountains...?

"Hey, hey, hey!" the lizard protested, scuttling its way over to nestle against the girl's thigh. "That's nonsense, you know that! You're not a *demon* of any sort! Your power makes you special and unique! *Not* evil! No one of an evil nature would have, or could have, saved that Sawmill Apprentice, and Duncan. *And* all those people down at the Medical Centre. Nor would they have *refrained* from harming Styrran and Cronuel, *especially* after what those two did to a dear friend! We both know you *could* have choked them. But you *didn't*! You are *not* a demon, Faye. And if you think Thayrille and Jack don't want to see you again, just you try and vanish into the forest! Jack will track you down within a week, mark my words!"

Faye released a small watery chuckle. Yes. The Forrester would undoubtedly search her out if she didn't arrive home at the appointed time.

"And I can just imagine what Thayrille would say." Faye offered with a sniff. "*One doesn't allow* paltry emotion *to dictate one's actions, Faye! Snap out of your self-loathing, if you please.*"

"Exactly!" Zen buzzed in amusement. "So. Let's get ourselves back home!"

Somewhat reassured, the girl bundled up the letters before tucking them safely into her pack. The sky lightened further, and a pink stain spread over the eastern sky.

"Time to go," Faye sighed heavily as she stood, collected her pack and staff, and then turned in the doorway to gaze at her room one last time.

"Rest easy, dear one. We'll be back before you know it," Zen crooned at her neck, once more burrowed beneath the riotous curls.

CHAPTER 26

THE POWERFUL STRANGER

As Faye left the great stone castle behind, knapsack and staff in hand, she had to marvel at the number of people who waylaid her, specifically to say goodbye. Despite the early hour, many other students were undertaking similar journeys and so were out and about organising themselves for their own departures. With the incident with Styrran and Cronuel still fresh in people's minds, she had thought that her leaving would be unremarked upon or completely ignored. But she hadn't taken into consideration people like Ross, Duncan, Tryllia, Rythin, Hanly, Merkin, and the whole Weaponry group, which included Sorwell. They weren't scared of her magical abilities, just respectful.

Each had wished her a safe journey and given her a brief hug. Even Duncan had risen well before his normal hour to wish her well. The boy would remain at the Academy over the summer, as he always did, since he didn't have a home to return to. Faye felt a small pang as she remembered the sad look in the boy's eyes as she told him she couldn't stay. Even though she was an orphan, she wasn't entirely unclaimed.

Duncan had merely given her a brief hug before melting back into the hallways that criss-crossed the school. He was too good a friend to make a big deal of their parting. It left Faye feeling forlorn.

"Oh-ho, young Faye! Will you be travelling with us? We can escort you as far as the Northern Crossroads if you're of a mind to travel the rest on your own?" a familiar voice called cheerily as Faye finally managed to pass through the front gates of the Academy.

Turning around in surprise, the girl was delighted to see Seeker Tyrone and several other young students ready to make the trek home.

"Oh, that's a kind offer, Tyrone. Really. I was planning on travelling the backroads, though, to avoid the highway. I loved the peace and quiet," Faye replied with a self-conscious smile.

"Really?" the young Seeker said with some surprise. "Are you sure you won't get lost?"

"Not likely! Besides, I grew up in the woods, and I know my way around them. It won't be too difficult to keep heading south," she assured him with a confident grin.

Tyrone's doubtful expression turned thoughtful as Faye allowed a small glimmer of her silver power to enter her eyes.

"Yes. Yes, I suppose that would be the case. Just... Take care, Faye. I expect to see you back here at summer's end." The Seeker finally relented, offering her a formal handshake before they parted ways.

Faye eyed over the motley group Seeker Tyrone was planning to guide down the southern highway and felt secretly glad she was escaping into the woods on her own. She would much rather spend the next week or two with just Zen for company rather than experience the sensory overwhelm that had plagued her all year from being in close quarters with so many strangers at the Academy.

Faye sighed quietly before turning and marching down the cobbled path that would take her through the city, much as she had done many a Resday with her Weaponry friends.

Thinking of those friends, Faye hesitated and glanced back at the castle.

Where was Jeremy? she wondered.

She hadn't seen the boy in the last week – he had been too busy studying for exams. She also wondered if he would be travelling home. It occurred to her that she should have planned for them to travel together. Having only *one* other Human companion would have been quite tolerable, especially as he was already a friend. Perhaps it might even be nice.

Faye shrugged sadly to herself and resumed her step.

"I wouldn't worry, Faye; he'll catch you up," Zen said contentedly from its position around her neck.

The small reptile, it turned out, was completely right. Within half an hour of walking down the large, cobbled street of Tryssdale, a large panting figure was lumbering after her.

"Faye! Wait!" gasped Jeremy.

"Jeremy! I was hoping I'd run into you!" she said cheerfully as the boy reached her.

Faye had been worried for a moment that the boy had planned to travel with Tyrone and his crew, after all. She had even dawdled quite a bit through the wending city streets just in case he decided to search for her.

Faye gave the sweating, heaving boy a quick hug and used a spark of silver magic to soothe him. The glow of power dried the sweat from his brow, cooled his red face and slowed his breathing.

"Cheers," he said with a grin.

Over the past semester, Jeremy had grown to accept Faye's magical ability and had even become accustomed to receiving its benefits.

"So, remember the way, then?" Jeremy asked as they continued through the city streets to the southern road.

"Of course. I have an innate sense of direction, you know," Faye grinned, giving the boy a confident wink.

Jeremy laughed, delighted. "Thank goodness for that! Because I think, if I were leading the way, I'd have us lost within the hour!"

In companionable silence, the two walked toward home together, reflecting on the vast differences between the trip to Austin Academy and the one away from it.

One evening, towards the end of their trek, Faye and Jeremy sat comfortably around a small campfire. It was peaceful, and the gentle tunes of ghostly music that only Faye could hear once more wafted on the breeze.

Faye was itching to get her pipe out and play. It was the first time in months that Faye had felt that silent summons. In a bustling place like Tryssdale, the call of the land was muted and easily lost in the hubbub of the Academy.

After careful consideration, Faye reached out to Zen with her innate power.

Do you think he'll understand the power beneath the music? Faye asked the lizard.

Doubtful. He'll probably enjoy a tune, though, Zen replied deep in her mind.

Decided, Faye retrieved her pipe and gave in to the ghostly demands. Jeremy sat there and gazed at her with avid admiration as the small girl played a rippling tune of joy, peace, and celebration. He didn't ask how Faye knew how to play or even wonder at the complexity and beauty of the music. Being a straightforward sort of boy, he merely enjoyed it for what it was.

Faye kept playing, and playing, one tune after another. She hadn't been free before to endlessly follow the ghostly notes.

After almost an hour of music, with the forest glowing brightly and the air shimmering with silver magic, a bright figure appeared at the edge of the clearing. Faye stumbled on the following notes, wary of this strange presence. Slowly, her silver magic faded, leaving only the glowing stranger.

Jeremy drew his hunting knife. Faye held up a hand as the tall, lithe stranger approached. The man was unarmed, and distinctly Fey.

His hair was a shimmery white blonde, his cat-like eyes bright blue. His face was even more delicate and pointed than Faye's, and his entire body radiated with a soft white glow. He was like someone out of a fairy tale book, or an elaborate historic tome. Jeremy glanced between the stranger and Faye, his eyes as large as saucers. Faye and the boy realised simultaneously that their impromptu visitor was a fabled Elf!

"Where did you find that pipe, Human child?" the Elf demanded, his face tight with anger and pain.

Throat dry, Faye whispered, "My mother."

The Elf paused for a moment, before stepping closer. He peered down at Faye's small face, illuminated by his shimmering white glow. Her blue eyes glittered and her blonde hair shimmered as she stared up at him in wonder.

"Your mother? What was her name?" the Elf demanded.

"I do not know, sir. She died soon after birthing me," Faye answered quietly, her voice pained. "She wasn't Elvish, I don't think. No one knows which Fey Clan she belonged to; her description matches nothing in our recorded histories. I don't know how she came by this pipe, either."

"Can I see the pipe?" the man asked, his eyes mistrusting

Faye felt herself compulsively hand over the slim instrument, complete with beaded cord, unable to resist the command. The Elf held the slim metallic instrument, causing it to glow in a series of blues, silvers, reds, oranges, and greens. The script on the flute shimmered, becoming easier to see.

"This was my sister's pipe," said the Elf, clutching the thing tightly.

Faye didn't want this strange Elf to confiscate it! It was the only link she had with either one of her parents!

"It was my mother's," Faye repeated stupidly, fear gripping her heart.

How on earth had her mother ended up with an Elvin pipe? Thayrille's description of her sounded like nothing Faye had ever heard of, or seen. This Elf before her was a creature of beauty and power, with his flowing hair, gleaming pale skin and electric blue eyes. Nothing at all like the description Thayrille had provided of Faye's mother.

"What did your mother look like? Perhaps I know her race," the Elf said slowly, his eyes glinting with tears as he examined the pipe closely.

"She... she was strange. Not Human," Faye whispered around the lump in her throat. "Her face was really pointy; it looked like an insect. She was spindly and bony, with hair as white as death and coarse like cows' hair, except longer. Her eyes were glassy and grey, almost white... She... She was not like you or me. She was completely alien."

Faye trailed off, realising that she knew no more than that. Thayrille had only spoken of the unfortunate waif once when she had gifted her ward with the pipe.

"I see," the Elf said, his eyes shuttered, his face pained.

After many moments of silence, he returned the slim metallic instrument to Faye. As her hand closed around it, the rainbow shimmer faded, and it became mundane looking once more.

"As this was in your mother's keeping, and my sister is long dead, you may have it," the Elf said, his voice sounding oddly choked.

Faye grasped the pipe, unsure what to say.

"My name is Fey'Thorl. What is yours, child? Something *Human*, no doubt," the Elf said sardonically, his white gleaming brows dipping in annoyance.

"My mother named me Faye," Faye said indignantly.

"Fey'...?" he trailed off in question as though expecting more to the name.

"Just Faye."

Fey'Thorl frowned slightly as though it were ludicrous. "She said this, to your Human guardian?"

"Yes. It was just as she died," Faye replied sadly, biting her lip to keep from saying something stupid.

She had a burning pain in her chest that ached to be released, probably in the form of angry tears and accusations. However, this Fey stranger didn't deserve that, so she kept silent. The Elf sighed deeply.

"I see. The Fey do not normally name their children simply 'Fey'," he said, somehow annoyed, sad, and angry all at once. "It would be like Humans naming their children simply 'human' or 'boy' or 'girl'."

"It's spelt differently," Faye protested, becoming increasingly upset, tears glittering in her blue eyes.

This criticism of her dead mother was eroding her self-control.

"I'm *sure* it is," the Elf murmured with a slight sarcastic inflection, shaking his head. "I journeyed far to discover the origin of this music, played by my sister's pipe. I never dreamed I'd find..." He broke off, paced a little around the clearing, then stopped before Faye again so he could stare at her some more.

"Do you know what Fey clan my mother was from?" the girl asked, hesitantly breaking the brooding silence.

"Perhaps," Fey'Thorl said after some time, his eyes still shuttered. "I'll need to look into it."

Faye felt this was a very odd answer to give. "Does that mean I'll see you again? When you have the answer?"

"Yes. I believe it does," he replied, appearing reluctant and unhappy about the fact.

"You could just leave me a note, then!" Faye spat waspishly, feeling put out by this contrary attitude, even if he were an immortalised Elf.

Something in the Elf's expression softened, and the corners of his mouth even kicked up slightly in a smile.

"We will definitely see each other again, child. Hopefully, I'll have more satisfactory answers for you then," he said, his eyes crinkling at the corners. "I must go now."

Just before he vanished into the night, Fey'Thorl frowned at Jeremy, then issued a small flash of white light. "He will not remember. It is better that way."

The Elf was gone.

To all appearances, Fey'Thorl blinked out of existence the moment the sun vanished behind the horizon.

Jeremy still stood there with his hunting knife hanging limply in his hand, a dazed look on his face. He shook his head once, twice, then sat down heavily on the log.

"That was beautiful music," the boy said, yawning, as though the past twenty minutes had never happened. "If it's okay, though, I'm going to get some sleep."

Faye nodded, and the boy slumped over to his blankets. Within moments, he was snoring.

"Poor Jeremy," Faye sighed.

"I wonder if it will affect his intelligence?" Zen asked as it made its first appearance of the evening from under her collar. "I dare say he hardly needs any tampering."

"I'd hardly think so," Faye retorted, and then her voice became concerned. "It may affect his memory, though."

The lizard clicked deep in its throat.

"I was only sassing," Zen said with a reproachful gaze.

Faye rolled herself into her own blankets, deciding she had enough for the evening, too.

"Who do you think this Fey'Thorl character is?" Faye asked, staring up at the stars.

"An Elf," Zen replied.

"I *know* that!" hissed the girl. "I mean in the scheme of things. My mother somehow had his sister's pipe. That means his sister was someone named Fey'Rhain. Is it just coincidence?"

"Perhaps you'll find out more when you see the Elf again," the lizard replied in an evasive tone, then chirruped a short tune.

"Zen, did you just...?" Faye felt her brain grow sluggish as sleep stole over her.

"You need sleep, Faye. Meeting a member of a supposedly extinct race is a bit overwhelming..."

Faye tried to protest, shout and glare at the lizard in disgust, but she was already lost to the sleep spell.

The two companions stumbled into Grydin Village after noon on their tenth day of travel, relieved to finally lay eyes on the familiar sight of the towering evergreens surrounding the Common Green, the single road lined with shingled cottages and their stout wooden signs squeaking in the light breeze.

"Come on, not far now!" Jeremy grinned at her, launching ahead towards the cottage that belonged to his happy family.

The girl hesitated a step, her return smile fading somewhat as she recalled the censure she had received all her life from the local villagers. Perhaps... Perhaps returning here *hadn't* been the best idea after all.

"Don't look so worried, Faye! Things will be different now, you'll see." The boy stopped midstride as he realised she had lagged behind. "Dad says the worst troublemakers are still rotting in gaol, and many of the others were moved on by the Constabulary. The town is much different to how we left it."

The girl drew a deep breath and nodded thoughtfully. Yes, she recalled just how many people had been shifted out of Grydin after the debacle of the Forrester's cottage burning. Jack was lucky to have survived that incident!

Faye caught up and they walked the rest of the way down the cobbled street, stopping only when they reached Jeremy's front gate.

"Ma! Dad! I'm home!" Jeremy hollered as he jumped the gate with athletic grace, too excited to bother unlatching the thing.

Faye remained outside, leaning on the picket fence with a bemused smile.

"Heya! There's a lad! Look at ye, son!" a deep voice called in return.

Father and son embraced before Jeremy was jerked around to be squeezed heartily by his mother.

"My boy! You're home!" she cried, face awash with happy tears.

Feeling like an interloper, Faye stepped carefully back from the fence, intending to slip away unnoticed. However, Jeremy's father, Mister Bloomsbry, stopped her with his steady gaze. He looked her up and down, noting her sturdy boots, travel gear, and knife that hung from her belt. Her sturdy staff added to the appearance of casual confidence.

The man nodded once, acknowledging the girl that had been the focus of so much vile slander all her life. Faye nodded in return, accepting that if she continued her friendship with Jeremy, his parents wouldn't object. It was a nice feeling.

"I'll see you around, Jeremy," Faye called, giving the three a jaunty wave as she turned and headed for home.

"Later, Faye," he called after her, returning her wave.

The girl continued up the road, determined to stay on the main street rather than slipping over to Shepherds Lane. If anyone left here in Grydin objected to her presence, then let them say it to her face.

To her surprise, Faye was greeted by a range of faces – some old, and some new. Many seemed eager to give her a friendly word, as though trying to make up for their previous lack of kindness. Even Mistress Brianey, the Baker's wife, offered the girl a fresh loaf as a welcome home present as she passed by. The Forrester's Cottage was quiet and dark, and Faye thought sadly that Jack would likely be off completing his usual summer duties. So up the cobbled path she ran to the stout stone building she had lived in all her life.

Finally, Faye arrived home.

She climbed the front steps with a measured pace and pushed the heavy front door open.

The girl had to admit that she was eager to see the Healer again, but as Faye walked through the front door, she found things were very different to what she had left.

The Forrester's Cottage was rebuilt just down the hill, *with* a back door, yet, as she stepped inside she was surprised to find Jack skulking and engrossed in a book in Thayrille's study.

"What are *you* doing here?" Faye demanded, mystified by his inexplicable presence in her home.

"Faye!" Jack gasped, head jerking up from the book he was reading. "Ye're home!"

With a relieved grin, the big man was on his feet and wrapping her in a massive hug.

"And ye've grown!" he commented, holding her at arms-length.

Faye noticed that Jack did seem at least five centimetres shorter than when she last saw him. His chestnut hair was as unruly as ever and tied firmly back from his square face, emphasising his hazel eyes. His beard was, as always, wild and woolly, hiding half his face.

"Nay, you've just gotten shorter," Faye said with a grin.

Jack let out a surprised laugh. "And making jokes, I see! Whatever happened to my serious little girl?"

"She got pummelled good and proper by a range of strange friends at the Academy," Faye replied with good humour, her blue eyes crinkling as she grinned.

"I'm glad Faye. Really glad," the burly man said, his eyes glistening a little with emotion. "That ye made friends, I mean. Not the pummelling."

"Where's Thayrille?" Faye asked then frowned as she saw the cautious look that crept over Jack's smiling face.

"Oh, in the kitchen," he said, a flush coming to his cheeks.

Faye glared at him through narrowed eyes. He was acting odd.

"Indeed? Is she in good health?" Faye asked, hands on hips as she caught on to his nervous air.

"Oh yes! In very fine health!" the Forrester rushed to assure her, then mumbled, "Just not in fine humour."

Faye looked curiously at him, but he waved her away towards the study door. The girl went down the hall to the kitchen and saw Thayrille angrily banging pots and vigorously stirring some serum on the stove.

She didn't look as though she was in any sort of fine humour. In fact, the girl couldn't recall a time when Thayrille was so... *forceful*... in her anger – barring the aftermath of Jack's near demise.

Faye frowned again, wondering why the Forrester was still in the house, hiding in the study while the Healer steadfastly ignored his presence. Surely, he'd be off doing Forrester duties? Or at least resting in his own house, now it was complete?

Then Thayrille turned, and Faye stared at her large, rounded belly in wide-eyed disbelief.

CHAPTER 27

SUPRISES

"Oh, *shut up*!" Faye gasped, unintentionally mimicking Britt's favourite term of surprise. "Since when?!"

Thayrille almost dropped the pot she was transferring to the bench. When her startled eyes registered the slim, blonde figure as Faye, her face broke into a radiant smile.

"Faye! You're home!" the Healer said, rushing to hug the girl, tears in her bright brown eyes.

Faye returned the hug automatically, stifling an exclamation of surprise, while noting that the round ball of a belly was kicking her energetically in the ribs.

"Where did this baby come from?" Faye asked, still completely astounded.

She couldn't imagine, for a moment, *any* man that would be game enough to try and get past Thayrille's prickly exterior. But as the Healer's eyes narrowed dangerously and she glared angrily down the hall at the study's closed door, everything finally clicked.

"Ohhhh! *Jack*."

The large, kind Forrester had always hung around the cottage. Faye had occasionally wondered at that, but no longer.

"Yes, *Jack*," Thayrille sniffed in annoyance then drew Faye to her regular stool in front of the kitchen counter.

"Never mind that! Tell me about school. Is Mistress Yvonne still teaching Healing?" Thayrille asked, wreathed in smiles once more.

Her pale freckled face had softened, and those genuine smiles made her look beautiful.

Faye felt floored. Thayrille had never been chatty, *never*.

Hormones, Zen murmured into her mind with a pleased chuckle.

Luckily, Faye knew how to respond to such overtures now, for she had spent almost a year amongst chatty, giggly teenage girls. After so many losing rounds of Prude Poker, Faye certainly was adept at *girl talk* – even if she didn't like it.

"No, she retired. Mistress Merkin is now teaching," Faye returned easily, as though nothing was wrong or out of place.

She expected the stiff expression, the flared nostrils, and the narrowed eyes when she mentioned Merkin's name. She wasn't disappointed.

"She's changed since your days together," Faye said with a grin, intensely amused by the clear rivalry between the two.

Thayrille nodded once, as was her way, then her tight shoulders relaxed.

"I suppose she's been teaching you all about those *foreign* plants," Thayrille commented dryly, starting to measure the serum into sterile bottles.

Faye neatly slid from her chair and rounded the counter. Within moments, she had confiscated the ladle and pot, taking over the task.

"Perhaps a cup of tea, and some lunch?" Faye suggested when Thayrille looked at her askance. The Healer smiled grudgingly and sat the kettle on the stove. Within a half hour, lunch was laid out at the counter, and the serum had been efficiently bottled.

"You've been volunteering at the Medical Centre," Thayrille noted approvingly as she eyed the sealed bottles.

The girl had completed the task more confidently than when she was last in the cottage.

"Of course! I have your reputation to live up to. Did you know they use you as a case study in various classes? To demonstrate that age is no barrier to greatness?" Faye asked in a teasing tone.

Thayrille flushed with pleasure and embarrassment combined.

"Oh, what a lot of tosh!" Thayrille said as she sat down to help herself to warm stew and fresh bread.

Faye noticed the extra plate, which was obviously set out for Jack. She glanced down the hall and saw the study door was still firmly closed.

"Should we call Jack to lunch?" Faye asked uncertainly.

Thayrille's nostrils flared, and Faye had the distinct impression that the Healer would rather they didn't. Then she sighed roughly.

"He knows. He's lurking just outside the door, waiting for an invitation," she replied, a hint of humour lightening her severe expression.

At that moment, Jack slunk sheepishly into the room. He really *had* been lurking just outside the door! Faye disguised her invasive giggle with a polite cough.

Before sitting down, Jack gave Thayrille a cautious kiss on the cheek. To Faye's amazement, this didn't produce the temperamental explosion she would have previously expected from Thayrille.

"How are ye feeling, dearest?" he asked tenderly, his large hand clasping her small one.

Dearest! Zen silently cackled, causing Faye to surreptitiously pinch its tail in warning as she bit her own lip in effort to prevent an amused grin.

"Better," Thayrille sniffed, her expression softening as she returned his grasp affectionately.

"Hmm, lamb stew!" Jack enthused as he sat down, eagerly helping himself to the buttered bread.

"You've been ill?" Faye asked, troubled.

Someone this far along in pregnancy shouldn't be troubled by morning-sickness. Or, at least, it was very rare and could be an indication of something else going awry.

Thayrille's expression hardened again as she glared at Jack instead of answering the question. Jack ducked his head and refused to say anything.

"I'm not physically sick, only tired. And a tad – *emotional,*" Thayrille admitted when it became clear Jack was going to continue wolfing down his lunch.

Perhaps Jack was afraid he'd be kicked out of the house before he was finished his meal, and be damned if he was still hungry. From the look on the Healer's face, the girl suspected the fear wasn't groundless. Faye felt a vague sympathy for the man.

"That's normal, though," Faye said with an understanding smile.

The young girl had spent plenty of time in the Maternity Ward over the last few months, studying the pregnant women of Tryssdale with fascination, watching their stomachs grow and change at all stages of gestation. She had even assisted with several difficult deliveries as part of her general duties.

Thayrille sniffed, and Jack stopped his vigorous nod of agreement mid-motion, changing it to a noncommittal shrug. Faye felt the greatest urge to laugh, mirthful tears were even pricking the back of her eyes, but she managed to control the urge. Zen's amused buzz was hardly helping her maintain her self-control.

"It will pass. How far along are you?" Faye asked, all sensible 'Apprentice-Healer' once more.

"I'm due soon after solstice."

"Solstice?" Faye frowned, tallying the days and months quickly. "But that would mean..."

Faye trailed off and flushed. The two had obviously become intimate not too long after she had left, probably while Jack was recovering.

"Humph," was all Thayrille said, glaring at Jack once more.

The Forrester winced, and despite the flush on his face, he decided to explain things more clearly.

"Ye should know, Faye, that I've loved Thayrille for many years. Since we first met, as it happens. I never thought she had feelings for me in return, though, she's such a closed person normally." Jack paused as though waiting for a reprimand, but Thayrille shrugged and sipped her tea. No point denying the truth, her expression said.

"I kept trying, making small indications that I was interested," the Forrester said, his cheeks stained pink and his earnest hazel eyes travelling over his love's freckled face. "Then one evening, one of Thayrille's patients had given her a few bottles of wine, along with the normal payment as thanks..."

"You got her drunk and seduced her, you sly old dog!" Faye burst out, finishing the story with a gale of laughter.

Jack grinned, even though his face turned an even deeper red. If he kept blushing like this, the poor man might rupture a vessel!

Thayrille sniffed yet again, her lips pursed.

"Indeed he did! I wanted to kick him out of the cottage the very next day, but he played on my sympathies, claiming he was still too ill to be out on his own. And the Forrester's cottage had not been completed," Thayrille snapped. "So, I continued to let him use the secondary healing room – *not* that he stayed in there…!"

The Healer cut herself off short, realising she was perhaps saying too much. Faye may have been a worldly child, but she was still only thirteen.

The girl's eyes widened further, and she looked at Jack in amusement. Having spent the past year with girls far older than herself, this conversation wasn't alien at all. She found she was coping very well with it, far better than the two adults, it seemed.

Jack shrugged self-consciously and sipped his tea. Faye didn't think his face would ever fade from that bright beet-red colour.

"Ye're my woman. I'm not about to keep sleeping alone, I've had enough of that all my life," the Forrester grumbled. "Now that Faye's here, we can tie the knot and make it all legal."

It was Thayrille's turn to flush, but Faye noted the Healer was secretly pleased by the simple sentiment. The girl sat back in wonder. Thayrille and Jack, getting married? What a turn of events!

"And now you've a baby on the way!" Faye said excitedly, breaking the silence.

Thayrille's face became shuttered, and Jack's was a mixture of silly pride and worry. Faye reached over the table and grabbed Thayrille's hands.

"Don't worry, Thayrille! You'll be a fantastic mother. Just look how well I turned out!" Faye exclaimed, smiling warmly, her blue eyes sparkling with sincerity.

The Healer met Faye's eyes, and her expression melted.

"I think that had much more to do with you, than me," Thayrille murmured, returning the warm clasp.

"You did more than you realise," Jack said, placing a comforting arm around the woman.

The Healer nodded and snuggled into his embrace.

So, that was it. Thayrille's scared about having her own child. That's why she's angry at Jack for getting her pregnant, and he's astute enough to know it, so he's not allowing her to scare him off with prickly attitudes and angry words, Faye thought to herself, her heart hurting for the woman.

They will be good for each other, Zen murmured. *And we won't have to worry too much about Thayrille's wellbeing while we're away Seeking.*

Some of Faye's delight faded as she looked at the two adults cuddling and whispering together.

They're having their own family now, Zen... Faye thought, sadness engulfing her.

They will always have a place here for you, Zen replied sternly. *I bet you a whole mango that your room is still untouched.*

That made Faye smile once more as she finished her lunch. The lizard would never idly bet a mango on any but a sure thing. Zen proved to be right.

After lunch, a much happier Jack returned to the study, and Thayrille walked with Faye up to her room. The attic was precisely how she had left it.

The small space was still decorated with the old lace curtains across the windows, and the deep bench seat was laden with her collection of colourful pillows. While clear of her usual bric-a-brac, the armchair and dresser still held a couple of decorative items she had left behind. A clumsy painting, some figurines and small stones...

The bed caught Faye's eye. It was neatly made, and an unfamiliar knitted quilt was tucked tightly around it. The afghan was new, and as Faye tenderly ran her hands over the textured material, she could feel the love and time that had gone into its making. It would seem that Thayrille had spent the winter evenings crafting this piece for her.

Faye felt her heart settle. Thayrille truly did care, and starting her own family with Jack wouldn't change that.

"Where is the baby's room?" Faye asked cheerily, setting her pack on the armchair.

"It will be down with us for the first year or so. Once as it's bigger, I'll have a cot placed in the next room," Thayrille said, indicating the right-hand wall.

The girl was glad that her presence wasn't taking up much needed space, and that the other two attic rooms were just as large as her own. Thayrille and Jack could fit four or more children between the other two rooms, and everyone would be perfectly comfortable.

"Are you happy, Thayrille?" Faye asked, taking the Healer's face between her hands so she would look her in the eye. The Healer seemed surprised as she peered down at Faye's concerned face, her eyes glowing soft silver. The silver mist spread from Faye to Thayrille, clearing away the fears and doubts like a fresh breeze.

The woman's tight face softened into a warm smile.

"Yes, I'm happy, Faye," she whispered truthfully.

The two smiled at each other for a long time, before Thayrille broke the contact and helped to pack away Faye's belongings.

Zen took the opportunity to slip from Faye's shoulder and flop onto the bed, kneading the quilt in pleasure.

"Why, Master Zen, you're looking very well fed!" the Healer said archly, in way of welcome.

The lizard clicked at her, returning the greeting. Faye grinned, noting the small reptiles growing paunch.

"It seems Zen's very partial to a particular fruit called a mango," she commented cheekily.

"Mangoes! Why, I haven't eaten one of those since I was at the Academy." the woman sighed; her brown eyes filled with longing.

"Thought so," Faye said in satisfaction. "That's why I brought some back. I've learnt the spell in Sorcery, to increase the capacity of my pack – and to chill the fruit."

"I thought your pack seemed to hold too much!" Thayrille exclaimed. "I could use a few boxes like that, it would make storage much simpler."

"I can help you with that, no trouble," Faye replied happily. "I have quite a few ideas for home improvements while I'm here."

Faye carefully removed the plump fruit from her pack. Each one glittered with silver magic and radiated an intense cold.

"So, you've learnt quite a bit of Sorcery, then," the woman said, a look of uncertainty crossing her face.

"Yes," Faye sighed. "You always knew I was half-Fey."

The Healer frowned, then sat on the bed and patted the spot next to her. The girl sat down heavily, leaning into Thayrille's one-armed embrace, resting her head against the woman's shoulder.

"Have you found out anything about your heritage?" Thayrille asked.

"No. No one can tell me anything. I've done some research, but there is nothing in the Academy library," Faye said softly. "Even after everything that's happened the past year, we're no closer to figuring it out."

Faye began to tell Thayrille all the adventures at the Academy, how she had discovered her intense, bottomless silver magic, and related the final confrontation with Styrran. Finally, she explained how she had mysteriously met an Elf in the forests outside Grydin, and their connection through the Elvish pipe.

"Oh, Faye! I never realised!" Thayrille sighed, hugging her close. "Perhaps this will be a new lead in finding out who your mother was."

The child chose to ignore the trace of scepticism on Thayrille's face at the mention of meeting an Elf. Faye knew that as far as anyone in Pendalin knew, the Elves were extinct. Meeting one at random was a highly unlikely event, especially so far south. Perhaps the mysterious man *hadn't* been an Elf, after all, but some other Fey creature.

"Perhaps," Faye replied heavily, feeling inexplicably despondent. "We'll have to wait and see."

"No matter what, you will always have a home here," Thayrille replied.

Faye smiled, her heart lightening.

ACKNOWLEDGEMENTS

First and foremost, I would like to acknowledge my family particularly my parents, Eric and Nadja.

Dad has been my number one fan and supporter from my very first attempt at fictional writing when I was a child. Dad is my Alpha Reader, my Beta Reader, my first editor, and my muse on occasion when I'm stuck for an idea. Thanks Dad. Without your support and encouragement, this book would not have been possible!

Secondly, I would like to acknowledge my teachers, Steven Green and Alice Johnson (from my years at Oak Flats High School – Graduate of 2002). Mr Green was the first person, aside from family, to tell me I had talent in creative writing. He gave me 19/20 for a history assignment and told me: "Now, Jess, the only reason I couldn't give you the extra mark was because your 'speech' ran well over the three minutes allocated. This was an engaging and creative piece of work, and was very well written!" I had never thought of myself as a writer, a potential future author, until that moment.

During my senior years, my English teacher, Mrs Johnson, actively encouraged my creative writing. She awarded one of my short stories full marks and the Literary Award for 2002. This was the first trophy my name ever appeared on, and I do hope it still exists at Oak Flats High, locked away on display in a glass cabinet in the front office. I also hope that the same trophy is awarded to other budding writers in the years since.

Thirdly, yet not least, I would like to thank my husband, Nicholas. Nick is not a reader, so he has not opened the cover of any of my books. Nick does not have much imagination - and I mean that in the most loving way! (He's an engineer) – So he has not been there to converse about storylines or other story items. He often wonders *'What is she doing for so long?'* whenever I'm at my laptop, tap-tap-tapping away.

However, in the early months of 2024, when I received rejection letter after rejection letter from publishers, Nick came up with a solution. He suggested engaging my own publisher and pursuing my lifelong dream. Having Nick say "your writing is worthwhile" and helping me to prove it has allowed me to turn a dream into reality!

Which brings me to my final acknowledgement - Wattle Tree Press. I'd like to thank Brooke and her amazing team. Without your support and encouragement, Faye would still be a tentative tale gathering dust on my bookshelf. I feel so blessed to be working with each of you, and I wouldn't change a single element of my journey to date. Thank you.

ABOUT THE AUTHOR

JESS SENFF writes MG and YA fantasy novels based in magical worlds and featuring strong young characters facing a variety of unique problems ... often involving evil sorcery!

She loves when these individuals prevail, reminding the reader that solutions can often be found in life - with a little perseverance and good humour.

Jess spends her days teaching science and maths in the Southern Tablelands of New South Wales, Australia. She lives with her husband, three children, four rescued shorthair felines, and a beleaguered Poodle x Border Collie.

Connect with Jess (Jess Senff Stories) on Facebook and Instagram or via her website: https://www.jesssenffstories.com/

ALSO BY JESS SENFF

The lands of Pendalin, once ruled by Elves, are in slow decline. In this time of turmoil, a child called Faye is born. Can she reunite the throne of Pendalin, locate the missing royal emblems, find the Royal Heir, and replenish the lands before it's too late? Find out in The Pendalin Chronicles.

Join Artura and the X-Calibre on their journey of self-discovery as they set out to save the Brittanian nation from the encroaching Mist of the Great Divide. Discover unlikely friends and miraculous magic in this contemporary take on the old Arthurian Legends.

Wattle Tree Press is an independent publisher
located on the picturesque Central Coast of Australia.
WTP believes that everyone has a story (or two) within them
and aims to bring Aussie storytelling to the wider world.

Their growing catalogue can be found at:

www.wattletreepress.com

www.ingramcontent.com/pod-product-compliance
Lightning Source LLC
Chambersburg PA
CBHW031742180726
48283CB00005B/1630